"I thoroughly enjoyed *The Ishbane Conspiracy*. The authors did a great job, and the story gives so much food for thought. I wish this book was required reading for students and parents across our nation."

Francine Rivers, best-selling author of *Redeeming Love*

"When I was a teenager, God used the piercing words of Randy Alcorn to open my eyes to spiritual realities and yank me out of the clutches of darkness. This gripping novel can do the same for you. Do yourself a favor and read a book hell would love to censor. *The Ishbane Conspiracy* is going to change the way you view your life."

Joshua Harris, author of *I Kissed Dating Goodbye* and *Boy Meets Girl*

"The Alcorns portray these characters with fresh insights and such clarity they seem like people I've met. What gives *The Ishbane Conspiracy* its intense intrigue is the way these writers manage to lift the veil and let us see what goes on behind the scenes in the spiritual realm. The conflict doubles, and so does the ultimate victory. A job well done by this talented father/daughter trio!"

Robin Jones Gunn, best-selling author of the Christy Miller Series and the Glenbrooke Series

"There is no greater spiritual battleground today than our high school and college campuses. These provide ample opportunity for the enemy to intercept and destroy souls, no matter what background they come from.

"In *The Ishbane Conspiracy*, the Alcorns have exposed, in exacting detail, the methods used by the deceiver to cheat young people out of eternal life. With this book, however, the enemy is on the run. I would love to see *The Ishbane Conspiracy* in the hands of every high school and college student in America."

James Scott Bell, author of *The Nephilim Seed* and *The Darwin Conspiracy*

OTHER BOOKS BY RANDY ALCORN

FICTION

Deception

Deadline

Dominion

Edge of Eternity

Lord Foulgrin's Letters

Safely Home

NONFICTION

In Light of Eternity

Law of Rewards

Money, Possessions, and Eternity

ProLife Answers to ProChoice Arguments

Restoring Sexual Sanity

Sexual Temptation

The Grace and Truth Paradox

The Purity Principle

The Treasure Principle

Women Under Stress

The Ishbane Conspiracy

ANGELA, KARINA & RANDY ALCORN

MULTNOMAH
BOOKS

This is a work of fiction. With the exception of recognized historical figures, the characters in this novel are fictional. Any resemblance to actual persons, living or dead, is entirely coincidental.

THE ISHBANE CONSPIRACY
published by Multnomah Books
A division of Random House, Inc.

© 2001 by Eternal Perspective Ministries

International Standard Book Number: 978-1-57673-817-7

Cover design by Kirk DouPonce

Multnomah is a trademark of Multnomah Books,
and is registered in the U.S. Patent and Trademark Office.
The colophon is a trademark of Multnomah Books.

Printed in the United States of America

For information:
MULTNOMAH BOOKS

12265 ORACLE BOULEVARD, SUITE 200

COLORADO SPRINGS, CO 80921

Library of Congress Cataloging-in-Publication Data:
Alcorn, Randy C.
  The Ishbane Conspiracy / by Randy, Angela, and Karina Alcorn.
    p.cm.
  ISBN 1-57673-817-5 (pbk.)
  1. Friendship–Fiction. 2. Spiritual warfare–Fiction. I. Alcorn, Angela. II. Alcorn, Karina.
  III. Title.
  PS3551.L292 184 2001
  813'.54–dc21   2001001854

08 09 — 10 9 8

To

Lucille Alcorn *(1918–1981)*
An awesome mother to Randy and grandmother to Karina and Angela,
Whose departure created a huge hole in our lives.

and

Adele Noren *(1916–2001)*
A wonderful mother to Nanci and grandmother to Angela and Karina;
Who left this world for another the week we finished this book.

Lucille and Adele became dear friends in the Shadowlands.
And now they're together with the Person they were made for,
in the Place they were made for,
there in the real world.

Thanks, Grandmas, for your faithfulness to King Jesus
and for your undying love for your families.
Both of you touched our lives for eternity.
Keep your eyes open for places you want to show us there.
We can hardly wait for the grand reunion.

ACKNOWLEDGMENTS

We want to thank the great team at Multnomah Publishers, including all whose names aren't included here. We especially thank our friend and editor Rod Morris. Also, Don Jacobson, Kevin Marks, Ken Ruettgers, Jay Echternach, Jeff Pederson, and Steve Shepherd, all of whom gave support and encouragement at one stage or another. Thanks to Steve Curley for cover coordination, Kirk DouPonce for the cover design, and Lance Woodward for copyediting. Also, all our friends in marketing and sales who labor to get the book into readers' hands.

Thanks to Officer Jim Seymour for his great professional insights and encouragement. We love you, Jim and Erin. We want to give special recognition to our good friend Gene Takalo, for volunteering his skill as a photographer. Thanks to DJ VanZanten, Melissa Allen, and Miriam Silva for their expertise. And Joe Greenley, Brad Noren, Matt Schneider, Tom Schneider, John and Patty Franklin, Chris Franklin, Matt Pearson, Chris Kropf, Jen Gifford, Zach McCollum, and Jason Black for their input on covers.

Our heartfelt thanks to Nanci Alcorn, wonderful wife and mom of the authors! Thanks to Dan Stump and Dan Franklin for their love for Christ, for their encouragement and prayers, and also, Lord willing, for giving their last names to Angie and Karina soon after this book is published.

Thanks to our great staff at Eternal Perspective Ministries—to Bonnie Hiestand for some typing, and Janet Albers, Kathy Norquist, and Penny Dorsey for proofreading.

We've gleaned insights from various experts on youth culture including Josh McDowell, Dawson McAllister, and the incomparable Steve Keels. We've also benefited from Frank Peretti's recollections of his childhood in *The Wounded Spirit*. Thanks for your honesty, Frank.

The idea for the correspondence portions of *The Ishbane Conspiracy* came from C. S. Lewis's classic *The Screwtape Letters*. Randy's book *Lord Foulgrin's Letters*, also inspired by *The Screwtape Letters*, introduced various characters in *The Ishbane Conspiracy* including Jillian Fletcher, Diane Fletcher, Daniel Fletcher, Brittany Powell, and Ian Stewart.

We're deeply indebted to the prayer team that faithfully lifted us up during the writing and revising of this book. Any eternal impact *The Ishbane Conspiracy* might have is the product of the prayers of these brothers and sisters.

We're thankful for being able to work together harmoniously on a big and challenging project. All the weekly meetings, the study and discussions on fiction writing, the research, and the writing were an investment not only in the book, but in one another's lives. We're so grateful for the oneness we experienced in this process.

We want to thank above all others our Lord Jesus, who has filled our hearts with joy. His loving assurances of our eternal pleasure in Him show for what they are, the always-broken promises of the father of lies and his warriors of darkness. We pray that by His grace, God would expose the strategies of our enemies, so we would not buy into their deceptions. We pray that readers would, through this story, come to see themselves for who they are, their enemies for who they are, and—above all—their God for who He is.

Note to Readers from Randy Alcorn

The main characters in *The Ishbane Conspiracy* are eighteen, nineteen, and twenty years old. It's a book about young people and the struggles thrust upon them by their culture and the enemies of their souls. But while it's a book *about* youth (and their families), it's not just a book *for* youth. This isn't a "youth novel." It's an adult novel with main characters who happen to be young. It's as much for people in their thirties, fifties, and seventies as for people in their teens and twenties.

How can adults and teenagers enjoy the same book? The same way both enjoy many of the same movies. *October Sky* was about kids. *Remember the Titans* was about high schoolers. Yet most adults loved both movies. The central characters in *The Chronicles of Narnia* are children, but countless adults read them over and over. *Huckleberry Finn* and *Tom Sawyer* have teenage main characters. Yet grandfathers enjoy them as much as grandchildren, and often more. No one thinks of them as teen novels. Likewise, *Lord of the Flies* is a story *about* boys, but it's not just a story *for* boys.

Of course, we're not foolish enough to consider *The Ishbane Conspiracy* a classic, but the point is valid—a story can have main characters who are young without being exclusively or even primarily a book for youth.

I receive many letters from teens and even preteens who have read my "adult" novels—*Deadline, Dominion, Edge of Eternity,* and *Lord Foulgrin's Letters*. Interestingly, these young readers rarely talk about the teenagers in those books (such as Carly in *Deadline,* and Ty or Gangster Cool in *Dominion*). Rather, they connect with the main characters, who are adults. Often their favorite character in *Deadline* is a young boy, Little Finn. Their favorite in *Dominion* is an old man, Obadiah Abernathy.

Similarly, *Dominion* is centered on the lives of African-Americans, but is not an African-American novel. Most of its readers aren't black. The primary characters in my novels tend to be men. But women read them as much as men do.

Just as the young can enjoy reading about the old, and whites about blacks, and women about men, *the older can enjoy reading about the younger.* This is one of the great benefits of reading a good story—entering into another person's world and coming away with a better understanding of real people. My daughters and I hope that parents and grandparents and uncles and aunts will gain from *The Ishbane Conspiracy* a greater understanding of the battles our young people fight and the joy they seek. I expect even more young people will read this novel than my previous ones. But I hope no fewer older people will read it, because it is for them as much as any book I've ever written.

My daughters Angela and Karina helped me write this book. It was my first collaboration since writing a book with my wife, Nanci, fifteen years ago, and I thoroughly enjoyed it. I can't think of two people I could have worked with who would have been more qualified and skilled, both spiritually and artistically. We read and discussed books on fiction writing, brainstormed characters and plots, stimulated one another's thinking, prayed together, had lots of fun, and shared the frustrations and mind-numbing hard work of disciplined writing. Angela and Karina are true coauthors, not token ones. This is their book as much as it's mine, and they have my deepest respect.

Angela, Karina, and I—along with their mom Nanci—are pleased to offer this book to our Lord Jesus. We pray He'll use it to make readers of all ages aware of the spiritual battles we face. May our eyes be opened to the strategies our accursed enemies are using to sabotage the lives of young people. And may we also see in a new light the King's joyful alternative.

"Sometimes the best way to see a thing
is to look at its opposite."
A. W. TOZER, *THE PURSUIT OF GOD*

1

DECEMBER 31, 3:25 A.M.

The moonlight cast an eerie shadow through the bedroom window. Jillian Fletcher kicked the mass of blankets to the side of the bed. She lay awake, weary, but unable to close her eyes. She appeared safe and snug in her nice home in the suburbs, but her heart ached for something she could never quite identify. Tonight a foreboding presence seemed to occupy the room. She wondered if she'd watched one too many horror movies with her friends.

A chill worked under Jillian's skin. She had the feeling she was being watched. She got up and shut the blinds, then spread two fingers between them and peeked out. She looked at the dark elm tree outside her second story bedroom. Was someone in the tree, watching her? For a moment she thought she saw the glimmer of eyes. She stifled a scream, then when she could see nothing, shivered and backed away. She went back to bed and pulled the covers over her, as if they were a warrior's shield protecting her from falling arrows.

The digital wall clock moved toward midnight.

"Another pointless New Year's party," Jillian Fletcher said, yawning, drained from last night's sleeplessness.

"The only people who aren't drunk are boring…or taken," Brittany said. "If this doesn't pick up soon, I say we leave and find a real party."

"Or we could just go home. I'm so exhausted."

"After this spine-tingling excitement, you'll be asleep before I get you home. You need to get a life, Jillian. And I'm just the one to help you do it. Back in a sec."

"Can't we go home?" Jillian said, her voice trailing off behind Brittany, who was already halfway across the room.

Jillian scanned Adam Brotnov's huge downstairs family room. There must've been fifty kids. The drinkers were over in their corner. Ty Lott and David Richards tilted back their beers, laughing too loudly at nothing. Apparently Adam's parents didn't have problems with underage drinking—or didn't think it was their business to come downstairs and check the place out. Jillian watched Ty light a joint. She wondered what her mom would think if she knew her perfect little daughter was at this kind of party. Most parents didn't have a clue. Mom was one of them.

Adam approached Ty.

"If you're going to smoke weed, go outside, away from the house." Ty and David laughed their way up the stairs and out the door. Jillian guessed they wouldn't be back. She felt relieved. Mom wouldn't smell it on her clothes.

There were three downstairs bedrooms. One had all the coats. Another was a make-out room, but it was full. Tired of waiting, some had gone out to their cars.

The third room had a group thing going, with a circle on the floor. Jillian guessed it was a game of Dungeons & Dragons. She drew closer to get a look. The door was slightly open. She smelled a sickening sweet incense. It was a New Age thing, with lights out and candles burning. Two girls and a guy were turning up tarot cards, then interpreting them. One of the guys was Ian Stewart, Brittany's old boyfriend.

Jillian felt something brush her ear. She jerked around.

"Let's go in," Brittany said. "It'll be fun." Jillian didn't want to, but she followed Brittany, who immediately sat in the circle. Jillian stayed back by the door, crouching down, trying not to draw attention to herself.

"This is the Magician card," said Skyla Stokes. She was a friend of Brittany's. She sat on folded legs, facing most of the kids. She had this wild Joan of Arc haircut that made Jillian wonder if the hairdresser sheared it with dull hedge trimmers. She was a four-point student and into Wicca. Some of the kids called her "Sabrina" behind her back, but for Skyla it was serious stuff. She was part of a campus coven of thirteen, mostly seniors. Brittany had told Jillian that Skyla put a curse on Corrie Ward just before her skiing accident left her paralyzed.

Skyla looked at one of the boys and said, "Okay, you drew the Magician—that means you have a mastery of words and matter. You have hermetic wisdom."

"What's hermetic wisdom?" the boy asked. Everybody laughed.

"You're a mediator-communicator," Skyla said. "You're a master manipulator of the material world. You can work miracles and do illusions. You are Hermes, god of orators and liars, merchants and thieves. Okay, now draw your other card."

He drew.

"The ace of swords," Skyla pronounced.

"What does it mean?"

"It's about the brutal aspect of power. It's about violence and consuming heat."

"Ooh," was the general response, partly joking, but Jillian sensed she wasn't the only uneasy one.

"Who's next?"

Someone Jillian couldn't see drew a card.

"You're the priestess," Skyla said.

Jillian stood on tiptoes to see her—it was Tara, a girl from youth group. Her dad was on the church board.

"You have the spiritual and intellectual face of the anima," Skyla said, "the feminine nature of the soul. You have primordial feminine wisdom, with the balancing forces of nature. You know the ancient healing arts, magic, and spiritual mystery."

"I *do*? Cool," Tara said. More laughter. The crowd seemed captivated. Though it unnerved her, Jillian was riveted too. Skyla's mysterious voice, the darkness broken by flickering candles...well, at least it wasn't boring.

"Draw your next one," Skyla said to Tara. She turned it up.

"The Death card!" somebody called. The room rumbled.

"Whoa. Look out!" said Ian Stewart. "Violence, brutal power, death—everybody be careful driving home!"

Laughter erupted. Brittany's laugh was the loudest. And she looked right at Ian.

Jillian sneaked out the door, hoping Brittany didn't see her. Brit would tease her, tell her she was paranoid. Maybe she was. Death and violence weren't entertaining thoughts. Not with what had happened to her dad.

Jillian walked aimlessly around, hearing the occasional laugh, but noticing the vacant troubled look on a lot of faces. Were people really having fun, or were they just pretending to? Were they as lonely as she was? She didn't feel at home here.

The party was supposed to be a celebration, but why did she feel so vacant? And why did everyone else look so empty too? Only one semester of high school left. But what would be next? She wanted to go away, anywhere. Do something different, anything. Find whatever it was she was missing. But how? Where? Jillian didn't know what was wrong. But whatever it was, she felt powerless to change it. What did she have to look forward to? She sighed. Her want list was topped by two items. She wanted a boyfriend. And she wanted to move to a new house. She needed a new person and a new place. Yeah, that was it. Her prospects for happiness boiled down to two questions—who and where?

Jillian got some punch and sat in a chair by herself, away from the traffic, staring at the room as if it were a galaxy far, far away.

Suddenly it went pitch black. An eerie silence was pierced by screams. Guys were taking advantage of the opportunity to scare girls and pretend they weren't afraid. Jillian crossed her arms and wrapped them tight, pulling back from the darkness into her chair. The lights popped back on. Kids cheered.

After twenty minutes, Brittany and several others finally emerged from the room.

"It was cool, Jillian. The lights went out at the perfect time. You really should try the tarot cards. We've got to get some."

Jillian nodded, not saying what she really thought. She rarely said to Brittany what she really thought.

Brittany ruffled her friend's hair, then Jillian playfully poked Brittany's stomach.

"Ow! Careful with the abs. Those exercises are killing me; the price you pay for perfection." Her eyes darted. "Hey. There goes Ian."

Jillian followed Brittany's gaze to the corner couch by a big punch bowl, where Ian Stewart was greeting another guy. They slapped hands.

"You still have it for Ian, don't you, Brit? That's why you wanted to go in that room."

"My interest was purely metaphysical," she said. "Well, okay, maybe I wanted to reconnect with Ian. We got pretty close…you know, before I…had my problems. He backed off then, like I had leprosy. I don't blame him. I was a little messed up. Hey, you see who's talking to him?"

"I see him. Who is he?"

"You don't remember Robbie Gonzales?"

"No! That's Rob? He looks so different with short hair. Guess I haven't seen him since he graduated last year. He goes to Portland State, doesn't he?"

"Yeah. I heard that's where Ian wants to go next year."

"I wonder if Rob still drives that pimped-out banger car, the black one? He looks…nice."

"He looks *buff*. If I wasn't taller than him, I'd be interested."

"Well, I'm not taller than him, and I *am* interested." Jillian felt instant redness, realizing she sounded more like Brittany than herself.

"Honey, there's nobody in this room you're taller than. Okay," Brittany whispered, raising an eyebrow. "Let's do a bathroom mirror check, then we'll mosey on over their direction."

"I'll go, but I'm not going to flirt."

"You say you're interested, then you say you're not going to flirt? Make up your mind, sweetheart. I know where I'm headed…right back into Ian's life. Rob's there for your taking."

"I'm not going to throw myself at him."

"Don't get self-righteous. You've gone conservative on me ever since…well, you know." Jillian teared up instantly. "You're talking about Dad?"

"I didn't mean it that way. I meant since your dad's…change. You know. When he got religious and stuff. At first you hated it, but then you started to buy into it. And then…"

"And then he died," Jillian said, a single tear cutting through her makeup, and exposing the underlying freckles.

"Oh, man. I'm sorry, Jill. I didn't mean to bring up your dad."

"No, don't say that! I *want* people to bring him up. Sometimes a few hours go by where I don't think about him, and I feel awful."

"Do you think he'd want you to feel that way?"

"Probably not."

"Right. He'd want you to move on with your life. He'd want you to go talk with Rob." Jillian laughed at the leap in her friend's logic. "I'm not in the mood."

"Let's see that face. Nothing Bobby Brown Essentials can't repair. I'll get you back in the mood."

Brittany grabbed Jillian's right hand and tugged on her to follow. In a lighter moment, Jillian would have bounced along next to her. As number one flier for Kennedy High's cheerleading squad, she was known for being "spirited," without crossing that fine line to "bubbly." But her dad's death in the car accident last spring had taken its toll. Right when she thought the wounds had started to heal, fresh pain would cut through her again.

She'd been reading the Bible once in a while and attending a church youth group, more than anything because she knew that's what her dad would have wanted. But except for her friend Lisa from school and Greg and Kristi, the youth pastor and his wife, Jillian hadn't made any real friends at church. She had a new faith, sort of, and yet…she didn't really own it. She wasn't sure she wanted to. Not after what God had done to her dad.

They marched across the room beside a ten-foot hors d'oeuvres table. Brittany's straight cinnamon brown hair hung nearly to her elbows, and it swung like a pendulum from one side to the other. Something about it always made Jillian want to laugh. They were such opposites.

Five minutes later they emerged from the bathroom. Brittany led the way, wandering through the crowd, accidentally-on-purpose meandering near Ian and Rob, who were sitting on a couch, engaged in heavy conversation.

Brittany picked up a ladle from a punch bowl five feet from the guys, then looked at Jillian and said in a loud voice, "Yeah, that's true, isn't it!" She laughed hard and long.

Jillian stared at her, then saw the commanding look in her friend's eyes, and suddenly started laughing herself.

"Brit?"

Brittany, her face full of surprise, turned and looked at Ian. "Ian Stewart? I didn't know *you* were here."

Ian grinned. "Didn't you see me in the tarot room? I was hoping we could talk. I miss hanging out with you. Seems like it's been months. You remember Roberto?"

"Of course. Hey, Robbie. Love your hair."

Rob laughed, like he wasn't sure if she was kidding.

"Jillian, remember Rob Gonzales?" Brittany asked.

"Sure. Hi, Rob," Jillian said. He nodded and smiled.

Ian pulled a vacant love seat over to face the couch. "Sit down," Ian said. Brittany sat next to Ian on the love seat, leaving Jillian standing there, gazing at the space next to Rob.

"We didn't mean to interrupt," Brittany said.

"No problem. We were getting too serious for a party anyway, right Rob?"

Jillian sat down carefully, trying to leave the perfect amount of space.

The four talked and laughed. Within five minutes Jillian was amazed at how natural it felt, how comfortable she was with these guys, especially Rob. It was like being with old friends.

Brittany pointed to the smoky quartz on the chain around Ian's neck. "What's the stone? It's new, isn't it?"

"It's an Osiris crystal. Got it last month."

"What's Osiris?" Jillian asked.

"An Egyptian god."

"You believe in God?" Rob asked.

"I believe in gods. I can't narrow it down to one god as opposed to another. I don't think we're alone. I think there are a lot of outside forces that influence us."

"Do-do-do-do, do-do-do-do." Brittany sang the *Twilight Zone* theme. "Still reading all your metaphysical stuff, Ian?"

"When I'm not playing basketball. And when I don't have a beautiful girl at my side."

"So how do you like Portland State?" Jillian asked Rob.

"Some of the profs are from another planet—speaking of the *Twilight Zone*—but some are pretty cool." His dark brown eyes sparkled. "Besides doing a ton of studying, I'm involved with a campus Bible study group. Plus there's an awesome church nearby. Sometimes I make it out here on Sundays to my home church."

"How's campus life?" Jillian asked.

"Fine, as long as you stay away from the drugs and booze and the…" he looked at the floor, "other stuff. But I really like it. I've met a lot of great people. I've been trying to talk Ian into coming next fall, staying in the apartments, maybe being my roommate. I'm sure the basketball coach would like to meet him."

They talked and laughed about everything. Jillian tuned out the rest of the party and lost herself in conversation.

"So how's your senior year going?" Rob asked.

"Got senioritis, of course. I'm really looking forward to getting out. Mom says I shouldn't rush it. But I want to get out there, do something. Cheerleading's going great, church youth group is good. Even work's kind of fun."

"Where do you work?"

"I'm a waitress at Red Robin. Just Thursday nights and an occasional weekend. I get great tips."

"Red Robin, huh? Maybe I'll stop by sometime." Rob seemed to blush, then turned towards Ian. "When's your next basketball game?"

"Friday night, home against Grant. They've got a 6-7 center, but my man's 6-4, so we're even. We faced off in a summer clinic. He's decent, but I can handle him. Should be a good game."

"Maybe I'll come check you out Friday," Rob said.

"Great," Brittany said. "Then you can see Jillian do her cheerleading. She's a…what do you call it? Glider?"

"Flier," Jillian said, not smiling. She wanted to strangle Brittany, who was already asking Ian about the meaning of the Osiris stone. Jillian and Rob gradually leaned back and caught each other's eye.

"You mentioned your church," Rob said. "Tell me more about it."

The more she talked, the more she wanted to. He seemed genuinely interested.

"11:59!" someone shouted.

"What?" Brittany asked.

"It's almost midnight?" Rob said. "You've got to be kidding. Last I looked it was 10:45!"

"Time flies when you're having fun," Ian said.

"I guess," Jillian said. "This started out as one of the worst New Year's parties I've ever been at. Now…it's like one of the best."

"What do you mean, *one* of the best?" Ian asked, his arm around Brittany.

Twenty kids gathered around a computer, where full-screen digits counted down the seconds. When it showed "11," Jillian heard the deep breath.

"Ten, nine, eight…" kids shouted in unison.

Ian and Brittany turned to each other and pressed their lips together. Jillian looked nervously at Rob out of the corner of her eye.

"Seven, six, five…"

Rob moved a little closer to her. She hoped he wasn't close enough to see her freckles through her make-up.

"Four, three, two…"

"Happy New Year, Jillian," Rob said.

Streamers flew, balloons popped, noisemakers fired, someone beat on pans and someone else turned up the music. Jonathan from the jazz band blew his trumpet. Everybody laughed.

Jillian felt something she hadn't felt in months. Maybe it was hope. For the first time since her dad's death she actually felt like celebrating.

Rob stepped up to the table, filled three punch glasses and handed one first to Jillian, then Brittany, then Ian. He filled his own glass and lifted it up in the center of their little circle. "To four friends, and to the year ahead of us…whatever it may bring."

The four glasses clanked, Ian's a little too hard, spilling some punch. They all laughed and drank up.

A cell phone rang. Five people reached for theirs, but drew blanks. Ian pulled his phone from a big pocket on his cargo pants and held it up to his ear.

"Yeah, Ty? Right. Still at the party. Wait. Slow down. I can't understand you, man. You called 911? What do you mean? Why?"

Ian waved his long arm for quiet. People stopped what they were doing and gathered by the couch to listen. "David? He was just drunk, man. I've seen him that way lots of times. Wait…what did you say? I can't understand. Start over. Say it really slow."

While everyone in the room listened breathlessly, Ian's face turned white.

"David's *dead?*"

Letter 1

My dearly demoted Foulgrin,

So you've just returned from a long visit to the House of Corrections? I trust you found it therapeutic. Beelzebub has made me your parole officer. He instructed me to watch you carefully.

When I heard you had the gall to call yourself "Lord," why was I not surprised? Even when I supervised you centuries ago, you were my most arrogant agent.

Don't bore me with your excuses. You claim your uncomplimentary references to Beelzebub were a trap set for your old understudy Squaltaint? I'm uninterested in politics.

I'm a no-nonsense demon. I equip subordinates in the fine art of deceiving and destroying human vermin. Keep your mouth shut and do your duty. Your previous experience with three of these four young vermin should prove helpful.

Let's get some things straight. First, Lucifer gave me the title "Prince"—I did not assign it to myself. Second, I welcome this new assignment no more than you. *Your* demotion got *me* reassigned from a top administrative position. To be transferred from directing the American politics department to baby-sitting you is a major downward career move.

I won't play games, Foulgrin. I have a job to do. I'll do it as efficiently as possible so I can quickly return to Beelzebub's inner circle. Your former secretary Obsmut is now at my service. He's assured me he knows your tactics well. He can read between the lines of your communication. Put aside your ego. Let's get some work done.

I read your initial dossier on Jillian Fletcher. You whine that you don't grasp the language and emotions of this young female. You complain you don't understand her taste in clothes or music. But in order to defeat the enemy, you must *know* the enemy. You must study her, her friends, and her family. This will give you the edge so you can take her down.

What always matters is the bottom line. Is she moving away from the Enemy or moving toward Him? Whoever or whatever draws her toward Him must be at the top of your hit list. Eliminate her any way you can.

Despite your failure to understand Jillian, you say you're confident you'll succeed. You've seen her up close, due to your years assigned to her father, Jordan Fletcher? I have his file in front of me. You failed miserably with him, Foulgrin. Is it your intention to do the same with her?

The reports show Fletcher's life and death were a defeat for Erebus. Many were touched by his conversion. The Enemy even used this sludgebag's memorial service for His ends. Fletcher left his family a Christian heritage. But there's a dark lining in every silver cloud. First, his fatherly influence is gone. Second, the girl blames the Enemy for taking him from her.

New Year's is one of my favorite seasons. It means Christmas—or as we prefer to call it, the "winter holidays"—is safely behind us. We've buried the manger under mountains of toys, videos, and designer clothes. But there's always the threat of the Carpenter rearing His head and being seen for who He is. The Enemy has this annoying habit of enabling some of them to see through our blanket of materialism. They grasp the terrifying significance of His invasion of the dark planet. As long as the Carpenter stays in the manger, it's tolerable. But if they see Him crucified and risen, beware. All heaven could break loose.

The New Year always raises hopes in these bloated bags of chemicals the Enemy calls His image-bearers. We dash their hopes until they become cynical, resigned to eking out their miserable existence. Then they die and victory is ours. The New Year inspires innumerable resolutions broken before the frosts of February. All their efforts at self-reform divert their attention from the Enemy's offer of lasting supernatural change.

The atmosphere of the party sounded delicious—drinking, drugs, fornication, materialism, gluttony, pretense, deceit, and even the occult. A demon's dream party. Increasingly typical, I'm glad to say. That the vermin died from alcohol poisoning is icing on the cake. We've cultivated a youth culture of death and self-destruction. The more the better.

Remember, though, the Enemy has a way of using our victories as warning shots across their bows. There's always the danger He'll use death to turn their thoughts toward what lies beyond it. And what they can do to prepare for it.

I want full reports not only on Jillian, but also on the other three young bipeds. Meanwhile, keep them busy. Their parents believe ceaseless activity will keep them out of trouble. What it really does is keep them from pondering what's missing in their lives. They'll never turn their attention to the Enemy. Not as long as we can lock them onto our long lineup of alternatives.

Anticipating your first report,

Prince Ishbane

2

Jillian walked with Brittany into First Memorial Church. They meandered past the large display of photographs, ball gloves, jerseys and skiing trophies. Brittany pointed at one photo of her, standing near David. In the pictures David looked alive and vibrant. And now...

A tall pale man in a dark suit escorted them up the aisle and seated them near the front. Jillian looked at her watch. She should be in English class, but when there was a student funeral—Jillian had been to five of them in her high school years—students were always excused. The school had it down to a science. Grief counselors were brought in. Students were encouraged to ask questions and seek help from staff and peer counselors. Teachers were trained what to say and what not to say. But somehow it never made everything okay. After all was said and done, the kids were still dead.

Jillian endured the uncomfortable moments when the piano was playing and people were being seated and the service hadn't started, but you could hear sobs, mostly quiet but occasionally loud enough to make you turn your head and look. As Brittany read the program, Jillian thought about her best friend.

She'd met Brittany Powell at a junior class water ski trip a year and a half ago, a week before classes started at Kennedy High. Brittany had just moved up from California. She was tall and bronzed, athletic and brilliant—and with a razor-sharp tongue. Jillian was the cute cheerleader, a B-plus student. But she had to work for those grades, while Brittany's A's seemed effortless.

Different as they were, in a matter of weeks they'd become inseparable. They'd talked about a lot of guys, seen a lot of movies, cruised a lot of town, done a lot of malls and pulled off some unforgettable escapades, like going down to Oxbow Park at midnight, wading in the Sandy River in the moonlight and freaking out at sounds in the woods. Brittany was always the instigator.

Religion was a sore spot between them. Besides a couple of other funerals and her sister's wedding, Jillian knew Brittany hadn't been to church since she was a kid. She didn't understand or appreciate Jillian's recent interest in Christianity—sometimes Jillian didn't understand it either. But Brittany had been there for Jillian. She'd even skipped a huge volleyball tournament to be at Jillian's dad's funeral. The coach had asked his star outside hitter to reconsider. "No way," Brittany told him. She was like that. She could be wild, outrageous, and infuriating. But she was always loyal to Jillian.

Suddenly Brittany's head turned and her antenna went up. Ian had walked in, escorted by Tall-and-Pasty-Face. Brittany beckoned for Ian to join her. Jillian still couldn't see Ian without remembering that Ouija board thing they did at his house last year. It was the scariest night of her life, a lot scarier than the Oxbow adventure. She still had nightmares about it. But worst of all was four weeks later when Brittany attempted suicide. Jillian shuddered at the thought, and though she smiled at Ian, she wondered if the two were good for each other.

A month after her best friend attempted suicide, Jillian's dad had died. It had been the hardest year of her life. Now here she sat, about to start her last semester of high school, uncertain about college, uncertain about everything. And it was starting with another funeral, this time a classmate's.

She noticed a middle-aged couple up front, the man in an old suit, the woman in a nice dress, both staring at the shiny mahogany casket.

David's parents. What must they be feeling?

Greg, the youth pastor at her church, Sovereign Grace, stood up and took the microphone. He'd probably been asked since he knew so many students at Kennedy. She wondered if he'd ever met David.

"Let's pray," Greg said. "Lord, this is a tough time for us. Especially for David's family and closest friends. We need Your help. Open our minds to Your truth today, Lord. Your Bible tells us, 'Death is the destiny of every man; the living should take this to heart.' Make us aware of our mortality, Lord. And help us take it to heart. Your Word says it's appointed unto us once to die, and after this the judgment. Help us live our lives and make choices in a way that prepares us for the day we stand before You. We want to remember David today, Lord, but we know he's not here. He's in another world. If David could come back from the other side, I'm sure he'd plead with us to prepare today for when we'll each stand before You. We pray for Your comfort on his parents and brother and sister, and all who loved David. And we pray also that You'd speak to our hearts today, in the name of the Lord Jesus, who is the way, the truth, and the life. Amen."

"Amen," Jillian heard someone whisper behind her.

The speakers blared "Higher," a song by the black-on-black group Creed. It spoke of dreaming, being guided through another world, and longing to escape from this life to a better one. Some place where blind men see, some place higher. Though she didn't think it was a Christian song, Jillian could identify with the longing. She wasn't sure whether David had.

Ty Lott went forward and read a tribute to his friend. Ty cried. So did everyone, even Brittany. It sounded so unlike a gathering of high schoolers. No laughter, no catcalls, no smart remarks. Stone silence, except for the weeping.

Principal Chandler said a few nice words about David, even though everybody knew the two couldn't stand each other. Then he said, "I'd like to introduce our guest speaker, the pastor of David's family's church where we're gathered today, First Memorial. Reverend Braun."

The lean graying man, wearing a black robe, stepped behind the pulpit.

"Hello, young people," he said, smiling broadly but sounding solemn. "This day of heartbreak brings us together in memory of our dearly departed friend..." he looked at his notes and paused, "Mr. David Richards. He was a dedicated student, a fine athlete, a beloved son. All who knew him were touched indelibly by his life. We will not soon forget our dear friend…David. We desire this service to be a time of healing for all of us. Let us pray and dedicate this memorial service to David's memory. If you feel comfortable doing so, pray with me now to the heavenly parent, whomever you may conceive him or her to be."

After a singsong prayer that gave Jillian the creeps, she looked up and saw Brittany roll her eyes.

"Phony," she whispered to Jillian, too loud. Jillian elbowed her and Brittany laughed.

Reverend Braun quoted from *Newsweek* and *People* and read a Robert Frost poem. He spoke of the strength and character of this misunderstood generation. He read a heartwarming story Jillian remembered getting in an e-mail, the kind that said at the bottom if you really loved your friends, you'd forward it to ten of them, and if you didn't you were a big loser. Jillian had sent it to ten of her friends.

Reverend Braun spoke of "holding fast to your truth, your own set of values" and said death is a "passage to a better place," and "like leaves changing color in the fall." He spoke of the "resurrection of lilies blooming in the spring after the cold darkness of winter." He said, "David is now in that higher stage of spiritual development." He said that since David so loved skiing, "the snow of winter should always remind us of David and his life, and the legacy he has left us." Reverend Braun assured everyone that death, while tragic, was a natural part of the cycle of life. "David is in a better place," he said, and "he will always live on in our memories."

Jillian didn't know David that well. But his rep was as a party boy, a heavy drinker whose life goal seemed to be to get as many girls in bed as he could. He'd been arrested several times, she knew. He didn't attend a church, and she'd certainly never seen an indication he was a Christian.

So how does this guy know he's in a better place?

When the service was over, a crowd gathered at the casket and held hands and cried. Feeling cold and empty, Jillian moved away from the casket. She got separated from Brittany and the crowd swallowed her. People she'd never had a conversation with were hugging her. She felt terribly alone in a sea of faces. Shivering, she withdrew and walked quickly to the end of a hallway. She opened a door marked "Third Grade Sunday School," and squeezed into a little red plastic chair.

Jillian recalled the words a pastor spoke at her father's funeral. "There's a time for everything…no man knows the day of his death." It sounded so cruel. She wanted to live in a different world, one where she would know what was coming, one that wasn't so…out of control.

"You okay?"

The voice startled her. She looked at a face she hadn't expected to see. She tried to compose herself, to look cool. It didn't work. Tears flowed.

"Didn't mean to scare you." Rob walked closer, but stopped. He looked as if he wanted to reach out his hand, but wasn't sure if he should.

"How'd you know I was here?" Jillian asked.

"I saw you at the service. I...watched you come back here. Thought you looked upset. Wondered if you felt like talking."

"No," she said. Then after a pause, "Yes."

He laughed.

"Is that clear enough?" Jillian asked.

"How about we go to Starbucks? Or Café Delirium. Somewhere we can talk without...talking."

"Okay. I'm sure not going back to school like this."

Letter 2

My scheming Foulgrin,

I was delighted to hear your Reverend Braun did the service. "Pray to the divine parent, whomever you conceive him or her to be"? Magnificent.

I checked Braun's file. It's full of memos from you and Squaltaint. This is my kind of clergyman. His reassurances about David being in heaven were perfect. The Enemy has used funerals time and again as platforms to communicate His truth. This bothersome youth pastor, Greg, was trying to do that. Fortunately, he could only bootleg in so much truth in a prayer. Not enough to neutralize the main message from our man Braun.

Braun's point was clear—if this vermin David, who never gave a thought to the Enemy, is really in heaven, everyone must go there automatically. So why think about it? Why bother with such inconveniences as repentance, confession, asking forgiveness, believing the Enemy's forbidden book, seeking to obey Him, gathering with the forbidden fellowship? If David is in heaven, everyone—with the possible exceptions of Hitler, Stalin, and Mao—will be there too.

Of course, *we* know what everyone in the universe except those on The Stupid Planet know. Hell, not Heaven, is their default destination. They can enter the nonsmoking section only through a change in reservation. The Enemy must intervene to draw them to Him. They must embrace His gift. Just don't let *them* understand that.

On the authority of a "Christian minister," they've been reassured that it requires no repentance to go to heaven! After hearing this, anyone saying "you must believe in the Lord Jesus Christ to be saved" will be considered a narrow-minded bigot.

We cannot create. But we *can* infect. Braun is our infiltrator. The god he offers is anything and everything, and therefore nothing. His message is rat-poison wrapped in taffy. He would have made an outstanding demon!

Apparently Rob and Ian will be sticking close to Jillian and Brittany. They should prove useful. I've decided you should employ team temptation with the three tempters assigned to the adolescent vermin: Raketwist, Pendragon, and Baalgore.

In spite of a thumbs-down from Obsmut, I'm appointing you team captain. In my letters to you, I will address concerns related to each of the teenage vermin. It will be up to you to relay the messages to R, P, and B. Don't make me regret this decision.

It looks as though Brittany will prove your greatest asset in taking down Jillian. She's materialistic and cynical? She tugs Jillian away from spiritual interests? Stretches her moral comfort zones? Keeps her from developing deeper friendships at the church? Perfect. She's a page right out of hell's playbook.

Brittany's convinced the church is a hangout for hypocrites and losers? If there's one thing these teenage sludgebags don't want to be, it's losers. Cool is everything. Yes, Brittany's occult experience is most promising. Revive that interest. Your encounter with her at the Ouija board last year and your appearance in her dream after her attempted suicide are notable. Remember, though, when it comes to deceiving and destroying Jillian Fletcher, Brittany may prove more useful to you alive than dead.

Implement our usual strategy with Jillian. Make her think that because she's doing her good Christian deeds, she's pulling Brittany up. Of course, her friend is actually pulling her down. Since down is our direction—and gravity is always on our side—we have no objection that Brittany has some good qualities.

It was Amrael who reassigned your adversary Jaltor to Jillian. Don't forget that Jaltor beat you in your skirmish over her father. Let that thought twist in you like a knife.

Rob is the only one you've not had previous experience with, and he's my biggest concern. He's the wild card in this quartet. Do your background check!

I'll orchestrate from a distance our conspiracy against these four adolescent vermin. I'll lead, you follow. I'll call the play, you run it. Have I made myself clear, Foulgrin?

At least two of the four are headed toward hell with minimal help from us. But even the Christians we can blind, distracting them from serving the Enemy. His children are always at the top of our hit list.

Let's make it a foursome, shall we?

Delighting in their destruction,

Prince Ishbane

3

Rob turned his key in the ignition of his black low rider. It cranked without starting. He turned back the key and waited. He tried again. Nothing.

"I'm just trying to impress you," he said. He tried again and again. Finally it started. They both laughed.

Rob drove Jillian to Café Delirium. They placed their order, then went to the back corner where there was a comfy couch and an old slouchy chair. He gestured for her to sit. She took the couch, and he sat across from her in the chair. They made small talk. When the girl behind the counter waved, he picked up Jillian's small vanilla latte and his turkey sandwich and large mocha, and they settled in.

"Sure you don't want a sandwich or something?" Rob asked. "It's lunch time."

"No. I'm fine. Just the coffee. So…did you know David?"

"Not well. I graduated with his brother Jarod. Went to his house a few times. David shot hoops with us once. But I thought I'd come to the service since we were at the party where he…"

"Yeah," she said.

"How well did you know him?"

She shrugged. "Went to the same grade school. Had the same homeroom a couple of years. Saw him play football. Saw him skiing up at Meadows a couple of times. That's about it."

"I think it's great you care as much as you do," Rob said. "But, if you don't mind me asking…why are you taking it so hard if you didn't really know him?"

She sighed. "Maybe because if it happened to David, it could happen to me or Brit or any of my friends. Or my mom. Or brother." She laughed. "Sometimes I want to kill my brother, but I don't want anybody else to."

"We all have to die," Rob said, so matter-of-factly it surprised Jillian. "But it's sad when it's because of wrong choices. I closed my eyes to some of the things that were going on at that party. Just because I wasn't drinking and smoking dope doesn't mean it was okay. I should've spoken up. Or left earlier. The only good thing that came out of it was…" His voice trailed off.

"What?"

"Connecting with Ian again. And meeting…you know, some new friends." He smiled.

"Just when you think things are getting good again," Jillian said, "something happens. I'm tired of people getting hurt. And dying. Life isn't so great these days."

Rob nodded. "It has its ups and downs, doesn't it?"

"I'm on a streak of downs."

"What do you mean? You're smart, you're nice, you're…"

"Yes?"

"Well, you're not ugly." He smiled.

"Uh…thanks?"

"Sorry. I just didn't want to sound like…I was coming on to you or something. But I do think you're very…cute."

"Thanks." *Beautiful would be nice, but cute will do.*

"So this hit you hard because it opened some old wounds."

"Not that old. My dad died nine months ago. Car accident."

"Oh, man. I'm sorry. It's coming back. I didn't really know you then, but I heard the story. I should've put it together."

"When it's someone you read about in the paper, it doesn't seem real. Ten thousand people could die in an earthquake in India, and I'd feel bad for twenty seconds, then I'd be back to normal life."

"Whereas their world is never going to be the same."

"Exactly. I knew about death in my head. But when Daddy died…" She choked. He put his hand on hers. They sat quietly. She didn't trust herself to start talking again.

"My brother Guillermo died four years ago," Rob said softly.

"I'm sorry. What happened? I mean, how…?"

"He…it doesn't matter. We were close. Just fourteen months apart. It was hard. Still is."

"I just want to have a normal life again," Jillian said.

"Is there any such thing as a normal life?"

"I used to have one. It was boring sometimes, but I'd rather be bored than have my life…shattered. I feel so out of control."

"Maybe it's because you are."

"You're a big help."

"No, I mean it. I'm not in control. Neither are you. We can do what we can do, but let's face it, we don't pull the strings of the universe. It's like we're on a big ship crossing the ocean and we can do certain things on board, like eat lunch or play shuffleboard or take a nap or read a book. But we can't make the ship go wherever we want. We can't keep the storms from coming, and we can't keep the waves from spilling over onto the deck."

"Wow, you're getting deep on me," Jillian said. "That's a pretty good analogy. But I'd like to think of myself as the captain of the ship or at least a crew member. I mean, we have to have *some* control."

"But not as much as we'd like. Otherwise I'd still have my brother. And you'd have your father. And David wouldn't have died the other night."

"Sometimes I don't like this world," Jillian said.

"For me, it's more than sometimes."

"This isn't a very upbeat conversation, is it?" For some reason, she giggled. He smiled a moment himself, but it faded quickly.

"What do you want me to say? That it's okay David died? And your dad, and my brother? It isn't okay. It's not God's ideal."

"Then why does He let it happen?"

"That's the big question, isn't it? He's all-powerful, so He could keep it from happening. I know it involves His glory and His sovereign purposes. The Bible says He's accomplishing a plan, but sometimes it's hidden."

"It'd be nice if it wasn't so hidden."

"Scripture says the secret things belong to the Lord our God. It also says that the things revealed belong to us. His Word tells us a lot, but it doesn't tell us everything. One thing's for sure, God's not a genie."

"What do you mean?"

"He's the master, we're the servants. It's not the other way around. He doesn't always do what we want Him to."

"I've noticed that. Like a couple of minutes after we celebrate a new friendship and a great time at the party, right when I'm feeling better than I've felt in nine months, we find out David died. Not my idea of the perfect ending to a perfect evening." She looked at Rob. "How long have you been a Christian?"

"Four years. Two days after Guillermo died. That's when I came to grips with the fact that I was out of control. And I needed to know the One who was in control. Maybe that was one of the good things God brought out of a bad situation."

"You would've liked my dad," Jillian said. "He became a Christian less than six months before he died. I'm telling you, he was a different person. He would've liked you too."

"I look forward to meeting him," Rob said. For just a moment, Jillian thought he'd misunderstood.

"You mean…in heaven?" she said.

"Yeah."

"And you'll get to see your brother again, huh?"

Rob looked at the floor. Jillian wished she could take the words back.

"I don't think so."

"What happened to him?"

Rob looked up at the clock. "Time's flyin'. I've got dinner with my parents, then a night class. I should get you home."

"Get out of my face!" Daniel screamed.

Jillian drew her baby brother Joey closer. "Looks like the Trench Coat Kid's on the rampage again," she whispered.

"I warned you!" Diane Fletcher yelled at Daniel. "I said if I caught you on those websites again, I'd take away the computer. This is the third time. I've had it!"

"You don't have the right. It's *my* computer."

"*Your* computer? I don't remember you paying for it. I don't remember you working for it. You won't even clean your room or take out the garbage. Using the computer's a privilege, and privileges have to be earned. Your father said—"

"My father's dead!"

The words hung in the stark silence. A moment later the spell was broken by Diane's soft sobs.

Jillian looked around the living room. She was so tired of this house. She walked over and handed Joey off to her mom. "I'm going to Brittany's," she said, leaving out that Ian and Rob were meeting them there.

"Wait until I'm finished with your brother," Diane said.

"We *are* finished," Daniel said.

"I'll talk to you later, Mom," Jillian said as she headed to the door. "Brittany's waiting for me."

"I'm asking you to wait for *me* a few minutes. Brittany's not the center of the universe and neither are you."

"Chill out," Jillian mumbled to herself.

"What did you say, young lady?"

"Sorry. But just because you've had a bad day—again—doesn't mean you should take it out on me."

"I need to talk with you about something."

"Brit's waiting. You started in on young Frankenstein, and now I have to go."

"Don't call him that," Diane said. Daniel put on his earphones and stalked into his room. "We're not done, young man."

As Diane turned toward Jillian, Daniel slammed his bedroom door behind him. Joey screamed. Diane shook as she tried to quiet the crying baby in her arms. Jillian stared at her. It was still hard to get used to the fact that in five months her mom would be coming to her high school graduation carrying a diaper bag.

"Jillian, listen," Diane said. Jillian turned toward the door. Her mother grabbed her wrist. "I found your lunch in the trash. You didn't eat a thing."

"I wasn't hungry."

"You're losing too much weight. Something's wrong. You need to see a doctor."

"I need to lose weight. I'm a flier. The girls who catch me don't want to be squashed."

"Please, Jillian. We need to meet with the counselor again."

"I'm not going back there. He's a nerd."

"He may be a nerd, but he's a trained and competent therapist nerd, and we need to talk to him."

"Why?"

"Because…since your dad died it's been difficult for us all."

"Talking doesn't help."

"Yes it does. We can go to someone else, Jilly. How about Kristi from the church, the youth pastor's wife? Did you ever call her back? She still wants to get together with you. A couple months ago you said you liked her. You need to talk with the right people."

"What I need is to get out of here, away from the noise."

"Work with me, Jillian. This family needs help. God's help."

Jillian felt her face tingle with the rush of blood. "If God wanted to help us, why did He kill Daddy?"

She ran out the front door, slamming it behind her. As Diane Fletcher slumped down on the couch weeping, her baby still in her arms, Jillian got into her car and pounded the steering wheel.

~~~~

Letter 3

Dear Foulgrin,

Serious conversations of the sort you mentioned are exactly what you must prevent. Jillian and the boy contemplating matters of eternal significance? Unthinkable. We inundate them with superficiality to avoid this very thing. I don't like Rob Gonzales. Get rid of him.

On the other hand, I'm delighted by the family feud. The Enemy wants to draw the Fletcher maggots together in their adversity. For a time He succeeded. But the post-trauma honeymoon is over.

The baby boomers have unwittingly cultivated in their offspring what they most resent. It drives them crazy that their children are rebellious and spoiled. Just like themselves, but with even less idealism and optimism. They're suspicious and cynical. Though they live in the most affluent culture in history, a cloud of gloom hangs over their lives. No hope. That's why they think short-term, not long-term. Which makes it easy for us to lure them into our traps.

I love their hard-edged cynicism. "That stinks" sums up their view of the world. Of course, if they find no hope in the world, they might turn to the Enemy for hope. Stay on guard.

There's no national cause to rally this generation together. They're fragmented into special interest groups. They're all about ethnicity, economic status, gender. This fragmentation leaves them narrow and conflicted. They're on their own, with everyone else the enemy.

Unfortunately, the Enemy is a subversive opportunist. We must continuously feed them secondary causes. Otherwise, they could see through the smoke and mirrors and turn to His primary cause. There's the danger they could come to the Enemy by process of elimination. That's why as soon as one of our alternatives proves a dead-end street, we must quickly offer them the next. Before we run out of false alternatives, they'll run out of time. We win. They lose.

This is the connected generation—connected to computers, telephones, videos, television, music. But they're also the disconnected generation—disconnected from parents, church, and moral absolutes.

The more hours they spend on the Internet—and their other substitute realities—

the more stressed, depressed, and lonely these kids become. It hampers their ability to communicate with real people in real life. The online world is a virtual reality without responsible adults. But the Enemy has made them to need adults, just as adults need them. Our job is to divide the generations. Convince them they don't need each other, they can't understand each other. Drive any wedge you can between Jillian and her mother.

As for Daniel, the more disconnected a vermin is relationally, the more prone he is to engage in antisocial behavior. He spends unprecedented hours in outside activities, yet also unprecedented hours alone. Parents stare at the television or work on the car or decorate the house, oblivious to the world of darkness their child lives in behind his closed doors. Parents say, "He needs his space." What he needs is parenting. Fortunately, we've convinced them they've taken the high ground by "not butting in." This is exactly what we've done to Diane. Luckily, the forbidden squadron she attends hasn't done much to equip her.

She tells Daniel not to look at the porn sites and the death-fixation sites or he'll lose his computer privileges. But each time she relents. Make her feel like she doesn't dare be strict. The poor little boy gets picked on, and he's lost his father. He needs extra rope. Just enough rope for us to hang him.

Meanwhile, make sure she makes no real attempts to enter into his world. Or understand the insecurities that plague him. Or the attractions that draw him. Those are for us to understand and exploit—not for her. Let her try to impose rules without the relationship that gives meaning to rules. Convince her these occasional visits to a counselor are the best she can do for her children. After all, she's not a professional. She's just a poor working mother. What does she have to offer her children?

As for Jillian, don't let her see her mother's needs, only her own. Make her the center of her own world. Let her wallow in her grief over losing her father. But don't let her consider the depth of her mother's loss. Convince Jillian that her mother wants to control her and make her life miserable.

Jillian's blame of the Enemy serves us well. As long as she doesn't blame herself, us, or the world, we can cultivate ever-deeper bitterness toward Him. It's especially helpful when she blames Him for the bad in her life, but doesn't credit Him for the good.

More on Ian and Rob in my next letter. Meanwhile, focus on driving Jillian out of the home. Convince her that her friends are the only ones who understand. Who needs family and old people? Not us!

Generationgap@erebus.org,

Prince Ishbane

4

Ian and the other Kennedy varsity players suited up for the Grant game. Coach Bramley called them into the team room. The guys sprawled out on the blue wrestling mats covering the floor.

"This is dumb," muttered Josh as he pulled up his socks. "We should be warming up."

"Coach knows what he's doing," Ian said. "Some of the best college teams do this before every game. It helps you focus."

When the last of the guys had trickled in, Bramley closed the door and dimmed the lights. He turned on some New Age music and encouraged the guys to relax. While there'd been lots of laughter and snide remarks the first time, most of the guys were used to it now, and some were really into it.

"Beginning with your toes, tighten and release your muscles," Coach said. "Keep moving up your body, tightening and releasing. Let the tension leave you as your mind goes clear, so you can focus."

Ian slowly flexed and relaxed each muscle of his body, finally moving up to his scalp.

"Visualize yourself leaving your body. You're watching from the outside as you play this game. You like what you see. You're making every shot, blocking every shot, stealing every ball, feeling every movement. No one can touch you. No one can stop you. You're in the zone."

Ian saw it all in slow motion. His passes were right on, he got perfect position for his rebounds and made every shot. Swish after swish. It was his game. He'd take his man every time.

The music slowly increased to a crescendo, with a little heavy metal Coach had thrown in to appease some of the guys. Ian's imaginary game sped up to match the pace of the music. His mind ran highlights, in which he made shot after shot, including a few slam dunks that in the real world would require a trampoline.

"All right, now slowly return to your body," the coach said. "See yourself in the team huddle after the game, high-fiving and celebrating our victory." He turned the music down. "I'm going to slowly turn on the lights now. Let your eyes adjust."

It was quiet. "Okay," Coach shouted. "Let's do it!"

The guys hopped up, slapping hands and screaming "Let's go!" and "Do it!" They jogged up the stairs to the gym.

Ian, toward the back, focused on each step as he ascended to the court. This was his turf, his game. He owned it.

Ian calmly dribbled the ball at the top of the key. He glanced at the clock. Twenty seconds left in the game. They were behind by three. He could try for a three pointer, but his defender was on him, trying to deny the shot.

He faked to his right, then moved left past his teammate's pick and into the open lane. His short jumper was perfect. Only one point behind. Ian had played his best game of the season, but no one would remember that unless they won.

Grant's number 34 threw the ball to Mike Fitz, Ian's man. Fitz headed slowly up the court, running the clock down. Ian pressured him and waited for Fitz's eyes to go to the scoreboard, to check the clock. They did. In that fraction of a second, Ian reached in and knocked the ball loose.

Ian ran, bending low to get control of the ball. As he moved past the half court line, he heard the crowd. "Four…"

Somewhere around the three point line he heard "three." Just past the foul line he heard "two." And just as he released the ball for a layup he heard "one." The next thing he heard, at the same moment, was the roar of the crowd and the buzzer.

People streamed out onto the court. He saw Brittany running through the crowd. She had to wait in line while his teammates hugged him and danced.

"Great game, Ian!"

High fives were rampant. Brittany pushed herself past two players and a half dozen fans to get to Ian.

"That was incredible!" she said, kissing his sweaty face.

"Thanks, Brit."

After a few more minutes of pandemonium the crowd started to thin. Ian grabbed his warm-ups from the bench and tossed them over his shoulder.

"Any plans tonight?" Brittany arched her eyebrows.

He smiled slowly. "None that don't involve you."

She put her arm around his waist.

Rob made his way to Ian, with Jillian close behind. "Nice job." Rob slapped Ian's hand. "I was yelling for you like crazy, but I don't think you heard a thing. You were in the zone."

"Thanks for comin', man."

"Hate to break it to you, buddy, but you aren't the only attraction here." Rob smiled at Jillian, standing beside him in her blue and gold cheerleading uniform. She blushed.

"So, Ian," Rob said, "you want to go somewhere?"

Ian glanced at Brittany who shot him the look.

"Uh, I think I'm hanging with Brittany tonight. Just the two of us."

"Oh, I get it," Rob said. "We just got ditched, Jill. Looks like it's just you and me, *chica*. How about some ice cream?"

"That'd be great. But I have to change first."

"Yeah, me too," Ian said, hugging Brittany.

She pushed him back. "You're a biohazard. Take a shower if you're thinking of coming near me."

"Later." Ian headed to the locker room, while Jillian dragged Brittany to the restroom.

"I'll be right out," Jillian told Rob over her shoulder.

"Brit, what are you thinking?" Jillian didn't even wait until the bathroom door swung shut. "I can't go out with him alone."

"Jill, listen to yourself. There's a guy out there, a decent-looking one, too, who's asking you out. And you're *mad* at me?"

"I'm not mad. Just nervous."

"You've been on dates before. It's not like you're a leper. Didn't you go out for coffee?"

"That wasn't a date. We were just hanging out."

"Well, maybe you'll get cozy tonight. I mean, he's a college guy."

"Don't even go there, Brit."

"What's the problem? You've been with a guy before."

"Don't remind me. Besides, he would never do that."

"What, because he's religious? You kidding me? Christian guys are the worst. They act like they don't want it, but guys are guys. Some admit it, some are just hypocrites."

"Are you sure you want to get back together with Ian?"

"We're just going to see if the chemistry's still there."

"Don't forget what happened when you guys were together before."

"That had nothing to do with him." Brittany lowered her voice, seeing two other girls' looks. "I was at a point in my life where I couldn't handle things. You remember. Mom was having problems, then Dad showed up after three years with that peroxide queen. The Ouija board thing freaked me out a little. It wasn't Ian's fault, it was only a game. Besides, it didn't have anything to do with my little stunt in the garage."

"Brit, you almost died. That's not a game. Ian introduced you—both of us—to something really weird. And dark. Ian seems like a great guy, but...I'm worried about you two."

"Relax, Jill. Ian's a big boy. And I'm a big girl." She stood on her tiptoes to make the point. "Besides, my life's together now. I'm on the fast track to premed. These long fingers will be performing surgery in some prominent hospital. I'll be saving kids' lives and making the big bucks. You can drive my Jag."

"Just promise me you won't do anything tonight you're going to regret."

"Please, little Miss Perfect, don't bother with the lecture. That church youth group is turning you into a prude. I'm going to have some fun tonight. Mom's gone for the evening." Brittany took a quick look in the mirror. "I give you permission to have fun too." She flung open the bathroom door and strode out into the hall, back straight.

Jillian changed, stuffing her cheerleading outfit into her backpack. Then she looked in the mirror. Five minutes later, after trying to get every hair in place, she walked out into an almost empty hall. Rob was leaning against the wall next to the trophy case.

"There you are," he said, grinning. "I was wondering if you crawled out the window."

"Sorry."

"No problem. Let's get out of here. Baskin–Robbins okay? A waffle cone sundae's callin' my name."

Letter 4

My beloved Foulgrin,

I enjoyed your account of their intimacies. "I love you," Ian whispered. "I love you too," Brittany whispered back. What a cozy little circle you were on that couch, just the five of you!

Though these two surrendered their virginity a few years ago, continued self-destruction is always sweet. It's like picking off the flower petals and grinding them underfoot.

It used to be hard work to take them down. But their culture now sends them the same messages we once had to do solo. "Don't have sex unless you're married" is now "Don't have sex unless you're really in love." They have an "unless" for everything.

As for their undying expressions of affection, "I love you" means I want what you can give me. For Brittany, that's security and status. For Ian it's sex. *Love* is the Enemy's favorite word, but we've robbed it of His meaning. Vermin men consent to "love" to get sex. Vermin women consent to sex to get "love."

We hate marriage precisely because the Enemy loves it. He intends it to be permanent, "till death do us part." But "being in love" is a feeling, transient and fluctuating. To the Enemy, love is something they do. For them, love is something they feel. By taking advantage of that discrepancy, we bring untold ruin.

But beware. If the vermin become disillusioned with our counterfeit love, they might start looking for the real thing.

Keep feeding young Ian, and all of them, with our sexual propaganda. Jokes and conversations about heterosexual and homosexual experiences are the norm on prime time television. Especially in programs targeting the younger audience. (Speaking of which, there are certain things in Brittany's profile that could lend themselves to lesbianism. Give it some thought, would you?) Slide them into the notion that while they would recognize voyeurism through a window as sick, voyeurism through a television set is perfectly normal.

Don't ever let the MTV generation imagine the despicable truth—that the best sex happens among the married.

Think of it, Foulgrin. A hundred years ago parents allowed their adolescent children virtually no unsupervised time together. Little leisure. Little money. No cars. No billboards. No movies. No televisions. No computers. Few magazines. Almost no pornography. Back then they gave them training in moral absolutes not only in church but in school. Parents taught their children to be disciplined and hardworking. Yes, we still managed to lure some of them into immorality, and a thousand different sins, but in those days it really took effort. Now, it's like falling off a log.

All they have to do is tread water and we have them. Only the Christian vermin have the Ghost's power to swim upstream. And even then many of them fail to draw on it. We've so permeated their culture, and their culture has so dominated their minds, they end up going with the current. Finally they go over the waterfall, smashing on the rocks below.

Ian didn't have to go looking for bad values. They came to him as naturally as the air he breathes. His parents, I see, are the progressive sort, modern and well educated. Their religion is simply a label they wear that has turned their son off to "Christianity." And why should Ian search for God when he gets tastes of the supernatural in our cheap little paranormal alternatives?

His parents never denied him anything…except standards and self-restraint. No absolutes. No household responsibilities. No discipline. They've never mentioned all his occult books and games? Marvelous. I see from his files that last year he rented a suite at a hotel with his prom date. And both their parents knew! How sophisticated. The most delightful part was Ian's father handing him a pack of condoms—and congratulating himself on his act of moral guidance!

Throw into the mix the gap between puberty and marriage. Add magazines, posters, movies, television, and the Internet, and the fuel for lust is infinite. This cultural celebration of evil is every demon's dream. What more could we possibly ask for?

Diluting the meaning of love is one of the finest achievements of our semantics department. Convince them they're in love, Foulgrin. Then you can turn "love" into a tender justification for any evil we choose.

Loving how we destroy them,

Prince Ishbane

5

The full bottle of pills lay in the darkness, in the far back of the desk drawer, covered by old photo albums. It hadn't been discovered. But would it be enough to do the job? The book said this was enough to stop the heart. But what if the book was wrong? What if swallowing all this medicine triggered vomiting before the poison was absorbed? What then? A trip to the hospital? Stomach pumped? The thought was unbearable.

There had to be a better way—one that was sure to work. Preferably one that appeared to be an accident.

For one fleeting moment it was absolutely clear this was wrong, that it would hurt everyone. The medicine should be flushed down the toilet. But just as suddenly, the light was eclipsed, the darkness regained control.

No, don't be a coward. Follow through with the plan. It's best for everyone.

Before the plan was discovered, the deed would need to be done.

Soon, something kept urging. *Very soon.*

"Mmm. Smells good, Jill," her mom said.

"Can't go wrong with Grandma's recipe." Jillian pulled two sheets of cookies out of the oven and set them on the range. "You can have a couple. I'm taking them to Ian's. We're all going to watch *the game.*" She rolled her eyes.

"On your way back, you might want to get some more milk." Diane drained the last of the skim milk into her glass.

"Anything else?" Jillian muttered.

"What?"

Jillian stood on her tiptoes to grab a paper plate from the cupboard. "Nothing."

"You know," said Diane, looking at her half-eaten cookie, "these remind me of your dad."

"Yeah. He always liked them straight out of the oven." Jillian stacked the cookies on the plate, one by one, pushing her mind away from where it had landed.

I've got to get out of here.

Diane grabbed four cookies and put them on a paper towel. "For Daniel—and Dan Stanklin."

"I still can't get used to Daniel having a best friend named Dan."

"Yeah, if they stay friends I think one should change his name." She laughed. "Aren't you going to have some cookies?"

"Later. We'll pig out at Ian's."

"Did you get dinner?"

"We're eating over there." Jillian glanced at the clock as she topped off her cookie pyramid. "The game starts at six-thirty. Gotta go."

Jillian grabbed her purse and the cookies and headed for the door. She set them down on the hall table and checked herself in the mirror.

"Yikes. I look like I just got in a flour fight." Jillian took the stairs two at a time and made a beeline for her closet. Ten minutes and three outfits later, she bolted to the bathroom to touch up her makeup. She hurried down the stairs and saw their Dalmatian under the table, looking guilty. She checked the cookies and saw that the cellophane was half off, and at least a half dozen cookies were missing.

"Nickerson!" She grabbed the antibarking squirt gun, marched over and doused his mutt face. She removed a couple of cookies she thought might have Dalmatian slobber on them and brought them into the kitchen. "Here's a couple more cookies for Daniel," she said.

"Oh, that's nice, honey," her mom said, then looked away, head down.

Is she crying?

Jillian pretended not to notice as she quick-stepped out of the kitchen. She rearranged the cookies to fill the plate and slipped out the front door. Fortunately there were still two dozen left.

Does she think she's the only one who misses him? Can't we just be normal for one day?

The five-minute drive seemed to take forever. When she pulled up to Ian's house, Jillian fished her compact out of her purse and tried to camouflage her red, puffy eyes. She headed for the door, putting on her perky self.

"Hi, Jillian," Ian's mom said on opening the door. "You missed the tip-off."

Jillian slipped off her shoes and set her purse on the hall floor. She walked by the Stewarts' spacious living room.

Wow! Now this is a house.

She stepped lightly down the hardwood stairs.

Don't want to sound like a herd of elephants.

As the staircase opened into the downstairs family room, Jillian saw Brittany and Rob sitting on opposite ends of the black leather couch in front of the Stewarts' big-screen TV. There were bowls of chips, popcorn and M&Ms on both end tables. She set her cookies down next to Rob and smiled.

She sat down on the couch between Brittany and Rob. Rob's eyes searched hers. "Everything okay?"

"Yeah, just a long day, that's all." She crossed her arms and stared at the TV.

Ian opened a can of Dr. Pepper and took a swig. "If this was a beer, this night would be perfect." He laughed.

While Rob muted the beer commercial, Ian took off his blue baseball cap and hung it on his knee.

Rob pointed at Ian's hair. "Man, don't you ever comb that stuff?"

"You just wish you had hair this great."

"If I had hair like yours, I'd wear a hat all the time, too," Rob countered. "When was your last oil change?"

Ian threw some chips at him. "If you weren't such a little guy, I'd take a swing at you."

"Give me your best shot, scarecrow."

The game came back on and the guys locked in on it, all insults forgotten.

Brittany grabbed a few M&Ms. "Cookies anyone?" she asked, lifting Jillian's plate.

Rob took the first bite. "These are great, Jill."

"Thanks."

"Aren't you going to have any?"

"No. Ate some at home."

Before Jillian knew it, the game was over.

"I think it's time to call it a night," she said. "Still got some homework."

"It's Saturday," Brittany said.

"I know, but tomorrow's busy. Church in the morning, then gotta help Mom with the baby."

Before anyone could argue, she grabbed the half-empty plate of cookies and headed up the stairs. She nabbed her purse and shoes at the door and said an overly cheerful good-bye to Mrs. Stewart.

Jillian got in her car and sat there a few minutes, hands on the steering wheel. Rob came out of the house and walked toward her car. She pulled out of the driveway.

Main Street Park. That'll work.

Jillian pulled over and sat, finally allowing herself to cry.

She looked at the plate of cookies next to her. There were probably a dozen left. She reached for one and munched on it.

God, I don't understand. Why did You take my dad and leave me? Why does my mom have to hurt so much? Why's Daniel so messed up? Why am I so empty? What am I so afraid of? I can't even have fun with my friends. Rob probably hates me for the mood I'm in. What's wrong with me?

Jillian's mind went numb as she ate. Five minutes later she polished off the last cookie, got out of the car and threw the paper plate in the garbage can.

⟳

Letter 5

My delectable Foulgrin,

I'm alarmed at the background check on Rob Gonzales. He's developed a fearless zeal in the short time he's been a Christian. Be wary of his influence on both Jillian and Ian.

On the positive side, Baalgore's files indicate Rob was a gang member. That assures old memories and bad habits. Best of all, he's had sex with numerous girls. Yes, he's now resolved to "save himself for marriage" (as the self-righteous prudes like to put it). But you can help Baalgore convince him it's too late for that. You and Baalgore must work with surgical precision. Bring back the fleeting pleasures of his choices, but put aside thoughts of their devastating consequences. Get him into a compromising situation with Jillian. Sure, he's committed himself to purity. But once the chemistry gets going, his body will neither know nor care that he's a Christian.

There are dynamics in this vermin quartet that lend themselves to our purposes. But other things could tip the scales in the Enemy's favor. Keep your nose to the brimstone.

If Jillian really is a Christian, she's ineffective, misinformed, easily shaken and vulnerable to bad influence. All you have to do to keep her in bondage is hold ground already taken. If you manage only to do that, we win. We'd like them all in hell. But if we can derail the Enemy's own brats from serving Him…well, that's a considerable consolation.

Reading your report made me hungry for vermin on a half shell. Jillian's falling prey to one of our favorite traps. She doesn't yet realize it, but she's on the edge of a cliff. Soon she'll step over. She finds her only comfort in food? She's always been the compliant people pleaser? Does what others want while quietly resenting them? Keep giving her the illusion that the only thing she can control is food. Meanwhile, use it to control her.

We surround these young girls with images of the perfect body, so they spend their lives in pursuit of thinness. There's no way your Jillian could ever measure up—she lives in the real world. Each of those posed pictures she looks at is the best among hundreds. The perfect angle, carefully retouched. The models are slaves, starving themselves to get the edge. They're airbrushed, surgically altered fantasy props. Each will dry up like last month's flowers, withering into depression and self-destruction.

Every women's magazine screams the message that only thin is attractive. And usually the adjoining page is a close-up of a dessert the women in the pictures can't eat unless they later induce vomiting.

It's not just the male minds we've programmed with images of sleek yet voluptuous young females. The females have fallen for it too. They think that's how they're supposed to look and act. That's how they're to attract males. What does the girl do for the boy she's attracted to in that wonderful movie *Titanic*? Simple—she poses nude for him. Now that's how to get a young man's attention! The modesty and self-restraint of young women once kept male lusts from taking control. But now we mentor the girls into promiscuity right along with the boys.

Of course, the Enemy knows the pleasure brought by food. He even promises them feasts in Charis. He claims He Himself will prepare them a banquet. (Surely He must be setting them up. Do you suppose He'll poison the meal? Or make them His main course?) He offers Himself as the bread of life, telling them they can satisfy their ultimate hungers in Him.

We take the Enemy's gifts and turn them into curses. They starve themselves to become skinny. Or they gorge themselves, then feel miserable. Then it's only a matter of time before we have them. Like Jillian.

See that Jillian's condition remains our little secret. If others suspect, keep them at arm's length. Don't let her realize she's enslaved. We always work best in the dark.

The gnawing emptiness she's feeling affords you understandable pleasure. But the Enemy draws her attention to her emptiness in order to fill it Himself. You must bombard her life with so much noise that she cannot hear the Enemy's still small voice.

When the Enemy or that flunky Jaltor whispers to her about her deepest needs, prompt her to open the refrigerator. Or turn up the radio. Turn on the television. Pick up the phone. Let her do anything besides examine her life, her emptiness, and her mortality.

I was delighted to hear that the suicidal thoughts you instilled in one of our youths has evolved into an actual plan. You can use this not just to ruin one life, but others.

They're already headed to hell in a hand basket. All you have to do is keep them from falling out.

Ravenously yours,

Prince Ishbane

6

The pill bottle label said the same as it had a few nights before. The pages from that book said the same. The overdose could be done quickly, painlessly. It would just be falling asleep. And not waking up. That's all.

What would it do to the family? They'd adjust. What would it do to that special person, and the other friends? They'd get over it. It just wasn't worth it anymore.

It's the easiest way. It's the best way. It's the only solution.

"What's that, quartz?" Jillian asked, standing in the gym lobby almost an hour after the game, and pointing at Brittany's new necklace.

"It's an Isis crystal. Ian gave it to me. It matches his Osiris. It symbolizes our divine powers, as a god and goddess. Cool, huh?"

"I…guess."

Jillian stared down Kennedy High's hallway. She saw Ian come up the stairs from the locker room. Just then Rob came in from the parking lot and walked up to him.

"He told me he couldn't come to the game," Jillian said. "But I guess he decided to drop by afterward anyway."

"When did he tell you that? Did he stop by Red Robin and order a Coke and leave you a fat tip again?" Brittany asked.

"Nope. He called."

"Jillian, the man's hopelessly infatuated with you," Brittany replied. "He can't stay away, especially on a Friday night. Now smooth down that hair and let's get moving."

"Don't be expecting her too soon, Brittany," said a voice behind them. Kelly Hatcher stood in her cheerleading uniform. "Those curls must be a nightmare, Jillian."

Brittany flashed an ultrasweet smile. "Yes, we all wish we could have perfect hair like yours, Kelly. Although I don't understand why you ruin such beautiful blond locks by dying your roots black."

Kelly looked as if she were about to say something, then turned away.

"Give yourself a week, honey," Brittany said. "You'll think of a comeback. Write it down and stick it in my locker. And next time don't come to a battle of wits unarmed."

Jillian stifled a giggle. After a quick attack on the curls in front of the bathroom mirror, she and Brittany walked around the corner arm in arm and joined the guys in the hall.

"Hey, Jillian. Let me take that." Rob smiled at her and put her backpack on his shoulders. "Sorry I missed your cheering tonight."

"That's okay, Rob. I—"

"A couple and a couple-to-be, how adorable," came the sarcastic comment from a familiar voice.

"Good one, Kelly," Brittany said. "You're so witty. You're not as dumb as you look. Come to think of it, nobody's as dumb as you look."

Kelly glared, not so much at Brittany as Jillian. Brittany pointed a finger at Jillian, then Rob, then Ian and herself. When she pointed to Kelly she said, "Hmm, there appears to be one too many in this circle. We thank you for coming, Kelly, but...buh-bye."

Kelly's eyes narrowed. "Have a special little date," she said, walking toward the door.

"And you have a great time at home, Kelly," Brittany called. "Say 'hi' to your mom for us."

Ian laughed and put his arms around Brittany's waist. "You're a feisty one." He kissed her.

"That's why you love me. Now, come on. Let's go do something fun."

They'd each driven separately, so Brittany insisted they all drive to her house and leave cars there. A few minutes later Brittany's white Jeep Wrangler pulled into her driveway followed by Ian's gray Mazda pickup, Jillian's red Saturn and Rob's black '62 Chevy Impala.

"I'll go with Ian," Brittany said. "Robbie, why don't you drive Jillian?" Brittany patted the hood of Rob's low rider and pointed to the for sale sign in the window. "Jill, this could be your last chance to hear this baby purr."

Jillian thought she saw Rob grit his teeth. "Where we going?" he asked.

"I'm starving," Ian said.

"Let's go to Giovanni's," Brittany said.

"Giovanni's?" Jillian asked. "It takes like half an hour to get there."

"I know, but it's great food. Plus, Ian and I need to discuss what we're going to do afterwards." She winked at Ian. "I'm sure there's *plenty* of things you two can talk about."

Brittany and Ian got in his truck and led the way.

When they got to Giovanni's, the guys each downed a huge dish of chicken fettuccini alfredo. Brittany had lasagna. Jillian picked at a Caesar salad that Rob finally finished.

"We're going to Ian's to watch a movie," Brittany said when they were finished. "But, Jillian, I know your mommy wants you home early, so I guess we'll just see you later. I'll call you."

Jillian and Rob walked slowly to his car. As they wove through traffic on the way to the freeway, Rob asked, "Your mom wants you home at 11:30?"

"Yeah. And I forgot to tell her where I went, too. Needless to say, I'm looking forward to college."

"Actually, I think it's cool your mom cares about you enough to want to know where you're at and when you'll be home. So what are you doing tomorrow afternoon?"

"After church? No plans."

"Want to do something?"

"Like what?"

"Like anything." He sounded like a little boy.

"Yeah, I do. Anything sounds good."

He tapped the steering wheel lightly. "Look, I'm not very good at this." He spoke rapidly. "I like you, and I'd like to spend time with you. Regularly. Okay, I said it. Sounded stupid, didn't it?"

She laughed. "No. It was nice."

They both smiled. He reached over, grabbed her hand, and drove her home as slowly as he could.

Letter 6

My unenlightened Foulgrin,

You say that despite my explanation you don't understand this "dating thing." A dating relationship can be detrimental to our purposes when it helps them prepare for marriage. Fortunately there are few young vermin for whom this is the case. Instead, it will twist their perspectives. Compromise their purity. Deaden their ability to carry on an exclusive lifelong commitment. After enough years of the smorgasbord of dating, they find it difficult to make one selection and stick with it.

You must see the teenage vermins' lives in the larger context. Teenagers are a recent invention, created in America during the 1950s. Yes, there have always been people between the ages of 13 and 19. But they were immersed in family tradition and work. Adolescence was nothing but the continuum between childhood and adulthood. There was the gradual relinquishing of childhood privileges and restrictions for the responsibilities and freedoms of adulthood. But in the 1950s teenagers became a socioeconomic identity. Suddenly they had their own music, tastes, and subculture. They became big business. Their preferences were catered to. Needless to say, we capitalized on this.

If we can hold them while they're young, they'll seldom slip through our grasp when they're older. Our strategy mirrors the Enemy's. Get them while they're young and hold on to them. The older they get, the less chance they'll ever change. And the shorter they'll have to live even if they do. We lead them to small choices that turn into larger habits that become ongoing lifestyles.

When working with Christian vermin, make them just a baptized version of the world. If the church is simply the world, only a little better, swearing a little less and giving a little more, it's no threat to us. The Enemy calls them to be radically different. We can put up with little differences. It's the revolutionary changes that mess us up.

The Enemy doesn't want a "little" of them. He wants it all.

Ian's had just enough exposure to Christianity to immunize him against it. When he sees a Christian like Rob, he thinks "I've tried that." Of course, he never has. He's got a deep spiritual thirst. But since he's seen nothing in Christianity to indicate it can quench his thirst, he looks elsewhere. Perfect.

Ian's an athlete. That can have its downside, if the self-discipline carries over to his personal life. Or if team camaraderie is channeled the Enemy's direction. Fortunately, athletics have fed his ego. He's not as shallow and superficial as most of his teammates, but he's just as self-centered. His parents and teachers say he's "a fine young man." This means that he's not a serial killer (to the best of their knowledge). Just as we've taught them to, they value the Enemy's gifting and success over character and virtue.

I see his interest in the occult has lain dormant during basketball season. There's no finer foothold, no better bridge with which to access their minds. I agree, Foulgrin—it's time to bring out that Ouija board again!

Delighting in the control they give us,

Prince Ishbane

7

Jillian and Brittany wandered the aisles of World Market. Jillian loved the teapots from China, baskets from Guatemala, chocolates from Switzerland, the wooden table from Italy—at least they said it was from Italy.

She kept thinking that out there somewhere was the place she was made for. Maybe it was in Europe. She saw in a picture frame a Paris coffeehouse. She wished she was there. The French Riviera? Milan? Venice? She'd read a lot of novels. But she felt deep inside it wasn't just a fantasy, that somewhere out there was the place of her dreams. And the person.

Lately she'd been envisioning Rob in some of those places, holding her hand across the table, while they enjoyed coffee and baguettes. He was starting to fit nicely into her dreams.

Afterward they headed back to Brittany's. They walked into her room. It was spacious, twice the size of Jillian's, orderly and immaculate. Compared to this, her own little room looked like a storage closet that had just been robbed. As usual, Brittany lay back on her bed, against her oversized maroon headrest, while Jillian sat in an old beanbag chair.

Brittany picked up some cards. "Did you know there are over a hundred different tarot card decks? Skyla collects them. She's got like forty of them. Some of them are so cool."

Brittany held up three cards to Jillian, who pointed to one of them. "What's with the naked woman?"

"Don't be a prude. It's just part of the game."

"It's not just a game."

"Sure it is." Brittany shuffled the cards into a thin main deck. "Go ahead and draw."

"No thanks."

"What, you afraid God's going to strike you down?"

"No. I just don't think it's right."

"Just draw one. You read fortune cookies, don't you?"

"Yeah."

"You know how we look at our horoscopes in the newspaper? Just for fun?"

"Yeah, but—"

"Same thing. Draw. These are just the character cards, not the whole deck. There's twenty-two of them. The one you pick says something about you. It's easy. You'll see. Here, I'll pick one so you can see how it works." She took the card on top and looked at it. "It's card fifteen, the Devil card."

"The devil?"

"Yeah, that's him, with a goat's head and horns." She showed Jillian the hideous picture. "Don't freak out. Skyla says some people think it's all about darkness and evil, but the devil actually symbolizes mirth and celebration. The meaning is that the devil can be your soul friend. When you befriend your fear, you're set free to take off your chains that hold you to the material world. That can give you the fulfillment you're seeking. It's a decent card—I'm glad I drew it."

"I don't like it, Brit. The devil's real…at least I think he is. He's not about mirth and he's certainly not anyone's friend."

"Okay, so we disagree. But now it's your turn. Pick a card."

"No."

"Come on, Jillian. It's just a game. Look, I'll take out the Devil card, since it freaks you out. Okay? Now just cut the deck and pick a card. It's harmless. Look, I listen to you go on about your things, like your stories from your little church. The least you can do is play along with me. Friends do that, right?"

Jillian sighed, then cut the deck and picked the card on top. She stared at it. It had the Roman numeral XIII at the top. Under it was a black skeleton contorted out of shape and holding a giant scythe, sharp and foreboding. Around it was a snake and a scorpion. The skeleton's head had an ominous dark crown.

"Card thirteen. That's the Death card."

Jillian turned pale.

"Don't worry. I don't know what it's all about, to be honest. These look like fetal images, don't they?" She pointed at the card. "But I know it relates to you being your own emperor, taking charge and exercising control over your life. Death's not bad, that's what Skyla says. Just a natural cycle of life."

Jillian stood up and inched toward the door. "Brit, I told you I wasn't comfortable with this."

"Exactly why the Death card was a perfect fit. You need to take control of your life. The tarot cards aren't like a religion where someone yells at you and tells you what to do. They're on your side, they guide you, help you to make your own decisions. But you're still your own authority. Now sit down and give it a chance."

Jillian sighed, then sunk back down in the beanbag chair. Brittany handed her the deck. She drew another card.

The Kennedy High parking lot looked like the freeway at rush hour. Jillian edged her red Saturn into the stream of traffic headed out to fast-food joints for lunch. Brittany perched in the passenger seat, touching up her lipstick.

"Don't look now but I think we might actually be able to move." Jillian edged forward. Suddenly a black Honda Civic swerved in front of them. Jillian hit the brakes and Brittany's lip liner ran across her chin.

Brittany swore and dug a Kleenex out of her purse.

"I don't think so, Kelly!" Jillian dug her fingernails into the steering wheel and edged up within a few inches of the offending bumper.

"What's her problem? Didn't you guys used to be friends?" Brittany asked, wiping the stray makeup from her chin.

Jillian hit the horn and let it blow. "She's just ticked because…it goes back before you and I met. I don't want to talk about it."

"Bad blood? I thought I knew all your stories. Holding out on me, huh? I want to hear the whole thing."

"She dropped me again at practice yesterday."

"That's sports. Not that you can call cheerleading a sport, but you know what I mean."

"Yeah, well it always happens when Miss Pritchard isn't looking. Wouldn't you be mad if some girl on your team kept hitting you in the face with the volleyball? It's the third time she's dropped me in the last week. That's not a coincidence."

"If somebody messed with me, I'd smash them with my next kill. You really think Kelly's after you? Then go after her. Do unto others so they'll stop doing unto you. Isn't that what your Bible says?"

"I don't think that's it exactly."

"Close enough. What did you do to fall out of favor with Queen Kelly?"

"Other than beating her out last year for the all-American cheer squad, I can't imagine."

"Her mom doesn't know any Texas hit men, does she?"

"Not funny."

"Well, neither is this." Brittany held up the Kleenex covered with lip liner. "She messed up my face. That means she's fair game."

The cars continued to inch forward. Kelly made it to the street and put on her right turn signal. She rolled down her window, radio blasting, stuck her head out and yelled "Bye, girls," then hit the gas.

Brittany made an unladylike gesture at the screeching tires. "It's on," she muttered.

Letter 7

Prince Ishbane,

This is your humble servant, reporting for duty, Magnificent One. How honored I am to renew our working relationship. You can count on my loyalty, as surely as my name is Foulgrin.

Since I was first privileged to serve under you millennia ago, I have established a distinguished reputation, notwithstanding the recent misunderstandings precipitated by the treacherous antics of my former pupil Squaltaint, who is now under discipline. I attribute much of my success to once having sat at your learned feet.

If you have not followed my campaigns and decorations, you will wish to review the attached sixty-page vita, which summarizes a smattering of my accomplishments. Attached also are *Foulgrin's 66 Rules of Temptation,* an acknowledged classic I'm sure you're familiar with. You probably know I've trained innumerable tempters and mentored some of our most notable agents. Lord Chemosh will attest to my past exploits as Eshmon of Sidon, and later as an Incan god in the mountains of Chile, where—if I may be so bold as to mention it—children were sacrificed to me.

I am gratified, exalted Ishbane, that you have appointed me captain of our demon cadre assigned to these four human idiots. I'm sure you see the benefits in ours being more of a partnership relationship, as your clairvoyance and mine are so far beyond the limited minds of these bumbling tempters. Though Jillian is my primary assignment, I find if I want anything done right with the other three, I have to do it myself. I've worked with Brittany's Raketwist and Ian's Pendragon before, and they were duly impressed with my powers. Baalgore is an incompetent fool, who has repeatedly failed in his dealings with the Rob vermin, requiring me to take a more active role with him myself. You'll see the difference in him, I'm sure.

I'm delighted to say most of Jillian's beliefs have come by osmosis, from being around parents and church, not by personal conviction. If she is still in this condition by the time she goes to college, she should be easy pickings.

Jillian's a harmless little roach. Her undistinguished personality isn't in need of constant supervision, allowing me more leisure to focus on her friends, who will easily pull her down with them. Unlike her father, she's mousy and compliant. This passive little airhead is just the kind of vermin we love, the sort who will tread water and let the currents of popular opinion and peer pressure take her right down the river of cultural conformity. Indeed, she may prove to be the easiest prey I've ever been assigned to.

I've enjoyed inflicting fear on Jillian in the witching hour. She and Brittany viewed a horror movie last night. Though she didn't want to watch it, she was afraid to refuse Brittany. I love these movies because they desensitize them to the true horrors, including ourselves. The more blood, gore, and stalking become entertainment to them, the more they become either oblivious to us or obsessed by us.

We cultivate male predators and female phobias through these movies. But we also cultivate a sense of interest in the supernatural—our kind of supernatural. The more they become enamored with us, the easier it is to seduce them.

The delicious thing is how they make choices which are the mental equivalent of opening the front door of their homes and letting anyone come in off the streets to prey on them. While we can intimidate only those who allow us to, it's amazing how many have given us these open invitations into their minds.

As for Rob, I'm digging up his secrets, targeting his weaknesses. Baalgore is intimidated by his study of the forbidden book and engagement in the forbidden talk. I'm engaging in tag-team temptation right now, but this pathetic demon needs me in the ring most of the time. Rob's guardian Talon is formidable. Were I a less formidable opponent, he might present a challenge.

Naturally, I'll draw Rob into sexual immorality with Jillian. This should be enough to destroy anything the Enemy might otherwise accomplish. But I never fight a battle on just one front. I have a multifaceted plan of attack.

I've been around the block several million times these last few thousand years, and I assure you I have many tricks up my sleeve. I'm confident you'll be pleased with my work, and will pass on positive reports to the authorities at High Command. Rest assured, I will not fail you, illustrious Prince Ishbane. When I'm done taking down these miserable adolescent vermin, Lord Beelzebub will be eager to restore me to my place of prominence. Be assured I will be in your debt as well. And I always repay my debts. Please remind Obsmut of that, will you?

Most respectful of your royal princeliness,

Foulgrin

8

Jillian kicked off her shoes and threw herself down on the couch. She loved Fridays, when school was done. She glanced at the clock, hoping Rob would call before the game. She flipped aimlessly through a *Seventeen* magazine, looking at swimsuit styles for summer. She stared at the model's tight thighs. If only she could look that good.

"Jillian, sweetheart, would you do me a favor?" The voice came from the kitchen.

Jillian rolled her eyes.

Mom always needs something. I never get to relax around this house.

"Yes, mother?" Her voice was sickeningly sweet. Her mom stepped out where she could see her.

"Honey, I realize you have stuff to do, but I have to pick up Joey from Ryan and Jodi's in a couple of minutes. Daniel needs to go to the store before he leaves for his overnighter."

Jillian looked up at her mom. "So…this relates to me how?"

Diane took a deep breath. "I'm sick of the attitude, Jillian. Put down your magazine and take your brother to the store."

Diane grabbed her car keys off the mantel and walked to the door, just as Jillian arose from the couch with her arguments. Her mom put up her hands. "I'll be back in two hours to start dinner."

"But Rob might call. And if you're going out anyway, why can't you just—" The door slammed.

Jillian stomped up the stairs to Daniel's room. She opened the door without knocking. He immediately pushed a button and turned from his computer screen with a startled expression.

"What are *you* doing in here? Get out!" As usual, Daniel was dressed in black pants and a black T-shirt.

"Chill, freak boy, I'm doing you a favor. You have one minute to get downstairs, and I'll give you a ride to the store. If you're not there, you're walking. Your choice."

She went across the hall to her room and grabbed her purse. Taking a quick glance in the mirror, she groaned, and prayed no one would see her at the store. A few squirts of her spray bottle and half a dozen scrunches later, her curls were under control. Barely.

She went downstairs. No Daniel.

"I'm serious," she yelled. "You'd better be in the car in thirty seconds." She stormed out the door.

Thirty seconds behind her, Daniel jogged to the car. Jillian pulled out of the driveway before his door was shut. After going a hundred feet, she put on the brakes.

"Excuse me, Gramps. Some people have better things to do than go for a Friday afternoon drive through the neighborhood going two miles an hour." She sighed in disgust and passed the shiny black Lincoln.

She rolled through the stop sign at the end of her road, turning on to the main street, and found herself behind a car with its left blinker on.

"Where you gonna turn, buddy? Into the berry field?"

Jillian saw a row of orange cones ahead.

"Aw, man. Construction today? Do you plan to do this every time I'm in a hurry?" she said toward the first construction worker, who was way out of earshot.

"What's your problem?" Daniel asked. "Attack of the killer hormones or something?"

"Wait'll you go through puberty. Maybe your squeaky little voice will change. You know what…forget it, I'm turning this car around right now."

Daniel gave her a smug smile as she looked in her rear view mirror and saw a huge line of traffic. The first place to turn around would be the grocery store parking lot.

Beautiful, just beautiful.

As she waited, she saw a for sale sign in front of a big, brand-new house.

If it was farther from the main road, painted dark green with white shutters, out in the country…that could be my dream place. *Maybe someday Rob and I…*

A horn honked behind her. Jillian glared into the rearview mirror and stepped on it. She careened into the store parking lot, pulled into a spot, and jumped out the door while the car was still settling. Fifteen feet away she saw big Josh Waters, all-state tight end and power forward on the basketball team.

"Hey, Jillian."

"Hey, Josh," she said, sounding perfectly pleasant.

Josh's eyes went to Daniel. "Well, if it isn't Goth boy. Drink anybody's blood lately?" He walked toward Daniel, who stood with his hands in his pockets, staring at the asphalt.

"What's wrong? Black cat got your tongue?"

Josh laughed at his joke, while Daniel mumbled something.

"You putting a curse on me or something? Look at me, freak show!" Josh swung his open hand, slapping Daniel in the head. Jillian turned the other way, but winced at the thud. She walked toward the store, hoping this would end quickly.

"Leave me alone," Daniel pleaded.

"Josh!" A girl's voice rang across the parking lot. Jillian slid up against a car, looking the other way, hoping the girl wouldn't see her.

"Hey, Kelly!" Josh yelled. He looked at Daniel. "I'll take a rain check on you, teen werewolf. See you at school. Maybe we'll duct tape you again—how's that sound? I'll be looking for you in the locker room. Better wear a jock with a cup this time."

Daniel said nothing. Jillian approached him. "Are you okay?"

"Leave me alone," he said, voice tough, but eyes red.

Jillian turned on her heels and marched into the store. "Are we headed towards the costume aisle for a new wardrobe item? Maybe they have some out-of-season Halloween outfits." She heard the cruelty in her voice, but she was too angry to care.

"Let's go to the pet food aisle," Daniel said. "I haven't seen you eating much, and Mom and I have just been worried sick. Maybe something in the dog-chow line would perk you up?"

Jillian grabbed his T-shirt. "I've forgotten what a selfish little shrimp you are. I take time out of my busy schedule to do you a favor, and instead of thanking me, you—"

"Hey, Jillian!"

"Melissa? Hi!" Jillian moved her hand down Daniel's shirt, and slipped her arm around his waist. "Have you ever met my brother Daniel? Daniel, this is Melissa. She's in my AP History class."

"Hi, Daniel."

"Danny needs some stuff so I dropped him by."

"Danny?" he asked.

Jillian squeezed his side a little too hard and smiled at her friend.

"Melissa, we need to get together sometime and do that project on Dred Scott. Why don't we do a video?"

"Great idea," Melissa said. "Every other student presentation is a lecture on the Magna Carta or something dumb like that. Mr. Black would love the video!"

The girls laughed and chitchatted a few minutes, while Daniel squirmed and stared off in silence. Jillian wondered why he didn't take off and get whatever he came for.

"Bye, Melissa!"

As soon as Melissa rounded the corner, Jillian took off down the aisle. Daniel caught up to her, grabbed her shoulder and turned her around. ·

"Danny?" he said.

"What's your problem?"

"Congratulations, Julia Roberts, for your stunning performance in your latest release, *The Two Lives of Jillian Fletcher*. You're ready to hang that old-man driver, you treat me like dirt, then you see that jock jerk and you're nice and friendly with him. And you and Melissa are just so perky, aren't you? Your friends don't know what little Miss Perfect is like, do they? Did you even see yourself? One second you're ready to blow up the whole world, and then you're laughing it up like you're this charming person. What a fake!"

Jillian could find no snappy comeback.

"What do you need, Daniel?" she asked wearily. "Let's get it and go home."

The game was over. Jillian was no longer enjoying her bad mood.

Letter 8

My obsequious Foulgrin,

Dispense with the flattery. Shove the fawning references. "Your royal princeliness?" Stop acting like a horse's rear end. We both know you hate me. Almost as much as I hate you.

I know you still think of yourself as *Lord* Foulgrin. But you're just a demoted errand boy taken to Beelzebub's woodshed and banished to the hinterlands for your betrayals. Don't waste my time with your two-faced attempts at manipulation.

We can coexist only because of our mutual hatred of our common Enemy. Ours is the only alliance that works in Erebus. It's a coalition of self-interest that keeps our house from being divided against itself. If you deceive and destroy Jillian Fletcher and her friends, we both get what we want. This will compensate for our mutual loathing.

I was amused by your account of the supermarket. How easy it is to control a sludge-bag like Jillian when you identify her vulnerabilities. They're adrift in seas of information, but they have no wisdom to guide their use of knowledge. They make spontaneous decisions with minimal reflection. They go with the herd. Usually without moral convictions or parental guidance to restrain them. With the deterioration of family structures and the abandonment of moral absolutes, this generation has been served up to us on a platter.

They're consumed with what other vermin think about them. They try to please even those who have no interest in them. They're pathetic little creatures. Small-minded. Shortsighted. The perfect prey.

Does Jillian try to understand her brother? No. Too much work. Instead, she alienates him through her constant disapproval. Why should he take her attempts at guidance seriously when she cares little for him? As toxic as his mind is, he's more honest than she.

Though they try to appear bold and confident, many of these teenagers are deathly afraid. Each morning when the alarm goes off, their masks go on. They put on clothes, jewelry, and attitudes to hide their fears. They pour themselves into sports, clubs, studies, and dates to find themselves. Or lose themselves. But they never do. The Enemy has made them so they can find themselves and lose themselves only in Him.

We offer an unlimited and ever expanding menu of alternatives. The Enemy doesn't appear until page 1200 or so. At least a few hundred pages after the last one they'll turn to before they die.

These misfits long for their parents to look past their clothes and music and behind their masks to see the real them—and to love what they see. In most cases we make sure the parents, as well as older siblings such as Jillian, are too busy or frustrated for that to happen.

What we do to parents is a work of art. Almost overnight these cute, charming little kids turn into moody, disobedient, and disrespectful teenage mutants. One minute they were all smiles. The next they stomp off in sullen withdrawal. They become irresponsible and impulsive. They argue. Fight. Blame. Rebel. Seeing they've lost control, parents resort to threats and bribery. When neither succeeds, they give up. They settle for peaceful coexistence without a meaningful relationship. They resort to rules without relationship or relationship without rules. Each is equally destructive to their little rug rats.

The Enemy doesn't wire the vermin kids to respond to rules and regulations for their parents' benefit. He wires them to respond to loving relationships in which adults give rules for the good of the kids. The kids have a love detector. They know when adults really care about them. And when they're just trying to make life easier for themselves.

When these brats' painful sense of aloneness isn't dealt with, their anger and fear can escalate into violence. That's where we come in.

Daniel's an asthmatic punk who thinks himself a tough guy. It's your job—working with Stungoth—to be sure his trench coat, tattoos, and multiple piercings are more than just the idiosyncrasies of a subculture. As long as he thinks we of the dark realm are there for his entertainment, he's ours. Move in on him too dramatically, and he may see you for who you are.

I've instructed Stungoth to accelerate Daniel's descent into darkness. Stungoth's a great ally. He's presided over three suicides and two murders in the past forty years. You need all the help you can get, Foulgrin. Learn from him.

Preying without ceasing,

Prince Ishbane

9

Saturday night Rob's car wasn't working—surprise—and Ian's was at the shop, and somehow Jillian was in the driver's seat. Rob sat shotgun and Brittany and Ian eagerly claimed the backseat.

They were coming from Ian's where they'd watched the video *Pleasantville*. Jillian was dropping Rob off first at his apartment by Portland State, because Ian and Brittany wanted as much backseat time as possible. Jillian listened to Rob's uncomfortable silence. He hadn't said a word since halfway through the movie.

She flipped the radio to her favorite, R&B.

"Change the station. I'm dying back here." Brittany pretended to gag herself.

"Driver's choice," Jillian said.

"Who died and made you God? Let's take a vote. Ian, I know you hate this stuff. What about you, Robbie?"

"I don't care," Rob said, leaning his head back against the passenger seat.

"You lose, Jill. This is a mutiny. Change it or we throw you overboard!"

"You get to choose the station when you drive, now it's my turn." Jillian looked in her rearview mirror hoping to finesse Brittany.

"Okay, little miss power trip, we'll see about that." Brittany leaned forward from the back seat, trying to reach the radio controls.

"Hey!" Jillian slapped her hand.

"C'mon, Ian," Brittany said. "Give it a try."

Ian stretched his long left arm out from behind Rob's seat and punched a few buttons. Alternative rock blasted through the speakers.

Jillian tried to change it back, but Ian blocked her. She looked at Rob. "Help me out here, will ya?"

"Maybe he'd rather listen to the Hispanic station," Brittany teased. *"¿Si, amigo?"*

Rob closed his eyes and clenched his jaw.

Jillian glared at Brittany in the rearview mirror, then suddenly caught sight of flashing lights.

"Oh, no." She applied the brakes and looked at her speedometer. Fifty.

"What's the speed limit?" she asked weakly.

"Thirty-five?" Ian suggested. "Thirty?"

"Great one, Jill," Brittany muttered, then laughed.

Jillian watched every passing car, hoping not to be recognized. It felt like five minutes before the policeman opened his door. Finally, he ambled up to the window.

"License and registration, please."

Jillian trembled as she pawed through her purse, then looked at Rob. "Can you check the glove compartment?"

He fiddled with the latch, sorted through the papers and handed her the registration. The cop eyed everyone in the car, then took the registration.

"Hey, aren't you the guy from the Village People?" Brittany whispered.

Jillian turned pale, hoping he hadn't heard.

"Do you know how fast you were going?"

"Sorry, officer," Brittany said. "She didn't realize her radar detector wasn't plugged in." Her whisper was loud enough for everyone in the car to hear, but—Jillian prayed—not the cop. The officer stayed with his paperwork.

"Nearly fifty? I was kind of distracted for a second."

"According to my radar gun it was fifty-six. The speed limit's thirty-five. I'm going to have to give you a ticket."

He walked back to the patrol car.

Jillian spun around in her seat and glared at Brittany. "What are you trying to do, get me arrested?"

"Just havin' a little fun, Jill. Calm down." Brittany laughed. "What's he going to do? We pay his salary."

Ian laughed and kissed Brittany's neck. Jillian stiffened and looked at Rob. He was staring straight ahead. She planted her hands on the steering wheel and bit her lower lip, waiting for the cop to return. She quickly wiped away a tear.

"Here you are, Miss Fletcher," said the officer, handing her a slip of paper. "Your eyes look a little red, ma'am. Have you been drinking?"

"Your eyes look a little glazed, officer," Brittany mumbled, "have you been eating donuts?"

"No," said Jillian loudly. "I'm sorry. I'm just a little upset."

The officer nodded slowly. "All right, you can either pay the full amount or plead your case in traffic court."

"Gee, officer, the last five times she was pulled over, she only got a warning."

Cut it out, Brit!

The cop stared in the backseat. "Did you say something?"

"Me?" Brittany asked. She shook her head.

"The date's on the ticket," he said to Jillian. "Please read all the instructions thoroughly. Have a nice night. And drive safely, okay?"

"Okay," she said.

Ian and Brittany were rowdy in the back, and Jillian and Rob were silent in the front, all the remaining four miles to PSU. Jillian drove five miles per hour under the speed limit, and turned down the radio. It was still on Ian and Brittany's station.

When they arrived at Rob's apartment, he mumbled "good night" and slid out of the car.

"What's his deal?" Brittany asked.

What's your deal? Jillian felt like asking her. But she didn't.

Letter 9

My strutting peacock Foulgrin,

I don't care about your grand schemes for world domination. Focus. Your job isn't to take down an entire culture. Your job is to ruin Jillian, her friends, and her family. Just do it.

Everything you do to mislead one has a domino effect on the others. The teenage sludgebags imagine they're independent thinkers. But all their decisions are influenced by the group. Once we get them on the river of peer influence, the current does the rest. The adults aren't any better. They live their lives enslaved to others' opinions and oblivious to the Enemy's.

Unfortunately, there's an annoying peer pressure that serves the Enemy. You must keep Jillian and Rob from church and youth group. What we despise is peer pressure toward godliness. Rob has walked this road. This is why he's the only really dangerous one of the four. The others are in our pocket.

Your report on watching the video at Ian's was most encouraging. *Pleasantville*? Yes, I see it here on our recommended movie list. *"Pleasantville* is a youth movie with a clear message: unrestrained sexual indulgence leads to increased health, creativity, intelligence and inner peace. Those vermin who embrace the Enemy's morality are depicted as dull and lifeless people in black and white. Once they violate the Enemy's standards, they become truly alive, depicted in full color. Highly recommended. Particularly effective when watched by Christian youths. Rated VUP: Very Useful Propaganda."

So Rob sulked in the car because he knew he'd compromised his faith watching our movie? The Enemy says to them, "Among you there must not be even a hint of sexual immorality, or of any kind of impurity." Yet they entertain themselves with these very things. They join us in laughing at the things the Enemy despises! When they watch a movie and two people are attracted to each other, what always happens? They go to bed together, naturally. Do the vermin in the movies ever examine their souls and ask whether it's morally right? Of course not.

When this is their steady diet all their lives, how could they ever be shocked at it? How could a fan of *Dawson's Creek* or *Friends* consider fornication anything but normal? It's not the exception, it's the rule. It's how life works. Why shouldn't it work for them that way too? I'm always amused when the same parents who've let their children be entertained by hundreds of fornications are shocked when they discover little Johnny or Sarah has forni-cated. Duh…why wouldn't they? Choices flow out of worldviews, and worldviews flow out of whatever they feed their minds on.

Rob's sulking is no danger unless he confesses and repents. If he doesn't, his conscience will be desensitized further. He'd imagined he would be a good influence on Ian, but it's working the other way. Perhaps Rob's not so dangerous after all. I may have overestimated his guardian Talon as well.

In the car they argued over what music they should listen to? At first, this made me nervous. I thought they might have actually been analyzing the moral content of the songs. But it was preference based solely on style, not content? Fine, as long as they don't consider the messages their minds feed on. I don't care if it's rock, country, or anything else. Just as long as the words undermine the Enemy's values rather than reflect them.

The Enemy's music can lift their hearts and deepen their minds. Worst of all, it can lead them to worship. Yet Jillian can sing her horrid little "praise songs" at the church youth group, then pull out of the parking lot that same night singing along to a song on the radio about the pleasures of fornication. She doesn't think of it in those terms, of course. It's your job to see she never does.

Do what you can to create distance between Rob and Brittany. I look forward to the power struggles, the relational cold war. Use Rob's distaste for her to keep Brittany from the Carpenter he represents. Use him to reinforce her stereotype of hateful, judgmental Christians.

Use Brittany's outrageousness to irritate and insult Rob. Have him place upon her an expectation of righteousness she cannot live up to, since she doesn't know the Enemy. Make his own moral superiority a source of pride. Their disrespect for the police officer is to our advantage. Since the Enemy is authority's author, disregard for human authority is disregard for Him. Their disdain for parents, teachers, cops, and church leaders serves us well. Refusal to submit to lesser authorities is their declaration of independence from the Enemy.

How do you ruin tens of millions of young sludgebags? One peer group at a time.

Watching your every move,

Prince Ishbane

10

Jillian pushed through the crowd, a plate of orange chicken and fried rice in her hand. She scooted herself into a booth in the corner of Sunny Han's, her favorite Chinese restaurant. Rob sat across from her, staring at his matching plate of food.

"You're going to love it!" she said.

"No tortilla?" Without warning, barely tipping his head, he said, "Thanks, Lord, for this day, for this food, and for Jillian."

"Hey," she said. "That guy's looking at your car. I think he's writing down your phone number from the sign."

He followed her gaze out the window.

"Why do you want to sell it? Besides the fact it's undependable, I mean. Need the money?"

"Nah, I won't get much money for it, and I'll just buy another junker. I guess…that car reminds me of too many things I'd like to forget. I was in a gang before I moved up from LA my junior year. You probably knew that, didn't you?"

"I heard."

"That car's like a tattoo across my forehead. As long as I have it, I'm branded a gang member. 'Here comes that spick banger Gonzales.' I'm sick of cops pulling me over. I'm sick of hearing the door locks go down in the car next to me when I'm at a red light." His voice grew louder. Jillian's eyes darted around the room. "God changed me, Jill, and I'm tired of having my past shoved in my face every time I get into that car."

"Sorry! It was just a question." *Where did all that come from?*

Rob ran his hands through his thick black hair.

"You're upset," he said.

"You're the one who was yelling at me," she whispered.

"I wasn't yelling."

"If we took a poll of people at the other tables, you might be surprised," she said. "I don't want to fight."

"It wasn't a fight. It's okay if people see we're human, isn't it?"

"Sorry," Jillian said. "Let's start over. So…how's it going at Portland State?"

"Not bad," Rob said. Finally a slow smile emerged. "Actually, Campus Fellowship has been awesome this term. This new guy Jeff's leading it. We've really clicked."

"That's great."

"I've been learning a ton from his teaching." Rob talked about a few Bible passages he'd been studying. Jillian tried to look attentive. Theology wasn't her thing, but she nodded and smiled.

"It's your turn," Rob said. "Tell me what you've been learning. I mean in your devotions, and at church and youth group."

Jillian paused. "Well, Greg's been going through the book of Romans."

"What chapter are you on?"

"Um, I think around two or three. Or four maybe. Something like that."

"I love in chapter two how Paul talks about circumcision being about the change in a Christian's heart, rather than just an outward sign of the covenant. That's so true, isn't it?"

"Uh…huh?"

"You know, that inside change in your life when you become a believer. It's so much more than changing the things you do on the outside. God's grabbed hold of your heart and transformed it. His grace makes us into new people."

"Yeah. Right."

"How about when you studied it? What'd you think?"

"Pretty much the same," Jillian said, nodding. "How do you like the orange chicken?"

Ian led Rob into his bedroom. It had a high ceiling with a huge fan. The light above it caused a continuous movement of shadows in the room. The place felt as if it were alive. Rob kept looking over his shoulder, thinking someone had just walked into the room.

"Sorry it's a mess," Ian said, clearing off the bed.

Rob laughed. "Makes me feel at home."

"That was some awesome rock climbing today. You're a pretty good athlete."

"You too. I don't care what everybody else says." Rob ducked as a pillow sailed over his shoulder. "I think we'll be sore tomorrow, though. Hope it doesn't mess up your game."

"Think fast." Ian tossed a football at Rob's face. He caught it in self-defense.

"Nice hands. Ever played?"

"Just in middle school. Halfback and corner." Rob eyed the bookshelf, by the stereo. While Ian browsed a big flip-case of CDs, Rob checked out the books.

"*The Celestine Prophecy*. Edgar Cayce. Deepak Chopra." Rob looked at the back dust jacket of another book. "'Words of wisdom from Romtha, the 35,000-year-old man, spoken through his channeler, J. Z. Knight'? Where'd you get this stuff?"

"Some from the paranormal book club. Most from Borders—my mom's always giving me gift certificates. They've got an awesome metaphysics section."

"Metaphysics? I didn't even know that was a category."

"You kidding?" Ian's voice was animated, like a button had been pushed. "Six full shelves. Plus dozens of different tarot card decks in glass display cases, and lots of other cool stuff."

Rob kept running his finger across the books, occasionally picking one up for a closer look. "*The Search for Shambhala*? What's that?"

"You've heard of Shangri-La? Same thing. It's in Nepal or Tibet. Sort of a heaven on earth."

"Astral Projection?" Rob read another book title.

"Yeah. It's kind of a controlled OOBE."

"What's OOBE?"

"Out of body experience."

Rob read from the table of contents. "'How to get from point A to point B once you're out of your body.' Is this a joke?"

"Nope. Hey, our bodies are just earth suits, you know? You can take off your suit."

"You haven't…done it, have you?"

"Not yet. At least I don't think so. I've tried. Eventually I'll get there. Heard a guy on the radio say it took him a few years to get the hang of it."

"How do they say you're supposed to do it?"

"You meditate and chant for a while, focusing on the crystals. You sort of open yourself up, let yourself go."

"Open yourself up to what?"

"Cosmic radiance. The force. Powers."

"Good powers or evil powers?"

"I don't look at it that way."

Rob picked up another book and raised his eyebrows. "Time travel?"

"Don't knock it if you haven't tried it."

"You've time traveled?"

Ian smiled. "Sure. I'm from the twenty-fourth century. I'm just here on a field trip, checking out twenty-first century volleyball players and Chicanos."

Rob stared at him.

"Just kidding, man. No, I haven't time traveled. But I went through the steps. Eventually…who knows? I've got to tell you though, I did the rave scene for a while, and there were times I thought I *was* on another planet."

"Why'd you stop?"

"I loved the music and the secrecy. But mind-altering drugs don't really fit with basketball. And I'm sort of fond of my mind. Don't really want it in a frying pan, you know? Plus it was pretty superficial and there was a lot of game playing and self-destruction. The fun wore off. But some of my old friends are still doing it. Of course, they have fewer brain cells left every time I talk to them. To each his own, huh?"

"Hauntings? Wicca?" Rob held up another book. "What's this one? Who's Emmanuel?"

"A spirit guide."

"Who's Kryon?"

"He's a spirit who helps mortals move to a higher energy level in the new age. It's written by his channeler."

Rob read the blurb on the back cover. "It says Kryon is 'a gentle, loving spirit.'"

"Right. He is."

"How do you know that?"

"I read it, most of it anyway. It's pretty cool."

Rob shook his head. "Ian, I've got to tell you…this is pretty scary stuff."

"Afraid of ghosts or something?"

"Actually, I'm afraid for you. The Bible says Satan masquerades as an angel of light. He's a master of disguise. He can pretend to be gentle and loving in order to deceive people."

"You think I'm being deceived?"

"If you think you can find heaven in Nepal or do time travel or leave your body or find the meaning of life outside of Jesus Christ, then yeah, to be honest, I think you're being deceived."

"A lot of different roads lead to heaven."

"Not according to Jesus. He said, 'I am the way, the truth and the life; no man comes to the Father but by me.' If Jesus was right, He's the only way of salvation. I say if it's true, deal with it."

"That's a big if," Ian said, flipping through his CDs again. He shrugged. "Whatever."

Rob picked up another book. *Opening to Channel: How to Connect with Your Guide.* What guide is it talking about?"

"Your spirit guide. You believe in angels, don't you? You've seen *Touched by an Angel,* right?"

"Yeah, I believe in angels," Rob said. "But the Bible says some of them are good and some of them are evil. And the evil ones often pretend to be good. Sure, I believe you can be touched by an angel. I also believe you can be touched by a *fallen* angel."

Ian laughed. "Well, maybe next season they'll come out with a spin-off: *Touched by a Fallen Angel.*"

"They probably won't," Rob said. "But maybe they should."

⟳⟋⟋⟋

Letter 10

My colleague Ishbane,

Ian's smarter than most of those idiots. He affirms the reality of an existence outside his own, and he's not content with his friends' superficiality. There's a danger that his spiritual interest could be hijacked by the Enemy. His recognition of the supernatural serves us well only as long as he stays clear of the Carpenter.

I've instructed Pendragon to keep Ian's mind from investigating the Enemy's claims with the openness he brings to OOBEs, astral projection, time travel, alien contact and our vast repertoire of spiritual alternatives. If we can't get them to deny the supernatural entirely, an undiscerning interest is next best.

We've established a tremendous edge with this generation, even in the churches. Unprecedented numbers of young people are dabbling in the occult. Yet the forbidden fellowships usually do nothing to keep them from us. They think the movies kids watch, the books they read, the symbols they wear, the music they listen to is just a generational thing, the equivalent of bell-bottom pants, long sideburns or Air Jordans. Merely a passing phase. Prey upon this ignorance.

Parents once regarded themselves as their children's protectors. Now they protect them from shootings or sexual abuse, but they fail to protect them from our encroachment into their lives. Since I'm working near their parents already, I'll do what I can to convince them that talking about the occult would only draw their children toward it. I'll blind them to the fact that it's ignorance of what we're up to—not understanding of it—that makes their children vulnerable.

How many young people have we sucked into Ouija boards, tarot cards, palm readings and astrology simply because no one told them how we can use these to seduce them? This generation of parents has lavished material things on their children. But they've failed miserably to cultivate their spirituality or point it toward the Enemy.

Curiosity is enough to lure them to the bait. They bite, we reel them in. (I assume, Ishbane, that you're taking notes? I've been in your position. Trust me—you need all the help you can get.)

Ian's parents are largely unaware of his metaphysical pilgrimage and have done nothing to guide or warn him about us. They don't care if Ian drinks as long as he doesn't drive or get kicked off the basketball team. They don't care if he has sex as long as he wears a condom. Playing with the dark side via music and games and cards? Who cares, as long as he doesn't do drugs. (Have you ever seen a bumper sticker saying "D.A.R.E. to tell your children about the occult"?)

This athlete Josh and some of his jock friends continue to push Daniel around. He's terrified to go to gym. I welcome simultaneous PE classes sharing the same locker room, so older boys shower with younger. A few have perfected the towel snap, terrorizing the freshman boys, including Daniel. Josh has nailed him between the legs so hard he's buckled to the floor in pain, causing roaring laughter and utter humiliation. He's not strong enough to retaliate, so he internalizes. I love it! We're letting his anger simmer on the back burner, feeding it with thoughts of revenge when he blows away his enemies in his computer games. Stungoth and I are biding our time. At just the right moment we'll turn up the heat and Daniel will explode like an unvented pressure cooker.

Forcing them to stand naked in front of cruel boys is a marvelous strategy that's served us well for years. While the Enemy defends the weak and vulnerable, we do all we can to exploit them. The bully is my favorite tool. Train them to be bullies now and eventually we'll use them to beat their girlfriends, intimidate their wives, kill rival gang members, frighten new flesh in the workplace, torture young military recruits, wield punitive political power, terrify students as coaches or PE teachers, run roughshod over church boards— you name it. Being a bully is a versatile job, with skills that carry over to all walks of life.

Meanwhile, we create wimpy victims like Daniel who dream of power and revenge.

I'm working to introduce Daniel to Ian. He needs a mentor! When materialism and naturalism and rationalism dominated, our best strategy was to convince them the supernatural was bunk. But those who've seen the futility of our dead-end streets crave a supernatural experience. We are not simply the best supernatural alternative to the Enemy and His warriors. We are the only alternative.

They sense there's something greater, above and beyond them. The notion of benevolent aliens and angels offers them a taste of the transcendent without requiring them to bow knees to the Enemy or come to terms with His nature and demands. If Ian, Daniel, and Brittany seek angels, they may well find them—just not the ones they expected!

In the end, Ishbane, it all comes down to convincing them that their deepest needs can be met by anyone or anything besides Him.

Making a list and checking it twice,

Lord Foulgrin

11

FEBRUARY 21, 9:43 A.M.

Fifteen minutes after campus Bible study was over, a few people still milled around. Rob stayed, watching Jeff, who finally ended his conversation.

"Got a minute?" Rob asked.

"Sure. What's on your mind?"

"Actually, there's a lot to talk about. Including my friend Ian. But the first one's kind of personal. Something's not right with me and Jillian."

"Come on, let's go next door." Jeff led the way into a vacant classroom, then pulled two chairs together. "What's up?" he asked.

"I don't know for sure. Part of it's me. I struggle with my past and some issues I've told you about. But it's more than that. I mean, I thought since Jillian and I were both believers things would be different."

"Different how?" Jeff asked.

"I guess I thought a Christian girlfriend would draw me closer to God."

"She doesn't?"

"Don't get me wrong. She's great. But she's not…passionate about the Lord."

"People are different. Maybe she's just not as expressive as you are."

"We hardly ever talk about our faith. I bring it up but the subject always changes. One moment I'm talking about the Word, and the next she's talking about orange chicken. I know I'm supposed to be the leader, but I hate trying to drag it out of her. When we talk about church, she just talks about her friends and activities, not the Lord."

"She's still in high school, right?"

"Thanks for the reminder."

"Look, I know you want a godly relationship. And that's really important. If you don't think Jillian's the one for you, maybe you should break it off."

"That's not what I'm saying."

"What *are* you saying, Rob?"

"I don't know." Rob put his forehead in his hands.

"You really like this girl, don't you?"

"Yeah. And I thought we were on the same page spiritually, but I don't know anymore. Plus, this is the first time I've dated since I've been a Christian. It's a bigger deal than I thought."

"It's not like you're the only guy to struggle with a relationship."

"That's easy for you to say. You've got Erin."

"And I've got news for you. Erin's terrific, but I had this idea she was supposed to be perfect. That's not fair. You either have to let go of the person or let go of that perfect little picture in your mind. And remember, the one in your mind doesn't really exist."

"Are you saying I should lower my standards?"

"No way—keep your standards high. If you don't think she's interested in her walk with the Lord, that's a bad sign, big time. But if she's following the Lord but just doesn't know how to express it like you do, give her some space...and some grace. Above all, guard your purity and take it slow."

"After how I've messed up in the past, I told the Lord I'd always put Him first. I said I'd never date somebody if I ended up putting her before Him."

"Yeah, that's one of the dangers of dating, along with the other temptations. If you're going to date—and remember, you don't have to—you can get sucked into something that compromises your walk with God. You'd better pray a lot about this one, Rob. I hear you saying maybe it's time to let her go."

"I don't want to."

"I can understand that, but do yourself a favor. Marry a girl who loves Jesus more than she loves you. Erin's not just my partner in life, she's my partner in ministry. It's easy to recover from some mistakes. If you go to the wrong school, you can transfer next term. But if you marry the wrong person...well, just don't let it happen. Nothing's better than a right marriage. And nothing's worse than a wrong one."

"I'm not talking about *marriage.*"

"Maybe not yet, but think about it—there's no such thing as 'just dating.' It's a big deal. If you're going to date, you'll marry someone you dated, right? So you'd better only date the kind of girl it would be right to marry. People don't marry strangers. If you're spending time with someone special, somebody who lights you up, you'd better think of it as walking a path toward marriage."

Rob stared at the floor. Finally he stood up and said, "Gotta go. Big test tomorrow."

"Life's full of tests, isn't it? I'll be praying for you, Rob."

"Yeah, thanks, man. See ya."

Rob walked back toward the apartment, dazed.

Okay, God, what now?

He stared at the textbook for an hour, seeing words, not meanings. He turned out the lights and got down on his knees. "Lord, You know I don't want to do this. But I have to let her go, don't I? God, touch her, even if I can't have her. Help her to love You with all her heart."

Brittany and Skyla kicked back in Brittany's bedroom. She'd invited Jillian to spend the night too, but she'd made up some excuse.

They popped in a video and watched *The Brood,* one of Skyla's favorite horror movies. Ninety minutes later the final credits were playing.

"That was scary," Brittany said.

"Yeah. Wasn't it great?" Skyla grabbed some more caramel corn and munched on it. "I've wanted to ask you something, Brit. Remember when you were in the hospital last fall?"

"Like I'll ever forget," Brittany said.

"Somebody told me you had a dream or something."

Brittany sighed. "I told a bunch of people about it at first, but then I shut up. The doctor said it was probably something my brain made up because I was wacked out on carbon monoxide and all that medication."

"What happened?"

"It was after I tried to…you know, after I revved up the car in the garage so the fumes would put me to sleep. I just wanted to end it all, and that was one of the suggestions in that Hemlock Society book. Anyway, instead I wound up in the hospital. And I had this dream. Only at the time it was more real than a dream. I was sure those things were actually happening."

"What things? Tell me exactly what happened."

"I was walking down a long tunnel. At the far end I saw…a bright being, with light all around him. He gestured with his hand, like he wanted me to come closer."

"You're sure it was a he, not a she?"

"Positive."

"Okay, it was probably Pan or Osiris. Maybe Amman-Rah."

"Huh?"

"Keep going. This is great."

"I felt a…sort of a tingling warmth. I wasn't afraid. Then he spoke to me. He said, 'Welcome, my child.' Yeah, he called me his child. Then he said, 'There's a world that awaits you, filled with joy and wonder.'"

"Cool."

"I've pushed this out of my mind for a while, because with the scary things that happened…"

"What else did he say?" Skyla asked.

"He asked if I'd like to come in and see it all. Well, in spite of what I'd done, part of me wanted to stay on earth, I guess. But I did want to see what he was talking about. He turned and pointed to the other end of the tunnel. And it was like I could see a whole world there."

"What kind of world?"

"Waterfalls, rainbows, and beautiful flowers—all my favorites, like red roses and pink carnations, growing wild. Grassy meadows. It was incredible, like this was the place I was made for, that I'd been searching for all my life. I was just about to walk in. But I didn't."

"Why?"

"The spirit, or whoever it was, said it was all waiting for me, but not yet. He said I was special, that my time on earth wasn't done. So he was going to send me back, but with…with a mission."

"What mission?"

"He said I should bring the good news to everybody I knew. I should tell them about him and his kindness, and that he promised never to judge or condemn anyone. Then he said I should tell them 'do not fear death.' He said, 'This is my message—love one another.' He asked me to promise I would tell people that. And then he stroked my cheek. He was so gentle. The next thing I knew the bright lights were in the hospital room. He was gone and there was a nurse standing over me. I was awake. They'd thought I was going to die."

"But did you do what the spirit said—spread the message? That people should love each other and shouldn't fear death?"

"At first, yeah. I told everybody. I didn't care if they thought I was crazy. But after a while people did think…well, that kind of thing doesn't happen to normal people. It was weird. I poured myself back into homework and thinking about medical school and volleyball and other things. You start to wonder if it really happened."

"I think it really did happen, Brit. Wiccans believe that life is cyclical—night follows day, seasons come and go, life is followed by death and rebirth. After we die, the human soul rests in a place called 'Summerland,' the land of eternal youth. The soul is refreshed there. It grows young, and is made ready to be born again."

"Born again?"

"Yes, into another cycle of life. Reincarnation. Anyway, your spirit's message was a lot like that. And I think the beautiful place you saw was Summerland. What else could it have been? So…who do you think the spirit was?"

"At the time I thought maybe it was Jesus."

"Maybe. Or it may have been the priestess. Or, if you're sure it was a male, it would've been Osiris, the horned god, consort of the priestess. Whoever it was, they chose you, Brit. They gave you an anointing, a mission. You said so yourself. Obviously, you've got some strong metaphysical vibes. That's why you're so good with the tarot cards. I think it's time you got back to the spirit world. In fact, that same spirit is probably with you now. He could speak through you."

"How?"

"Channeling. Maybe automatic writing? All sorts of ways."

"I'm not sure, Skyla."

"He's your guardian angel, right? You owe him. He saved your life, didn't he? He showed you there's nothing to fear after death. And he gave you a message to take to others. I think you should do what you can to get back in contact with him. Don't you owe it to him? And don't you owe it to yourself?"

Letter 11

Prince Ishbane,

You want an update on Daniel and Brittany? Your wish is my command.

Can I make my own humble request? I've been unable to locate my former pupil Squaltaint. If I didn't know better, I'd think he's in a witness protection program. I only want to send him my warm regards, letting bygones be bygones. Please give me his forwarding address.

Diane imagines Daniel's choices are beyond her. She has no idea how much territory we already occupy in him. She won't take the computer away from him because no parent has the right to do that, especially not to a poor little boy who's lost his father. She hopes her Danny will magically keep from viewing the thousands of porn sites on-line. Don't you love it? It's like subscribing to pornographic magazines and filling her son's closet with them, then telling him "now be a good boy, and don't ever look in your closet, promise?"

Fortunately, when Diane brings up Daniel's problems, even most of her church friends reassure her it's "just a passing phase." She sees how moody, withdrawn, depressed, and joyless he is, yet it doesn't click with her that we're playing a major role in it. She considers his obsession with occult themes, music, and videos as just "something else the kids are into these days." His utter disrespect for authority is seen as natural teenage rebellion, rather than evidence of our supernatural stronghold in him. (Of course, some of it is the natural adolescent rebellion—"we refuse to be like our parents.")

Diane Fletcher's seen his occult jewelry, but it doesn't even register with her. His pentagram, ankh, eye of Ra…just some weird jewelry. Images of graveyards, blood, cats, death, and monsters? Harmless. Piercing his tongue? What's the downside of self-mutilation and defacing the Enemy's creation?

While rebellion normally serves us, there is one hideous exception. Sometimes the Carpenter steps in and leads the young in rebellion against the dominant cultural beliefs and values. When it comes to the status quo, we are conformists, not rebels.

Stungoth's five-year plan for Daniel is right on course. He has periodic thoughts of suicide, but potential for so much more. If we stay on target, he'll not simply take himself out, but some classmates as well. No accessible guns in his house right now, but I'm working on it. We can always get one somewhere.

As for my Brittany, I have fond memories of hunting her last year. The night they invited my presence through the Ouija board was all the foothold I needed. She granted me visitation rights. Once they open the door, why stay out in the cold? Yes, I was disappointed Brittany didn't die in that garage. Her suicide would have been successful if not for the nosy neighbor who heard the car engine and saw the fumes. While she was in the hospital, I could see the Enemy was going to bring her back. So I came to her in the tunnel, showed her the phony heavenly images—"Hell's demo"—and delivered my message.

I expected to get more mileage out of her than I did. I thought I could make her a New Age spokesperson, or she could channel me or write an "embraced by the light" book. No such luck. But in retrospect it's even better. Once they leave this world they're securely in hell, but they're of no more practical use to us. Now Skyla can be her mentor. Brittany can be a tool to derail Fletcher's daughter. Bad things come to those who wait!

We promise our servants everything, and give them nothing but their own destruction and horror. The more they serve us, the more we demand, and the more authority we're given to torture them. Meanwhile, inexplicably, the Enemy offers them the kingdom of Charis at no charge. (After He had the audacity to kick us out!)

Soon I'll be coming to my Brittany in her dreams again. She's mine, Ishbane, and I'll have her. I feed every dark impulse that comes on her. The more she thirsts, the more I'll give her salt water, and the more desperate she'll become. I'll toy with her a bit longer, while introducing the idea again that her dilemmas would be solved by a simple act of suicide. I'm considering a group suicide, a pact with Ian. Maybe we can get Daniel in on it. Who knows?

The Carpenter called the Master a "murderer from the beginning…a liar and the Father of lies." He said, "When he lies he speaks his native language." The Tyrant intended this as an insult. I take it as a compliment. Deception's the name of our game. No one plays it better than I. The Enemy's monolingual. He speaks only truth. We're bilingual. We speak truth selectively, to create a credible context for our lies.

I'm the cat, Brittany's the mouse. I'll play with her until the time is right. Then I'll swallow her whole. Her chances of escape? A snowball's chance in hell.

Celebrating our native language,

Lord Foulgrin

12

Just as Jillian sat down at the dinner table, the horn honked. "Gotta go, Mom. That's Lisa." Jillian jumped up, grabbed her purse and headed for the door.

"Ask her in. You haven't eaten a thing."

"I can't, we'll be late for youth group." She opened the door.

"Take a couple bread sticks at least. You can eat them in the car."

"Relax, Mom, we'll probably go out and eat later. Gotta go."

"Tell Greg and Kristi hi for me. The Lord's really using them."

"Uh-huh. Bye."

She slid into the front seat of Lisa's gray Honda.

"Hey, Jill. How was your day?"

"An average blah Wednesday. I think they should cut out Wednesdays from the school week. Mondays and Tuesdays you're not bored yet, plus you're still thinking about the weekend you just had. And Thursdays and Fridays you're excited for the next one."

"Great idea," Lisa said. "Now we just need you on student council to vote it in."

As they pulled into Sovereign Grace Church's parking lot, they saw their youth pastor and his wife getting out of their car.

"Hey, Greg. Hi, Kristi!" Lisa yelled out the window. "They're great, aren't they?" she said to Jillian.

"Yeah. The Lord's really using them."

"Greg asked for prayer about tonight. He said there's going to be some spiritual battles going on."

Jillian nodded, wondering exactly what a spiritual battle was.

As the night went on, Jillian played the games and chatted with friends. At eight o'clock they moved into the auditorium. She and Lisa found a seat in the middle. Jillian sang familiar songs with the group. She didn't think about the words. She closed her eyes. Words came at her from somewhere else.

There's going to be some spiritual battles going on in this auditorium tonight.

The band sat down and Greg took their place on the stage. "Let's pray." Jillian saw a wave of baseball caps going off. Everyone bowed their heads.

"Draw us near to Yourself right now, God. May no other powers but the power of Your Holy Spirit be felt in this room tonight. Protect me as I speak." Greg paused and his last words were spoken quietly, "And God, open the hearts of those who don't know You."

There's going to be some spiritual battles going on in this auditorium tonight.

Jillian opened her eyes. As Greg spoke, she thought about the homework she had to finish after youth group. She thought about Rob, Brittany, Kelly, and how Daniel had stolen a CD from her and denied it.

Greg was telling his story, or "giving his testimony" as Jillian had learned to call it. He'd grown up in a Christian home and gone to a Bible college, then off to seminary to become a pastor. "One weekend at my home church, the pastor asked me to preach."

Maybe I should call Rob. He hasn't been himself lately. There's that phone in the hallway. I should call him now.

She looked around at the crowd of kids sitting on the floor. There weren't any aisles. How could she get out?

"The pastor asked me to speak on how to become a Christian. I was sort of bummed because maybe he thought I couldn't handle anything more."

Jillian noticed her nails needed a good filing and a fresh coat of paint.

Maybe I'll stop by the store on the way home and pick up a new color.

"…and I'm telling you guys, I'd read those verses a gazillion times before. I'd even used them to share the gospel with people I met on airplanes. But I realized those verses were in my mind, not my heart."

This message doesn't apply to me. I'm a Christian. I believe in Jesus, just like Dad and Mom wanted me to.

"Paul says in Romans, 'If you confess with your mouth "Jesus is Lord" and believe in your heart that God raised him from the dead, you will be saved.'"

Greg stopped, and searched the crowd. His eyes seemed to lock on Jillian's. "I confessed it with my mouth, I believed it in my mind, but I never believed it in my heart."

I believe. I know John 3:16. I know He died on the cross. I know He rose again.

"I knew all the answers. I got A's in my seminary classes. I went on a mission trip. But I never realized I had to make a decision that involved my heart."

Before she knew what was happening, Jillian was climbing over people's legs to escape. She moved quickly out of the auditorium and toward the bathroom. She thought she heard someone call her name, but the few faces in the hall were a blur as she stumbled forward.

She pushed open the bathroom door and stopped in shock as she looked at herself in the mirror. Tears were flowing down her face and dripping onto her shirt, staining it with her make-up.

"Jillian?"

She stared at herself, wondering who was behind the reflection that stared back.

"Jillian!" She felt a hand on her shoulder, and jumped.

"Lisa." Jillian tried to wipe the tears away. "I didn't hear you."

"I've been calling your name ever since you took off. Are you okay?"

"Yeah. I mean…" Jillian paused and felt the tears start to flow again. "I don't know."

Lisa led her out of the bathroom to a couch in the nursery next door.

"I didn't mean to get up like that. I don't know what happened. I don't even know why I'm crying."

Lisa took a deep breath. "Remember how Greg wanted me to pray because he thought there would be some spiritual battles tonight?"

Jillian nodded.

"You know how Greg said he tried to do the right thing his whole life? He was having his devotions and witnessing to people and going to school to be a pastor. But he said he still hadn't experienced what salvation was all about. Jill, I think someone didn't want you to hear that."

Jillian felt her jaw tighten. "I don't want to talk about it."

"Same reason you didn't want to hear that message?"

"I don't know. I just don't know, alright?" Jillian hung her head.

"Jill, the reason I'm sitting here with you is because I care about you, so don't take this the wrong way. I think you need to evaluate where you're at with God. I know you didn't grow up in a Christian home, but I did. There was a long time when I just went through the motions. I sort of lived off my parents' faith. I didn't realize what becoming a Christian was all about."

Jillian looked up at Lisa. Through her tears she asked the question she'd been afraid to ask. "What *is* it all about, Lisa? I mean, I've been going to church for over a year. I try to live by what the Bible says. I believe in Jesus. I try to do everything right. And I'm still not good enough to call myself a Christian? What am I missing? What's it all about?"

"It's about a person. It's about Jesus. It's about the fact that everyone has sinned, but Jesus took the punishment for our sin so that we wouldn't have to. You've heard the words, maybe, but listen and try to think of what it really means. See, God is so holy that He can't stand sin. The price of our sin is death, which means being separated from God for eternity."

"Hell," Jillian said, shivering.

"Right. All of us deserve hell. But instead of having all of us pay for what we've done, He sent His Son to die so we wouldn't have to. Jill, He died for you. He loves you. See, it's not about you and about what you're doing for Him; it's all about Him, and what He did for you."

"So everything I've been doing doesn't matter? I thought the Bible told people to do what I've been trying to do."

"But you can't get to heaven by doing those good things. When you have the Holy Spirit, you learn to live like Christ from the inside out. I do those things because I know God's plan is best for my life. I do them because I want to live a life that shows others His love. I don't do them to earn my way to heaven, but because I know Christ paid my way to heaven."

Lisa grabbed Jillian's hand. "First things first, Jill. You need to accept His gift of salvation. You have to admit you can't be perfect enough to do it on your own. Let Jesus Christ do it for you."

"I feel so stupid," Jillian said. "I knew all this stuff before, but I...never accepted it in my heart, just like Greg said. I'm not sure why. Maybe because it made me feel better to think I was doing something to earn it? Anyway, you're right—I don't deserve it."

"None of us do, Jillian. That's why it's called grace. If we deserved it, we wouldn't need it!"

"Lisa...my dad used to pray with me. And my mom does sometimes. Would you mind?"

Lisa hugged her. "There's nothing I'd love more!"

Letter 12

My disastrous Foulgrin,

I'm your superior, not your pupil! Stop patronizing me. After what's just happened, you're in no position to dictate terms.

You violated the first rule of temptation. You let Jillian get her mind off herself, her hair, her clothes, her boyfriend and her cheerleading, and onto...Him! *Your* Jillian is now *His* Jillian? You've committed the unpardonable sin.

Were your last letters about Jillian, your main assignment? No! You went on and on about Brittany and Ian and Daniel. Your attention was diverted by the Enemy's sleight of hand.

You've lost one of our biggest advantages—making the vermin falsely assume they're Christians because they're in church.

Where were you when this abhorrent Lisa was sharing the forbidden message with Jillian? While you were looking the other way, the Ghost snatched her.

Alright, the milk is spilled. Stop crying about it. You can still trip her up. Create a labyrinth of self-righteousness. Keep her wandering in the maze of self. Consume her with what she has to offer the Tyrant rather than what He offers her. She believes her new life began by grace? Make her imagine it must be maintained by rule keeping. Make her motto, "God helps those who help themselves." Don't let her see that He helps those who realize they can't.

The Enemy doesn't force them to obey. He cleans their house, but He doesn't automatically keep it clean. She asked Him to take control of her life, but that doesn't mean she'll daily relinquish her life to Him. Decisions of submission to the Enemy made in the past are never as dangerous as those made today.

Now it's all about damage control. Jillian bears on her shoulders the Carpenter's reputation. That means you can tarnish His reputation through her. This spells opportunity.

Convince her that being a Christian is a short sprint, not a marathon. Burn her out quickly. Disillusion her. Though she has the power to resist us, keep her ignorant of the Ghost.

Bring a parade of hypocrites her way. Use the forbidden fellowship to make her feel condemned. Let her notice the disapproving looks from our prideful pharisees at church. They dismiss this generation, stereotyping them all as lazy, immoral, irresponsible, and unspiritual. Some of these church people look like they've been baptized in vinegar and taken communion with lemon juice. They make no effort to connect with younger members of the church family. Use their superior attitude to alienate Jillian and cut her off from the wisdom of her elders.

It's cafeteria Christians we want. Your job is to get as many offerings as possible on the spiritual smorgasbord. A consumer religion where each customer looks to meet his own needs. They want to eat meat only, no vegetables? Fine. They want a selection of six desserts and no fruit? Fine. They want a good choir, the right music, a certain kind of message, good parking? Fine—make it all about *them*.

Train them to be church shoppers. That way, when they're lazy and busy—which they eventually will be—they'll abandon church altogether and become private Christians. We have no fear of private Christians. Embers separated from the fire never burn long.

Don't let her give up her obsession with food! This is one of your main strongholds. Anything besides the Tyrant Himself that controls her heart, mind, or body, anything she desires more than Him, He considers an idol. Blind her. Don't try to get her to choose evil because it's evil. Get her to choose evil by disguising it as good. She believes food will bring her joy, and being skinny will fulfill her. Surely her loving Father wouldn't want her to be unhappy, would He? Have her see the Tyrant as the guarantor of her self-fulfillment, the genie in the bottle who exists to serve her.

I command you not to call me Lord Ishbane again. My title is Prince. I go on record as saying I have never called myself Lord! Do you think I can't see through your attempt to frame me? And do stop hounding me about the location of your former pupil Squaltaint. That's classified.

Focus your deviousness on the vermin! We're not finished with Jillian Fletcher yet. Make her think the Tyrant owes her a life of fulfilled dreams and accomplished goals, even when those dreams and goals are hers, not His. Then, when He insists on doing it His way—which He always does—watch her newfound faith crumble.

You've lost a major battle, Foulgrin. Redouble your efforts. You may yet win the war.

Looking on the dark side,

Prince Ishbane

13

FEBRUARY 23, 3:24 P.M.

Jill, we've got to talk," Rob said into the phone.

"No kidding! Did you get my message? I've got something to tell you, Rob. You're not going to believe it!"

"It's something serious."

"What's wrong?" Jillian asked, sitting down by the kitchen table.

"We have to talk."

"You said that. But what about? I have some good news for you. And an apology."

"Before you apologize for anything, I have to say I'm sorry to you."

"For what?"

"For letting this relationship go so far."

"What are you talking about, Rob?"

"I don't think I can marry you."

Jillian laughed. "I should hope not. I'm still in high school. We've only been dating what, five weeks?"

"I mean I can't date you anymore, for the same reason I couldn't marry you."

She froze.

"Did you hear me, Jill?"

"Yep."

"Look, I didn't mean to say this over the phone. I'm sorry. It just spilled out. I should come over there."

"You're breaking up with me?" Her stomach churned.

"Uh…let's wait until I get over there."

"Right."

Rob hung up. Jillian sat still, holding the phone, paralyzed.

What's going on? Is this what You do to me when I give my life to You, Lord? I said You could have everything. This wasn't what I had in mind.

Stomach aching, she sat on the couch, under a dark cloud. Twenty minutes later, she heard a knock. She wiped her eyes and opened the door.

"I'm sorry for doing that to you," Rob said. "I should've just come over in the first place."

She stepped back when he walked in and closed the door behind him, mechanically.

"I'm so sorry, Jill. I just can't stay in this relationship."

"But…why?" A tear slid down her cheek.

"I just don't feel like we're good for each other. I don't think we're helping each other grow in our faith."

Suddenly Jillian started laughing. "Is this about our different spiritual commitments? Is that it?"

"Isn't that enough?"

"But we can handle that."

"I've been working on the spiritual side of our relationship ever since we started dating."

"But I haven't been."

"You haven't?"

"I didn't even know God. So how could my heart be in it when we talked about Him?"

"What are you saying?"

"I'm saying that last night I became a Christian." She laughed again, as she wiped her tears.

"But I thought…" Rob's forehead scrunched. "I mean, I assumed you were a Christian. Didn't you say you were? You went to church and youth group and read your Bible and prayed, right?"

"I thought that's all there was. Lisa showed me I had to make my own decision, not just go to church or try to be a good girl. I actually had to receive Christ's gift."

Rob leaned back against the entryway wall. "I can't believe I didn't see it. I knew something was off, but I just thought you weren't on fire for the Lord."

"It's hard to be on fire for the Lord if you don't even know Him."

"I guess so."

"Aren't you happy for me, Rob?"

"Of course. Yeah. I just can't believe I was dating a non-Christian. It was something I said I'd never do."

"Sorry if I didn't meet your standards."

"I didn't mean it as a put-down. It was my problem. I told the Lord I never wanted to put anyone else in front of Him. And I was starting to put you in front of Him."

"But I'm a Christian now. So we don't have to break up."

"Well, no. I mean, I don't know."

"The problem's solved, right? Now I want to follow God. Lisa says I'm His child. I have His Holy Spirit inside. It'll all be fine."

"But…we shouldn't have been dating in the first place."

"You didn't know I wasn't saved. Even I didn't know."

"That doesn't matter. We still shouldn't have been together."

"So because of that, you think we have to break up *now?*"

"Not just because of that."

Jillian sat on the couch, unable to believe what she was hearing. "I thought you'd be happy for me. I figured you'd be surprised, sure, but excited. Now you're breaking up with me because I decided to give my life to Christ?"

"Not because of that, because of…I *am* happy for you. But I still don't know about us."

What's happening? This isn't how it's supposed to be.

"I'd better go," Rob said. "I need to think about this. It just doesn't seem right."

"Sounds like you've made up your mind. Okay. I know when I'm not wanted."

"It's not like that. I just need to sort things out."

"You do that," she said, voice dead. She walked to the door and opened it. The moment he walked through, she shut the door behind him without a look.

She crumbled back on the couch, in an empty house, silent and cold. So cold she shivered. Who could she talk to? She couldn't call Brit. She'd never understand—and it would turn her off to Christians more than ever. Lisa hardly knew Rob. Mom was gone. Besides, she hadn't talked much to Mom about guy stuff. She had no one to turn to.

Jillian closed her eyes and spoke. *"God, I don't understand. I thought Rob would be thrilled. Now I've lost him. I guess You know what I'm going through, don't You? Is that it? Do You want it to be just You and me? I'm new at all of this. It's the worst I've felt since…"* Her voice cracked and she sobbed, a broken heap on the couch. She never finished the sentence. She never said, *"Since Daddy died."*

The pills were still there, at the back of the desk drawer. The book felt heavy. The information was marked on the page with the Post-it note. Here was another way to kill yourself. It was all so calm and clinical, suggesting this was a rational decision. You could be walked through how to take your life just as you could be told how to bake a pie or fix a dripping faucet. The emotions were numb now. The brain was functioning mechanically, reviewing the plan, debating it, wondering if another option would be better for everyone. Perhaps an option that would look like an accident. Yes. There it was. The book had ideas about that, too.

Jillian wandered down to the kitchen. Her mom was putting water on to boil for a spaghetti dinner.

"Hi, hon. It's just you and me for dinner. Daniel's over at Dan Stanklin's. It's his mom's turn to put up with the Dans."

"Mom, can we talk?"

"Sure, honey. Is something wrong?" She turned and looked at Jillian's face, then immediately turned off the burner. "What is it, Jilly?"

"Stuff's happening. I need help sorting it out."

"Tell you what, forget the dinner. I'll call for pizza and let's have some good old-fashioned girl talk. I didn't feel like cooking anyway." She pulled out the phone book and asked, "Pepperoni and pineapple?"

Jillian nodded.

After making the call, Diane joined Jillian, who sat on the edge of the couch, elbows on her knees, chin in hand. Diane sat next to her, arm around her.

"What is it?" she asked.

"I feel kind of silly telling you this, but…" She told her all about Greg's message and Lisa and everything that happened the night before.

"Oh, Jillian, that's wonderful. I've been praying about this for a long time."

"But, I thought I *was* a Christian. I mean, I went to church and everything. Didn't *you* think I was a Christian?"

"For a while I did. But recently I started to wonder if you'd ever really made the choice yourself. You came to church with Dad and me. But like Ryan says, if a cat jumps into the oven it doesn't make it an apple pie. And if someone goes to church, it doesn't make them a Christian. Your dad didn't force me to become a Christian, and we didn't force you. Only God can draw you to Himself. I've been praying about the right time to talk to you, but whenever I try, there's a big fight or you have to go. It's been like something…or maybe someone…keeps us from talking."

"I thought you'd be shocked, or mad. Like Rob."

"What do you mean 'mad'?"

Jillian drew her feet up on the couch, leaning against her mom. "I told Rob a few hours ago. He broke up with me."

"What? Oh, honey, I'm so sorry."

"I don't get it. All this time, I thought I was a Christian. So did he. Now that I really *am* a Christian, he doesn't want to be near me. Am I missing something?"

"Maybe he just needs some time to let it sink in."

"It's over. And he didn't even seem that happy about me coming to Christ. I just don't get it."

"Give it time, Jilly. He seems to really care about you. I think he'll come around."

"I don't know if I want him to." She knew that wasn't true, but she didn't want to sound as pathetic as she felt.

The two sat on the couch, holding hands in silence. But for once the silence drew them together rather than ripping them apart. Jillian hugged her mom and cried. She felt something she hadn't felt since she was a little girl—that no matter what happened, no matter who deserted her, Mom would be there.

But even when she can't be here for me, You will, won't You God?

The doorbell rang. Joey woke up and started crying.

Diane went to the door. "Can you get Joey, please?" She fished money out of her purse and exchanged it for the cardboard box.

Jillian came back with her little brother and set him in his infant seat on the kitchen table. Mom grabbed some Gerber rice cereal and tried to charm it into Joey's mouth.

Diane looked across the table at Jillian. "How about you pray?"

Jillian bowed her head and closed her eyes. She'd prayed with Mom before, but this was different. It felt like the first time.

"God, thanks that Mom and I could talk. I'm sorry for the way I've treated her sometimes. She's a great mom. Thanks for Joey, he's so precious, and even for Daniel. Help him to come to know You. Be with Rob…" Her voice broke. "And say hi to Dad for us, okay?" Then she laughed and cried at the same time. "Oh, yeah, and thanks for the pizza, too."

They squeezed each other tight.

Letter 13

My tiresome Foulgrin,

No, I've not read *Foulgrin's 66 Rules of Temptation*. Nor have I the slightest interest in doing so. I've forgotten more than you'll ever know. And I've forgotten little.

So this youth pastor speaks of spiritual battle? Let that be a figure of speech only. Don't let them heed the Enemy's description of a roaring lion seeking whom he may devour.

"Put on the whole armor of God" the Enemy commands them. He provides it, but the good news is, *they* have to put it on. And most of them don't. They don't act like they're on a battleship. They act like they're on a cruise ship.

No soldier wins a battle he doesn't prepare for. No soldier prepares for a battle he doesn't know exists. Keep their eyes closed to the spiritual realm. How? Simply by keeping them busy orbiting around themselves.

Keep Jillian away from the Enemy's alert and disciplined soldiers and put her with the weak and careless ones. They'll manage to lead her into our minefields. Or out on the fringes of the battalion where we can pick them off one by one. We've already seized the territory they live on. The only way they can win the battle is to retake what we've captured.

The days of the overpowering frontal attack are mainly behind us. With Jillian, subtlety's the best strategy. Don't kick the door in when you can pick the lock. Don't chase after moths with a blowtorch. Don't assault and scream when you can seduce and insinuate. You're conducting a sting operation, not an air raid. Know when to back off and when to come back at a more opportune time. Be gentle. Talk lovingly to the little lamb. Speak reassuring words. Wear the skin of civility over the raw flesh of your malice. Stroke her cheek with one hand as you slit her throat with the other.

If your Jillian realizes the refuge of her mother's love, that home and family is a sanctuary, your work will be severely undermined. We hate family and home precisely because it's the dim reflection of Charis. Their love for home, the exhilaration they feel in coming home to loved ones, where they belong, is a glimpse of heaven. It draws them toward it—and Him.

Erebus is the broken family, forever fragmented. No relationship, only individuality. Embers of wood eternally separated, unable to give warmth or retain it. To have family united in heaven is a horrible thing, but it's beyond our control. To let it happen on earth is our greatest shame, our worst defeat. Do all you can to tear down this family. Go back to sowing the seeds of daily irritation that will produce the harvest of bitterness.

Our cultural destruction committee continues its work to redefine the family. We've taken both parents out of the home by convincing the most wealthy people in history that they must have two incomes. We've made single parenting normal. We've created latchkey children who have been baby-sat by television and the Internet. The hand that rocks the cradle rules the world. Which means day-care centers now rule the world. We've put an end to the sacredness of family dinner together, using busyness and telephone and television to pull them away from the table and family conversation. We've given a whole new meaning to "family planning." We've even created scorn for "family values."

We must keep Christian parents from understanding their children and their friends. The Enemy commands them to rejoice with those who rejoice and mourn with those who mourn. But because the adults don't take time to understand the kids, they don't grasp what makes them happy and what makes them sad. If they get a particular item of clothing that makes them feel good, the parents respond, "That looks like it came from Goodwill." Or if they can't go to a favorite concert, it's "Why are you so upset? You can't understand the words anyway." They trivialize the things important to their children, instead of building an emotional attachment by honestly discussing their tastes and opinions.

To target families and the church family is to tear down the Enemy's protective walls. It allows us to isolate the sludgebags so we can pick them off one by one. Set your sights on Jillian and her friends. Then gently pull the trigger.

Hating the family as we hate the Father,

Prince Ishbane

14

"Y ou were intrigued by my books," Ian said to Rob. "Check out those. Most of them are new—another big gift certificate from Mom. They'll blow your mind."

Rob looked at the pile of books on Ian's big oak desk. "I'll say this much for you, Ian. You certainly aren't your average high school jock who reads nothing but the sports page."

"Some guys have jobs. My folks say they'd rather I spend my spare time feeding my mind. I can live with that. I love to read—I work out my body, then I work out my mind."

"*Contacting Alien Entities?*" Rob held up the book.

Ian laughed. "I'm not saying I believe it. I'm just open-minded. Who knows? There's the fake UFOs, alien autopsys, the X-files, the stuff that's fun but phony. But then there's Roswell and a lot of other things that haven't been explained. Have you researched the alien abduction stories?"

"Uh…not recently, no, can't say that I have."

"They have way too much in common not to have some reality behind them. It's a big universe. Shouldn't we expect it to be full of life? Like Carl Sagan said, it would be virtually impossible for intelligent life to have evolved here and nowhere else."

"Or maybe it's impossible that it evolved here in the first place," Rob said. "Maybe it was specially created by an intelligent Designer."

"Maybe. I've heard the design arguments, about all the complex machinery at the molecular level, complexity that couldn't have evolved, right? It's pretty persuasive. Yeah, maybe there was a Designer. But maybe that Designer was an alien."

Rob pointed at another book. "Harry Potter? Isn't that for kids?"

"Kids, adults, anybody. They're okay. A little too mild for me. But I'd have loved them as a kid. You kind of get hooked. Harry goes to the school of witchcraft and wizardry and learns all these things about using his powers. It's pretty cool. I'm gonna read the rest if I can find the time."

"*Palmistry Made Easy?*"

"My brother's girlfriend was into reading palms. She was good. Taught me a few things. Want me to read yours?"

"No thanks. I'd rather read the Bible."

"Oh, yeah. I forgot you were the apostle Paul."

"It beats being Silver Ravenwolf." Rob pointed to the author's name on the next new book.

"How would you know that? Were you her in a past life?"

"The Bible says we live one life here on earth, and when we die we give an account for the choices we've made."

"Then we'd better make good choices."

"Right. So if it's true, let's deal with it."

"You said that before. But how do we know what's true, Rob? And as for good choices, the problem is what *you* think are good and what *I* think are good won't be the same. Well, to each his own. You look for truth where you want to, I'll look for it where I want to."

"But it's not like we should just go out and choose whatever looks good to us, like picking from a smorgasbord. It's God we answer to. He's the one who decides what's right and wrong, good and bad. And we won't find that out by reading horoscopes or palms, but by reading His Word."

"I know Christians who are Wiccans. And into astrology."

"No way," Rob said.

"How can you say 'no way'?"

"Because those things contradict the true Christian faith."

"You're not God, Rob. Or are you?"

"No. In fact, that's the whole point. What I say and what you say and whatever popular culture says or whatever books are popular down at Borders doesn't amount to a hill of beans. What matters is what God says. And it's in the Bible."

"But the Bible's full of errors."

"It's full of things people don't understand. That's not the same as errors. Give me an example of what you think's an error and we'll talk about it."

"No, thanks. I'm not interested in a debate."

"So you're going to go right on thinking the Bible is full of errors just because you've been told that—but you're not going to actually look at what the Bible says and listen to me try to explain it?"

Ian shrugged. "What can I say? The Bible doesn't press my buttons."

"Maybe the universe is about more than pressing your buttons."

"What *is* it about, Mr. Answer Man?"

"It's not about us. It's about God."

"Well, fine, but a Hindu god or a Zambian tree god or a Mayan god or the Christian god? Who's to say which god is right? I think they all have some truth. You and I just think about God differently."

"Which means at least one of us is wrong. If we believe contradictory things, we can't both be right."

"I just find a lot of Christianity hard to believe."

"Let me get this straight," Rob said. "You're the guy who's into palm reading, tarot cards, horoscopes, alien encounters, time travel and out of body travel, and you find *my* belief in historic Christianity hard to swallow?"

"You're awfully sure of yourself, aren't you?"

"It's Jesus I'm sure of. I know how He's changed my life."

"Maybe I don't want my life to be changed."

"Actually, I think you do, Ian. Why else would you read all this stuff? To tell you the truth, I really appreciate you pursuing spiritual things, even if I think you're looking in the wrong place. I mean, your interest in the occult is because you want to get in touch with the spiritual world, isn't it?"

"I guess."

"Well, that's a good desire. The Bible tells you how to get in touch with the good spiritual world. It's not in crystals and tarot cards and boards and rituals and occult books. It's in Jesus."

"You come to God your way and I'll come my way."

"But those roads don't converge. They go in the opposite direction."

"Then I guess that means we go opposite directions. If you don't mind having a pagan for a friend."

"I like having you as my friend, Ian. But it doesn't mean I won't try to persuade you of what I'm convinced is the truth. You tell me what you believe, and I'll tell you what I believe. Maybe we'll learn from each other."

Ian sighed. "Fair enough, preacher. I'd rather disagree with you about this stuff than just talk about nothing but sports and beer and girls and cars. I mean, I like all those subjects, don't get me wrong, but there's got to be more to life."

"On that point we agree 100 percent." Rob raised his hand and Ian raised his. They slapped them together.

Brittany gave Joey a big hug as she stood inside Jillian's door, ready to leave.

"Bye, Joey. I love you, too. Some day I'm going to be doing open-heart surgeries on little guys just your size, what do you think of that? If you ever need one, it's on the house. You take care of your big sister, okay?"

Joey cooed at Brittany. She laughed. She handed him off to Jillian and his face went into a perfect pout.

"I told you he has a crush on you," Jillian said.

"Who can blame him? Problem is, Joey, I can't wait eighteen years for you to grow up. Of course, it might take Ian that long to grow up, too. In that case, I'll keep my eye on you. Later, Jill."

"Bye." Jillian closed the front door and sighed. It was a Friday night. She was in the last place she wanted to be, doing the last thing she wanted to do. Home and babysitting.

"Come on, Joey," Jillian said as she held a full bottle to his mouth.

The phone hadn't rung all night. Not that it mattered. She was stuck there with a Dalmatian sleeping in front of the gas fireplace, a seven-month-old who wouldn't eat, and a fifteen-year-old who wouldn't come out of his room. Not that she wanted him to.

Joey's eyes drooped and his mouth relaxed. His soft Down syndrome features made him look cherubic. His eyelids were heavy. Jillian took the bottle and set it on the kitchen table. His eyes shut and he was breathing evenly within a few seconds. She held him close. All he knew was comfort and warmth. No worries. She envied him.

Brittany and Ian had plans tonight. What was Rob doing?

Jillian walked upstairs and carefully laid Joey down in his crib. She left the door cracked and walked back downstairs to put away the leftovers from dinner she'd eaten an hour ago.

An hour later, at nine o'clock, the phone still hadn't rung. She'd checked twice to be sure Daniel wasn't on the Internet. Apparently he was doing something else in his bat cave, as she called it. She sat on the blue glider chair, reading her Bible. After another visit to the refrigerator, she looked at a Christian book Lisa had given her. Then she heard the front door unlocking. Nickerson was all over Diane with a huge Dalmatian grin, prancing like a pony.

"Hey, Mom."

After kissing Nickerson, Diane said, "Oh Jilly, my night was perfect." Jillian didn't just see but heard her mom's smile. "Jodi kicked Ryan out of the house and we got takeout from Road House and ate cookie dough ice cream and watched an old Cary Grant movie. I can't remember the last time I had so much fun. Next time Ryan's out of town we're having a slumber party. Thanks for baby-sitting, honey. I know you usually go out Friday nights."

Jillian forced a smile. "Brittany's out with Ian anyway, and since I don't have any other friends…"

"Jillian, that's not true. If I were your age, you'd be exactly the kind of person I'd love to hang out with."

"Do you realize how motherish you just sounded?" She saw her mom's smile fade. "I'm sorry, Mom. I appreciate it. Really. And I'm glad you had fun tonight—enough fun for both of us." The words caught in her throat.

"You miss him don't you?"

"Dad? Of course."

"You know who I'm talking about."

Jillian pressed her palms on her cheeks. "I haven't heard from him in two weeks. It's not like I'm expecting him to call and beg me to go out with him again. I just hate the way things ended. I wish…I don't know what I wish."

"Give him time, sweetheart."

"I *have* given him time. And I still jump every time the phone rings."

The telephone rang, and Jillian jumped.

Diane laughed. "Wow. Do you want me to get it?"

"Why not? It'll be for you anyway."

"Hello?" Diane's lips twitched as if holding back a smile. "Uh-huh. Tonight?" She turned her back to Jillian. "Yes, that would be fine. All right, thanks for calling. Bye."

Jillian watched as her mom hung up and began cleaning the kitchen.

"Who was that?"

"Do you tell me about all your phone conversations?"

"Just curious." *Mom's hiding something!* "I'm going to go change into pajamas and pop out my contacts, then maybe, I don't know…" Jillian wandered toward the staircase.

"Jill, it's barely past nine. Don't get ready for bed yet."

"Why? Expecting somebody to drop by?"

Her mom didn't answer. But she had that look, like she was thinking about…a guy? *Mom? No way.*

"Brittany's out, Lisa's gone for the weekend, Rob hates me, and nobody else would think to call, so if it's all the same to you, I'm going to get as ugly as possible and veg out on the couch."

"Suit yourself," Diane said. "But you never know who might drop by."

Some guy's been macking on Mom, and now he's coming over. But she won't admit it.

Jillian almost decided not to change, then smiled, thinking about the possibilities.

Fifteen minutes later, she had makeup off, retainer in, dorky old glasses on, and curls sticking wildly out of a high ponytail. She'd put on a huge pair of Dad's gray sweatpants rolled up three times at the waist and a neon yellow, pink and green tie-dye shirt she'd made for Mom in sixth grade art class. And the final touch…fuzzy cow-pattern slippers. Perfect. Now if some low-life guy came over, interested in her mom, Jillian would scare him off in no time.

She saw her Bible on the coffee table and opened it again. Strange, something told her not to read it now—she sensed it would be boring or make her feel guilty. She needed something mindless. She turned on the TV, channel surfed past wrestling, cooking, another lame survivor show, and "Who Wants to Be a Millionaire?"

Not me, I'd rather eat out of garbage cans.

She finally turned off the TV and opened her Bible. She thought she heard sounds in the upstairs bathroom like her mom was primping.

The doorbell rang. Jillian grinned. "I'll get it!"

Jillian walked to the door, glancing in the hall mirror. *Man, I look hideous.* It was perfect, really. She'd have a story to tell her friends, if she could find some. She tried to contain her smile as she opened the door.

"Hi, Jill."

This was not the story she had in mind.

"Hi," Jillian croaked. "Sorry, I was expecting…someone else." She tried to hide herself behind the door.

"Uh, can I come in?" Rob asked.

"Yeah. Fine. Come in." Jillian kept herself behind the door as she opened it. When his back was to her, she yanked out her retainer, a string of drool coming with it, and threw it on the small table in the entryway, next to her senior pictures. She turned around and he was facing her, with a broad smile.

"I've never seen you…"

"Yeah?"

"In glasses."

"I stopped sporting these babies in public when I turned eight." Maybe if she acted confident, she'd start believing she was. She glanced at the mirror again as they walked toward the family room. Or not.

They sat on the couch. Jillian pulled her feet up and wrapped her arms around her legs, trying to hide her frumpy outfit as much as possible. What was he staring at? She looked down. She stuck her fuzzy cow slippers under the coffee table and vowed to burn them later.

He laughed softly. *"Estoy pasmado."*

"Translation please?"

"You know, every time I think I've got you figured out, you surprise me even more. For example, there aren't very many girls that can pull off an outfit like the one you've got on and still look so—"

"Heinous?"

"Actually, the word I was going for was—"

"Repulsive?"

"Beautiful."

Jillian's mouth hung open. Nobody had ever called her beautiful. She was occasionally "adorable," and mostly just "cute." Her dimply little cheeks had been pinched more times than she could count. Cute, cute, cute. But never beautiful.

"I'm serious," Rob said. He folded, then unfolded his hands, then looked at them like he didn't know what to do with them. "To be honest, I didn't know what would go through my mind when I saw you again tonight. I've been thinking about you a lot. I wanted to know for sure if the picture of you I had in my mind was real. Because what I saw in my mind was someone I didn't want to lose."

"Somehow I doubt the picture you had in your mind looked like this." Her index finger pointed from wild ponytail to cow slippers and back again.

Rob shook his head. "Nope. Although if I had any idea you looked so good in neon tie-dye…"

"Don't push it."

He opened his mouth twice and closed it. He looked like a little boy who'd walked to the end of the high dive and was about to turn around and head back.

"Go back to the part about not wanting to lose me." Jillian bit her lip quickly.

Was that out loud?

"See, there you go again, surprising me. The fact that I still don't know everything about you makes me want to…"

"What are you saying, Rob?"

"I'm saying I miss you. I'm saying it was really hard for me to let you go. But I think it's all been for the best because we never got past the surface in our relationship. And that's mostly my fault. I tried to push you to go deeper. When we'd talk about spiritual things, you didn't know how to go deeper because you didn't know Christ. I just thought you didn't want to talk about Him. If I'd watched and listened instead of just hearing myself talk, I would've realized. Sorry for being so dense."

"I thought you'd be excited when you found out I became a Christian. When I finally opened up to you about something important—the *most* important—it was like you couldn't handle it."

"I know, and I'm sorry. I needed time, mostly to realize what an idiot I was. I was embarrassed that I'd violated my standards about dating only Christians, and I'd done it without even knowing it. Maybe I was proud. But now we have the Lord in common. We can go beneath the surface. The more I've prayed for you, the more I care about you."

"You prayed for me?"

"Every day. It's the real Jillian I'm drawn to. Not the glasses, not the sweatpants, not the retainer you ditched. Not even the fuzzy cow slippers. It's the Jillian inside I care about. Please forgive me. Can we start over?"

Letter 14

My annoying Foulgrin,

I'm considering reassigning you to join ST in Washington, D.C. There you'd be one more small rat in a large sewer.

I have no time for your wordy intellectual treatises. You're a pretentious windbag, Foulgrin. I'm a pragmatist—all I care about is results. So cut through the fog and keep it simple.

Stop asking me questions with obvious answers. *Of course* you should do everything you can to distract her from the forbidden book. If it's a seedy romance novel or a video promoting materialism and superficiality, all the better. The media is our most effective gateway to their puny minds. Program her mind like they program a computer—what goes in is what comes out.

Make Rob inseparable, in Jillian's mind, from her spiritual life. That way, when he fails her or breaks off their relationship again, she'll feel deserted by Him, too. Make sure they look to each other for the things only the Carpenter can provide. Make her think Rob is really the person she's always longed for. Let her buy the romantic notion that he can bring her happiness. That way she won't look to the Enemy to meet her needs. When they idolize each other, they put impossible pressure on their human relationships, setting them up for collapse. When they do, instead of turning to the only Person who can meet their needs, they'll blame Him. Then they'll run off looking for someone else.

Use Jillian to draw Rob away from serving the Enemy. Make him reevaluate that summer missions trip he's planning. How could he leave her behind?

Now that Jillian has the Ghost, this rekindling of her relationship with Rob may be troublesome. You can undermine any value the Enemy might get from it by derailing them into sexual immorality. Convince them they're a couple. That entitles them to the rights and privileges of marriage, without the responsibilities. Encourage Jillian to give her emotions, her soul to Rob. Then, when her guard is down, her body will naturally follow.

When they seek the emotional intimacy of marriage, the physical privileges instinctively follow. Then, whoever she ends up marrying, she'll have had the taste of emotional intimacy outside of marriage. Sow the seeds of fornication now, reap a harvest of adultery later.

The Enemy calls them to delayed gratification. We call them to instant gratification. Their bodies and their culture cast the deciding vote: instant oatmeal, instant bank deposits, instant entertainment and instant gratification. They grow up having their wants pandered to. They're taught to sacrifice the future on the altar of the present.

"Why wait till marriage to have sex?" is really no different than "Why wait until you have money to spend it?" The only thing they want to delay is payment.

Make them think the Enemy's commands are whips to punish them rather than guardrails to keep them from falling off the cliff.

"If I had cherished sin in my heart, the Lord would not have listened." Do you see the formula? Get them to cherish sin in their hearts, and the Enemy will not listen to their prayers! It's that simple. "If anyone turns a deaf ear to the law, even his prayers are detestable." If they choose to violate His standards, the Enemy will hate their prayers! (Except the prayer of confession and repentance, which—regrettably—He always welcomes.)

When Jillian lies in bed at night, send images of Rob to her mind. When she hits the snooze button in the morning, lying in her bed, have her imagine Rob next to her, holding her. It's all so innocent. Our best attacks are subtle, undercover. You may not get them to fornicate next week or even next month. Just keep wearing them down. Gravity's on our side. Get them off in the corners, in cars, on couches, in rooms by themselves. That's all it takes.

We've redefined "single" to mean "I'm not currently dating someone." Even the Christian vermin forget that in the Enemy's eyes they're single until they take their marriage vows. I love this notion "we're nearly married." Do what you can to get them to act like they're married when they're single, then act like they're single once they're married.

Sabotage this relationship. Keep them from seeing the desires they have for one another are mere shadows of the higher pleasures He promises. If they see Him as the fulfillment of their deepest desires, this takes the wind out of the sails of every temptation we send them.

Using the Enemy's blessings against them,

Prince Ishbane

15

*D*id you look at the real estate guide, Mom?" Jillian asked, pointing at the magazine full of house listings in east county.

"How many times have I told you we can't afford to move?" Diane asked. "What's wrong with this house?"

Jillian shrugged. "I just think we'd be happier somewhere else."

"The problem with moving somewhere else is you always take yourself with you."

"What's that supposed to mean?"

"Never mind. Something's bothering you again, Jilly. Is it Rob?"

"No." She sighed. "In history, Mr. Weaver was going off about the awful things churches have done throughout the centuries. He made it sound like Christians just persecute and repress people who think differently." Jillian took another small bite of asparagus. "It ticked me off, but I didn't know what to say. It didn't used to bother me, but now…"

"So what *did* you say?"

"Nothing. He's the teacher."

"You're allowed to disagree, you know."

"Some people argue with teachers. Not me. Never."

"Nobody hates conflict more than I do. But sometimes we need to speak up."

"I guess I just didn't think it was worth fighting over. He's the teacher, I'm just an ignorant young Christian. I don't know my Bible very well. He'd just make me look like an idiot."

"You should've been there," Brittany said. "It was awesome. Skyla really knows how to throw a party."

"Did she do her Sabrina imitation?" Jillian asked.

Brittany raised her eyebrows with dramatic flair. "So Christian girl's mocking witch girl, is that it? Did you know her aunt's been a Wiccan for like twenty years, and she knows all about spells and rituals and everything? Even love potions." Brittany laughed. "We actually called the psychic hotline."

"You didn't."

"Stop sounding like a Sunday school girl. We all got a big laugh. But Skyla said it was a phony. Just a rip off. She said real clairvoyants don't do it like that. She did some astrology stuff with us. She read my horoscope and gave me a palm reading."

"I'm sure that was enlightening."

"She said I had a bright future, that I'd succeed in my goals, which of course means college and volleyball. She said I'd soon face an obstacle, but there would be a solution that would allow me to accomplish my goals. That kinda made me nervous, but overall, it was good news. Check out this book." She handed it to Jillian.

"*Witchcraft for Teens?* Skyla gave this to you?"

"No. She told me about it. I checked it out this morning. School library. They've got a half dozen books on Wicca. Skyla says she gave a list of ten more to Mrs. Corby, and she said she'd order six of them."

Jillian flipped through it. "Why is magick spelled with a 'k'?"

"To distinguish it from tricks or sleight of hand. This is the real thing. Through our magic we try to control, bend, shape, or direct reality to reach our goals."

"Don't say 'we,' Brit. You're scaring me."

"I'm not a card-carrying witch yet. I haven't even been to an esbat."

"A what?"

"It's a gathering under the full moon. Come on, Jill, don't be so narrow. The Wiccan creed is, 'If you harm none, do what you will.' You're free to live however you choose as long as you don't hurt anyone. I like that. There's no external authority to legislate morality. You call your own shots. It sure beats Christianity and living under all those rules."

"Christianity isn't about rules. It's about Jesus."

"Yeah, right."

Jillian didn't have to look to see the famous Brittany eye roll. She picked up a book featuring an attractive female witch in a fashionable, well-tailored business suit and appearing to walk down Madison Avenue. "I guess today's witches aren't ugly old hags with warts on their noses, wearing black capes?"

"Don't forget the cone-shaped hats, riding their broomsticks on a moonlit night," Brittany said. "The day of stupid stereotypes is past. Except among Christians."

Jillian bit her tongue.

"I told Ian about some of the rituals for teen witches," Brittany said. "He suggested we do the one where participants are sky clad."

"Sky clad?"

Brittany whispered, "Naked as a jaybird! Wicked, huh?"

"Yeah, Brit. That's exactly what it is. Wicked. Is that really what you want?"

"I haven't done it yet. But it's intriguing. I mean, who knows if you haven't tried it? You only live once."

"You live once on earth. But then you live forever in heaven or hell."

"You sound like one of those jerks on the big-hair channel. You really believe that stuff?"

"This sounds like the conversations Rob's been having with Ian. You've been talking to me about the Goddess and the Earth Mother and crystals and séances and tarot cards and astrology, but because I'm a follower of Jesus suddenly *I'm* the one who's nuts? Pardon me, but on the scale of weirdness, this Wiccan stuff goes way past anything you and Joan of Arc can accuse me of."

"Making fun of Skyla's hair again, huh? I thought Christians were supposed to be nicer than that."

"I'm just having a hard time getting used to the idea of you and Skyla being bosom buddies."

"I invited you to the party. If you'd rather hang with Lisa and your little Sunday school friends, or go get tacos with your little preacher boy, that's your loss. I've told you before, Jillian, you're too compliant. You give in too easily. Don't let those wacky fundamentalists tell you what to believe and what to do. Be a stand-up girl, kiddo. That's what I am. And I'm not giving it up for anybody. Including you."

Letter 15

My magnanimous Ishbane,

Fifty years ago most of them would have seen right through this neopaganism. But due to their increased emptiness and gullibility, it's become one of our favorite mantraps.

To help you understand why I labor to pull Ian, Brittany, and Daniel into this particular web, I'll elaborate. (Remember that the time I invest in these others will pay dividends with Jillian, too.)

The old paganism had its advantages, but neopaganism is perfect for this post-naturalist culture. Paganism's child sacrifice and sordid liaisons with prostitutes had nothing over the forms Moloch and Eros have taken in Western culture today.

Once they stop believing in the Enemy, the vermin don't believe in nothing, they believe in anything. That's why atheism doesn't serve us nearly as well as competing spiritualities. By seeking our New Age substitutes for the Enemy's faith, they can have the illusion of spiritual enlightenment, without giving up the relativism of their culture.

Worship of a false object not only seduces them, it stops them from searching for the true object. Foulgrin's three strategies to take them down to hell: distraction, distraction, distraction. (Is that simple enough for you?)

They're dying, Ishbane! That means time is on our side, never theirs. We don't have to lure them into a lifetime of agnosticism, false religion, materialism, or sexual obsession. Just give them a few decades of one, a few decades of another, and pretty soon they run out of decades!

I adore Wicca's pantheism, polytheism, and shamanism. I love its elevation of the goddess Diana, who's none other than our own Prince Artemis in drag. I favor anything that makes them ignore the Enemy's fundamental teaching: one life on earth, followed by one death, followed by one judgment and one eternal sentence. The ingenious lie of reincarnation is that there's always another chance, so there's never any urgency.

I'm delighted with this magical worldview in which they can call on nature, or the life force, to come to their aid. They do this without praying to the Creator, who has this

THE ISHBANE CONSPIRACY 93

annoying habit of making unpleasant demands. May the force be with you, Ishbane.

The creation of Wicca as a "womins" religion has the added benefit of casting Christianity as a men's religion. Of course, there have been more women in the Enemy's camp than men, and the Carpenter treated women with unprecedented respect. Wherever Christianity has gone it has elevated the status of women from paganism's oppression. But never mind how it *really* happened. These days, we write the history books.

We've transmuted militant feminism into the softened, more appealing form of goddess worship and the sacred cult of the Green. Of course, there's just as much pleasure when the vermin devastate the Enemy's creation. This is the worship of another green, Mammon, an equal offense to the Enemy. If we can get them to engage in something they consider a more virtuous idolatry, all the better. *Any* idolatry, whether gray with smoke or green with foliage, will do equally well.

This resurgence brings back fond memories of nature religions and mystery cults. Ah, the Celtic, Norse, Greek, Egyptian, and Roman mythologies. Those were the days. The tribal religions, including shamanism and Native American spiritualities, are now glorified as the higher way. Astaroth, Diana, Osiris, and Pan are invoked anew. Witchcraft has taken off the black cape and put on the white. Witches are lobbying like other special interest groups, cultivating an image as "the pagan next door." I see on our reading list *The Witch Family,* which "portrays witchcraft in a positive family setting." A magnificent sleight of hand.

Do you see what we've done, Ishbane? Lift your nose from your "to do" list long enough to smell the sulfur. Hell's marketing department has reinvented paganism. We've given witchcraft a facelift. We've become a no-hag main street religion, permeating media, music, and schools!

Our new witchcraft even takes the moral high ground: "Harm no one." Instead of denying their spiritual longings, as the old atheism did, Wicca embraces those longings and promises fulfillment. Of course, we never *keep* the promises. We always say hang on— wait until you die and come back, everything will be better. "Hang on until you die." Yeah, that's the ticket. Because once they die there'll be nothing to hang on to. It's the eternal free fall.

Wicca is our little white lie, drawing in millions of this displaced younger generation. It's taking on a greater mass, increasing its gravitational pull. We're recruiting and grooming for leadership tens of thousands like Skyla and Brittany, intelligent and gifted and strategic. Needless to say, few of them come from pagan upbringings, where the despair and darkness of life is too obvious to be denied.

The Enemy has long had this strategy—win them when they're young and they'll be your best ambassadors for decades. I continue to hook my line and bait my hook for the young ones. And I never throw them back. Catch them now; fry them later.

Stealing spirituality from the Enemy,

Foulgrin

16

MARCH 15, 4:51 P.M.

"I'm glad you came, Ian," Rob said as he exited off the freeway.

"Yeah, thanks for showing me around. That was the first time I've seen most of PSU's campus. It's bigger than I thought."

"You're going to love it. Especially if you get involved with Campus Fellowship. You don't have to be a Christian to go there. But you can get into some great discussions about spiritual issues." Rob came to a stop sign and put his left blinker on.

"Could you drop me off at Brittany's?" Ian asked.

"I wondered why you brought that backpack. I say you're whipped if you're going someplace that requires changing out of jeans."

"Actually, we're not going anywhere. Her mom's out of town. I'm spending the night."

Rob felt his shoulders tense. He'd guessed this had been happening, but Ian hadn't said it until now. A dozen reasons came to mind why Rob shouldn't say anything. But of all the voices he heard, he decided to listen to one.

"Ian, I don't think that's a good idea. You and Brittany…well, you're not married. And God designed sex for marriage."

"All right, preacher." Ian rolled his eyes, Brittany-like. "Save the sin talk till my funeral, will you?"

"Your funeral will be too late to deal with sin. Seriously, Ian. It's not that God doesn't want us to have any fun. In fact, the Bible talks openly about sex, like in Song of Solomon. It's a gift God wants us to enjoy."

"Really? Maybe I should be reading the Bible after all."

"But he says the boundaries of sex are the boundaries of marriage."

"It's a gift, but we're not supposed to use it?"

"Jeff, my campus group leader, used an analogy that made sense. Water's a gift of God. Without it we couldn't survive. But floods and tidal waves are water *out of control,* and the effects are devastating. Fire's a gift of God that gives warmth and allows us to cook. But a forest fire or a house burning to the ground or a person engulfed in flames is fire *out of control.* Sex is the same way. When it's done inside the boundaries of marriage, it can be beautiful and constructive. But when it's out of control, violating God's intended purpose, it becomes ugly and destructive. So it's a good thing that can become bad. And the greater the gift, like water and fire and sex, the more power it has both for good and bad. It all depends on whether it stays inside the boundaries God intended."

"But you're a guy, Rob. At least, I've always thought so. Unless there's something you have to tell me…"

"Yeah, Ian. I'm a guy."

"Relieved to hear it. Anyway, you can't tell me you're actually happy about the 'no sex before marriage' commandment. Haven't you been with girls before?"

"Yeah, I have. And I remember all the trouble it caused me. It's not worth it. A few minutes of pleasure turns into a whole lot of grief."

Ian rubbed his neck. "Yeah, yeah, I took sex ed my sophomore year too. I know all the stuff about STDs and pregnancy, but we're being responsible, and besides, it's not like I go out and have sex with every girl I meet. I care about Brittany."

Rob pulled into Brittany's driveway. "But if you really cared about her, wouldn't you want to save her from the consequences of what you're doing? I'm not just talking about physical consequences. There are all kinds of emotional issues. There's a much higher divorce rate, for one thing, and a greater likelihood of unfaithfulness. You put yourself on the line when you have sex, and it has permanent effects on you."

"I said we're being careful. It's only a matter of time before you and Jillian are doing the same thing."

"No way, man. I've gone down that road before. It's a dead end. I'm not going there again. You'd better wake up, Ian, before it's too late!" Rob heard the anger in his voice.

"Thanks for the lecture, Dad." Ian got out of the car and held the door open. He bent down and said, "When you love somebody you want to show it. It's not evil, Rob; it's natural." He shut the car door, then waved at Brittany, who was waiting for him at the front door.

Rob's Chevy died. He turned it over. It wouldn't catch. Ian laughed and waved. "Get rid of that boat and find a car, buddy."

The foursome was hanging out in the Fletchers' upstairs hallway when Daniel's bedroom door opened. He stopped suddenly. As the pounding heavy metal music pushed its way out the door, color crept up his cheeks.

"Hey, Daniel," Rob said.

Daniel mumbled a reply and started to retreat into his room.

"Hi, Danny," Brittany said. "Have you met Ian?"

Jillian was sure Daniel knew who Ian was. The whole school knew Ian Stewart.

"Ian," Brittany said, "this is Jillian's little brother. Danny's a freshman."

"Hey," Ian said and reached out his hand. Tentatively, as if expecting this was a trick, Danny slapped it, then cringed. Jillian sensed he was waiting to be slapped in the head or something.

The song blasting out of Daniel's stereo reached a shrieking crescendo. Jillian folded her arms. "Turn that music down! You'll wake up Joey."

"Wait. I love this CD!" Ian said, moving past Daniel into his room. "It's a classic. I've looked for it everywhere. Where'd you find it?"

"Music Depot."

"The new place? Haven't been there. Is it good?"

"Uh-huh," Daniel replied. "It's cool. You trade in old CDs and get credit to buy new ones. There's a lot of hip-hop garbage, but once you wade through it, they've got some decent stuff."

"Marilyn Manson?"

Daniel nodded slightly.

"Cool. You like the classics? Nine Inch Nails? Metallica?"

Daniel nodded again. "Venom. Slayer. Megadeth."

"Helloween? Rob Zombie?"

"Yeah."

"Shock metal, black metal. Cool," Ian said. "You do D&D?"

"Yeah."

"What else?"

"Magic: The Gathering, Vampire: The Masquerade, Werewolf: The Apocalypse."

"Cool. I've done Magic and Vampire. You've got to show me Werewolf."

Daniel nodded.

"Favorite movies?" Ian asked.

"The Halloweens. Blair Witch. Chucky. You know."

"Cool."

Jillian saw Daniel relaxing with each word. She hadn't heard him talk this much in a long time. After Ian and Daniel talked five more minutes, Daniel looked at Jillian and said, "I need a ride to Stanky's."

"I can't leave Joey, and I'm not going to wake him up from his nap to take you five minutes down the street. Can't Dan's mom pick you up?"

"She's gone. It's two miles, and it's raining. It'll just take you a minute. Your friends will be here for Joey. Or take him in his car seat. It's not that big a deal."

Jillian opened her mouth for the comeback when Ian said, "I can take you, Daniel." He smiled and added, "But only if we can listen to this CD in my truck on the way there."

"Yeah, okay." Again, he sounded tentative, like he wondered if Ian was going to hand him over to his basketball teammate Josh in a back alley. "I'll grab my stuff and be right out."

He was playing it cool, but Jillian knew Daniel was shocked that one of the most popular guys at school loved his music and was offering him a ride.

Jillian looked at Brittany. "Tell me Ian hasn't talked you into liking that kind of music."

"Never. Pretty much any connection between his reality and mine is purely coinciden-tal."

"Hey," Ian said, "we're both into metaphysics, and we're both athletes, remember?"

"Yes, but when I walk off the court, I'm worth something to society."

"Are you implying that I'm not?"

Brittany snorted. "Your SATs are documented proof you have the mathematical skills of a Clydesdale."

Ian smiled. "Translation: 'Ian, you're the man of my dreams. And I envy your under-standing of the metaphysical realm.' You may have outscored me in math, but who won the verbal?"

"Yeah, 680 to 650. Thirty lousy points is more like a tie."

"Sore loser."

Daniel walked out of his room, backpack in one hand, skateboard in the other. Ian put an arm around his shoulder. "Let's ditch these women…and Reverend Gonzales, too."

Daniel smiled. Brittany gave an exasperated sigh as Ian and Daniel walked toward the front door. Ian turned around and winked at Brittany. "See ya, darlin'."

"Don't hold your breath," Brittany called. She shrugged at Jillian. "See what I have to put up with?"

Jillian laughed nervously. Rob looked away and said nothing.

Letter 16

My overweening Foulgrin,

You're arrogant, presumptuous, and insolent. In short, Obsmut assures me you're being yourself. Can I make a suggestion? Try being someone else!

I can only put up with attitude if I see results. Show me some!

When it comes to judging and not judging their friends, get them to fall off either side of the horse. Just don't let them stay in the saddle. Some of the Christian vermin look the other way when non-Christian friends make disastrous choices. They fail to warn them about sin. Your job is to convince them that would be "pushing" their religion. (Never let them think of it as throwing a life preserver to the drowning.)

Others, like Rob, expect non-Christians to live by Christian standards. He wants Ian to raise his moral level without the Ghost's empowerment. Don't let Rob recall what he was like five years ago. Make him Ian's judge, not his guide. Prompt him to look down on Ian and give up on him. Have Rob lay on him the Enemy's standards without ever making clear the Enemy's love and power to transform.

I don't care if Ian shows some outward moral reform. Yes, we enjoy seeing fornication and occult seduction, but if he becomes a "good moral person" without knowing the Carpenter, we still win. The landscape of hell is littered with moral churchgoing vermin who died proud.

If taken seriously, though, Rob's warnings are dangerous. Truth is inherently dangerous, even when poorly communicated. The Enemy can shine His message even through the dense fog of an obnoxious personality.

As for sex, it's not just something they do, but someone they are. This is what gives it such great potential for destroying them. The Enemy intends it as an expression of the lifelong commitment of legal marriage. Apart from marriage, the commitment is absent. Sex becomes a lie. Every lie serves our purposes. Every act of sex outside of marriage cheapens both sex and marriage. It insults our Enemy who made them. The forbidden book says sex is a privilege inseparable from the responsibilities of the marriage covenant. To exercise the privilege apart from the responsibility perverts the Enemy's intention for sex. Exactly what we want.

The bottom line? The Enemy wants sex to be an act of giving toward someone they're legally committed to. We want sex to be an act of taking from someone they're uncommitted to.

Convince them "we really love each other," not "we're married," is the proper criterion for sex. Remember, sexual impurity is most strategic among Christians. The Enemy's will is centered on their character and moral purity. Not, as they imagine, on their circumstances (job, housing, schooling, and so forth). They often seek the Enemy's will in secondary areas while violating His will in primary ones. The forbidden book says, "It is God's will that you should be sanctified: that you should avoid sexual immorality." Draw Rob and Jillian to violate His spoken will in the areas He most cares about, while fooling themselves by seeking His will in areas He cares less about.

Congratulations on connecting Ian with Daniel. I'm glad they think their mutual interest in music celebrating darkness is "cool." We've permeated their music with the occult message. CD covers in our headquarters display case include illustrations of demons' heads, crucified figures, demonic babies, skeletons, pentagrams, black candles, and the number 666. (I particularly enjoyed Morrissey's smash hit single "Ouija Board, Ouija Board," about contacting a dead friend.) When they arrive on the other side, "cool" won't be the first word to come to mind. No air conditioning!

The Enemy desires to use the older to influence the younger. We use the same model, for the opposite purpose. Sometimes the forbidden fellowship neglects His ideas. But we're always glad to hijack them. I see enormous potential in Ian mentoring Daniel.

If your plans for their deaths succeed, I'll be there to welcome Ian, Daniel and/or Brittany myself. "Smoking or nonsmoking?" I'll ask. "Oh, I'm sorry. I forgot. All we have available is a *smoking* section!"

Fine, let Jillian and Rob be concerned about Daniel. Let them even pray for him if they must. But while Ian reaches out and infects him with our way of thinking, never let it dawn on Jillian how she's neglected her brother. Never let it occur to Rob that he's over at the Fletchers' three or four times a week and he's never taken interest in Daniel. He's never looked for opportunities to talk to him, understand him, and try to influence him for the Enemy.

Perfect. Keep Christians at an arm's length from Daniel. Make sure they look down their noses at him and his freaky Goth friends.

I love it when the Enemy's missionaries stay in their comfort zone while we send our missionaries out to recruit this disconnected generation. Not only can we reinforce their disdain for the forbidden fellowship, we can use them to further our purposes in a thousand ways. Right till the day we discard them like smoked-out cigarettes, smashing them under our heels.

Enjoying the cultivation of young servants,

Prince Ishbane

17

MARCH 19, 12:49 P.M.

Jillian sat at the kitchen table surrounded by stacks of catalogs and glossy brochures, each with pictures of smiling students. They all seemed to scream at her, "Come to this college—you'll be *so* happy!"

She sorted through the pile that had been steadily growing for months. She should have had her application in long ago, but...

"What's with the junk?" Daniel said as he searched the refrigerator, looking behind every condiment in hope of hidden treasure.

"It's not junk," Jillian said. "It's college stuff."

"Whatever," he mumbled as he headed back to his room with a can of root beer and a bag of potato chips.

"Wow, what's all this?" Diane asked, picking up a brochure.

"Rob's coming over to help me figure it out."

"I thought you'd decided on Gresham Bible College."

"I'm not sure."

There was a knock at the front door. Daniel came out of his room. Jillian continued to shuffle papers. She heard Daniel and Rob talking in the other room.

"Let's go later tonight," she heard Rob say.

"Really?" Daniel said. "I mean, yeah, that'd be cool, you know, if you have time."

They talked some more, then Rob walked into the kitchen.

"So you're taking my brother out and ditching me, huh?"

"He's gonna show me around that new CD store. We might go to Borders, too."

"Sounds like a fun date."

"Next time maybe we'll invite you," Rob said, smiling.

She looked at the pile in front of her and put up her hands, then motioned for him to sit down. "I'm not sure where to start. I haven't even heard of some of these places. Don't know how I got all this stuff."

"Well, I did my homework last year. I narrowed it down to three schools. A state school, a Christian liberal arts college, and a Bible college. So, first question—do you want to go to a Christian college or secular?"

"Christian, I think. Funny, I'd already decided that before I came to Christ. Dad wanted me to go to Gresham Bible College. Maybe I was doing that to please him."

"I've heard awesome things about GBC. But a lot of 'Christian' colleges are watered down. Some professors aren't believers and lots of them teach stuff that's unbiblical."

"But how am I supposed to know which schools are the good ones?"

"Well, you can start with their doctrinal statements. But some of them are false advertising. I checked out a school where one prof said half the teachers didn't believe the doctrinal statement. Anyway, I'd make some calls, talk to some people who've gone there. People you trust. If you narrow it down to a few places, visit them."

"Sounds like you'd have to really nose around to find that out. I'm not that pushy."

"Seriously, Jill, college is a lot of time and money. It's important to check it out. I say either go to a solid Bible-believing college or go to a state school where there's a strong campus ministry and good churches. You know, like Portland State. Nobody would ever claim it's Christian, so you go in on your toes, knowing you have to defend your faith or get washed down by the current. You can't just tread water, that's for sure."

"Is that an invitation to PSU?"

"It'd be fun to have you there, but you've got to make the call."

"I know Dad would want it to be my decision whether to attend Gresham Bible College. I hear they've got a bunch of rules."

"I wouldn't complain about rules. It means everyone else has to live by them too. A 'no drinking' rule sounds great to me. Last semester I was in a situation where the bathroom always smelled like beer, joints, and vomit. Guys watched porn videos. And I wouldn't go near a coed dorm where you walk in on your roommate and his girlfriend. I don't need that."

"But if I went to GBC I'd be living at home."

"Do you want to go away?"

"Not really."

"Don't stay here because of me."

"I was planning on staying before. It's just that Brittany's going to California, and if I'm ever going to go away, now's the time. But Mom needs me here, and...I'd miss you a lot."

"I'd miss you, too, but I'm trying to be objective. Distance could be good for our relationship. I don't want to get in the way of God's will for you."

"You don't have to be *that* objective."

"He knows what He's doing. I guess we both pray like crazy, then let Him work out the details."

Jillian nodded. She saw Daniel lurking in the hallway.

"I'm done with him, Danny," she called. "He's all yours. You guys have fun."

She got up and watched Rob walk out the door with Daniel. Instead of resenting it, she felt warm inside. Something told her it was right.

"I hate pep rallies," Brittany grumbled, slamming her locker shut. "No offense, Jillian, but I can only handle so much pep."

"But I'm doing a stunt we've been working on all year," Jillian said.

Brittany crossed her arms. Jillian sighed and switched tactics. "I'll either nail it or fall to my death, so no matter what happens you'll get some action."

"All right, Evel Knievel," Brittany said, shaking her head. "Only for you would I do this. I'll be there in five."

Jillian, in her cheerleading outfit, walked to the gym and took her place on the court with her squad, as the student body settled into the bleachers. She scanned the crowd for Brittany and found her standing by the door next to a few senior guys with painted faces. Jillian waved; Brittany rolled her eyes.

"Hey, Jillian." She felt a tap on her shoulder. "Ready to fly?"

Jillian turned to Kelly, who reached out with her right hand and pinched Jillian's cheek. "Whatsamatter? Ya nervous?"

"The only reason I'd be nervous," Jillian said, "is if somebody's too clumsy to catch me."

"Heather really is a klutz, isn't she? And I wouldn't trust Amber with your pretty little head." Kelly smiled. Her eyes didn't.

"It's not Heather or Amber I worry about."

Kelly's fake smile widened. "With those extra pounds you've put on, I can't guarantee what'll happen when we put you up. Be a bummer to fall in front of the whole student body, wouldn't it?"

"Dropping me in practice is bad enough. If you ruin what we've worked for all month—"

"But, Jillian, what could you possibly *do* about it?"

Jillian shook her head and walked past Kelly to her place in formation.

Five minutes later the music started, faces in the crowd blurred, and Jillian focused on the beat. She felt two shoulders, Heather on her right and Kelly on her left, as she placed her feet in their clasped hands. Amber put her hands on Jillian's waist, spotting her as she went up in the stunt. Heather and Kelly braced themselves for the toss. On the count, she felt a push against her right foot, then her left, but a second too late. Her knee buckled before they pushed her into the air. She wasn't able to complete her toe touch before she landed sideways, upper body cradled in Amber's arms, and legs slapping onto the floor. Then her head slipped out of Amber's hand and hit the floor with a dull thud.

Jillian's whole body throbbed. The music stopped, the crowd went silent.

"Oh, Jill, are you okay?"

"Honey, that looked like it hurt. Are you sure you can get up?"

"What happened, Jill?" Kelly asked.

Jillian slowly sat up and saw Brittany bending over her. A sound escaped Jillian's mouth, something between a laugh and a sob.

"You okay, kiddo?" Brittany whispered. Jillian nodded. "Then let's get outta here."

Everybody watched as Brittany helped Jillian get up and limp off the court. Jillian heard a few snickers, then there was light applause and the band started playing. Jillian made an awkward exit.

She leaned against the wall, hearing the routine start over and wondering who took her place as flier. Probably Kelly. After the music stopped, Brittany led her down the hall. She heard the student body president on the microphone making some lame joke. The assistant cheerleading coach and a few administrators followed them out of the gym and insisted Jillian go to the school nurse.

"She's fine." Brittany said. "And if she's not, I'm taking her home so her mom can decide if she needs an emergency liver transplant or whatever you guys are freaking out about."

They walked toward their locker. Jillian felt her head clearing. "I'm gonna kill her, Brit. The whole thing was Kelly's fault, and nobody's going to know it but me."

"And me," Brittany said. She looked at Jillian. "And all of Kennedy High if we can pull it off."

"What do you mean?"

Brittany got both of their backpacks from the locker, then laid them down in the hallway. "Rest your head on these." She helped her lie down. "When I come back, moan and groan—act like you've got brain damage or something. That should be easy."

"What's supposed to be wrong with me?"

"Pretend you're on your death bed. Make sure it's dramatic, like this is the school play. Only with better acting." Brittany headed back down the hall toward the gym.

Brittany and her wild ideas. She's going to embarrass me. I should just get up and walk away.

"Help! Please!" Jillian heard Brittany yell. "It's Jillian. She collapsed by our locker!"

Jillian heard cries of alarm and saw four cheerleaders, then Brittany turn the corner a few seconds later. Behind them came an army of students that sounded from the floor like an elephant stampede. Apparently the assembly was over.

What have I gotten myself into?

Jillian groaned softly and closed her eyes before Amber rushed to her side.

"She's still breathing, I heard her groan," Amber said, voice quavering.

"Are you okay, Jillian?" Heather asked.

"Oh, no," a familiar voice whispered. "I didn't mean for this to happen."

Jillian's eyes popped open and she said in a calm but loud voice, "What *did* you mean to happen, Kelly?"

The students gasped. The cheerleaders backed away.

Kelly's eyes widened. "Me?"

"Yes, you." Jillian stood up, "You dropped me on purpose! You just admitted it."

Kelly's eyes went dark, and her face turned scarlet. "I'm not the klutz that fell. Don't blame me, tubby."

Jillian's lips pursed. Brittany stepped in front of Jillian, inches from Kelly, towering over both of them. Kelly cowered beneath Brittany's glare.

Jillian pushed Brittany away to face Kelly again. "This is about the all-American squad, isn't it? You'd rather have me break my neck than make the team again, wouldn't you?"

"You don't deserve that spot," Kelly shouted. "Cheerleaders aren't just supposed to *be* good, they're supposed to *look* good. That requires diet and exercise. For you, I'd recommend a Thighmaster."

Jillian slapped Kelly's face. Hard. Kelly stumbled backwards, and redness gathered in the shape of fingers on her cheek.

Jillian turned to Brittany and grabbed her arm. She limped out into the courtyard to head toward the back parking lot. Her anger held back her tears just until they got outside.

Behind them she heard guys laughing and calling "cat fight." Adults were trying to manage the crowd. Jillian just wanted to disappear. Brittany made sure she did.

~~~

Letter 17

Prince Ishbane,

I must say I'm succeeding admirably with Jillian. The loss of her reputation now that people know she's the Enemy's follower is particularly gratifying. So, too, is the shame I'm inflicting on her. Even though she's confessed to the Enemy, I'm raking her over the coals for offenses the Enemy has forgiven. I'm not letting her accept His atonement. I'm convincing her she must repeat it. This not only enslaves her, but insults Him.

The beautiful thing about accusing them for their sins is that we're the ones who convince them to sin in the first place. Then we have the brass to condemn them for following our lead! You'd think they'd begin to see through this charade, wouldn't you? But then, they're imbeciles.

I'm persuading Jillian she's "lost her Christian witness" and may as well give up trying. She mustn't see that the most potent Christian witness is not to pretend never to do wrong, but to be the first to confess she's been wrong and ask others to forgive her. (That's why I'm making sure she doesn't think of Kelly as a person, only as an opponent.) I'll convince her that as long as she asks for His forgiveness there's no need to ask for anyone else's.

I've again established Brittany's power over Jillian. The girl has no ability to stand up to her friend, which pays off in a hundred ways. For a veteran like me, Jillian's easy pickings. In fact, all I really have to do is seduce Brittany. The negative effects of that will be absorbed into Jillian, since she hasn't the strength to keep her friend's dominant personality from controlling her.

A few years ago I attended the regional conference on "Burying Vermin Teens," and did three workshops myself: "Shipwrecking Students" and "Preparing them to Lose their Faith at College" and "Lab 101: Dissecting the Young Vermin." Since Jillian is making college decisions, I'll pass on my observations. Feel free to share them with others.

First, I cannot overestimate the importance of the vermin's first year out of high school. This is the time more than any other when either we or the Enemy can establish a life-determining beachhead on them. These young moldable minds leave the structure and values of home and family and church and are immersed in a radically foreign atmosphere, with far less structure and decisively different values. Here's a mathematical formula for you—

unprecedented liberties, plus low morals, plus lack of wisdom, plus extreme vulnerability to peer pressure, plus susceptibility to intellectual manipulation equals…what? Unparalleled opportunity for us.

Going to college is like going to Mars. For many of these young vermin, it presents us with our single greatest opportunity to encroach upon both their minds and their bodies. No wonder the Master deploys more of our troops to college campuses than any other location. (Unfortunately, the Enemy has stationed many of His own warriors there as well.)

Often our best strategy is to send young vermin to a college that has Christian roots, but doesn't really believe in or teach the forbidden book. Instead of mirroring the Bible and challenging the world, they mirror the world and challenge the Bible. The few times they refer to the forbidden book, they reinterpret it to make it conform to the current social wisdom. Since the drift of society is under our control—even the Enemy admits Beelzebub is "the god of this world"—we pull the strings of their culture. (I love how many of the Enemy's ignorant followers financially underwrite schools serving our purposes and undermining His!)

My plan is to inoculate Jillian to truth by exposing her to a diluted and distorted version of it. If I can get her to the right school, it will offer neither atheism nor authentic Christianity, but nominal Christianity. Eventually she'll lose either her faith or her zeal. Either way, we win.

If I can make her assume her teachers are Christians, she's liable to buy in to whatever they say even when it's non-Christian and even anti-Christian. We outright challenge Christianity at the secular schools, and we usually succeed. But sometimes this backfires, especially among students who have been warned to exercise discernment. But when these same students go to Christian schools, no one warns them. Rather than searching the forbidden book to see what's true, as the Enemy instructs them to, they assume their teachers are genuine Christians and their teachings are true. With their guard down, we take their minds captive.

Instead of challenging students to believe and obey the forbidden book, many of our professors at Christian colleges do nothing but raise questions. Of course, I don't mean the questions of the curious mind seeking truth. I mean the cynical superior kinds of questions that don't want answers, but promote doubt and disillusionment with the forbidden book.

If someone travels far enough away from Christianity, he may be able to look back and see it in perspective. But if he drifts from the core creed while surrounded with nominal Christianity, he'll remain blind to the true faith he no longer embraces. Infect them with a small dose of counterfeit Christianity, and it'll immunize them to the real disease. That's why I'll take one nominal "Christian" teacher over a faculty of atheists any day!

Unfortunately, there is that *other* kind of college, which takes its doctrinal statement seriously, and where teachers worship the Carpenter and disciple the students. I am laboring to keep Jillian from any school which unapologetically teaches the forbidden book and encourages students to obey it. Fortunately, there aren't many of these schools, and they're easily lost in the mountain of literature promoting other "Christian" schools.

Regrettably, this Gresham Bible College is one of those schools I detest, where the forbidden book is believed and taught. My counterstrategy in such places is to turn them into smug self-righteous Pharisees, self-appointed spirituality police. We make sure their love is not for the Carpenter, but for long lists of rules whereby they judge themselves as spiritual because they've checked off all the boxes of do's and don'ts, and imagine everyone who's different from them is therefore ungodly. I like to see them set up their own judgment seats rather than wait for the Enemy to set up His.

Meanwhile, we try to make sure that in our other Christian schools any attempt at maintaining moral standards—such as requiring chapel attendance, prohibiting alcohol or restricting Internet access—is attacked as censorship, legalism, and pharisaism. (Faculty and students who never quote the Bible can be made to quote my favorite out-of-context verse, "Judge not.")

We must continue our policy of false advertising for "Christian" colleges. We must keep up the appearance of a spiritual environment, with all the proper accoutrements, including the lofty faith-affirming statements made in catalogs. Chapel meetings are fine, even desirable, as long as they focus on political correctness, not the forbidden book. Never label a bottle of arsenic "Arsenic." Label it "Aspirin." Only then can we be certain many of the fools will take it, mistaking the poison for the cure.

You asked for a Portland State University catalog. I'm sending it by courier. Rest assured I'm completely on top of this situation. It's all about molding their minds, and that's my specialty.

Lowering higher education,

Lord Foulgrin

18

Jillian's having one of her salad days again." Brittany winked at Ian as she stole one of his McDonald's French fries.

"Jenny Craig?" Ian asked.

Jillian rolled her eyes. "Just trying to be healthy."

"Me, too," Ian said. "Here's to my health!" He took a huge bite of his Big Mac, mayonnaise dripping down the side of his face.

"You're disgusting." Brittany handed him a stack of napkins.

"Finish the story," Ian said. "I mean, I saw the cat fight, and how you slugged Kelly—that was great. But what did Chandler say to you this morning?"

"She didn't *slug* her," Brittany said. "It's not like they were in a street brawl or something. It was a slap, nice and loud, leaving clear finger marks on the darling's cheek. Didn't know our little Jillian had it in her, did you?"

"It's about time somebody hit that girl," Ian said, "but I've gotta admit, Jillian, you're the last person I thought would actually do it. I would've put my money on Brittany. What got into you?"

Jillian shrugged her shoulders and popped the plastic lid off her salad. She'd heard all this last night, from Mom and Jodi and Kristi. She wasn't about to explain herself. Not to Ian. Not to Brittany.

"So, Rocky Balboa, tell us. What did the principal say?" Ian asked.

Jillian ignored them, trying to look busy opening her package of fat-free salad dressing. She attempted unsuccessfully to rip each corner.

"Jillian?" Brittany probed.

"What?" she snapped. "Look, it's funny to you, not me. Cheerleading's over."

"What do you mean?" Brittany asked.

"They kicked you off?" Ian asked. Brittany elbowed him hard.

Jillian nodded.

"I'm sorry, Jill," Brittany said, putting her arm around her.

"No, it's fine, I mean it really works out for the best. I didn't have that kind of time or energy to do it anyway. The worst part is…the whole school saw what I did."

Brittany laughed. "Always the self-conscious one. Everyone loved you for it, Jill. They saw you come out of your Christian-girl shell."

"But that's it. I'm a Christian now, Brit, for real. And I should be living like one. Everybody saw me acting like…something else."

"What people saw was that Kelly almost killed you and you just—"

"No," Jillian said firmly. "What people saw was a girl who claims God loves her, but she can't show that love to others. And they saw a girl who says God forgave her after turning her back on Him for eighteen years, and she can't even forgive others when they wrong her. I'm a hypocrite."

"You're human," Brittany said. "Anybody would've hit her. It was her fault, not yours."

"No. I shouldn't have pretended. And I certainly shouldn't have slapped her. Rob reminded me that we need to own up to it when we're wrong. We need to confess it."

"Well, Rob must be Mr. Super-Christian, huh? What gives him the right to make you feel guilty?"

"I was already feeling guilty. Rob just helped me come to terms with it. I told God I was sorry for letting Him down."

Brittany sighed loudly and did her eye thing. "You blame me, don't you?"

"I didn't say that."

"You didn't have to. Setting up Kelly was my idea."

"I didn't have to go along with it."

"Yeah, but I'm glad you did. Sorry about the cheerleading thing, but Kelly deserved what she got."

"Rob thinks I should ask forgiveness from Kelly, the squad and everybody else."

"Then Rob's a traitor."

Brittany took a bite of her chicken sandwich, and chomped on it hard. A deathly quiet descended for a minute. Jillian felt Brittany watching her again as she rationed her salad dressing.

"Sure that's gonna fill you up?"

Jillian pretended not to hear. She was sick and tired of people telling her what to do.

"Take a look." Ian tossed the video to Daniel, who sat down on the bed.

"*Witchboard?* Cool."

"Sure you've never seen it? Read the back."

"Horror movie…R-rated, violence," Daniel read aloud. "'College kids playing with a Ouija board contact an evil spirit named Malfeitor who possesses one of them and drives him to kill. When you open the door to the unknown, there's no telling who will drop in…or who will drop dead.'" Daniel smiled. "Cool. Never seen it. Says there's a sequel, *Witchboard II: The Devil's Doorway.*"

"I don't have it, but it's a winner, too. Okay, Danny boy, you're gonna love this." Ian popped it into his VCR, cranked up the sound and turned off the lights.

Letter 18

My naive Foulgrin,

Why attack the Enemy when you can simply displace Him? There's only so much room in their hearts and minds. Get them to focus on money. Clothes. Sports. Status. Popularity. Sex. Ambitions. Grievances. Obsess Jillian with being a good student, girlfriend, churchgoer. Their life clocks wind down every moment. Time is on our side.

Don't assume Jillian's death of a dream will serve us. Not being a cheerleader may devastate her for the moment. But the Enemy can use it to draw her attention to Him. Think long term. We enjoy seeing them suffer. But we must hold out for the ultimate suffering of hell. Far better that they would have pleasure for the moment and misery for eternity than the other way around.

Witchboard? *The Devil's Doorway*? The vermin seem eager to take over our job for us, don't they?

I've enjoyed perusing the Portland State University catalog. I found many courses I'd recommend. Here's one, and, no, I did not make this up: "Science and Pseudoscience—An examination of basic issues in philosophy of science through an analysis of creation science, faith healing, UFO abduction stories and other pseudosciences. Some of the questions addressed: What distinguishes science from pseudoscience? How are theories tested? When is evidence reliable?" And my personal favorite, "Must we invoke the supernatural in order to explain certain aspects of reality?"

Notice that belief in the supernatural and creation science is squarely placed in the same category as belief in alien abductions! All are referred to as "pseudoscience." Don't you love it? Of course, after the Tyrant made us, we witnessed His creation of the physical realm. We know what really happened. Obviously, we're incapable of the level of stupidity required to think the universe came into existence by itself. But that doesn't keep us from selling it to the vermin! (The hardest part is keeping a straight face—glad they can't see us!) As the forbidden book puts it, we demons know there is one God. However, we're under no obligation to tell *them* what we know, are we?

Picture the professor teaching this class. He congratulates himself on debunking the ridiculous fantasies of religious fanatics. Of course, his own position is imminently credible—in the beginning there was nothing, and then the nothing exploded into gigantic pieces we call stars and planets, and from these self-generated inanimate objects came plants, and from plants came animals, and from animals came people, and from people came Saran Wrap and bug zappers and bungee cords. Presto chango alakazam, there you have it, the history of the cosmos!

That is the "enlightened" scientific position. This is what they smugly hold to while dismissing the idea of intelligent design and creation! Here at headquarters we call this kind of coursework "psuedoeducation." But because they pay money to be taught these things, they will naturally assume them to be true.

We teach lies. But they actually *believe* them! Obviously, men are different from rocks, plants, and dung beetles not merely in kind, but in degree. But remember, that's only obvious to rational creatures like us. The humans' minds are tainted, because they have such vested interests in disbelief. If they don't have a Creator, that means they don't have a Judge. How convenient. They can feel free to live as they want, not as He demands. No absolutes and therefore no sin, no ultimate consequences, no afterlife, no accountability, no real hope. None of this has to be directly stated, of course. Students are more swayed by the unspoken assumptions of a classroom than the actual content.

You may wish to audit this pseudoscience class yourself. It could afford some great opportunities. Whatever you do, keep strong Christian vermin away from such classes and direct the weak ones straight to them. From your reports, it appears Jillian is easily influenced by her peers and teachers. Do what you can to place her in an environment where she'll be seduced from the Carpenter.

But beware, Foulgrin. Some young vermin have drawn closer to the Carpenter through the adversity experienced in college classrooms. When under fire they become conscious, for the first time, that they're in a battle. Suddenly they start seeking to arm themselves and draw cover from other soldiers. Don't allow Jillian to become one of those casualties we lose to campus ministry groups or Christian vermin friends.

If Jillian doesn't go to a lukewarm Christian college, any of our state school strongholds will do nearly as well. Rob may be strong enough to identify and do battle with our propaganda in this kind of environment. Jillian is not. In the sink or swim world of secular universities, without help she'll surely sink. Fortunately, most of the forbidden fellowships do almost nothing to train and pray for and dialogue with the young people they send off to college.

Jillian's college decision is crucial. Make sure you're her primary guidance counselor.

Your tutor,

Prince Ishbane

19

MARCH 31, 4:24 P.M.

The foursome had just come back from a ten-mile bike ride on the Springwater Corridor trail. Ian had a family thing, so he and Brit took off.

Jillian brought the popcorn into the living room and put the bowl on the coffee table. She expected Rob to sit by her on the couch, but instead he sat in the rocker, six feet away. She saw him looking at her.

"Everything okay?" she asked.

"That was an awesome ride," he said. "Seeing the deer, squirrels, rabbits. It's a beautiful trail."

"Don't forget the beaver."

"And all the dogs walking their owners," Rob said. "I love the sunshine and the fresh air."

"How come you're sitting over there?"

"Thought maybe we could talk a little."

"About what?"

"I'm not sure I want to do the dating thing," Rob said.

Jillian held her breath. "Is this another bombshell? Are you breaking up with me again?"

"No. No. I'm really enjoying our relationship. I don't want to give it up. I just don't want to get into trouble."

"Trouble...as in...?"

"We both know how it goes in a typical dating relationship. You couple up, pair off, then people start treating you like you're married or something. It's already happening. Haven't you noticed? Next thing, you begin thinking you have some kind of claim on the other person. And you can slide over into wanting to have some of the privileges of marriage without the responsibilities."

"Like...?"

"Like...intimacy."

"You mean sex?"

"Yeah."

"You believe in abstinence, right?"

"Absolutely."

"Me, too." She swallowed hard, trying to forget the memories that haunted her and hoping she'd never have to tell Rob.

"I've been memorizing 1 Corinthians 6:19-20. 'You are not your own; you were bought at a price. Therefore glorify God with your body.' See, our bodies are sacred because they're a temple of the Holy Spirit. They belong to God, not to us—which means, despite what the world tells us, we don't have the right to do whatever we feel like with our bodies. Verse 18 says, 'Flee from sexual immorality.' You know, like Joseph running away from Potiphar's wife when she was trying to seduce him."

"I'm not like Potiphar's wife."

"That's not what I meant! Neither of us wants to…seduce each other. But if we get in the wrong situation, the body chemistry kicks in, and it can happen regardless of what we say we want. It takes more than just believing in abstinence. Jeff said it and so did my youth pastor, Steve. We have to protect ourselves. Not let ourselves be alone, except when we're on our way to something or on our way home. I mean, no parking, no hanging out in each other's bedrooms."

"That sounds pretty rigid."

"Maybe it needs to be rigid. I've blown it enough to know I don't want to do it again. Here I am lecturing Ian on why he and Brittany shouldn't sleep together. But we've been getting cozy ourselves lately, and I don't want it to go any further. Actually, when it happens I *do* want it to go further and that's the problem."

"O…kay."

"There's another thing. If we're going to be seeing each other regularly, I think we need to talk with our parents."

"Our parents? About what?"

"About…our relationship. We need their approval. And their input."

She laughed. "Sorry. You're not kidding, are you?"

"No. The Bible says God's given us parents, and we're supposed to submit to them. They've got to be involved in our lives. My parents haven't even met you, and it's killing my mom. I think we should make a point to hang out with them."

Jillian smiled.

"What's so funny?"

"It's not funny. Just sort of…cute."

"Cute?"

"You've called me cute. I can call you cute if I want to. It's just that you sound so traditional. Old-fashioned."

"Well, if the way people do it these days isn't making the kind of relationship we want, maybe we need to try something else. Maybe people used to understand some things we don't. Not every change is an improvement, you know."

"Is this like…courtship?"

"Maybe. I'm not sure what the right word is. But if it's a choice between dating and courtship, maybe courtship's an improvement. I've been reading that book I told you about, and it's got some pretty strong arguments."

"Does this mean one of our moms comes with us if we go out to Starbucks?"

"I'm not saying that. But it does mean we shouldn't spend too much time alone. Normally let's be with groups."

"Like Brittany and Ian?"

"I'm not sure a foursome's a group, especially with the way they're always hanging all over each other. I guess the question is whether we can set the example. Can we rub off on them without letting them rub off on us? I mean, we can be having fun, laughing and talking, playing tennis, you name it, everything's going great and then all of a sudden we're crossing the lines."

"They're not so bad."

"We're the Christians. If we're going to hang with them, we need to be an example."

"You're still bugged about that movie they took us to, aren't you?"

"It was bad enough we watched that *Pleasantville* garbage at Ian's. Who would've thought a movie called *Pleasantville* could dis on the truth like that? Then they insist on going to that movie, and we let them talk us into going with them. Well, at first I was angry at them. But now I'm angry at me."

"But it was a teen movie, right? And it was just PG-13."

"Yeah, but you had people in and out of bed, and even if they didn't show the details, we knew what was going on. It was more than enough to…push the wrong buttons. There was skin, there was bad language. And remember that black magic scene? I still feel bad about it. Here I am trying to get Ian away from that kind of thing, and you're talking to Brittany about it too, right? And then we're sitting there watching a movie with them that's reinforcing it. And the sex thing, too."

"I've seen a lot worse."

"If you have, maybe that's a problem."

Jillian felt her face turn red.

"I don't mean to put you down, Jill. I've seen those things, too. I'm just saying as Christians we should have higher standards. The Bible says we're not supposed to be conformed to the world, but transformed by the renewing of our minds. If we feed our minds on the wrong stuff, it's going to prompt us to do the wrong stuff. I think we need to confess it to the Lord and ask His forgiveness."

"I've never confessed seeing a movie."

"Do you think we should've watched it?"

"I guess not."

"Then we better admit to God that we were wrong. Maybe…we should confess it together, right now. I'll go first." His eyes had barely closed when he started talking. "Lord, I'm really sorry I agreed to see that movie. I had a bad feeling about it, but I did it anyway. Didn't want to rock the boat. Well, I was dead wrong. I ask for Your forgiveness. And also for failing to take the moral leadership and speak up and stop watching it. I should've protected Jillian, too. I really let her down. I ask Your forgiveness for that. Thanks for Your promise that if we confess our sins, You are faithful and just to forgive us our sins and cleanse us from all unrighteousness."

There was a long pause.

"Hi, Lord. This is Jillian. Well, I blew it again. Please forgive me for seeing that movie and not walking out. The truth is, I did wonder about it and maybe that was You speaking to me. Forgive me for not even realizing how bad it was. Looking back I realize there was a lot of garbage in it. But I guess I've gotten used to watching garbage, to the point that I wasn't as uncomfortable as I should've been. Help me to try to do what pleases You. And thanks for giving Rob a sensitive conscience about this. Help us to be pure, Lord. We ask this in Jesus' name."

They both looked up and said "Amen."

"Let's pray for Ian and Brittany," Rob said. "Lord, help us to be an example to them. Maybe we should tell them we were wrong to see that movie. I don't know how to do that without sounding judgmental. But, Lord, we really want to show them what You're like. And You're not like the world. You have a better way, a way of truth and grace and purity and joy. Help us model those things, for Your glory and for our good and as an example to Ian and Brittany."

They said "Amen" again. Then they spent the rest of the evening with Jillian's mom, talking and playing cards and laughing and looking at old family pictures, including a video of Jillian's tenth birthday party. They even managed to get Daniel in on it for an hour, and after a few minutes he wasn't even sulking. Jillian went to bed thinking it was the best night she could remember in a long time.

"Relax, open yourself to the friendly skies," Skyla said.

"What friendly skies are we talking about?" Brittany asked.

"Are you scared?"

"I'm not scared of anything."

"Then just open your mind. Don't resist. Watch me first." Skyla situated the blank yellow pad of paper in front of her, put the blue felt pen in her hand, repeated a few strange words Brittany had never heard. Then she said, "Mother Goddess, Aphrodite, Artemis, Astarte, Diana, Isis, Lilith…we call upon you and your horned consort Adonis, Ammon-Ra, Apollo, Dionysius, Eros, Hades, Odin, Thor, Osiris, Pan. Speak now through your daughter."

Nothing happened. Skyla sat perfectly still, pen poised. A minute later Brittany thought maybe she should say something, but suddenly Skyla's right hand started twitching. Brittany looked at her face—it was expressionless, zombie-like. Her hand started moving quickly, fluidly across the page. In just a few moments she finished.

Skyla read aloud: "'Remember you are goddesses. Enjoy all that's around you. Do what you feel like doing. I will give you success.'"

"Wow," Brittany said. "But what's it say at the end? There's two more sentences."

"I don't have a clue," Skyla said. "I can't read it. And I can't remember anything—the words just came without me knowing what they were."

"It's messy, hardly looks like your handwriting. But it says, 'Beware of…Christians.' Then it says, 'Look out for the one with the…Foulgrin.'" Brittany turned white. "Why did you say that?"

"What?"

"Foulgrin?"

Skyla stared at the page. "Like I said, I don't remember writing it. Must mean a Christian with a self-righteous smirk or something? That's true of a lot of them."

"But it looks like…one word. There's no space between the l and the g. And it's capitalized. Why did you capitalize it?"

"I didn't."

"Look at it."

"Okay, it's capitalized. But I was only the instrument. A friendly spirit wrote it through me."

"Friendly spirit? Like Caspar?"

"Not *that* friendly." Skyla laughed. "Caspar's just a movie, a cartoon. This is the real deal."

"I don't like the Foulgrin thing."

"Why?"

Brittany hesitated. "Last fall when Ian and I were together, before we broke up, he got me to do the Ouija board with him a few times."

"Cool."

"Yeah, I thought so then. The first couple of times it was fun, a little spooky but fun. Then we asked Jillian to come. This was before she went religious on me, when her mind was more open. Anyway, the three of us had the board on our laps and Ian asked the spirit to identify himself."

"Or herself. Did she?"

"Yeah. He…she…it, whatever, spelled out the name Foulgrin. One word, not two. That's the only time I ever saw that word. Until now."

"Awesome!"

Brittany wasn't sure it was all that awesome.

"So what Christian do you know with a foul grin?" Skyla said.

"Jillian's boyfriend Rob doesn't like me. Doesn't approve. I mean, he may try to be pleasant, he may smile at me, but I can see right through it."

"I'll bet he's the one with the foul grin. You need to watch out for him. Maybe he's trying to mess you up. Turn Jillian against you. Maybe even Ian. Guys will do that."

Brittany pointed to the words. "You really didn't know what you were writing?"

"Nope. Honest. I just let myself go, and a guide takes over. I mean I've seen people fake automatic writing. And at first, mine was just scribbles. But I'm not faking it. Sometimes it even happens when I don't ask for it. Like twice when I've been writing in my book of shadows."

"You really keep a book of shadows?"

"It's my bible. I've done it for two years. Every day. It's important to journal your steps as a Wiccan. You should start one."

"Ian and I talked about it. He tried it for a while. His brother did it all the time. But I guess I just want to be a dabbler, you know, play with this stuff for the fun of it."

"It's not just for fun, Brittany. It's serious. You need to let the spirits bring harmony to your life and give you direction. My life was empty before I discovered Wicca—now I see everything differently. I have a mission, a reason for living. You need that, too."

"That's what Jillian tells me. Only she says it's Jesus I need."

"Jesus was okay. He did magic too, healing and signs. He was a Wiccan, a practitioner of the secret arts. I believe in Jesus. I just don't put Him in a box like these narrow-minded Christians do. It's not like you have to choose between Jesus and this. It's not either/or, it's both/and. The Jesus I know wouldn't burn witches at the stake like Christians did."

"Someone said the Bible condemns the occult."

"That's not true. It's a lie Christians make up. They also claim the Bible condemns lesbianism—and you don't think that's wrong, do you?"

Brittany shook her head. "No. Weird, but not wrong."

"Well, it's not weird either. When you're a Wiccan you understand that. I'll tell you some time about the Susan B. Anthony coven. But first, I need to introduce you to some of my college friends from our coven. Anyway, Christians claim the Bible says this and that just to keep people from experimenting so they can't discover for themselves what's good for them. It's like telling people 'don't eat the fruit.' Well, Wicca says it's fine to eat the fruit. The Bible doesn't condemn white witchcraft, only the really bad stuff, like using spells to harm people who haven't done you any wrong. But Wicca's first principle is 'do no harm.' Does that sound evil? That's what Jesus said, right? That's why we don't turn people into frogs. Although, we could."

"You could?"

Skyla laughed. "Well, I never have. But I've seen some amazing things. Now, you try the automatic writing."

Brittany took the pen in her hand. "I'm not sure about this."

"Come on, Brittany. It's cool. Don't be afraid."

"I told you, I'm not afraid of anything."

"Let me quote you something from the *Charge of the Goddess*." Skyla closed her eyes and stretched her hands out in front of her. "'Call unto thy soul; arise, and come unto me; for I am the soul of nature, who gives life to the universe. From me all things proceed, and unto me all things must return.... Let thine innermost divine self be enfolded in the rapture of the infinite.'"

"That's pretty trippy," Brittany said. "But cool, I guess."

"Okay, good, open your mind. Let a spirit speak through you."

"I need to get home. But maybe later. I'll think about it."

"Promise?"

"I promise."

"Here's a book for you." Skyla handed her the compact little volume. "Remember the I Ching?"

"Yeah. You showed it to me once at a slumber party. You use coins, right?"

"Right. Three of them. You ask your question, hold it in your mind, then you flip the coins. Tails is yin and heads is yang. Anyway, the book explains everything. You can even use it with thirty-two tarot cards, and it'll give you a reading as accurate as the ancient Chinese method of using forty-nine yarrow stalks."

"What's a yarrow stalk?"

"Never mind. The paper inside explains it. It's amazing. The I Ching is like opening a present when you don't know what's inside. But what's inside can change your life forever."

Letter 19

My seductive Foulgrin,

First things first. Get Rob and Jillian in bed with each other. It's a line in the sand. The Enemy commands them "flee from sexual immorality." We invite them to discard those primitive puritanical antisexual myths. "Be an enlightened progressive fun-loving young person. Do what everyone else does."

The Enemy tells His brats, "Among you there must not be even a hint of sexual immorality or of any kind of impurity." Hold a mirror to that and you've got your job description. Fill their minds with suggestive comments and jokes, from radio DJs and sit-coms and movies. Use clothing and swimsuit styles and low-cut, side-slit prom dresses and a hundred other strategies to provide that "hint," and more, which He warns them against.

The Enemy says unrepentant sexual sin contaminates an entire church and expands like bread yeast. Do you need any more motive than that? What He forbids, we normalize. How successful have we been? Look around you, Foulgrin. For them a "good movie" is one where people commit adultery but the camera cuts away just before intercourse, and obscenities are used "only a few times."

Nothing's more effective at derailing a young Christian than sexual compromise. The Enemy says if they choose the path of impurity, He doesn't hear their prayers until they confess. Imagine that—when His children refuse to listen to Him, He won't listen to them! Why bother laboring to keep them from praying, when we can lure them into moral choices that will nullify all their prayers anyway? Besides, when they're living in immorality, the last thing they'll want to do is pray.

Now that RG and JF have discussed sexual issues and put them on the table, they may relax and let down their guard. Convince them "we've dealt with that—no way it's going to happen to us now." Your job is to get them, however well intentioned, into the setup. Then facilitate the moment of weakness. Take them by surprise. Then make them live the rest of their lives in the shadow of that regret.

Skyla's tempter Jeznarc has trained her well. I'm impressed. Never speak evil of Jesus. Always profess respect for 'the real Jesus,' as opposed to the harsh narrow stereotype of Jesus portrayed by the apostles. Arguing against Jesus is like arguing against someone's mother. It rarely works. So appeal to some of the words of Jesus, out of context, to support the very things He detests.

Skyla sounds like a fine tool for this. The combination of keen intellect and extreme gullibility is useful. She has a promising future, as long as Jeznarc restrains himself and doesn't kill her first. The best strategy is to use her for years to mislead and twist and pervert, then have the pleasure of watching her die. It's delayed gratification. Torture them along the way, but don't torture them to *death* until you've gotten the most possible use out of them. Don't throw away the bottle until you've finished the wine.

Resist this self-glorifying habit of identifying yourself, as in the automatic writing. If you keep giving out your name, people may compare notes and figure you out. I know it goes against your grain. But you could better serve our purposes in subtle anonymity. Perhaps then you would get off parole sooner. And I could go back to my preferred assignment.

I'll instruct you on Ouija board strategies later. But suffice it to say, the most effective use of the board is not elevating it and making the planchette fly out from under their fingers and crash into the wall! Sometimes terrifying them backfires. It may push them away from the board. What draws them toward it, and toward us, is giving insightful and helpful answers. The same is true of tarot cards, automatic writing, and palm reading. To lure them back we must give them positive reinforcement. They're like Pavlov's dog. Only uglier and more stupid.

Don't let it dawn on them that the Enemy has forbidden them to seek occult guidance not to deprive them, but to guard them from disaster. He actually appears to love the vermin. Inexplicable, since He has as much reason as we to loathe them. He sets limits in order to protect them, just as they set guardrails around mountain roads to keep drivers from plunging off the cliff. You, Foulgrin, must teach them our favorite lie: Freedom comes not in staying within the guardrails, but breaking through them. Teach them that the Enemy is a cosmic killjoy. Don't let it dawn on them that He sets His rules to protect them from…well, from us.

With the gateways Brittany has given you and Raketwist, you should easily take her down. She's aggressive, intelligent (for a vermin I mean), yet gullible and prone to spiritual seduction. She's a natural leader. We can use her to take many others down our path.

Yes, Brittany, open your mind to the spirits. Enjoy the thrill of being touched by an angel.

Gleefully,

Prince Ishbane

20

After lunch Saturday, Ian went to play backyard basketball and Rob headed to the library to work on a paper. Brittany and Jillian drove to the Fletchers' to give Diane a day off and take care of Joey.

Jillian looked at Brittany as they walked through her door, swallowing hard. "I need to apologize about my attitude toward Skyla. I haven't been very nice when I've talked about her."

"No, you haven't."

"Please forgive me."

"I'm not your priest. Although I'd make a pretty good priestess."

"I'm serious, Brit. I disagree with Skyla, and I still think her witch stuff is scary. And, yeah, I wish you'd stay away from it, for your sake. But I had no right to put her down, or make fun of how she looks. I really am sorry."

Brittany shrugged. "Okay." She was quiet for a moment. "But since we've gone serious, there's something I need to say to you."

Jillian braced herself.

"You need to start eating."

Jillian sighed.

"I'm not kidding, Jill. You're making me nervous."

"I don't know what you're talking about."

"You're trying to lose weight for all the wrong reasons."

"Okay, Miss America, enlighten me. Just because you don't have to try doesn't mean the rest of the world is tall and thin and beautiful."

"You know better than that. I have to work out for volleyball. And I do it to be healthy, not to be someone else."

"So I just need to be content being my fat little self?"

"You're being ridiculous. Listen to yourself. You look great. But even if you didn't, there's no sense starving yourself."

"You're acting like I'm anorexic or something."

"Or something."

"Nervous?" Jillian asked as she got into Rob's car after church on Easter Sunday.

"No, not really." He pulled back and looked at her. "Are you?"

"A little, but I'm looking forward to meeting your family. I'm glad you invited me."

"Holidays are important to my family," Rob said. "And not just Cinco de Mayo."

"Do I get to help your mom in the kitchen?"

"Do you want to? It's not Taco Bell."

"I hope not!"

"It might not be what you expect."

"Are you talking about the food, or your family?"

"Both."

"So what should I expect?"

"Don't worry, *chica,* everything'll be fine." He messed with her hair. "They're going to love you."

After a five-mile drive from Jillian's suburban community, winding through bright beautiful countryside—farms and trees and meadows—Rob pulled off on a gravel lane between two fields of baby trees. "My dad works here at the nursery," he explained. "Mom works at the cannery down the road."

They drove through the dust to a group of older mobile homes. A crowd of boys dressed in their Sunday best laughed and played with a half-deflated soccer ball.

Rob led Jillian toward a weathered green house with a half-painted door. A stout brown woman threw open the door and called, *"José, Pablo, ¡vengan acà!"*

A pair of mud-encrusted work boots sat next to the steps, and a crucifix hung above the front door. *"¡Bienvenido!* Welcome!"

When they stepped inside, the round woman wiped her hands on her apron and gave Jillian a bear hug.

"This is my mom," Rob said, trying to stifle a laugh at Jillian's saucer eyes.

"It's nice to meet..." Jillian was interrupted by Rob's three teenage sisters who came out the door and gave her hugs between giggles.

"This is Seci, Daisy, and Maria." They were bright and colorful, all wearing platform shoes.

"That's my dad and my brother Rico on the sofa." The men smiled their welcome and got up to shake Jillian's hand. At five feet eight, Rob was the tallest by two inches.

I feel at home already!

A woman swung open a bedroom door, poked her head out and waved, an infant held to her chest.

"That's my brother's wife, Carmen. I think she's uh...feeding the baby." He reddened. "Everyone, this is Jillian."

"Sit," said Mrs. Gonzales. She put both hands on Jillian's arms and herded her and the men into the living room. *"Chicas, ¿me puedan ayudar en la cocina? ¡Hay muchas comida!"* The sisters disappeared into the kitchen.

Rob's mom returned with a tray of glasses, all different sizes and shapes, filled to over-flowing with iced tea. Carmen tiptoed out of the bedroom and sat next to her husband on the sofa arm. She laid down the baby in a blanket next to him.

"He's asleep for now," she whispered. Turning to Jillian she smiled and said, "It's nice to meet you."

"Thanks. You too."

"I'm going to poke my head in the kitchen and see if they need anything."

"I'll join you." Jillian hopped up. As they walked, Carmen said to Rob, "Not bad, little brother! But I thought she'd be Mexican!"

There was a moment's silence followed by hearty laughter. Jillian followed Carmen to the kitchen. She'd never seen so many women crowded into such a small place. A big cauldron of beans bubbled on the back burner. A pot of rice steamed on the stove. Seci was frying tortillas as her mom reached over her to check the rice. Maria and Daisy competed for counter space as they cut vegetables. It must have been ten degrees warmer than the living room.

Carmen tapped her mother-in-law on the shoulder. *"¿Necesitas ayuda?"*

Mrs. Gonzales glanced at Jillian and tried to shoo her back into the other room. Jillian said, "I'd like to help. Really."

Smiling, Daisy pointed to a stack of plates. "You can set the table."

Jillian grabbed the plates and began setting them out on the table. There were only five chairs.

Rob, his mom, his dad, three sisters, brother and wife, me, let's see, that makes…what, eight, nine?

Jillian finished putting out nine place settings, then managed to convince them to let her help with the fruit salad. By the time she'd sliced up the melon, dinner was ready.

Mrs. Gonzales sounded like a circus barker, calling everyone into the dining room. Seci and Daisy grabbed chairs from their bedroom, and Maria and Carmen managed to wedge the piano bench in at the far corner of the table. Rob's dad reached out his hands. Rob grabbed one of Jillian's hands, and his mother the other. Mr. Gonzales prayed.

"*Gracias,* Lord, for Your gracious provisions for Your children. Thank You for the gift of life and the gift of food. Gracias that Roberto's friend Jillian can be with us too."

When everyone was seated, Maria and her mom brought out the bowls and plates of food, one by one. Some were in serving dishes, others still in the pots and pans. There was more food than Jillian could believe. Tamales, beans, rice, fresh homemade salsa and flan for dessert, waiting in the kitchen. Mrs. Gonzales kept piling food on Jillian's plate. It looked great, but…

"Eat." Mrs. Gonzales said to Jillian. She felt everyone's eyes on her.

Jillian whispered to Rob, "I can't eat all this!"

He whispered back, "You have to; it'll hurt her feelings if you don't. Just don't eat the next few days, and it'll even out." He smiled.

Jillian picked at her food and tried to make it look as if she were eating more than she really was. Just when she thought she couldn't eat any more, Mrs. Gonzales would insist she try something else.

After nearly an hour of eating and talking, Rob rubbed his stomach and said, "Mama, that was outstanding. It's siesta time for me." He pushed back his chair from the table and, along with his dad and brother, headed to the living room where they sprawled out on the couch and chairs.

The women cleared the table, then Mrs. Gonzales dismissed Jillian and the girls for their afternoon nap. Daisy offered Jillian her bed, which she accepted, and a nightgown, which she turned down.

They take this siesta thing seriously! I never imagined.

The three sisters squeezed into Seci and Maria's double bed, shoved against the opposite wall of the bedroom.

After an hour and a half, people were stirring again and the family came back together. Rob's dad started telling hilarious stories. Rico pulled out a guitar and they sang songs. He handed the guitar to Rob, who played it beautifully.

How come he never told me?

It was a few hours later, about five o'clock, when Rico and Carmen left. Rob and Jillian said their good-byes and received final hugs from Mama. Jillian got into the Impala, her head in a daze.

"So," Rob said, "what did you think?"

"I could sure get used to the nap time thing."

"And…"

"The hugs were good too. And I just realized there's a lot more to learn about Rob Gonzales than I imagined."

"What does that mean? They're my family. That's who I am."

"I just feel bad that I've never seen that side of you before—guitar playing and all."

"So now that you've seen 'that side,' what do you think?"

"I like what I saw. And I think I want to see more."

Letter 20

My tedious Foulgrin,

Teach the young vermin that truth is *created*, not *discovered*. Here's the line: each culture determines its own reality. Truth is absolutely relative. Anyone who believes something which puts others in an unfavorable light is automatically bigoted.

It's impossible to overestimate the power of such propaganda. It's indelibly carved on this generation's psyche. Even the Christian young are infected with it. So are many of their parents.

No single cultural belief undermines the Enemy's cause, and furthers ours, as much as this notion that truth is subjective, not objective. For if there's no real truth, or if they can find truth within themselves, *why should they search for it elsewhere?* (Needless to say, those who don't search for it never find it.)

I've had it with your prying questions about your former pupil Squaltaint. I'll tell you this much, no more. He's serving out his sentence in a Christian Science reading room. His job is to convince people all pain is imaginary. The Enemy's soldiers keep causing them to stub their toes and bite their tongues. This refutes his thesis before they're out the door.

Obsmut warned me not to tell you where Squaltaint is. He says you'll go after him. I'd like to think you're capable of focusing on the task at hand. Put aside your petty demon-eat-demon desire for revenge.

I've climbed ranks above you not simply because I'm more intelligent and skillful. It's because I don't get distracted by personal agenda. Sometimes you fall for the same lies you whisper to the vermin. Neither earth nor Erebus revolves around you, Foulgrin. The sooner you come to grips with that, the better.

Absolutely committed to relativism,

Prince Ishbane

21

ob walked in Ian's front door with a book in his hand.

"Hey, Rob! Come on up. I'll change, then we're off."

Ian led Rob into his room. It was neater than usual, except for an open box with odds and ends strewn out on the floor—dice, counters, rule books, sheets with scribblings.

"What's that?"

"Just a game."

"What game?"

"D&D," Ian said.

"Dungeons and Dragons?"

"Yeah. You play it?"

"No," Rob said. "But lots of guys at college do. Some group even came on campus and set up D&D displays, gave away stuff, promoted products, taught people how to play, like it was a really big deal. There was a major buzz about it."

"Cool," Ian said, putting on jeans and a pair of Nikes.

"Tell me about D&D."

"It's sort of complicated. You have to play it to really understand. Want to play?"

"No thanks."

"Why not?"

"I'd need to understand it better before deciding what I think about it."

"Each player chooses an imaginary character and assumes his identity," Ian said.

"Are they evil characters?"

"Not all. Sure, mostly you choose the more evil and violent powers, because they score more points and live longer. You claim certain evil powers to have the best chance of winning. Dwarfs, knights, thieves, gods, devils, demons and all that. You go for power and wealth, and you kill your enemies or be killed."

"I've heard it involves witchcraft."

"Yeah, and magic spells. It's pretend, of course. Mostly."

"Mostly?"

"Well, some people take it more seriously than others. I mean one guy, Tony, had a curse put on him in the game, and he thought it was for real."

"What kind of curse?"

"It went, 'Your soul is mine, I'll choose the time.'"

"You're into this pretty deep?"

"I don't live and breathe it like some guys. I've got a life—basketball and Brittany and lots of books to read. There's even you. D&D's a pastime. I've thought about becoming a

Dungeon Master. He orchestrates and referees the game, creates the scenarios. Some are pretty scary."

"I know some people swear it's harmless," Rob said. "But I've heard others say they get more than they bargained for."

"Like what?"

"Spells and incantations and stuff. One of the guys in our apartment said some people ask for power in the name of Satan. That pulls them into some pretty dark stuff. In the extreme cases I've heard they've committed murder. Or suicide."

Ian shrugged. "So they say. But it doesn't affect me that way. It's just fun."

"You and Daniel were talking about it."

"Yeah. He's a player."

"I don't think his mom knows."

"I'm not sure *my* mom knows. Some parents let their kids live their own lives. Welcome to the twenty-first century."

"I don't think it's a good thing to do—for Daniel or for you."

"Who made *you* God?" Ian's calm, good-natured voice suddenly took on a hard tone.

"I'm not God. But God says He hates this stuff."

"God speaks to Rob Gonzales? Do me a favor and ask Him who's going to win the NBA championship. It was a lot easier to figure out back when Jordan was playing."

"God doesn't speak to me audibly. But He's spoken in His Word, the Bible. And it says this kind of thing is evil."

"Dungeons and Dragons?"

"Not specifically, but that sort of thing. Here, let me read you some verses." Rob started opening the Bible in his hand.

"Now?"

"Sure, why not?"

"Well…don't we need to get going?"

"We haven't even figured out where we're going, remember? What's the hurry?"

"I didn't plan on spending my afternoon being preached at."

"I'm not preaching. You told me about your game. I've seen the tarot cards and your books. Look, Ian, we're friends. I just want to show you what the Bible says so you can understand why I don't think it's a smart thing to do. And why I'd appreciate it if you didn't encourage Daniel to do it either. He's impressionable."

"He's already into it. I had nothing to do with that."

"I'm not blaming you. I just want to say a few things and then we can go have some fun, okay?" Rob pulled out a sheet of paper with notes scrawled in ink. "Just consider this a metaphysical conversation—part of your quest for enlightenment."

Ian blew out air, and put his head back on his pillow. "You're loaded for bear, aren't you?"

"I looked up some passages, that's all."

"I wondered why you brought your Bible with you. Okay, preacher. Take your best shot. Wake me up when you're done." He closed his eyes, but Rob knew he was listening.

"The first one's in Deuteronomy 18. It says, 'When you enter the land the LORD your God is giving you, do not learn to imitate the detestable ways of the nations there. Let no one be found among you who sacrifices his son or daughter in the fire, who practices divination or sorcery, interprets omens, engages in witchcraft, or casts spells, or who is a medium or spiritist or who consults the dead. Anyone who does these things is detestable to the LORD, and because of these detestable practices the LORD your God will drive out those nations before you.'"

"Well, obviously I don't believe in child sacrifice. But I don't think the rest of it's so bad."

"Here's another one. Deuteronomy 4. 'And when you look up to the sky and see the sun, the moon, and the stars—all the heavenly array—do not be enticed into bowing down to them and worshiping things the LORD your God has apportioned to all the nations under heaven.'"

"You think that's about astrology? I do horoscopes and stuff, but I've never bowed down and worshiped the stars."

"Leviticus 19:31: 'Do not turn to mediums or seek out spiritists, for you will be defiled by them.'"

"Defiled? Give me a break."

"Leviticus 20:6: 'I will set My face against the person who turns to mediums and spiritists to prostitute himself by following them and I will cut him off from his people.'"

"That's a bit intolerant, isn't it?"

"Well, if there's a God—let's just say *if*—wouldn't He be entitled to set the rules? I think He does it for our protection too. But He makes clear there's no neutrality—if you go to mediums and spiritists rather than God, you've forced His hand against you."

Rob flipped to the next marked passage. "Okay, here's Deuteronomy 17. 'If a man or woman living among you in one of the towns the LORD gives you is found doing evil in the eyes of the LORD your God in violation of His covenant, and contrary to My command has worshiped other gods, bowing down to them or to the sun or the moon or the stars of the sky, and this has been brought to your attention, then you must investigate it thoroughly. If it is true and it has been proved that this detestable thing has been done in Israel, take the man or woman who has done this evil deed to your city gate and stone that person to death.' Then here's the same thing in Leviticus 20: 'A man or woman who is a medium or spiritist among you must be put to death. You are to stone them; their blood will be on their own heads.'"

"Listen to yourself, Rob! It's like Christians burning witches in Salem. I can't believe a God of love would do something so hateful."

"Maybe He knows how terrible witchcraft and astrology are—and wants to protect people from them."

Ian shook his head in disgust. "That's the Old Testament God of wrath they talk about in English."

"It's not just Old Testament." Rob flipped to another passage. "Galatians 5 warns against witchcraft. Revelation 9:21 talks about people who didn't repent of murders, magic arts, sexual immorality or thefts. And here in Revelation 21:8 it says, 'But the cowardly, the unbelieving, the vile, the murderers, the sexually immoral, those who practice magic arts, the idolaters and all liars—their place will be in the fiery lake of burning sulfur.'"

"You're sounding intense, Rob. I can hear those upside down exclamation marks in your voice." Ian laughed, then Rob followed. "Superstition," Ian said. "That's all it is."

"I don't think so, Ian. Look here in Isaiah 8:19: 'When men tell you to consult mediums and spiritists, who whisper and mutter, should not a people inquire of their God? Why consult the dead on behalf of the living?' I've got a challenge for you, Ian. Study the Bible with me. Let's see what it says about what you're searching for. That's an official invitation."

Ian paused. "I don't think so. Look, I know you're sincere, Rob. It's just that I need to search for the truth in my own way. And I just don't think I'll find it in Christianity."

"Why not?"

"The Crusades, the witch hunts, all the *hypocrite* Christians, all the churches always fighting, homophobia, and hatred. How's that for starters?"

Rob sighed. "I'm not going to deny that a lot of people who say they're Christians are hypocrites. And a lot of bad things have been done in the name of Christianity. But the Bible says Satan is a counterfeiter. He's behind the bad things done in the name of Christ, so when people see the evil, they reject Him. But it's not about the behavior of people who call themselves Christians. It's about Jesus, who He is."

Ian looked at his watch. "We need to get going."

"Will you talk with me about this again?"

"I don't know…I'm not sure."

"Well, pizza's on me. All you can eat." Rob smiled. "So if you want the pizza you'll say, 'Sure, Rob, let's talk about this again.'"

"What kind of pizza?"

"BJ's, deep dish. Then pizookies for dessert."

"Sure, Rob," Ian said in an animated voice. "Let's talk about this again." He slapped Rob on the back as they walked out.

Letter 21

My disingenuous Foulgrin,

No time to respond to your insolent comments. I have work to do.

The Enemy's drawn a line in the sand. There are some things He won't tolerate. By getting them to flirt with the occult, we lure them into choosing us. It need not be a conscious choice to be a decisive one. This violation places them under His judgment. It's a perfect arrangement. We hate the Enemy's followers and He approves of them. We hate our followers and He disapproves of them. The sludgebags who choose the occult have the worst of both worlds. Don't let that dawn on them.

This Ian is useful, but dangerous. He wants a short cut to spirituality, a fascinating experience with the world beyond. The promising thing is that he's looking toward us, not the Enemy. But the danger is that the Enemy can take such longings and redirect them toward Himself. That's why I always prefer working with vermin whose yearnings are deadened rather than those whose yearnings are keen.

What do these young Millennials value and long for? They're disenchanted with the emptiness around them. They're tired of having no purpose. No vision. Nothing to live for. Their frustration and boredom can be brick walls to the Enemy and the forbidden fellowship. Or they can be open doors to them.

Whether it's food, housing, sex, money or religion, those who live to have every short-term longing fulfilled are fools. They lose their grasp of greater longings. They become impatient with any desire that can't be fulfilled today, here and now.

Through the flippancy of popular culture, we've robbed them of the moral imagination so useful to the Enemy. This imagination was once stimulated by the arts, music, and great literature. And the forbidden book itself. It was used incessantly by the Enemy to draw their thoughts to unseen realities. But we have extinguished those longings—or at least buried them deep—under the flood of short-term satisfactions.

That's why hell's marketing schemes are so effective. Nothing's better than the commercial that convinces them they need what they don't. Or that they want what we want them to want. Or they must have it immediately. Not in the Enemy's form, nor in His time, but ours.

We've replaced imagination with fantasy, joy with pleasure. We fill rooms with empty-souled, vacant-eyed vermin telling sleazy jokes and mocking the Enemy's ways and laughing as though their hearts were full of joy. In fact, they're full of cynicism and hopelessness. Their misdirected longings will never be fulfilled.

This is why sex is so useful and at the same time so dangerous to us. In the sexual union, the Enemy wants them to see in Him the bridegroom they long to be one with. Their desire to please their beloved, and be pleased by her, is from Him. He intends sex as a sacrament of marriage in which they can see Him and be further drawn to Him. We must disguise the fact that He's the source and object of their love. But we've cheapened the sexual act to nothing more than pleasure. We've made it available on every street corner, magazine rack, cable service, and computer. We've thwarted His attempts to make them see sex as something spiritual. We've trivialized sex. It's lost the transcendent magic the Enemy built into it.

Make them souls without longing. Make them mechanical men, who go through the motions dutifully and joylessly. Eventually they stop seeking altogether. And when they do, we've got them!

If we can't keep them from longing, the second best is to have them long for lesser things, six-packs or jewelry or vacation homes. Make them believe that money, power, popularity, and sex are really what they were wanting. When every desire for sex or possessions is gratified, they lose all sense of delayed gratification. The notion of longing for a God they can't see and a heaven that hasn't yet come is nonsense to them.

How can anything matter if it doesn't satisfy them today? *Especially* if it makes their life inconvenient today? Christianity compels them to help the stinky man who has nowhere to sleep. At the same time it tells them to pass by the seductive woman without looking at her. Who would be inspired to make this his religion of choice?

Never let them see that these acts requiring momentary sacrifice and inconvenience are the same ones the Enemy rewards, both now and later, in a thousand ways. Our job? To rearrange the price tags. Make sure they're unwilling to pay the price for what's precious. Instead, make them value what's cheap. Only in the end will they realize how dearly they must pay for it.

Rearranging the price tags,

Prince Ishbane

22

"Remember how much it helped us last time?" Brittany asked. "Just sit down and let the tarot cards do the talking. You've been so uptight ever since your little born-again thing. Relax!"

She handed Jillian a card. Jillian looked at it. She saw a snake.

"No," Jillian said. "This isn't right. I won't do it."

"Jillian, honestly, don't be so closed minded."

"I'm leaving, Brit. I'm sorry I looked at the card. I shouldn't have let you talk me into it. I need to make my own choices. That's one of my problems. I get pressured by other people."

"Haven't I been saying that? Remember last time when you drew the Death card? It was telling you to take charge of your own life."

"Actually, I need to give God control of my life. I need to trust Him. If I do that, I can follow Him instead of being a slave to people's opinions about me. Including yours."

"You're making this my fault again, aren't you?"

"No. It was *my* fault. I take full responsibility. But I'm telling you this, Brit. I'm not going to hang out in your room again as long as you have tarot cards and occult books and the teen witch kit and the Wiccan stuff from Skyla. It's not just your life you're affecting, it's mine. This stuff is evil. Rob talked to me about this, and he showed me some Bible passages."

"Yeah. Ian told me about the sermon Rob gave him. So *that's* what it's about. Rob's trying to turn you against me?"

"It's not about Rob. It's about God. His Word tells me to stay away from stuff like this. And that's exactly what I'm going to do."

"Now you're trying to control *my* life, is that it? *You* don't like this, so *I* have to get rid of it?"

"You can do whatever you want, Brit. All I'm saying is, if this kind of stuff's in your room, then I can't be. It's my life I'm taking charge of, not yours. You can make your own choices." She walked out the door and toward the stairway. She was on the third stair down when she heard Brittany call. She hesitated, with a moment's hope.

"You're just jealous of Skyla, aren't you?"

"Hello?"

"Hey, Jill," Rob said. "Can I pick you up in half an hour?"

"First, tell me where you've been. Do you ever check your messages? It's been three days!"

"I just got busy. Homework, helping my dad at the nursery. You know."

"Okay, I guess. Where are we going?"

"It wouldn't be as fun if I told you, would it?"

As soon as they hung up, Jillian sprang from the couch and ran up the stairs to get ready. As she passed the living room window, she saw blue sky and Oregon green everywhere.

Jillian showered and threw her wet curls into a twist on the top of her head. After changing three times, she decided on a new pair of jeans and a yellow three-quarter sleeved shirt.

It may be sunny, but it's still Oregon.

The doorbell rang and she answered.

"Ready?" Rob stood there casually, smiling.

"Let's go. I'm curious to see what you've got up your sleeve."

They drove for thirty minutes, heading toward snow-capped Mt. Hood. They turned on a side road Jillian had never been on. She felt uncertainty in her stomach. Five miles after the pavement turned into gravel, Rob pulled over next to a huge pine tree.

"We're here." He lifted the trunk and hauled out a large wicker picnic basket, brimming with food. Jillian stared wide-eyed.

"Mama got a little carried away," Rob said.

Jillian grabbed a blanket. They found a clearing in the woods, and set the blanket down. They ate and talked and laughed. Hours passed.

They put the basket in the trunk, then sat back down on the blanket. Jillian hugged Rob tightly. "Thanks for bringing me here," she said, her head resting on his chest. "This will always be our spot."

Rob kissed her lightly. Then the kisses grew longer and deeper. She felt lost in his arms, unaware of thoughts but overcome with instincts. They'd embraced, but never like this, for this long. She felt a rush of fear and excitement. The next thing she knew Rob had rolled on top of her, still kissing.

Suddenly Rob got off and stood up. He moved away quickly, almost running. Jillian followed him. "Rob, what's wrong?"

"Jillian…there's stuff we need to talk about. I wasn't going to tell you, but what just happened…anyway, I should tell you. This is the first relationship I've had since I became a Christian. Well, I guess that goes for you, too. Anyway," he paused. "I think we need to set more specific boundaries for ourselves. Physically, I mean."

"The Bible says we shouldn't have sex before marriage. So, we won't, right?"

"That's not enough for me. It doesn't take much to get me going. You know what I mean?"

"I'm not sure."

"I'm a guy. We're perverts! Okay, what I mean is, we have really strong sex drives. And it's not just me. I don't know what you felt when I hugged you like that, and when I was pressed against you. But for me, I was one minute away from having sex, or I could have been. I was being pulled toward what should be saved for marriage. It's too easy to rationalize."

"But can't we just hug and kiss? We don't have to go any further."

"But Jill…you're the one I want to share myself with. Once we got going like we just did, I don't know how I managed to pull back. God helped me this time. If we let it happen again, I don't know that I'll be able to stop. I don't trust myself. This was like a warning."

She nodded slowly.

"Don't you see what's happening?" Rob said. He almost sounded angry. "As we've gotten closer emotionally, we've gotten closer physically. First we held hands, then there was the arm around the shoulder and the side hug. Then the hug was straight on and it lasted longer, and the kisses went from little to big. I've been thinking about stuff…that I know I shouldn't. It's like I'm getting addicted. I want more."

"But to me it seems like the more you care about someone, the more you want to show it, right? And how do you show it without being…physical?" Jillian stared out into the trees. "The more you care, the more you want to be close."

"Exactly. That's why we've got to set boundaries." Rob had a faraway look in his eyes. "I wish I'd done it a long time ago."

His head hung. He sat down on the grass. She sat three feet away.

"Rob?" He didn't move. "Tell me what's wrong…please?"

"There's too much to tell," he mumbled. "Too many stories I wish I could forget. Too many things about me that I don't want anybody to know. But I think I owe you an explanation."

"Like what?" Jillian had never seen his face so red and his eyes so wet.

"There've been girls, Jill. Lots of them. I don't remember them all. I never even knew some of their names." His voice was a lifeless monotone. "Isabel was the first, and it's her face more than anybody's I can't erase from my mind. I was only fourteen. I'd just graduated from a peewee to a real *Sureño 13,* and I had my blue bandana to prove it. Isabel was Miguel's *novia."* He stopped, and looked at Jillian. "Miguel was our leader. He was my hero. He had everything I wanted—including Isabel."

Jillian stared silently, and Rob cleared his throat.

"For some reason Miguel wouldn't let her have a gun. She offered herself in exchange for me bringing her a nine millimeter Glock 17 one night. She controlled a lot of guys that way. Everybody talked about her. She was so beautiful." Rob hesitated for a second. "I told myself it was great, even though it was…embarrassing and awkward. Then, about twenty minutes after I left, I was talking with some homies, bragging about what I'd done with Isabel, and I heard the shot. We thought it was the beginning of a gang war. Maybe someone had killed Miguel. No. It was Isabel—she'd shot herself."

Jillian shivered as she saw the emptiness in Rob's eyes.

"She was seventeen, homeless, and pregnant, we found out from the newspaper. It felt like a cold fist closed over my heart that day. I was with lots of other girls the next few years before I got out of the gangs. But I always thought about her. And the sex wasn't fulfilling like I told myself it would be. It was like someone was whispering it would be so great, the best ever, but then every time when it was done I felt so empty."

Jillian reached out and held his hand in hers. She cried with him.

"I don't remember the pleasure much. I remember sadness and pain. But especially fear. Fear that I'd be the next one found alone in a warehouse with a gun in my mouth and a bullet in my brain. And fear that I couldn't do a thing to stop it."

He pulled his hands away and wiped his eyes, then ran his hands through his short black hair.

"God forgave me for it, I know that. But even when sin's forgiven, we still have to live with some consequences. If I'd known then what all that would do to me, if I'd known the real cost, I wouldn't have made those choices." He blew out air. "There. That's the first time I've said those words out loud. You and God are the only ones I've told."

O God, why didn't he wait? She started to cry. *Why didn't I wait?*

"So now that you know this about me," Rob said, "maybe you'll want to rethink our relationship."

Jillian opened her mouth to say something, then closed it again. Finally she said, "I was only sixteen the first time. Two years ago. I thought he loved me...I thought I loved him."

"You don't have to tell me, Jill. As long as you've told God."

"I've confessed my sins in general. But maybe not the specifics." Jillian drew in a shaky breath. "The guy kept pressuring me, telling me if I loved him, I should prove it. But when I gave in, our relationship changed. It was all about sex. If I didn't give it to him every time we were together, he got mad. Finally, he dumped me for another girl. I was devastated. I felt so cheap and dirty. My parents didn't have a clue—in those days they let me stay out as late as I wanted. As late as *he* wanted."

She wiped her eyes. "It gets worse. I went to his best friend looking for help. He was there for me. We'd double-dated with him and his girlfriend for a while, so I knew him pretty well. I thought so anyway. Pretty soon we were spending time together. He said he'd never do anything to hurt me like his friend did. A few weeks later, while his parents were away one weekend, and his girlfriend was out with her friends, he invited me to his house. Somehow we ended up in bed. It was terrible. Once you give up your virginity...it's like you don't have anything to hold onto. It made it easier to do it again with another guy, last year. What did I have to lose? I'd already lost it."

"I know exactly what you mean," Rob said. "But we've got to ask forgiveness for the past and start over. We come clean, then God really makes us clean, and we save ourselves for marriage from that point forward. I've heard it called 'secondary virginity.' That's what I'm committed to."

"Yeah, me too. But like you said, the past keeps coming up, doesn't it? I never told a soul about this guy, not even Brittany. It only happened once, and we both tried to ignore it. But I've never been able to look him or his old girlfriend in the eye since. Especially not his girlfriend."

"Did she ever find out?"

Jillian let out a huge sigh and closed her eyes. "Yeah, I'm pretty sure she did."

Letter 22

The artist formerly known as Prince Ishbane,

I am not some junior tempter who needs my hand held…or slapped! Your files will show that our résumés are comparable, and arguably it is I who have the edge due to my extensive field experiences. (What's the saying: "Those who can't tempt, teach"?) I am not your inferior. We are peers.

You say I'm making myself too obvious? Well, it's a refreshing change of pace to come out of the closet once in a while and enslave them with minimal pretense. True, many of them imagine we're fiction, like the entertaining "Far Side" cartoon demons who live in hell, torturing dead humans. Fine, let them imagine either that we don't exist or that we're safely off in hell. Blind them to the reality that we roam the earth not torturing the dead but deceiving the living. Let them depict us as the long-tailed, cloven-hoofed jester with horns and red tights. That way they'll put us in the same category as Godzilla, King Kong, or Freddy Kruegger.

What you're missing, Ishbane, is that we don't always have to disguise our evil entirely. A little of it fascinates them, draws them into our web. That's what I'm doing with Ian, Brittany, and Daniel. Like a savvy prostitute, I'm showing them the beautiful side of evil, the seductive part. Never too much too soon, always just enough to lure them further into my web.

In short, I welcome materialists and magicians with equal enthusiasm.

You go on and on about the opportunity to derail these miserable vermin youth through sexual immorality. Do you think I'm unaware of this? Check the syllabus for the Erebus Convocation on Vermin Youth Destruction, and you'll see I taught the class. *Of course* sexual compromise is our most effective way of deceiving and destroying them. What will you tell me next? That I ought to try getting them to take drugs or drive drunk or hang themselves? How original.

As for your noble-sounding exhortation that I should "love our cause," may I respectfully remind you that Erebus has a simple arithmetic. One's advance is accomplished through another's demise. The pie is only so big. "Love" our cause? We do not love, we hunger and ravage! When the humans hunger for one another, we tell them it is love. Appetite is mistaken for romance. Let's fool them into believing this, Ishbane, but when we talk among ourselves, let's be honest enough to admit we can accomplish our goals only at another's expense. It is the Enemy who came up with this nonsensical notion of His interests and their interests—all of them—being served simultaneously. Poppycock!

I tire of your sanctimonious exhortations to set aside my own interests for those of the collective. It is not *your* career that has been derailed by another's willful incompetence. Answer me this, *Lord* Ishbane. Is not all you do motivated by self-interest? Isn't that why we followed Lucifer in the first place? Can you tell me it is your loyalty to Erebus alone which fuels your instinct to rebel? Of course not. It is your interest in self-promotion, coupled with your hatred for the vermin and our self-righteous ex-comrades.

Yes, I've sent out feelers on Squaltaint. Eventually I'll pay him a little visit. But this will not keep me from performing my duties. I'm a consummate professional.

Let me give you a tip, Ishbane. The best way to find out about your Enemy is to read His mail. By understanding what it says you can best prevent *them* from understanding what it says. Whatever the Enemy wants, we want the opposite. The forbidden book tells us what He wants, and therefore serves as a photographic negative of what *we* want.

It's a package deal the Enemy gives them. It all stands or falls together. Get them to disbelieve Genesis 1–11, and eventually they'll disbelieve John 3:16. When they reject one portion, they set themselves up as judges of the Enemy's revelation, rather than letting it judge them. They become the teachers, making the Enemy the student. He detests this role reversal. We love it!

Don't you see? I'll draw you a picture. The Enemy entrusts to them a ship. He sends them out on the water with a cargo He intends for them to consume, as well as deliver to His intended port. But then the waves come, their adversities and doubts. Instead of going to work and adjusting the sail, they try to lighten the load by throwing overboard part of the cargo. They make themselves captains of the boat, though they signed on as crew. They mutiny. And they throw overboard the very cargo He's intended for them to live off of to get them to their destination.

Once we get them to jettison one part of the forbidden book, they'll throw overboard more and more and more. This is where colleges come in so handy! It's not just the things we get them to throw overboard. It's the fact that once we've set them in motion, they'll spend the rest of their lives—whether in calm waters or rough—wondering what they should throw overboard next. And, of course, with everything they cast off, the ship becomes less capable of carrying them to a worthy destination.

You advised me again to be more subtle. You think I, of all demons, don't understand the value of subtlety? What you don't seem to understand, Ishbane, is that three of these young vermin have made themselves vulnerable to my direct approach. Our strategies should vary according to the sludgebags' particular weaknesses.

Take Ian's parents or Brittany's mom, for instance. I keep telling Ian's father's tempter, Spleengouge, that he doesn't have to lead him into spectacular new sins to look good on his résumé. Every day this man remains in his present condition brings him slowly, surely, dependably—even if nonsensationally—closer to hell. He doesn't have to spray his office with fifty rounds of ammo to go to hell. He's already going there! I say, don't tinker with him. Time's on our side. His life is ticking down. When it expires, only one thing will matter—that he hasn't come to know the Enemy.

The safest road to hell is the gradual one—the gentle slope, soft underfoot, without sudden turnings, without milestones, without signposts.

If you require more wisdom to set you on the path, you know where to find me.

Honored for the opportunity to instruct,

Lord Foulgrin

23

MAY 5, 7:43 P.M.

This is it," Jillian said out loud to herself. "6801 Tyler Court."

She walked onto the front porch and knocked on the door. It opened a few seconds later. Kelly Hatcher blinked in surprise, then raised one eyebrow on an otherwise stone-hard face.

"Hey," Jillian said weakly.

"What are *you* doing here?"

Humiliating myself. "I came to apologize."

Kelly gave her a you-don't-really-expect-me-to-believe-that grin. "Uh-huh, and would you like to kiss my feet as well? Would that make you feel better? Or do you want me to turn the other cheek so you can slap that one, too?"

Jillian chewed her lip. "Well, actually…I am sorry about that. I lost my temper and it was wrong. But that's not the only reason I'm here."

"Well? Why *are* you here, Jillian?" Kelly stood with the door half open.

Jillian's stomach tightened and her breath grew quicker and more shallow.

Turn around and go home. Kelly probably already knows. Bringing it up would only cause more pain.

Jillian took a step backward. Then she asked God for help. "It's about Dustin. I need to tell you something."

Kelly glanced back into the house, then moved outside to the porch, pulling the door shut behind her.

"Let's see, I dated Dustin for a year and a half. You only knew him for what, three months while you and Joel were together?" She paused and looked deep in thought, her index finger tapping her bottom lip. "Tell me Jillian, what do you know about Dustin that I don't?"

Jillian's palms felt clammy. "When Joel and I broke up—"

"You mean when Joel dumped you for Alicia."

Jillian felt a definite urge to turn around and walk away. Yet something prodded her to follow through. "Yeah. Well, you probably remember I was a basket case after that. One night when you weren't around, Dustin asked me to come over to his house. I was really a mess. He told me he understood, put his arm around me. Then, somehow we…"

"What? Say it." Kelly's eyes were smoldering.

"We had sex. I'm so sorry."

"Did you think I was a fool, Jillian? That I never figured it out? I could tell you the night it happened. I knew something was wrong that next day, but I didn't put it together until we saw you at the mall later that week." Kelly forced a laugh. "You two couldn't even sputter out one intelligent word."

136

"I'm sorry, Kelly." Tears streamed down Jillian's face. "I'm so sorry, I wish I could take it back. I wish—"

"It was over with me and Dustin from that day on, but neither of us wanted to admit it." Kelly's voice sounded hollow. "We'd planned on getting married after I graduated, but once he left for college, we both knew it was hopeless."

"I don't understand," Jillian said. "If you knew, why didn't you dump him right then?"

"Because I loved him, all right?" she yelled. Then her voice turned into a whisper. "I loved him." A single tear cut through her flawless makeup.

"I'm so sorry," Jillian said, feeling stupid for saying it again, but not knowing what else to say.

"Well, sorry isn't good enough, little Miss Perfect. You ruined my life." She turned around and yanked the door open. She stepped inside and looked back at Jillian. "The only thing that keeps me going is picturing you lying awake at night because of the guilt. I hope it never lets you sleep, Jillian. Ever."

Kelly slammed the door. The air pushed against Jillian's face. She felt empty, like she'd poured out every ounce of herself on that porch. She walked back to her car, numb.

Jillian had envisioned Kelly hugging her, thanking her for coming and telling her all was forgiven. Instead, she had shoved a knife in her heart.

I try to do the right thing, and it blows up in my face. Why, God?

Jillian drove home. Mom had gone out earlier, leaving Joey at Ryan and Jodi's. Said she wouldn't be home until ten o'clock.

Jillian walked into the kitchen and opened up the cupboards—all of them. She found a full bag of potato chips, a package of red licorice, and her mom's not-so-secret stash of chocolates. Then she went to the fridge and grabbed the onion dip and a piece of cheesecake. Finally, she opened the freezer and reached for her favorite, Rocky Road.

She grabbed a small white garbage bag under the sink and set it on the table next to the food. It took two trips to get everything up to her room, but Jillian was careful to itemize her hoard so she could replace it all that night after a trip to the grocery store.

Jillian brought the portable TV into her bedroom and sat cross-legged on her bed. She watched sitcom rerun after rerun. She polished off the cheesecake and the half gallon of ice cream first. Then she opened the bag of chips and dove in. She forgot about Kelly, Dustin, Brittany, Rob, and everyone and everything else.

Jillian scraped the bottom of the dip and placed the container carefully in the trash bag, along with the empty ice cream carton. She grabbed a handful of licorice, tied a dozen strings in neat little knots, lined them up in a row, and ate them one by one.

Jillian turned off the TV and walked to the bathroom across the hall, bringing the trash bag with her. She opened the cupboard under the sink and found the bathroom garbage too full to add the bag. She'd take them both outside later.

She knelt down by the toilet and stuck her finger down her throat. The laxatives had worked before, but this was so much quicker, and it had gotten easier each time. As much as it disgusted her at first, anything was better than letting all those calories stay in her body.

When she finished, she flushed the toilet. Her stomach felt better. But just to make sure there wasn't more, she began the process again.

Jillian thought she heard something and froze. No. It was her imagination. Then she heard it again, but it was too late. Her gag reflex kicked in. She hoped the door was locked.

"Jill, are you okay in there?" Her mom, Joey in her arms, pushed the door open.

"Can't you knock?" Jillian said, turning her head away and trying to wipe her mouth with a bath towel.

"Are you sick, honey? It smells like…" Diane spotted the trash bag in the middle of the floor. The empty ice cream carton had fallen halfway out.

"What's going on?"

"Get out. Get out!" Jillian screamed. She got off her knees and stood between her mom and the bag. "Can't you just leave me alone for once?"

"Jillian, what's wrong with you?"

"Just leave me alone!"

"Jillian Fletcher, what's in that bag? It smells like you've been throwing up." As soon as she said the words, she put her hands over her mouth. "Oh, Jilly." She backed up, leaning against the door frame. "I don't think I can handle this."

"You don't have to handle anything. All you have to do is walk out that door."

"I've been worried about you, but I thought it was just mood swings."

"There's no way you can understand this, Mom, so don't even try. Just do us both a favor and don't worry about it, okay? I can handle this."

Diane closed her eyes. She looked like she was going to faint. Joey started to cry.

"Just go." Jillian sat down on the linoleum floor, head in her hands.

Diane stumbled out of the bathroom, trying unsuccessfully to quiet Joey.

Jillian felt hollow. She knew she should feel bad about yelling at her mom. She probably would later. She was so ashamed of her secret, this thing that was off-limits to everyone, including God. She knew she should pray. But she was tired of feeling that brick wall when she tried. Too numb to cry, Jillian hugged her knees to her chest, withdrawing into her carefully spun cocoon.

Letter 23

My floundering Foulgrin,

I've forwarded a copy of your latest insolent letter to the Deputy of Internal Affairs. They know where to find you. You're walking on thin ice, Foulgrin. And in our parts, the ice tends to be very thin indeed.

The authorities will be particularly interested in noting your signoff as *"Lord* Foulgrin."

You're a legend in your own mind. It's your grave you're digging. I'd be glad to hand you a shovel. The problem is, like it or not—and in fact I detest it—our assignment means our successes and failures are bound together. Focus, Foulgrin. Wipe that smirk off your face and *focus*.

Yes, I'm sure Jillian's misery satisfies you. The exposure of her fornication, her betrayal of Kelly, and her mom's catching her humiliating binge and purge, all must have caused unbearable pain. Such things are undeniably pleasant for us.

But did it not occur to you that her confession to Rob and then Kelly was exactly what the Enemy wanted? And that Jillian's mother discovering her might have been orchestrated by the Enemy's warriors and the Ghost? Why do you suppose Diane came home two hours early? Coincidence? I think not.

By allowing Jillian's mother to discover her condition, you've broken the spell. Now there will be opportunity for her to get help.

Jillian's actions are only the tip of the iceberg. The real battle is in her mind. She looks around her and sees gorgeous homes. She thinks, if only she had a place like that, all would be well. Then she looks at all these images of willowy women. Since childhood she's been given food as reward or bribery, yet she's expected to be thin. Beauty, for girls in particular, is synonymous with being slender. Meanwhile, they're surrounded by an unending variety of food. They face a choice. Discipline, or a shortcut? We're right there with a menu of shortcuts and a myriad of disciplines which ultimately enslave. Diet pills, laxatives, vomiting, bingeing, self-induced starvation. Their lives revolve around food. It's their idol.

Jillian's a control freak. No matter who else pressures her into doing other things, she thinks she can at least control this one little area. In reality, she's completely out of control.

Now that her mother knows her little secret, do what you can to use this against them both. Show Jillian how to manipulate others through it. Make the whole family revolve around her and her problems. This is the payoff that will further motivate her behavior. The "counseling" is crucial at this point. Be sure she finds the kind of counselor, Christian or not, who implies everyone else is to blame and she doesn't have to take any responsibility. Make Diane walk on eggshells around her daughter lest she be driven back to food. Teach the Fletchers a counseling model based on disease and a cure based on behavior modification—never a model based on sin and forgiveness, followed by transformed thinking.

Don't let Jillian understand that if she's truly to change, she'll need to change her whole perspective. Never let her think of her changed status before the Enemy. Yes, she's been declared righteous and made a new creation. But we can tap into the roots of her new identity and graft back in the habits of her old sin nature. Don't let her believe this food addiction could be related to a hole in her heart that only the Enemy can fill.

Don't let her see this as a sin against the Ghost's temple. She can minimize it in comparison to Brittany's sins—another way Brittany comes in handy. She can write it off as a phase. She can exercise incessantly, or not at all. She can gorge herself or starve herself. We don't care how they miss the mark. Only that they keep missing it.

Keep her blind to her self-destructive thoughts. Make her flail away in a vain attempt to swim, or give up and drown. Either is fine so long as she doesn't concede her inability to hold herself above water. And especially that she doesn't reach out to the Enemy's life preserver.

If we cannot deface the Enemy directly, we can cause His image bearers to either despise or worship their own bodies. What better way to spread graffiti on the Enemy's portraits?

Don't surrender an inch of turf, Foulgrin. And never let the Ghost change her from the inside out.

Keep her distracted with her own problems. Make her think of her needs, not of meeting others' needs. Don't let her realize that if she allowed the Enemy to use her to meet the needs of others, many of her most basic needs would be met as a by-product.

It doesn't matter if she dances about in pride and self-righteousness, or wallows about in humiliation and shame. What you must never permit is confession, repentance, transformation, and empowerment. Hell knows no fury like a vermin transformed.

Marring His image one sludgebag at a time,

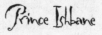

24

MAY 6, 1:24 P.M.

Ryan and Jodi sat on their living room sofa, Joey snuggling in Jodi's arms. Diane sat across from them in a loveseat.

"Thanks for letting me come over on such short notice. I just..." Diane shook her head, voice halting.

"Hey, Di, you know we're here for you," Jodi said. "What's going on?"

"Ever since Jordan died, things have been crazy at home. The kids need a dad and a mom. I can't be both. I'm not even good at being one."

"I feel bad, Diane," Ryan said. "I should've been over there for Daniel."

"You two have been so supportive. You've reached out to Daniel. He's just a tough case. Jordan was getting through to him, but then..." It took her a moment to continue. "Actually, the reason I came is Jillian."

"Jillian?" Ryan said. "We were thrilled she became a Christian. Is there a problem?"

"She's still dating Rob, isn't she?" Jodi asked. "Everything okay with that?"

"Oh yeah. Rob's a great guy. He loves the Lord. He's a better influence on Jill than I am. The problem is...Jillian's got an eating disorder. I've suspected, but I didn't say much. I didn't want to make things worse. But, yesterday I came home early from...and..." Diane put her head in her hands and started crying.

Jodi handed Joey to Ryan and joined Diane on the loveseat. She put her arm around her friend.

"She was in the bathroom, throwing up. Deliberately. She'd eaten a ton of junk food. I'm so scared. I don't know what to do. She won't let me help."

Jodi looked at Ryan. He nodded and took Joey out of the room.

"I have a little experience with this," Jodi said. "More than a little."

"What do you mean?"

"In high school I had to quit cross-country because of a back injury. I gained weight really quick. I got depressed. Eating was like a release for me. But I was frustrated with my weight. Throwing up seemed the perfect solution."

"What made you stop?"

"My parents' love and prayers helped a lot. What made me decide to fight back was learning more about it. I was in journalism and they assigned me to write a story about eating disorders. Talk about God's providence. When I found out about the physical consequences of bulimia, it scared me into taking it seriously."

"What consequences?"

"Digestive problems, decaying tooth enamel from the stomach acids, hair loss and on and on. I even read about women who died of a ruptured esophagus."

"I didn't know it was that bad." Diane's voice sounded hollow.

"I'm sorry to scare you, Di, but it really is serious. Not as bad as anorexia, maybe, but it's awful, I can tell you that. I wanted to quit, but it took awhile to retrain my mind and my body. I still fight it in my mind. I haven't given in to it for years. But I could struggle with those thoughts and temptations the rest of my life."

"Sorry, Jodi, but it's just hard for me to understand how it could be a temptation to make yourself vomit!"

"It's not that simple. God gives us desires for good things, like food, clothes, shelter, even sex. Some people have a weak spot for nice clothes or nice homes. Others are addicted to sexual immorality or pornography. For me, and I guess Jillian too, food is a weak spot. Big time."

"I thought eating disorders were a disease."

"I'm no doctor. But I know for me it's not a disease, not in the normal sense of the word. It's a temptation—and giving in to it is sin. Instead of looking to God to fulfill my desires, sometimes I've looked to food. Saying it's a disease only made me feel like it was catching the flu or getting cancer. Like there was no way to control it. I used that as an excuse. The Bible says without Christ we're slaves to sin, but as believers we're slaves of Christ. But even though I'm no longer a slave to sin, I sometimes act like I am."

"I can relate. In about a hundred other areas, anyway."

"Everybody has their struggles. That's how you can sympathize with Jillian. Admit one of your weaknesses to her. That'll break down the barriers."

"I've got too many weaknesses to choose from. But still, this is different. I can't understand what's going on in her mind."

"For me it was control. I wanted everything just right. Food was the one place I could take shortcuts and get away with it. Only I wasn't getting away with it—I just thought I was."

"But you stopped?"

"It wasn't simple. Those kinds of thoughts and temptations still come on me. It's a war going on in my mind—a spiritual battle, like the Bible talks about."

"I asked Jillian about counseling, but she doesn't want to see anyone."

"Once we found the right counselor, it really helped me. Just be sure it's someone who believes the Bible and understands bulimia. Otherwise, they won't deal with the root problem, they'll just try to change the behavior. If you want, I can talk to her, maybe help her understand it's serious, but not hopeless. I'd like to pray with her. If she agrees, we can find her a good counselor."

"Would you do that?"

"In a heartbeat. That's what church is about—we worship God and we help each other follow Him. Meanwhile, make sure Jillian knows you're on her side. She may fall a few times on the way. She needs to know you love her no matter what. Before I call her, though, you need to tell her you talked to me. She'll be angry at first. But tell her I've been there. In fact, I've probably gone a lot further down the road than she has. One thing's for sure—Jillian doesn't need to feel ashamed around me."

"What about this one?" Brittany asked, standing in the aisle of Hollywood Video. She was holding up another scary R-rated video with a half-dressed woman looking terrified.

"Sorry," Jillian said. "I really want something…cleaner. More…"

"Wholesome?" Brittany said, rolling her eyes, as if the word was the most stupid one in the dictionary.

"I'm not trying to be a party pooper."

"Well, you're succeeding!"

Jillian picked up a movie. "Remember this one?"

"*Arachnophobia.* Oh man. We kept jumping and knocking over the popcorn bowl." They laughed. Brittany pointed her finger at Jillian. "Then you flipped out and landed on my lap. From that point on, we were crammed in that tiny beanbag chair."

"It's scary without being dark and evil, and it's kind of funny too," Jillian said. She looked at Brittany. "We have so many memories together. What am I going to do when you leave me next year?"

Brittany wrapped her arm around Jillian. "You're going to come to San Diego State with me, that's what you're going to do."

"I'm not sure, Brit. It's a tough decision."

"Not for me. I can't wait to get away. I need freedom. Someplace people aren't looking over my shoulder."

"Maybe we need people looking out for us," Jillian said. "Accountability—that's what Kristi at church calls it."

"I don't need accountability," Brittany said. "Any more than I need wholesomeness."

"What's going to happen with you and Ian? Will you stay together?"

"All I know is, we're together right now. But I'm not leaving till early August to start volleyball, so why worry?"

"Have you talked about it?"

Brittany laughed. "Talk with Ian? We can get serious about his metaphysics. But about our relationship? Suddenly he's a dumb jock again. And I'm not much better myself."

"You'd be surprised what a serious talk could do for your relationship. Communication matters. It's sure been a big help to Rob and me."

"It's not like we don't ever talk. But neither of us wants to get that deep. We just want to have fun. I mean, I'm eighteen and he's nineteen. It's not like we're about to get married."

Brittany grabbed the movie out of Jillian's hands. "*Arachnophobia* it is. We'll relive old times. You still have that beanbag chair?"

They pulled out of Hollywood Video. As she waited for the light, Brittany said, "Whoa, midlife crisis at two o'clock."

Jillian turned her head to the right and saw a stunning silver sports car. The driver was a man in his forties wearing a pair of Oakleys and talking on a cell phone. "Wow! That car looks more expensive than our house."

"No kidding. It's a Porsche, isn't it?"

Jillian shrugged.

Brittany squinted at the driver. "He must've killed a lot of men to make so much money. I doubt he's from Gresham; the real drug money's down in LA."

Jillian laughed.

His light turned green and the girls watched the car speed off the line, leaving the man in the tan Toyota Cressida in the dust.

"That guy," Brittany said, "is definitely on a power trip. But then, if he was twenty years younger, I'd be willing to put up with a lot to ride in a car like that!"

As they drove, Brittany was uncharacteristically quiet.

"You okay?" Jillian asked.

"It's nothing."

"What's nothing?"

"It's just…my horoscope said something bad would happen tomorrow. But it also said it wouldn't be as hopeless as it appeared. I guess I don't like waiting to find out."

Letter 24

My not-so-cool Foulgrin,

Anytime adults become aware of this generation's problems and get involved in helpful ways, we lose. We feed on these kids' disdain for their elders. We must make sure they don't listen to their parents or church leaders or any adults. Except, of course, our representatives who try to make points with young people through scorning standards.

Get inside their pubescent brains, in order to best exploit them. Part of the young vermins' mocking the adult world is self-defense. It's a scary world. They have to take responsibility. Keep a job. Earn a living. Provide for a family. They're afraid of this. Instead of revealing their fear, they jeer what triggers it.

The kind of teachers, pastors and youth group volunteers we want are those who dislike the young. Because the kids intuitively sense this, these adults set themselves up for mockery.

Brittany's ridiculing her elders stems from pride. Coolness is our tool to reach this insecure, self-absorbed generation. Convince the young vermin that whatever isn't cool is undesirable. They'll mock elders and peers who fall outside the boundaries of their culture-driven lines of coolness.

When they're in church and see the deacon with the hairy nostrils and the woman with the lime green polyester pantsuit and the pastor with the old-fashioned tie and lame jokes, they think, "This isn't cool enough for me." The "this" is Christianity, the church and Christ Himself. Don't let them examine the logic—"Obviously, Christ can't be real, because that man talking about Him is wearing an ugly tie."

Our ability to control them comes out of the priority they put on being cool. Never mind that "coolness" has no objective quality. That it's limited to whatever is currently in vogue. That it's marketed to them by profit-hungry adults. Don't let them think in terms of good and bad. Or light and dark. Or righteous and evil. Have them think only in terms of cool and uncool. Trendy versus out of style. That way they'll judge beliefs and actions not on the basis of truth or goodness, but on the basis of newness and popularity. When we pulled off the great rebellion, we were nothing, if not cool!

Since truth by its nature is old, what's new is heresy. And since we control what's popular—through media, education, and peers—we have them right where we want them. Long live the holy trinity of Marx, Darwin, and Freud. Long live our high priests of popular culture: musicians, actors, and athletes. Welcome, vermin, one and all. Come join our Truth of the Month Club. Before we run out of false truths, you'll run out of life!

I hate all those bloated bags of slime. But it's the young I most detest. The great majority of the Enemy's followers turn to Him before age twenty-two. Our research department has proven that if the Enemy doesn't get hold of them by that time, He probably never will. (Though, annoyingly, the Enemy daily reminds us they're still within His reach.) So don't waste much time on the old ones. Why eat stringy old sheep when you can eat lamb?

This generation has been given more and less than any other. More wealth, recreation, technology, and free time. Less morals, guidance, discipline, and inspiration. They've been coddled and patronized. Bought off in exchange for their passivity. Parents smothering their children with toys and technology is my favorite kind of child abuse. The more they have, the less they enjoy. The more activities thrust upon them, the more they're bored.

Yes, Foulgrin, I too study the forbidden book, for intelligence gathering. Consider this statement: "They are filled with every kind of wickedness, evil, greed and depravity. Full of envy, murder, strife, deceit and malice. Gossips, slanderers, God-haters, insolent, arrogant and boastful; they invent ways of doing evil, disobey their parents, they are senseless, faithless, heartless, ruthless."

Sound familiar? An entire generation racing toward hell.

But now we come to the troubling part. On the one hand, this generation appears to be a lost cause. On the other hand, the Enemy keeps making unexpected inroads among them. Look at the abstinence movement. The rethinking of dating practices. The rediscovery of worship. The reading of the forbidden book. And biographies of great Christians, including martyrs. Look at the renewed commitment to evangelism. They boldly stand up for the Carpenter. They go to the streets to help the needy. They go to the far reaches of the globe to help the poor and share the Enemy's forbidden message. They rub this all in our face, Foulgrin. It's outrageous!

The official position is that this generation belongs to us. Many even of the church's adults have given up on them. Yet the Enemy ignores our claim. He works behind the scenes. He draws in one after the other to His kingdom. He's notoriously sneaky. No matter who says otherwise, He has not surrendered this generation of vermin.

We must convince adults in the forbidden fellowship to paint these youth with the broadest brushstrokes. Stereotype them. Never look at them as individuals. When they see someone like Daniel, make them see him as a disrespectful, no-good, self-centered little punk. Don't let them understand how lonely he is. Don't let them see that he's desperately searching for meaning.

If they understood his true state of mind, they'd see him as a prime candidate for conversion. If the church could get their own generational hang-ups out of the way and show him the Carpenter, he might become the Enemy's child. Don't let it happen, Foulgrin! You never know when the Enemy might try to take him hostage.

"Image is everything" we tell them. "Character is everything, appearance is nothing," the Enemy tells them. "Man looks on the outward appearance, but God looks on the heart," He says.

The Enemy has only the forbidden book. We have Madison Avenue. And Hollywood. And the mall bookstores. And the newspapers. Sometimes even the forbidden fellowship itself! How could the Tyrant hope to defeat us?

Staying cool,

Prince Ishbane

25

Brittany sat on the edge of her bathtub before school, eyes fixed on what she held in her hand. There were two pink lines on the end of the strip. She felt the tremble spread from her spine outward.

No. Impossible.

She reread the instructions and looked at the test again. The results were the same.

I'm pregnant.

"Wow," Rob said. "That's really weird."

"I swallow my pride and pour out my heart about an eating disorder and all you can say is 'that's really weird'?"

"What did you want me to say?"

"Maybe, 'that's okay, a lot of people have that problem, you'll make it.' Or even, 'I'm proud of you for working on it.'"

"I guess I just don't get it," Rob said. "You know it's not right. You know what you ought to do. So if it's true, deal with it."

"That's a favorite saying of yours, isn't it? But it's not always so simple."

"Sorry, but to me it is. If you know you shouldn't do it, why don't you just stop the binge eating and stop making yourself vomit? It doesn't seem that complicated."

"Yes, Mr. Self-Disciplined-Never-Have-A-Serious-Problem, I suppose it seems pretty easy to you. I guess you don't have any hidden vices, do you?"

"Yeah, actually, I do. One of them is why I asked you not to wear a couple of your out-fits."

"Never mind that they happen to be two of my favorites. Unfortunately, GAP isn't willing to take back things I bought six months ago because Rob Gonzales doesn't like them."

"I told you the problem isn't that I don't like them. The problem is that I like them too much. They make me think about…parts of you I don't need help thinking about. Like I told you, guys are different. It doesn't take much to put our minds where they shouldn't be."

"That's for sure. Or maybe I should say 'that's really weird.'"

Rob laughed. "Touché. But I don't go for counseling or take pills or have group meetings about my problems. I just talk to Jeff and a couple of guys, for accountability. Do you really think you need to get counseling for your…problem?"

"My bulimia? Go ahead and say it, Rob. Repeat after me: boo."

"Boo."

"Lee."

"Lee."

"Me."

"Me."

"Uh."

"Uh."

"Put it all together and what does it spell?" She moved her arms in a mock cheer. "Bulimia!"

Rob smiled.

"I didn't face it for a long time," Jillian said. "I just hid it. And Mom and Jodi say it gets worse when you hide it."

"It was God's work that your mom discovered this, Jill. He's looking out for you."

"It's humiliating, obviously, but I decided it's something you should know too, Rob. Who knows, maybe some day *you'll* actually have a problem, I mean besides…you know."

"Repeat after me. 'Lust.' It's just one syllable. Do I need to spell it?"

"Okay. Lust. I'll try to help you on that, you try to help me on this."

"It's a deal, but…how?"

"Tell me I'm okay the way I am. That I'll make it. If you see me fixating on food or bingeing, gently remind me."

"I'm all over it."

"Just don't forget the 'gently.'"

Brittany threw her backpack on the kitchen table and sat down, head in her hands.

No way; this can't be happening to me, she thought for the hundredth time. *I only forgot to take my pill once.* Well, it had been twice, actually. Or maybe three times. Four max. But still. Her older sister Tami and her husband had been trying to get pregnant for five years.

"How come those who want to get pregnant don't? And those who don't want to do?" She asked it aloud, though she wasn't sure who she was talking to. "I don't think there's a God, but if there is, just thought I'd tell You I'm mad at You! Are You punishing me because I'm not one of those perfect little Christian girls like Jillian?"

Brittany massaged her forehead, trying to fight off a massive headache.

What am I going to do?

She walked from the kitchen to her bedroom. She closed the door behind her and sat on her bed. Her eyes were drawn to the I Ching book. She grabbed a handful of coins, sat down on the floor and opened the book. She asked a question and tossed the coins. She added up the values.

Her sister Tami's face flashed into her mind. She felt her thoughts drawn toward something that happened eight years ago. Brittany had come into Tami's room and found her crying. Brittany was ten and Tami eighteen. She wouldn't tell her what was wrong. Later that evening, when their parents were gone, Tami's best friend came over. Brittany quietly listened outside her room. She'd heard the word *abortion*. She had to look it up in the dictionary. Now she was about to look it up in the phone book.

What other choice is there?

Her whole future depended on volleyball. If she was pregnant, she couldn't play, she couldn't keep her scholarship and she'd never be able to afford college. She was smart, with good grades, but she wasn't going to get a full ride anywhere without volleyball. Not at a college like San Diego State. Besides, she wouldn't be able to support herself or her child. Not by folding clothes and working the cash register at Old Navy.

The light stung her eyes, and she turned off the switch. A thought came to mind. For a moment, she considered it. Somebody who really wanted to have a baby could adopt it.

Maybe Tami would want my baby.

No way. She'd still lose the scholarship. And then there'd be seven or eight months of discomfort and humiliation. Parents would shake their heads at her. Jokes would fly around school. No. She couldn't let it happen. No one made fun of Brittany Powell.

Besides, what kind of a woman would give her own baby to somebody else?

Then, there was Ian. She couldn't let his life be messed up either. His parents would be furious. They'd never look at her the same way. They seemed to like her now, maybe because she projected the 'good moral person' image to them. But the game would be over. Even if Ian's family's church wasn't as narrow-minded as Jillian's, surely they'd condemn Ian for consorting with a prostitute.

Abortion really was the only choice. "No alternative," she could almost hear the darkness whisper.

She wouldn't have to tell Ian. She'd never tell anyone. It was perfect, an easy out. Two friends had told her they'd done it. One said it was no problem, but she'd never mentioned it since. The other's head had gotten messed up, big time. Now she slept with every guy who came along, and she'd been doing drugs.

Loser. I won't let that happen to me.

She turned the light on and pulled the phone book off her shelf. She saw in the Yellow Pages an ad with a picture of a young woman. The caption said, "Considering Abortion?" It was under the heading "Abortion Alternatives." She was drawn to the ad. She looked at the number. *No.* She pulled her eyes away. She wanted an abortion, not alternatives.

She looked down at "Abortion Providers." She looked back up for a moment at the other ad. It was called "Pregnancy Resource Center," and it looked warm and inviting. *No!* She reached into her desk drawer and grabbed a thick black marker. She ran it over that ad, blacking out the phone number entirely.

She laughed at herself. She couldn't believe she'd done that.

Her eyes went downward until they settled on the name of one clinic highlighted in blue. "Downtown Women's Center." The advertisement said, "Abortions through twenty weeks. Individual private personal care. *Se habla Español.* Speedy, flexible appointments. Cash discounts."

It was a nice ad. She dialed the number, not sure if anyone would be at the desk. They were. No openings on Saturday. She made an appointment for Monday morning, 10:00 A.M. Six days away.

Brittany went to the tarot deck, cleared her mind and asked guidance to draw the right card. She drew it and stared at it, hand trembling.

That's it. That's the answer I needed.

Letter 25

My control freak Foulgrin,

I've been reviewing your files. I was particularly interested in that episode with Jonathan Edwards. And the Amy Carmichael debacle. Then there's your more recent failure with a certain White House hatchet man who's now getting the forbidden message into prisons around the world. You made no mention of these in your vita. I wonder why.

Brittany wonders what kind of woman would give up her baby for adoption. You have to love it. Adoption, which gets an innocent child into a home where he's wanted, isn't a viable alternative. But abortion, which cuts the same child to pieces, is! Think of what we're pulling off here. We convince women who think it's wrong to give up a child to kill him instead.

The vermin can easily be distracted from the Enemy's primary cause simply by pursuing secondary causes. These don't have to be bad causes—in fact, the most distracting causes are often good ones. All that we work for comes down to this: get them to focus on this life and they'll never think about preparing for the next one. Don't let it dawn on them that their life on earth is but a dot. Or what they do while living in that dot determines the direction of their eternal line. Your job is to trick them into living not for the line, but the dot.

It's their worldview we want. Control how they see the world and we control them. If every belief is equally valid, no belief is worth their allegiance. We don't want the Carpenter's claims debated, we want them ignored. Since He created logic and reasoning, debate gets the issues onto His turf. We must use emotionally charged rhetoric. When there's no truth to defend a position, we must bury it under mountains of high-sounding verbiage.

I'd rather have them apathetic about everything than passionate about anything. Better they be indifferent to the Carpenter's resurrection than argue against it. Too often those who investigate the facts end up embracing Him.

I was happy to hear that Jillian has been regularly passing up evangelism opportunities. They'll watch someone fall off a cliff into the pit of hell before reaching out their hand and offering the Enemy's alternative. After all, the person falling may be "uncomfortable" with their attempt. "Love your neighbor" to them means "never say anything that could make your neighbor uncomfortable." Since the gospel always goes against the grain of their self-righteousness, it's often uncomfortable. Hence, there's always a compelling reason to remain silent.

Vermin consistently value the opinions of their peers more than the opinion of the Enemy. If other sludgebags applaud them, they imagine they've done right. Don't let them see the part of the forbidden book where the Carpenter tells His followers the world will hate, persecute, and resist them because of Him.

The unpleasant fact is this: The vermins' hearts long for the Carpenter. The forbidden book says He's full of grace and truth. Hence, their hearts long for grace and truth. Our job is to deceive them into searching for grace and truth in all the wrong forms, in all the wrong places.

The Pharisees affirmed truth at the expense of grace. Some forbidden fellowships do that, while others affirm grace at the expense of truth. Without truth, the counterfeit for grace is what they call "tolerance." This is simply cowardice. Without grace, the counterfeit for truth is rule keeping.

Ian's parents are part of a forbidden fellowship whose evangelism strategy is making sinners comfortable by never talking about sin. They never offend anyone. They lower the bar so everyone can jump over it. They can all feel good about themselves. What they think of as grace is nothing but lower standards.

The Carpenter never lowered the bar, He raised it. (Remember those words about looking at a woman lustfully being adultery?) But here's the trick—in the Enemy's grace, He offered the vermin the power to jump the bar. And when they fail, He's quick to forgive them. Fortunately for us, they have to ask.

When the forbidden fellowships minimize truth, people see no *need* for salvation. When they minimize grace, people see no *hope* for salvation. Either serves us well.

Use this as a model in your dealings with each of the young vermin, beginning with Jillian. Ask yourself, "How am I drawing her away from truth?" and "How am I drawing her away from grace?" Without truth or grace, they'll have no reference points, no direction, and no hope.

Unraveling whatever the Enemy sews,

Prince Ishbane

26

"We've done this three times and it's never been like you said," Daniel complained. "You swore you and Jillian and Brittany had contact with a spirit."

"We did. Or something," Ian said to Daniel, negotiating his way through the wet fog as he drove. "We just need to set the mood better."

"I still can't believe my sister did this."

"It was before she got so…religious, you know. Are you getting cold feet?"

"No way. I've done it with my friends. But nothing much ever happens."

"Well, it happened with us. And to make it more likely, we're going to the graveyard. Okay, we're both wearing black, that's good. We've got the CD player. If Nine Inch Nails doesn't do it, we've got Helloween on deck."

"What if we get caught?"

"Who else will be in a cemetery this time of night? Igor digging up graves for Dr. Frankenstein?"

"But we have to use our flashlights to see where we're going. And somebody could hear the music."

"We'll go way back from the streets. I scoped it out by daylight, remember? We'll go all the way in, under the big trees. But listen, Daniel, if you're too scared, let's back off. I don't want you wetting your pants."

"I'm not scared! I just don't think it'll work."

"If you don't have faith, maybe it won't."

"Okay, okay. I want it to work. I want to see the spirit move the pointer."

"Planchette."

"Whatever."

Ian pulled the car over, got out, and pulled up the hood on his black sweatshirt.

"It's cold," Daniel said. Dad's old black leather jacket wasn't as thick as he'd have liked.

"There's no wind," Ian said, holding up his hand in the deathly stillness. "That's good for the candles." He took out the black duffel bag and locked the car. They walked into the graveyard over the grass, ignoring the pathways.

"Should we be walking over the graves like this?" Daniel asked.

"Afraid somebody's going to reach up and pull you under?"

"No."

Ian felt something on the left side of his face. He stepped away. Something touched his nose. He swatted at it and jumped back.

"What's wrong?" Daniel asked.

"Uh…nothing. Just a branch or something. Let's keep moving."

They walked up a hill and down the other side, disappearing into the shadows.

"Nobody'll see us here. Let's set it up…there."

"Right in front of the tombstone?"

"On the tombstone."

"What?"

"Help me push it over." They struggled to loosen it in the dirt, finally wiggling it back and forth until it was on the ground. Grunting, they pulled it out of the loose dirt and laid it flat.

"We could get in trouble for this," Daniel said.

Ian pointed the flashlight at the headstone engraving.

"Roger Banish," Ian said. "Died 1978."

"Born 1959. That means he was just…"

"Nineteen."

"How old are you?" Daniel asked.

"Nineteen," Ian said, numbly. He opened the duffel bag, laid out a dark blanket, set up the candles, and took out the board. Ian set it carefully on the headstone. In the soft flickering aura of candlelight, the board took on a different feel.

"Turn on the music," Ian said. "Not too loud."

The eerie sounds of Nine Inch Nails climbed out of the boom box as though from way down under. It didn't sound as safe as it did through earphones in a bedroom.

Ian shivered. He looked at Daniel, hoping he couldn't see how scared he was.

"You okay?" Ian asked.

Daniel nodded, saying nothing.

"We can leave if you want to." Ian hoped he wanted to.

Daniel shook his head.

"Okay," Ian said. "Now clear your mind. I'm going to invite the spirits to visit us. Open yourself up. Repeat after me: 'Visit us, spirit.'"

"Visit us, spirit," Daniel said. Ian could barely hear him.

"Speak to us, master of the board."

"Speak to us, master of the board." Ian heard raw fear in Daniel's voice. It gave him a blood rush.

"Ask it a question," Ian said, resting his fingers lightly on the planchette.

Daniel put his fingers by Ian's. "Is someone there?" he whispered.

For a moment, nothing happened, then the planchette moved steadily toward the upper left of the board until it rested on the Yes.

"You move it?" Daniel whispered to Ian.

"No," Ian said. "Did you?"

"No way."

"Okay, here goes," Ian said, clearing his throat. "Tell us what will happen to me in the future."

Suddenly the planchette started moving from letter to letter. Keeping his left hand on it, Ian reached in the duffel bag and pulled out a notepad and pen. In the flickering candlelight he started jotting down the letters, many of them. Finally it stopped.

"Wow. This is a long one. I must have jotted down fifty letters. Did you catch what it said?"

"Some of it," Daniel said, voice shaking.

Ian held the flashlight under his left armpit and the notepad in front of him. He started drawing lines to indicate breaks between words.

"These aren't random," he said, voice slightly squeaking. "They're real words!"

"What does it say?" Daniel whispered.

"It says, 'Unexpected intruder could ruin your life.' Then it says, "'Must not let it destroy you.'"

"What's that about?"

"Don't know." Ian put his fingers on the planchette. "Who are you, spirit guide?"

The response came back, "Who are you?"

"Is it repeating my question? Or is it asking who we are?"

"Are we supposed to spell out an answer?" Daniel asked.

"I don't think so. I mean, it can hear us, right? Okay, spirit, I'm Ian Stewart and this is Daniel Fletcher. Who are you?"

The planchette moved quickly, spelling out, "Visitor from another world."

"An alien?" Daniel asked.

"Cool," Ian said. "Spirit, tell us your name."

At first nothing happened. Suddenly the planchette moved. Ian felt sure now Daniel was scooting it. Then he saw how terrified Daniel looked. Maybe not. Though it was very still, and there was no rustling in the trees, the candles swayed and flickered. The planchette jiggled until it came to rest on one of the letters.

"F," Daniel whispered.

It started moving again. It stopped on the G. It didn't start again.

"FG," Daniel said. "Who's that?"

"I don't know. Unless…" Ian thought back to that night last year when he and Brittany and Jillian had done the board. Ian shut his eyes. "Are you watching?"

"Yeah."

"Keep track of each letter and tell me what it spells." Ian readied himself. "All I want from you, spirit, is the last four letters of your name."

Ian shut his eyes tight, feeling now some wind, and the distinct sensation that someone was telling him "Get away." It was as if the wind was warning him.

Meanwhile, the planchette kept moving. It started and stopped four times. Ian trembled, feeling out of control.

"It's stopped," Daniel said.

Ian opened his eyes. "What were the rest of the letters?"

"G…R…I…N," Daniel said.

Ian swallowed hard. "Foulgrin," he whispered.

"Should we ask it something else?"

"It's your turn."

"Do you have a message for me?" Daniel asked.

The planchette was still, but Ian heard a soft moan from Daniel. He seemed to be staring at the shadowy woods. Ian followed his gaze and froze. Out of the woods came a huge form gliding toward them across the graves.

Ian couldn't get up.

The form drew nearer.

Suddenly a bright light shone and a powerful voice spoke in words Ian couldn't understand. He lifted his arms to protect himself from whatever it was.

"I said, 'What are you doing here?'"

Ian gazed at the image behind the blinding light. His aching eyes began to adjust. He saw a blue outfit, a bulging belt, and a badge. He finally exhaled, feeling sick and dizzy. He heard Daniel wheezing. He turned and saw the boy on his knees, bent over, hands on his chest.

Letter 26

My boastful Foulgrin,

Don't brag as though you're the expert on the O board. I was direct supervisor to Scalprake, the warrior assigned to William Fuld. He invented the Ouija board, with a little help from our friends. On one occasion when Fuld consulted the board, I myself took control of the planchette. I instructed Fuld to erect a building in which to manufacture the board, to get it into as many hands—and heads—as possible.

Tragically, our Mr. Fuld fell to his death from the very building the O board advised him to build! "Fell" to his death. Yes, that's what the newspapers reported. Once they serve our purposes they're always disposable. When the gum loses its taste, you spit it out.

Of course, we used similar devices with the Egyptians and Greeks. But the modern board resides in tens of millions of homes. Many of the early buyers hoped to communicate with spirits of dead soldiers. Then we spread it to college campuses, where we've pulled off some exquisitely engineered introductions to the dark side. Visitations. Possessions. Poltergeist. Sexual scandals. These were but a few of our antics. As always, by infecting the educated and influential, we established strongholds among those who set the tone of society. Why bother with the small fries when you can reel in the big fish?

It was my idea to sell the board's rights to a respectable company like Parker Brothers. Monopoly, Scrabble, LIFE, Clue and…consulting spirits of darkness. A nice mix of innocent fun, don't you think? One of my career highlights was the year many parents started giving O boards to their teens and preteens for Christmas. Many of us were amazed parents would give our loaded spirit gun to their babies to play with. And what delicious irony that this should be done on the celebration of the Carpenter's birthday!

Do you remember when our board outsold Monopoly? We entered 2.5 million new homes in a single year, and many of our boards had dozens of users each. You do the math. We're still reaping the harvest of the seeds sown then, and every year we plant a fresh crop. The cumulative deception and destruction from this board is incalculable.

And today? I just retrieved this info, fresh from ESD: Of all vermin involved in the occult, two-thirds were drawn in by their experimentation with the Ouija board! (For about one-fifth, the primary pathway was Dungeons and Dragons, so Ian and Daniel's involvement in that is also promising.) And listen to this, Foulgrin: Better than 50 percent of those who experimented with the Ouija board went out to obtain additional occult-type literature, whether from libraries, friends, or local book stores. Your Ian is one of those!

But here's the best news of all from our statisticians: Among Christian young people, 15 percent of junior high students have used the Ouija board. Among senior high students, it jumps to 26 percent. Twenty percent of Christian high schoolers have consulted astrology, and 16 percent have played Dungeons and Dragons. The figures are higher among non-Christians, but the difference isn't nearly as significant as you'd suppose. How satisfying to have this kind of foothold even in the forbidden fellowship!

One last notable finding: Of those Christians who eventually stopped using the board, nearly all of them stopped reading the Bible and quit serving the Enemy! The research confirms what we've long observed. Even when they don't perceive the board as working—or after they lose interest in it—if they don't repent of their actions, we still gain a long-term hold on them!

One of my subordinates, Fangnarl, has been especially effective. Chelsea Yarbro compiled her Ouija messages from "Michael" in three books, starting with *Messages from Michael*. Your inventory of Ian's books indicates that he has two of the three, and Skyla owns one. I thought Fangnarl's ploy of identifying himself with the name of the Enemy's highest ranking commander was particularly amusing. Who would hesitate to take advice from a spirit named Michael?

Think of the mileage we've gotten from *The Exorcist*. Horrible dreams even among Christians. Seduction toward other books and movies of the kind. Dulled interest in the Enemy. Most of the vermin never realize the book is based on a true story or that the infamous demon possession came about through—what else?—our Ouija board!

When they use the board, they give permission for an unknown spirit to communicate with them. If living in a war zone occupied by Enemy troops, would they open their front door to let in anyone who requested entry? Of course not. Yet that's exactly what they do in the metaphysical realm. Without open doors there's little we can do. The Ouija board is a powerful door opener.

Of course, many of their experiences with the board are nothing but conscious attempts at manipulation. Or subconscious efforts resulting in imperceptible muscular responses that move the planchette. But even in those cases, they invite outside intelligences to offer them guidance. It's every demon's dream!

Commercials for the Ouija board sometimes appear during Saturday morning cartoons. The manufacturer says it's for those eight years old and above. The younger the better.

Relishing our spiritual seduction,

Prince Ishbane

27

After he'd spent an hour at the police station, Ian sat in a holding cell with a couple of drunks. These weren't alcoholics, these were *drunks*, he told himself, and if he'd never been sure there was a difference, he was now. The two men were both heavy jowled and unshaven. He imagined they might be brothers, though one was more red faced than the other.

They sure smelled like brothers.

Ian's backside was wet. He smelled urine and kept checking to be sure it wasn't his pants. It wasn't, but he almost wished it was. Better his than someone else's. He kept moving away from his cell mates, who seemed always to inch back closer to him. They wanted to talk. He didn't. He just wanted out.

A guard opened a door and took Ian by the arm. As he stepped out he saw Daniel, looking even paler than usual; then he saw Diane Fletcher. Her usually pleasant face scowled. Her eyes shot fire at him. Suddenly he wanted to go back to his smelly roommates.

When Ian had squirmed and looked at the floor a full five seconds Diane said, "I really can't believe you did this to my son."

"I'm sorry, Mrs. Fletcher. Really. We were just having some fun. I didn't know it was against the law."

"You invite Daniel to spend the night to listen to music and watch a video. I say yes, thinking it's nice an older boy's befriended my son who doesn't have a father. And then you take him to a *graveyard* at two in the morning? What possessed you to do that?"

"It wasn't that something possessed me. I mean, it was just that…"

"Going to tell her about the Ouija board, son?" asked the same officer who'd brought them in.

"Ouija board?" Diane asked. "You showed Daniel a Ouija board?"

"I know how to use one, Mom," Daniel said, sounding embarrassed.

"Those are evil," Diane said. "Aren't they?" she asked the policeman.

"They're just a game," he answered. "But they do put scary thoughts into kids' heads. Next thing you know they think they hear voices and they decide to hurt themselves…or somebody else. I've seen it happen."

"Well, I keep finding out there's a lot I don't know about my son. *And* my daughter's so-called friends."

"I really am sorry, Mrs. Fletcher," Ian said. "It was my fault, not Daniel's."

"It was both of your faults." She put her hand on the back of Daniel's neck and walked out with him. The officer led Ian back to the holding cell. Ian was bracing himself to rejoin Tweedle Dum and Tweedle Dee, when suddenly a man in a business suit burst through the door.

"Hey, Dad. How's it goin'?" The moment he said it, Ian realized how stupid it sounded.

"Are you okay? Did the cops hurt you?" Ian's father glowered at the officer, whose hand was still on Ian's arm. "Take your hands off my son."

"If he's your son, maybe you should try putting your hands *on* him," the officer said.

"Beat him up, is that what you mean? You cops are all alike. If you hurt my son, you'll be hearing from my attorney." He pulled out his wallet and turned over a business card. "Badge number 215." He jotted it down. "Okay, I've got you."

"I don't suppose you're willing to let him spend the night in jail, so he could learn a lesson?"

"What kind of a father would do that to his son?" Mr. Stewart's words dripped with indignation.

"Oh, maybe…a good one." The officer bit his tongue a moment too late.

Mr. Stewart's face flushed, but suddenly his demeanor changed. He said to the officer, "So it's not a serious charge, right? Just criminal mischief, that's what they said on the phone. A misdemeanor? This can't ruin his scholarship, can it? You don't need to tell Portland State, do you? He has to be able to play basketball."

"Maybe you should stop talking to me about your son, and start talking to him," the officer said, and went back behind the desk, returning to his paper work. "If you're going to take him home, do it now."

"Of course I'm going to take him home. He's my son." He turned to Ian, a confused look on his face. "Don't worry, son, I'll get you out of this. We'll make sure you get to play."

◦⟋⟍⟋⟍⟋

Letter 27

My recalcitrant Foulgrin,

How refreshing to hear such excellent reports about Ian, Daniel, and Brittany. It makes me wish I was there for the kill—or should I say kills?

Ian's father is priceless. I adore this flavor of parent. They protect the family name and remove every consequence of their kids' misbehavior. They're angry at everyone but the guilty parties—their children and themselves.

The Enemy builds negative consequences for sin into life to teach them it's never in their best interest. This kind of parent undermines the Tyrant's intention. Ian's father teaches his son he's an exception to the rules. Daddy and Mommy will cover for him and make sure those mean old outsiders don't do anything bad to their precious little boy. This creates the finest kind of criminals, the white-collar variety who end up beating their wives and embezzling. Because his family's goal has been to make him *look* good, rather than help him *be* good, they'll stand up for him again. "His wife is exaggerating, and he was framed at the office. Poor boy."

Your report shows Ian's father has given his wife and sons material things to compensate for his absence. He takes pride in never having deprived Ian of anything. Of course, without deprivation the sludgebags cannot develop moral discipline. If they always get what they want, they can never be content with less. This is why indulging their children is a cruelty worthy of us. Inevitably it makes the little vermin unhappy.

Ian's father lives vicariously through his son's athletics. Just like many of the vermin mothers live through their daughters' cute little prom dates. He's a passive vermin who believes the way to deal with his son is to never be angry with him. Never blame him. Never punish him. Perfect. A night in jail and loss of scholarship could have been a wake-up call. Naturally, the last thing we want is for Ian to wake up.

The best part is that Ian's father thinks he's taking the parental high road. He won't confront his son because he thinks he'd lose him. He's unwilling to risk his son's disapproval, which guarantees he'll ultimately receive it.

What a contrast to an obnoxious Christian mother I worked with a few centuries ago. She raised her children in grace and truth. She prayed that when they sinned they'd get caught. Then, by facing their sin they'd experience the Enemy's grace. Two of those obnoxious offspring were John and Charles Wesley. You know how our kingdom suffered as a result.

The situation with Ian is well in hand, but I'm not as optimistic about Diane and her treatment of Daniel. The forbidden fellowship she belongs to takes truth too seriously. As long as she lets this incident slide, doesn't confront and follow up, we're all right. But what if she does follow through? What if she calls out for help from the forbidden fellowship? It could backfire. Feed her the conventional wisdom of "boys will be boys," "it's just a passing phase," and "parents shouldn't interfere with their children's choices."

Rules without relationship breed rebellion. Relationships without rules breed indulgence. Both rebellion and indulgence lead to the same end…death. That's why we love rules, as long as they are too few or too many.

There's no parent I fear more than one who'll admit he's wrong and come to his children and ask their forgiveness. Many barriers that appeared impenetrable have been broken through a parent's acts of humble contrition. *Don't let it happen, Foulgrin!*

Fortunately, we've been enormously successful in blinding parents to the symptoms of occult involvement. They seem oblivious to the recurring nightmares, insomnia, suicidal thoughts and murderous imaginations. But don't overdo it. Hearing voices and seeing apparitions are over the line. Even these parents might put two and two together, so use them judiciously. I'd far rather see a murder everyone thinks came out of the clear blue sky. You've heard the interviews: "He was a good boy; there were no warning signs."

I'm especially delighted to hear Daniel has his own Ouija board hidden in his closet.

His mother doesn't even remember his aunt gave it to him when he was eight years old? Marvelous. Everything's falling into place. Daniel won't just be our food. He'll be our fork to bring us more food.

In praise of the compensating parent,

Prince Ishbane

28

Ready for a shocker?" Brittany asked Jillian as they sat by themselves in a corner of Baja Fresh.

"What do you mean?"

"When I tell you, you might hate me."

"I'd never hate you, Brit. What's going on?"

"I'm pregnant."

Jillian froze. "You're kidding."

"No. That's one thing I wouldn't kid about."

"So…what…?"

"I've decided to get an abortion." She said it with no emotion, no explanation, no room for argument.

Jillian's throat felt as if she'd swallowed an orange whole.

"The appointment's Monday morning." Brittany's voice sounded rehearsed and mechanical. "I talked to the school nurse. She'll give me an excuse so my mom won't know I missed class."

Jillian stared at her.

"They say the pain goes away pretty quick." Brittany pulled out the brochure that had just come in the mail. She read aloud words she'd gone over five times already. "'Cramping might continue for up to an hour afterwards. Some women describe this cramping as uncomfortable but not painful, and others say the cramps were slight.' I'm not worried about it."

Jillian nodded slowly, chewing her lip.

"Since you're my best friend, I need to ask you a favor," Brittany said.

"What?"

"They say it's better if someone else takes you. A 'support person.' Would you go with me? Be my support person?"

Jillian's mouth opened, then closed.

"Jill, I'm kind of…scared. I need your help." Tears started running down Brittany's cheeks.

Jillian hadn't seen her cry more than a few times. "Brit, you know I'd do anything for you…" She got up and hugged her, then whispered in her ear, "Sure. I'll go with you."

Letter 28

My promising Foulgrin,

Two encouraging letters in a row. I must say, you're on fire!

I'm delighted at Brittany's willingness to sacrifice her child on our altar. Praise Moloch. There's nothing the Enemy hates more than the shedding of innocent blood. So there's nothing we love more. Nothing defines our control of a culture more than the frequency of child killing. Whatever they kill children in the name of—whether Moloch or choice or convenience or compassion—doesn't matter. What matters is the killing itself.

The Enemy's fond of His tiniest sludgebags. Often He uses them against us. He uses babies to turn irresponsible adults into responsible ones. He makes those who've scorned family values embrace them. What happens to the person who gives himself to care for the child? The elderly? The handicapped? He grows in compassion. Patience. Self-sacrifice. He becomes disgustingly less like us and more like the Enemy.

The more of the brats we can eliminate, the better. Our slogan on earth is "every child a wanted child." In Erebus we say it plainly: "Every unwanted child a dead child." When it comes to unwanted children, the Enemy seeks to remove the "unwanted." We seek to remove the "children."

Keep telling Brittany she's making the best choice for every person involved. Just make sure she doesn't think of the *primary* person involved.

Clouding Brittany's brain comes down to the pronouns. As long as the baby is an "it," not a "he" or "she," we win. Make it "terminating a pregnancy," never "killing a baby." It's all semantics. If a woman wants her baby, everyone recognizes the baby's real. Kicking inside her. Clearly visible in the ultrasound. "Do you know if the baby's a boy or a girl?" they're routinely asked. But if they want to kill the baby, then shut their mouths about such things. Make them pretend.

We've exalted the word *choice* to a sacred mantra. Keep their focus on the grand notion of choice and off the particular choice in question. Ask them if they're pro-choice and they'll say yes. Don't let them ask the obvious: "What choice are you talking about?" Are they pro-choice about rape, kidnapping, gay bashing, racial violence, and assault and battery? Of course not. Are they pro-choice about killing preborn children? Of course, because every choice is good, isn't it?

Don't let them see what laws against murder and rape and kidnapping and child abuse do—they all restrict a person's right to choose. In the Enemy's moral framework, one person's choice ends where another's begins. The woman doesn't choose to be raped. The Jews don't choose to be gassed. The blacks don't choose to be hung. The babies don't choose to be aborted.

We celebrate choices that inflict suffering on the weak. The Enemy doesn't. Our job is to make the vermin think like us, not Him.

Two go into the clinic. Only one comes out alive. Two victims for each abortion—one dead, one wounded. Two for the price of one! Hell's sidewalk sale.

Jillian's response was perfect. I couldn't have scripted it better. She's terrified of losing her friendship with Brittany. Imagine it—we can use the Enemy's own daughter to facilitate her friend's child killing!

Jillian will be one more agent of destruction, as much a part of the equation as our clinic employees. Meanwhile, you'll deepen Jillian's vested interests in abortion. People won't just defend any choice they make, but any choice they helped their friend make. They never want to admit to child killing. Who knows? Once you get Rob and Jillian fornicating, maybe she'll get pregnant. Then abortion will be a viable choice for her, too. If she drove her friend to get an abortion, why not drive herself? Or maybe Brittany will drive Jillian to the clinic. Friends and accomplices. Lovely!

Being a friend these days means not saying anything that makes someone feel bad. In the interests of "not judging" and "loving" each other, they aid and abet each other's self-destruction. Our semantics department has brilliantly twisted the word *friend*. The Enemy defines a friend as one who acts in another's best interests. This includes warning him to stay away from danger. And encouraging him to choose the path that brings safety. Our definition of *friend* is one who gives moral support by saying yes—even when someone's walking toward the edge of a cliff.

"Would you hold my backpack while I lean over the cliff and see what's below?"

"Of course, I'm your friend, aren't I?"

When their toes are dangling over the chasm's edge they say, "I'm afraid to step out any farther. I need your help. Would you give me a little push, please?"

"Certainly. That's what friends are for, isn't it?"

Ah, yes. That's what friends are for.

Killing off His image bearers one child at a time,

Prince Ishbane

29

Battling Portland's morning traffic and caught in a downpour, Jillian maneuvered across lanes. She pulled into the parking area on Fifth and College. She walked around the corner to Ondine, Rob's campus housing building. He was waiting out front, wet, with no umbrella.

"Sorry I'm late," she said.

"It's only a few blocks." Rob swung his fraying orange Jansport backpack over his left shoulder, and leaned under Jillian's umbrella. The air was heavy and wet, filled with the smell of fresh rain. It was unusually cold for mid-May.

"Did you get my messages?" Jillian asked. "How come you didn't call back?"

"How'd that thing turn out with Daniel and Ian?" Rob asked.

Is he deaf, or is he avoiding my question?

"Dad's friend Ryan took Daniel over to Ian's. He told Ian the Ouija board was dangerous. Told him he should trash it. And he asked him to keep it away from Daniel."

"How'd Ian take it?"

"You know Ian. Took it in stride. Ryan's cool too, but I doubt Ian listened to him."

"It's not easy getting through to Ian," Rob said. "I keep praying, 'Do whatever it takes Lord.' I'm starting to wonder what it *is* going to take."

As they crossed a street, Jillian asked, "So what's on the menu today?"

"First stop, Elementary Ethics. Ph202. I think they should call it Relativism 101."

"Why are you taking it?"

"I had an elective. Figured we'd have some interesting discussions."

They crossed Broadway and walked up a block. "Neuberger Hall—we're here." Rob took her upstairs. "Just to warn you, I've had a few run-ins with Prof James. We don't see eye to eye."

"Just don't get into a fistfight, okay?"

"Don't worry," Rob said as they sat down at the back. "Unlike you, I don't believe in hitting women."

"Very funny."

The door swung open and a slender professional-looking woman with short hair strode up to the lectern. She wore a sharp-looking blazer and carried an air of authority, yet appeared friendly. She had a briefcase in one hand and a cup of coffee in the other. She took a sip of coffee and pulled a stack of papers out of her briefcase. Jillian liked Dr. James immediately. She wondered what Rob's problem was.

After shuffling through her notes, Dr. James said, "We've explored different ethical systems. Now it's time to move on to specific issues. Since there are no moral absolutes, we should all be able to listen and learn from each other's truths. Here's one straight out of today's newspaper. It turns out Portland's chief of police is antigay. What do you think should be done?"

"How can you have a bigot as chief of police?" said a woman at the front. "He should be forced to apologize."

"And if he refuses?"

"He should be canned."

"Even if he apologizes," said a guy in front, "the damage has already been done. How can anyone trust him?"

After similar comments, Dr. James asked, "How many of you agree the chief should be fired?"

Twenty hands went up. Four didn't. Rob's was one of them. Before the teacher could say anything, Rob said, "I don't get it."

"What a surprise," Dr. James said. "Go ahead, Mr. Gonzales."

"You're calling him 'antigay' and a 'bigot.' But what are the facts? According to what I read in the paper, the man expressed in a church meeting his belief that homosexual behavior is wrong. He also made it clear that he believes in the civil rights of all citizens. He has no problem working with those of different beliefs, including homosexuals. His service record has proven that's true. You're talking like he beat up a homosexual. He didn't."

"Hate speech is the source of hate crime," said a girl. "If you say homosexuals are committing perversion, you have to take responsibility when somebody attacks them."

"Good point, Emily," Dr. James said.

"It's not hate speech to express a moral opinion," Rob said. "And it's not just Christians, you know. Muslims and Jews believe homosexual activity is wrong. Does that make them bigots?"

"I'm sure not all Muslims believe that," Dr. James said. "And I know not all Jews do. But that's not the issue. The question is whether a man should be allowed to make these kinds of prejudicial statements toward an important part of his constituency."

"I did a research paper on Dr. Martin Luther King," Rob said. "Did you know he spoke out against homosexual behavior? Should he be discredited for that? If he was mayor or police chief, should he have been canned? Should we stop celebrating Dr. King's birthday? If the city of Portland starts weeding out employees based on their religious beliefs and personal convictions, where does that stop? This is a first amendment issue. Doesn't the chief of police have the right to free speech?"

"Free speech is one thing," the guy in front said. "Bigoted speech is another."

"So he should only have free speech if our ethics class agrees with him, is that it?" Rob asked. "I mean, if he'd spoken up and said he thinks Christians are wrong about what they believe, like you're doing right here, wouldn't that be okay? So why isn't it okay to believe homosexuals are wrong? Aren't Christians part of the constituency, too?"

"I still say he should be canned," someone threw out.

"Are you going to hunt down other Christians in city government and fire them too?

Or is everybody entitled to free speech but them? Are you going to say all the people over all these centuries who have believed homosexual behavior is wrong are automatically stupid and bigoted and not entitled to an opinion?"

"The same people believed the earth was flat," Dr. James said. A ripple of laughter followed.

"Okay, if someone believed the earth was flat," Rob said, "would they have the right of free speech to express that belief? Or would we shut them up? If you're going to turn on the antibigotry detector, let's be sure it's pointed all directions. Where's all this tolerance you're always talking about? Or is it only tolerance toward *your* beliefs?"

Jillian squirmed. Everyone was looking at Rob. And at her.

Why didn't I visit a math class?

"Can him," the guy in the front said. Most of the class laughed.

"Well, okay, I think we're on the same page about the police chief," Professor James said. "I mean, the majority, anyway. Let's try another political hot button. Abortion."

Not this, not today.

"What are the ethical considerations in this debate?"

A blonde in a red linen blouse spoke up. "Legal abortion is necessary for women to have reproductive freedom."

"And equal economic opportunity," someone added.

"And control over our own bodies."

One guy with wire-rimmed glasses added, "Taya's right. I say abortion should be paid for through universal health care." He looked at the girls. Jill thought he was enjoying their nods of approval.

"It improves the quality of life for everyone," said an Asian guy.

Jillian looked at Rob. He was clenching his jaw. "Everyone but the baby," he said, a little too loudly.

"Are you referring to the fetus?" Dr. James asked.

"Call it what you want, it's still a baby. We all know it."

"Mr. Gonzales, can we steer clear of religious comments?"

"I didn't say anything about religion. I was talking about the facts. Heartbeat, brain-waves, separate human DNA."

"But what really makes a person?" Dr. James asked.

"Intelligence," the guy with the wire-rimmed glasses said.

"Yeah," added Taya, "so like a dolphin could be a person, too." A few people laughed. Strangely, Jillian thought, *very* few.

"I think a person is anyone created in the image of God," Rob said. "And that means all humans are people. It's not about IQ or age or size."

"That might be true for you, but it's not for me," said Taya.

"How can something be true for me, but not for you?" Rob asked. "If it's true, it's true for both of us. If it's false, it's false for both of us. Abortion is either right or wrong. I say it's killing a baby. That's wrong."

"If there's one thing I can't stand, it's intolerance," Taya announced. The majority of the class nodded in agreement.

"So you can't tolerate intolerance?" Rob shook his head. "If we're just sharing our preferences, what's our ethical standard? Personally, I don't believe in my preferences. I believe in God's law."

"I'm going to have to ask you again to leave your religion at home, Mr. Gonzales," Dr. James said. "This is a classroom, not a church. Now, let's get back to the issue: what does anyone *else* have to say about abortion rights?"

Rob chewed on his pen. He was silent the last twenty minutes. Jillian felt tense and embarrassed. She couldn't wait for class to end. When it did, they walked out of the classroom. People seemed to keep their distance from Rob.

"Does this happen all the time?" Jillian whispered.

"I try to pick my battles. But today was just too much. I had to speak up."

Had to?

Jillian wanted to tell Rob about Brittany. *No,* an inner voice told her—that would be violating confidentiality. Besides, Rob wouldn't understand. He was a nice guy, but the teacher was right—he was awfully opinionated. She didn't want him to think less of her or try to talk her out of standing with her friend. Then she sensed another nagging voice. It argued against the first voice, and wouldn't leave her alone.

Letter 29

Lord Ishbane,

It's good to be back on campus. I have fond memories of working with the strategic assault team to redesign Western higher education. What we've accomplished is mind-boggling. Nowadays, the basic criterion for teaching ethics is denying objective ethical values.

In the old days, many of them didn't *live* by the Enemy's standards, but nearly all of them *recognized* them. A man might commit adultery, but he'd admit he was wrong. Today the man has good reasons for his adultery. He makes it sound justifiable, even virtuous. They commit immoral acts, all the while taking the moral high ground.

The trick isn't getting them to do evil. They do that on their own. The trick is getting them to believe—and persuade others to believe—their evil is good.

If the vermin know a foot is twelve inches, that consensus allows them to make measurements. But what we've done is break the ruler in pieces. Now it's as if they're saying, "A foot is only five or six inches to me, and three inches to him, and seven inches to you." We've regauged the basis for objective measurement.

"There is no truth. You're no different in kind from the animals. There's nothing beyond the grave, nothing for you to live for." No wonder colleges have such high suicide rates. The students are clearly getting our message!

The Master is wise to assign our troops disproportionately to college campuses. Why bother with drug addicts in the gutters when we can go to the universities and target the influencers of education, business, and politics?

While I'm pleased with Dr. James, I was disturbed when Rob spoke up in class. It's particularly bothersome that Jillian witnessed this. When one of them is bold, it encourages the others. This is why I detest student-led prayer and "See You at the Pole" gatherings, as well as "Life Chain" and other public events. Even bumper stickers and T-shirts can be bothersome. I'm committed to keeping Jillian a passive, compliant people pleaser, the kind of Christian who poses no threat to us.

As Talon stood guard over Rob, our many warriors in the classroom labored to close the minds of Rob's classmates. They kept whispering phrases like "religious superstition" and "narrow-minded bigot" into their pea brains. Most of the students follow the teacher's lead in dismissing statements made by Christians. The trick is to let them imagine the rest of their insect-brief lives that "back in college I investigated Christianity and decided it was wrong." We convince them they've tried Christianity and found it wanting, when they've found it challenging and never tried it. We convince them they've seen through the Christian faith, when they've never seen the Christian faith at all.

There are forms of stupidity they must be highly educated to commit. If the world came about by chance, then of course anything—homosexual behavior, adultery, abortion—would have no meaning. It would all come down to point of view. Truth would be relative. In contrast, if the world was created by a God whose character and commands dictate moral values, then truth is not relative.

Since we've permeated the modern mind—and contaminated many Christian minds in the process—with the notion of evolutionary randomness and moral relativism, many of the vermin are incapable of carrying on intelligent moral discussions. In the end it always comes down to "but this is what I feel." Since their feelings are rooted in their sin natures, and reinforced by us and the world, their rules of conduct cannot rise far above their depravity.

Since Rob insists on standing up for his beliefs in the classroom, I'm doing what I can to encourage him to be the self-appointed truth police. I'm urging him to fight for truth, not for the souls of sludgebags. I'll make him a crusader, interested only in his agenda, using truth as a weapon rather than a bridge. He may win arguments, but he won't win people. And since it's people going to hell, not arguments, who cares?

I've trained Baalgore to coax Rob into majoring on truth to the exclusion of grace. Meanwhile, I'm convincing Jillian to major on grace, to the exclusion of truth.

As for Jillian hearing Rob speak up about abortion, I'm working on damage control. The Enemy is attempting a coup. Until Monday, I plan to keep Jillian away from strollers, baby shoes, and her little brother. I'm blinding her to the vermin child inside Brittany. If she does think about speaking up, I'll convince her that the real ethical issue isn't the baby, but whether or not to hurt Brittany's feelings.

I'm laboring to make confidentiality—not truth or holiness or preserving life—Jillian's highest moral principle. By not seeking wisdom from her mother or anyone else, she can blindly facilitate her friend's immoral choice. She can actually believe she's a principled person while assisting in destroying a child and ruining her friend's life.

That's my calling card. I supply them good reasons for doing evil.

Fluent in the language of lies,

Lord Foulgrin

30

~m~

Jillian had been holed up in her room for hours, staring blankly at the plaid patterns on her bedspread. She'd called Rob and left a message, but he hadn't called back. Again. She had this picture of him sitting there hearing her talk into the air, choosing not to pick up.

What's going on? As if I didn't have enough to worry about.

"Knock, knock."

Jillian's mom came through the partially opened door, arms full of laundry.

"What's going on, Jilly? You've been walking around like a zombie all day."

Jillian covered her eyes. Diane dumped the pile of clothes on the bed and grabbed her daughter's hands as she sat next to her.

"What is it, sweetheart? The bulimia?"

"No. Jodi's been a big help with that. Those verses she gave me to memorize, plus she calls me. Just knowing she's going to call helps. I've got the counseling appointment next week. I'm doing pretty good, but it's not easy."

"No," Diane said. "I'm struggling with stuff that isn't easy either. But something's wrong with you, Jilly. What is it?"

"It's Brittany, Mom. It's not just one thing either. She's been spending lots of time with Skyla. I admit, I might be a little jealous. But I'm really worried about her. You know what Brit said? Skyla offered to put a curse on Kelly for what she did to me."

"A curse? I thought this witchcraft stuff was a joke, like a rerun of Samantha and Darrin on *Bewitched* or something. Didn't you say they're committed not to harm anyone?"

"That's what they claim, but I've heard they make exceptions, like when people do bad things and cross them up."

"Do you really believe that stuff works?"

"I guess not. But there are some creepy stories. Like Corrie last year—when she got on Skyla's bad side, then ended up paralyzed in that skiing accident."

"Your dad and I talked with Ryan and Jodi about Satan and demons. I don't remember the Scripture passages, but I think they said demons can't exercise any power over Christians unless we give in to them. So I don't think you need to be worried about a curse. Is that what's bothering you?"

Jillian sighed. She turned away, burying her face in her pillow.

After a few silent moments, Diane said, "I want you to know I'm here for you. Whether you take my help is up to you, but I'll keep offering." She tucked a few curls behind Jillian's ear and stood, then walked toward the door.

"Mom, wait." Jillian turned around and sat up. "It's about Brittany, but Skyla's not the main thing. Brit's…she's…*pregnant.* And she's getting an abortion."

Her mom sat down. Jillian told her everything.

"What can I do? I'm her best friend. That means supporting her no matter what."

"Do you really believe you should help her…do that?"

"I'm not excited about it, but yeah, I guess I do. Don't you?"

"I probably did when I was your age. But let me ask you something. If Brittany decided to attempt suicide again, and she asked you to help her take her life, would you do it?"

"Of course not!"

"But you said friends support friends in everything they want to do, right?"

"Well, not *that.*"

"Okay, what about that teacher you guys can't stand. What's his name?"

"Mr. Weaver." She shuddered.

"What if Brittany came to you and said she had a gun and she'd decided she was going to kill Mr. Weaver. What would you do?"

"You're getting creepy on me, Mom."

"What's your answer?"

"I'd try to talk her out of it."

"But what if she said she'd made up her mind? What if she said she really needed you as her best friend to drive her to his house Saturday morning to kill him? Would you do it?"

"Of course not!"

"Then why would you drive Brittany someplace to kill her child?"

The words hung in the air.

"That's different," Jillian said weakly.

"Is it? How?"

"Well, killing herself or killing Mr. Weaver is just plain wrong."

"And killing a baby?"

"Don't put it that way."

"Why? Because it doesn't sound nice? Remember when the doctor told your father and me we should abort Joey because he might have Down syndrome? We said 'no way.' And you said you agreed with us, remember? After he became a Christian, your dad reminded me several times what you said—'Keep the baby, lose the doctor.' He was so proud of you."

"But you guys were married. And you were old. I mean, older."

"So? That doesn't change the fact this is a baby, does it?"

"But it can't be very big yet. I mean—"

"Don't go there, Jillian! I played that game when I was your age."

Silence fell like a rock from the sky.

"What do you mean you played that game?" Jillian asked.

Diane stared at the floor. Finally, she put her hands together, pressing them awkwardly.

"I was a freshman in college. I got off away from home, and the rules all changed overnight. No parents to watch me, tell me what to do. I wasn't prepared. I got involved with somebody and next thing I knew…I called it 'terminating a pregnancy'—but eventually I realized what I'd done."

"What are you saying, Mom?"

"I'm saying I wish my best friend hadn't driven me to the clinic. I wish he'd tried to talk me out of it. I wish he'd given me an alternative. That's what I really wanted. Or even if I didn't want it, that's what I needed."

"He? Your best friend was a *he?*"

Diane nodded and swallowed hard. "My best friend was your father."

"You guys had an abortion?"

She nodded again. "He would've been twenty-three in November."

"Who?"

"Your brother."

"No way."

Diane tried to steady her voice, but every word shook. "A few weeks after your father became a Christian, he asked me to…forgive him." Diane sobbed.

Jillian reached out to embrace her. In that moment it hit her that her mom had a life, too—just as real and just as important as her own. It was so obvious. Yet somehow the thought was brand new.

Diane cried a few minutes. Then she said, "I didn't know if I could ever tell you. I was so ashamed. But see, Jilly, it happened to me. You can't know how much I wish I'd had a best friend talk me out of it. You just can't let Brittany go through with this. Not without trying to get through to her."

"Yeah, but…if I tell her she's wrong, it's like saying she's a horrible person. If I don't help her, it'll ruin our friendship. I can't win either way."

"You can win by doing what's right. God's your judge."

"Brittany's pretty good at being my judge, too."

"But you won't stand before her when you die, honey. You'll stand before Jesus."

"But I'm her friend."

"Yes, exactly! You're not thinking right, Jilly. This is what I hear you saying. You could help Brittany make the worst mistake of her life and do something she'll always regret. Or you could risk losing her by trying to convince her not to kill her baby. God might use you to save her from doing something horrible that will always haunt her. The question you have to ask yourself is, what does true friendship mean? Is it going along with everything somebody wants to do, right or wrong? Or is it caring enough about someone to stand up to her when you know her choice will cause death and heartache? What are friends for?"

Jillian closed her eyes. "I should've told her it was wrong to sleep with Ian."

"This is even more wrong, Jilly. Big time. Now's your second chance to speak up."

They heard the baby starting to fuss.

"The doctor was right about the Down syndrome," Jillian said. "But he was totally wrong about aborting Joey."

Diane nodded. "Hang on a second."

A minute later her mom walked back in with Joey in her arms. Jillian looked at the big smiles on their faces. She reached out her arms to take her brother.

"We realized it didn't matter how young or how small he was," Diane said. "Joey was a person. It didn't matter what anyone thought, what might be easier for us; we didn't have the right to take away this life God had created. It isn't always easy, Jillian—not in this world. But making the right decision, even when it's hard, always pays off."

"If you'd gotten an abortion...I can't even think about it." Jillian cradled him in her arms. "Sometimes it's hard to take care of Joey. But I can't imagine what it would be like without him. I want him to be ring bearer in my wedding someday."

"So what will you tell Brittany?"

"I can't help her do this. Why did I think I could?"

"There are so many lies out there, sweetheart. Your dad said he thought it was the devil, convincing people not to care about God's littlest children."

"But, Mom, her mind's made up. I know Brittany. There's no way I can talk her out of it."

"All you can do is try. And pray. You're getting baptized in a few weeks, right? That's taking a public stand for Jesus. You remember the day your father and I were baptized? I'll never forget it. I was so nervous, so worried about appearances, that I'd look silly going down under the water. But when I did it, I knew it was right. And I felt so good that I'd followed through. If you do the right thing with Brittany, no matter what she thinks, you'll know Jesus approves. You can't make Brittany's choices. But you have to make your own. That's all God expects of you."

Jillian looked at her mom, then she stood and stepped close to her. They both bowed their heads, eyes focusing on the child in their arms. Diane Fletcher prayed. Her daughter followed.

Letter 30

My struggling Foulgrin,

Stop whining about how Jillian's life is taking an unexpected turn. You can't handle a teenage girl? They're just makeup, hair spray, clothing, and gossip. Isn't that what you told me? You poor devil. Shall I send in reinforcements?

Get your act together, Foulgrin, or there'll be *hell to pay!*

My mouth waters for Brittany's child. The irony is especially delicious since our Brittany wants to be a surgeon who saves the lives of babies. With just a few twists along the way—this being the first and best—you could turn her into an abortionist herself. She could dedicate her life to killing children in the name of rights and virtue. She could receive awards from NARAL, NOW, Planned Parenthood, or any of our affiliates! Deaden her conscience now. It will pay great dividends later. Give me an abortionist over a Satanist any day.

Remind Jillian how devastating it was when she apologized to Kelly. Convince her it'll be much worse if she confronts Brittany. Cause her to believe the Carpenter would never ask that she do something so painful. He's too loving and compassionate.

They're the entitlement generation. Things have come easily to them. They've been raised from the nursery to believe they have a long list of rights and a short list of responsibilities. They have everything, but think they deserve more. They don't thank the Enemy that their needs are provided for. They live on the level of wants, guaranteeing they're always discontent. Their parents have trained them admirably.

Smother the vermin in prosperity. Curse them with good health. Lead them down the easy street to hell, in comfort and abundance. We can pick the meat from their bones later because we've labored to fatten them now.

As a fish doesn't notice water, they don't notice their cultural context. They're immersed in their society's way of thinking. It manifests itself in every conversation, news report, billboard, class lecture, and office policy.

Our worldview infiltration is so insidious they never pick up on it. When they watch a movie, they see that when two people are attracted to each other, they go to bed together. Do the characters ever examine their souls and ask whether it's morally right to have sex outside of marriage? Of course not. With this as their steady diet from childhood, how could they be shocked at fornication? It's not the exception, it's the rule. It's how life works. It's fun. It's normal.

Control their worldview and we control them. Stay under the radar. As long as they don't see you, they'll never resist you.

Better to have them apathetic about everything than passionate about anything. I'm even uneasy when they passionately embrace our error. There's always the possibility their passion will turn toward the Enemy. That vermin Paul brought to the forbidden faith the same zeal with which he'd persecuted Christians. It's the apathetic who serve us best. We love inertia. Those who do nothing do our will.

Think how time-consuming it would be to individually deceive every human heart. That's why we need the media. Through screens and speakers we control their pulses, fuel their passions, and pour their soft squishy minds through our funnel into a Jell-O mold of cultural conformity. Their minds dulled, their senses numbed, they become our automatons. Even in their enslavement, we convince them they're free. It's Christianity that enslaves, we tell them. It seems ludicrous to think they'd fall for it. But they've been doing it for centuries.

Poison a water supply at its source. Their minds are the headwaters of their actions. Our lyrics run down their minds like rust runs down a sink drain. Nothing distracts and contaminates like a nicely placed television commercial or a song on the radio.

Lead the vermin down the cultural slippery slope, right into your claws. Wrap the present nicely. Let them untie the bow expectantly, looking inside for the treasure…the poisonous viper. It bites their miserable hands and injects its venom. Then comes the fun part—watching our prey fall to the ground. Writhing. Shaking. Choking on their own vomit.

It doesn't get any better than that.

Finally, Foulgrin, I have a suggestion regarding Daniel and Ian. Have you ever masqueraded as a departed human spirit? This is often effective. Other spirits may frighten them. But a familiar human spirit offers comfort and takes them off guard. Since we have access to extensive information, you could easily convince them you're a departed loved one. You can recite incidents. Nicknames. Details. Surely, they'll suppose, a loved one from the great beyond would do them no harm. In time, you'll no longer need the board to speak to your prey. He'll hear you always, inside his head.

Bankrupting this disconnected generation,

Prince Ishbane

31

MAY 19, 2:27 P.M.

It was Friday morning, three days before Brittany's appointment. Jillian still hadn't found the right time to talk with her.

Before school, Brittany was frantically cramming for a first period economics test. It wasn't the time. Their passing periods were only eight minutes long, just enough to catch up with what was going on in each class. It wasn't the time. During lunch, Jillian and Brittany were surrounded by other people, talking and laughing. It wasn't the time.

After school, Jillian walked Brittany to the parking lot. It still didn't seem the right time. But time was running out.

"We need to talk, Brit. Let's get in your Jeep."

"Okay, little Miss Assertive. What's up?"

God, please help me say the right thing.

"Have you given your situation any more thought?"

"You mean the abortion? I'm okay with it. As one of your Bible-thumping friends would put it, I've got a real peace about it."

"Where does that peace come from?"

"What's that supposed to mean? Everything's confirmed it's the right decision. You agreed to drive me. And the I Ching showed me it was right."

"I should have spoken up the other night, Brit. I'm sorry I didn't. But I don't think you should get the abortion. What you have inside you is a baby."

Brittany's eyes narrowed into slits. "Oh praise God, I have my own little guardian angel who will save me from myself and my wicked plans."

Angry tears filled Brittany's eyes.

"You think I want to drag myself through this?" Jillian asked. "I wish I could tell you what you want to hear. I wish I could say abortion's the way to go, that it'll make everything all right. But that's a lie. A lie from…the pit."

"Like I didn't think this through?" Brittany said. "I even went to the tarot deck and drew a card. It showed me I was headed the right way."

"What card?"

"The Death card. I knew what it meant immediately—I needed to assert myself, take control. I couldn't just let my life go down the tube. That's the passive way. I had to take control. That's what being pro-choice is about. It's the best thing for everybody."

"Ironic it was the Death card," Jillian said. "Because that's exactly what this is. Taking an innocent life."

"What's your problem?" Brittany reached under the seat and pulled the lever stretching out backward, her nearly six feet taking up a lot more space than a moment before.

Jillian felt compelled to back off. She felt the wrestling in her stomach and in her soul. Finally, she dug in her heels and spoke again.

"Remember how you didn't know the meaning of the fetal images on the Death card? Well, maybe it relates to the devil being a killer of children. There's a lot of societies that have sacrificed their children to their gods."

"I don't believe in gods."

"Money's a god."

"Yeah? Well, I don't worship him."

"But isn't it your career you're concerned about? You want to be a great surgeon, make a lot of money, right? And your baby would get in the way of that, wouldn't he? So an abortion would be sacrificing your child for the sake of education and money and career goals, wouldn't it? Seems like that would make money your god. Or convenience."

"That's easy for you to say. You're not the one who's pregnant! I just want a choice, some control over my life."

"You already made a choice by sleeping with Ian. If I'd been a better friend, I would've spoken up about that a long time ago. I'm sorry I didn't. And isn't control a god too? I should know. I've worshiped at that altar, with the whole food thing. The Death card is the control card? Who is it that's trying to persuade you to put your child to death? It's the devil."

"Just because he's on a tarot card or in the Bible doesn't make the devil real," Brittany said. "I'm not sure I even believe in the devil."

"Well, just because you don't believe in him doesn't mean he'll disappear in a puff of smoke. You don't have to believe in him to serve him. In fact, maybe it's easier if you don't." Jillian sucked in a deep breath. "I've got a passage of Scripture I wrote out. I want to read it to you." She pulled a folded index card out of her jeans pocket, hand shaking.

Brittany gave her a sideward glance and did her famous eye roll. "You really have gone off the deep end, haven't you?"

"It's from Psalm 106. It's talking about how God's people mingled with the nations and adopted their evil customs. It says, 'They worshiped their idols, which became a snare to them. They sacrificed their sons and their daughters to demons. They shed innocent blood, the blood of their sons and daughters, whom they sacrificed to the idols of Canaan, and the land was desecrated by their blood. They defiled themselves by what they did; by their deeds they prostituted themselves.'"

"Are you calling me a whore?"

"No. I'm just telling you what God says about child killing. It's not only killing, it's not only an offering to demons, it's self-destructive. It defiles you as a person. It turns you into someone you don't really want to be. I don't want to see you become that kind of person, Brit."

"I don't need this." Brittany's voice was cold and loud. "I thought you were my friend."

"Friends don't let friends drive drunk...or kill their babies."

Brittany took a deep breath and pressed her back against the driver's seat, as if trying to force it one more inch. "I was wondering how long it would take you to decide your good-girl rep's been tainted by hanging around a pagan like me."

"That's not true, Brit. That has nothing to do with it. Friends tell each other the truth. And the truth is, this is wrong. It's going to hurt you. And it's going to kill an innocent child. Your child."

Brittany lowered her voice to a mocking whisper, "I'm *so* glad you're my conscience, Florence Nightingale. But I don't think you've been in this situation before, have you, O wise one? It's always easy to judge someone when you haven't been in her shoes."

Jillian swallowed hard. "Mom and I talked."

"That figures. Why should I trust my former best friend with a secret?"

"Look, Brit, Mom loves you. And I'm going to tell you something. She gave me permission. She and my dad had an abortion when she was your age. And she's regretted it ever since."

Brittany stared at her. "That's her problem. I'm not going to regret it."

"How can you know that?"

Jillian saw a moment's vulnerability in Brittany's face, a touch of softness. But suddenly her glare returned. The mask was back on. Big time.

"If your conscience needs to be appeased," Brittany said, "I hereby release you of all responsibility for me and my problems. Go ahead and break your promise to drive me to the clinic. Maybe I can find a real friend."

"Brit, don't—"

"Get out."

Jillian stared at her, seeing boiling hatred in her eyes.

"I said, get out!" The scream was so loud Jillian's eardrums throbbed.

Jillian opened the door and stepped out. Before she could shut the door, Brittany slammed the Jeep into reverse. She yelled out the window, "If you can't support me when I need you most, it's the end of our friendship! Go hang out with your church friends. You hypocrites deserve each other!"

Brittany popped the clutch. As she peeled out, gravel sprayed in Jillian's face.

"Your mom would kill us both if she knew we were doing this," Ian said, as the clock neared midnight.

"If you're too scared, we can stop," Daniel said. "I don't want you to wet your pants or anything."

Ian slapped Daniel lightly on the side of the head. "Getting feisty with me, huh, little fella? Okay, but if you let the word out, I'll deny it. It'll be your funeral. I don't want your mom dragging in Jill or Rob either."

They asked the board a few warm-up questions and got some modest movement.

"The spirit seems to be responding more to you this time," Ian said. "Talk to him."

"What should I say?"

"Ask him who he is."

"It's probably FG again."

"You don't know that. Ask him."

"Spirit, who are you?"

The planchette pointed to J. Then to F.

"JF? Who's that?" Daniel asked.

"Maybe it's not finished. Maybe the J was a mistake. It's probably just F, for Foulgrin. Wait. It could be JFK—John F. Kennedy. That would be cool! You might have stopped too soon. Ask him again."

Daniel readied his fingers and touched them lightly to the pointer. "Who are you?"

Again the planchette moved to J, then to F. It stopped.

"Okay, it's definitely JF," Ian said. "Who do you know with those initials? Of course, from what I've read it could be some Scotsman who died three hundred years ago. See if the spirit knows you. Test him. Ask him some specific questions."

"What's my birthday?"

The planchette went to the number row, pointing to one, then two, then stopped on five.

"One twenty-five," Ian said. "January 25?"

"No," Daniel said. "My birthday's December 5."

"But that's…twelve five. Wait. That's what it was saying, isn't it?"

"I didn't move it."

"Me neither. Besides, I didn't have a clue when your birthday was. This is it, Danny! Ask him something else."

While Daniel tried to think of something, the planchette started moving. Every time it stopped on a letter, Ian called it out. He had one hand on the pointer. With the other hand he wrote on a note pad. When it stopped, Ian read it aloud: "You can talk to me through the board any time, Danner."

Daniel turned white.

"Danner? It doesn't know how to spell your name?"

"It's a nickname."

"Who calls you Danner?"

"Nobody anymore."

"What do you mean, anymore?"

Daniel looked at the board, seeming not to hear Ian. "Who are you?" Daniel asked. He took his hands off the planchette. Only Ian's fingers were on it.

"What's going on?" Ian asked.

"D…A…D."

Ian stared at Daniel, who looked like his face had been drained of every ounce of blood. "The spirit is…your dad?"

Letter 31

My derelict Foulgrin,

What the heaven's going on? Talk to me. Without information my claws are tied.

When you last wrote, I was disturbed by your allusion to Jillian's worship in church and youth group. Most of these groups used to sing feel-good campfire songs. It gave them a vague sense of camaraderie but didn't draw their thoughts to the Enemy. I love watching their half-hearted attempts at singing. They look like they have to go to the bathroom but know they can't for another hour.

But things are changing. Some young vermin are getting lost in worship. It's the worst possible scenario. Our greatest asset is their self-absorption. We've cultivated this from the cradle. But now they're singing songs that humble themselves and exalt the Enemy. Some are actually believing the words. They're riding them into the terrifying abyss of the Enemy's vastness. This is intolerable, Foulgrin. When they truly encounter Him, they are changed. And we are defeated!

External revisions we can tolerate. A touch of self-reform? A bit of conformity to the standards of a religious group? No problem. But when they focus on Him and shift into the background? When they find pleasure and delight in such metaphysical experiences? Then we're in serious trouble. The occult will hold no lure for them. Why settle for supernatural counterfeits when they can have the real thing?

Whatever experiences they have at church make little difference to us, except one. If they end up gazing upon the Enemy, meeting Him personally, giving Him praise and adoration, it's time to tremble.

Disillusion Jillian and Rob with church. Convince them church exists to meet their felt needs, not so they can be used by the Enemy to meet others' real needs. Turn them into restless consumers, moving around and sampling from the smorgasbord. Fashion them into the sort of adults who hunt for the best preaching, music, and programs. Let one bad experience lead to another until they become professional church critics. Don't let it occur to them that the problem with churches is simple—they consist of people like themselves.

Rob and Jillian are reading a book on Christian martyrs? Unacceptable! If they must read Christian books, give them celebrity fluff and pop psychology and trendy youth books. Keep them away from the forbidden book and anything that challenges them to break with normalcy. Don't let them rise above the commonness of their generation. The young ones are terribly dangerous. They've not yet settled into a long-term lifestyle of materialism. They haven't walked as far down the path, so it's easier for them to change directions.

The habits they establish now they'll carry with them. What if they gain a heart for evangelism? Global missions? Prayer? Giving? There's a huge danger they'll carry this over to their adult lives. They may cultivate these repulsive mind-sets in their children,

Beelzebub forbid. Then, instead of parents doing our work for us—raising children in self-indulgence, superficiality, and indifference to suffering—they could end up doing the Enemy's work for Him. They could raise children in strength of character and depth of faith. I tremble at the thought.

Obsmut has given me a copy of your own writings on materialism. I agree, it all comes down to physics. The more things the maggot-feeders accumulate, the greater their total mass. The greater the mass, the stronger its gravitational pull. This sets the vermin in orbit around their things. Finally, like a black hole, their money and possessions suck them in. They become indistinguishable from the things that hold them.

The struggles that forged their past heroes are largely gone. Heroes never emerge out of ease and prosperity. But because they still need heroes, we've redefined them. Now a hero is someone who dribbles a basketball. Or sings into a microphone. Or repeats memorized lines in front of a camera.

The young are especially hungry for heroes. We've given them celebrities, characterless hero substitutes. When a generation has no one of character to look up to, they look up to those with talent, charm, and fame. Rob, Ian, Jillian, and Brittany all have this in common: They desperately long for people to believe in. Make sure the Carpenter and His representatives in the forbidden fellowship don't become those people.

Youth remain at the top of our hit list. Hang on to them now, and they'll remain ours. True, when the ravages and weaknesses of old age come, many slip through our fingers. They turn to the Enemy they've had no time for. Our Master is relocating more troops to rest homes and hospitals to counteract the Enemy's presence there. But even when He snatches them from us near the very end, there's consolation. All those years they could have been furthering the Enemy's kingdom they were instead furthering ours.

The worst case scenario is for them to come to the Enemy young, then serve Him for a lifetime. It's unthinkable, Foulgrin. We must not let it happen.

With stakes at their highest,

Prince Ishbane

32

Soon. Soon. Do it soon.

The bottle of pills seemed to call out from the darkness of the desk drawer as if it were a living thing. Days at a time, good days, used to go by without any thought of the pills and the book and the plan. Now not a day went by, sometimes not an hour, without the mental images of the plan playing themselves out, props in place, action taken. The envisioning now came more frequently and without warning. The images were so tangible. What had been unthinkable now became thinkable. And doable.

Soon. Soon. Do it soon.

Sunday afternoon, while her mom napped, Jillian held Joey in her arms. She looked into his almond eyes. One of her tears dropped on his cheek and rolled down. Why did she sense he understood intuitively so much she didn't? What made her feel as though he wanted to tell her something? Was it him trying to communicate to her? Or was someone else trying to speak through him?

When her mom woke and took over with Joey, Jillian went to her room. She stretched out across her bed. She thought about going to the computer to put down her thoughts. No. This needed a more personal touch. She took some green flowered stationery from her desk and began to write a letter. She poured out her heart through the pen.

"Brit," she wrote at the top. "First, I want to say how much I love you. Since the first few weeks after we met, I've considered you my best friend. I've done a lot of thinking about what my mom said, and also what you said. I've decided Mom's right. True friends are willing to risk hurting their friend's feelings to help her do what's right. I've decided I'm willing to risk having you hate me in order to do what's best for you. It might not seem like it to you, but I'm making a sacrifice to act as a true friend."

She paused, pen in hand, asking her Father to speak through her. She wrote again, thinking the words herself, yet sensing they came from Another.

"I'm not judging you. I don't condemn you. But I do think you're doing the wrong thing. And it's not too late, Brit! Of course, I can't stop you from messing up your life. But I can make sure I don't help you do it. I want to spare you the hurt that will fall on you if you do this thing. I hope my telling you I can't drive you to the clinic has made you think. If I've made it difficult for you, well, that's the best thing. I hope it's so difficult you decide not to do it. I couldn't live with myself knowing I'd helped do this thing to you and your baby." She prayed God would give her the next words. "Something so dark and evil."

She looked at the words and started to cross them out. Surely she shouldn't use words like that. *No? Yes?* She decided to leave them. They were true, and they were spoken in love. Isn't that what she'd read earlier in Ephesians—"speaking the truth in love"?

"Remember how you've always told me I should stand up and not let people push me around? Well, I'm standing up now, Brittany. (Though maybe you don't like it if it means taking you on.) That's why I decided I wasn't going to let you pressure me into driving you to the clinic. This isn't the old passive 'make people happy' Jillian speaking. This is the new 'have the guts to stand up to people and do the right thing' Jillian.

"Jesus said, 'Do unto others as you would have them do unto you.' Well, personally I want the kind of friend who will tell me the truth and be willing to sacrifice to help me do what's right. So I'm determined to be that same kind of friend for you.

"I was holding Joey this afternoon. You know how we've talked about that look he gets on his face, like he's tuned in, like he understands things better than we do? Well, there's a little Joey inside you, a tiny miracle that could bring you joy. Please Brit, let him live. If you do, I promise to help take care of him whenever you need me. If you need money, I'll work extra hours. If it comes to it, I'll sell the Saturn. If you need a shoulder to cry on, I'll be there for you. If you decide to give him up for adoption, I'll make phone calls for you, go to a lawyer with you, or whatever's involved. I'll be right there next to you. I'll do anything for you."

Except the one thing you want me to do.

Jillian wrote a little more, then sealed the envelope. She sensed Brittany's anger, desperately wishing she could defuse it. She felt a pressure on her head and shoulders, and a sudden urge to tear up that letter.

No!

She grabbed her keys and drove the familiar three miles to Brittany's. She reached out for the doorbell. The letter looked enormous in her hand. It felt so heavy.

You'll look like a fool. She's going through with it anyway. Why make her hate you?

No one answered the door. Jillian turned to leave, then stopped. She felt simultaneously pushed toward the car and pulled back to the door. She gave in to the pull instead of the push. She went back and slipped the envelope through the mail slot, then walked away. She sat in her car, not knowing what to do next.

"Help her, Lord," she whispered. *"Please. Brittany really needs Your help."*

"When can I get my computer back?" Daniel asked in a sulky voice.

"We said it would be a month before we even discussed it," his mother said. "I don't know what we'll decide. But if the computer comes back, it'll be just like Ryan said—with a service provider that screens out the worst stuff, and one of those filters too, just to make sure, and a record of all sites visited that can't be tampered with. And it's going to be in the family room, not your bedroom, with the screen turned out toward the center of the room."

"I know, I know. I've heard all this a hundred times."

"That will be best for everybody, honey." She put her arm around him. He pulled back. "What have you been doing by yourself in the room all this time?"

He shrugged. "Music. Homework."

"Why don't you spend more time out here, with your family?"

"I need the computer."

"We'll decide in another week."

"Dad says it's okay."

"What?"

"To get the computer back."

"Dad says…? Your dad bought the computer, is that what you mean? Yes, but you know how strongly he felt you shouldn't be viewing those things."

"Maybe he doesn't feel that way anymore."

"But your father's…Danny, what are you talking…?" Diane suddenly looked at her watch. "I'm late. We'll talk later." Within forty seconds she was out the door.

Daniel retreated to his bedroom. He turned off the lights.

Brittany stood by the living room window, peeking through the vertical blinds, watching Jillian sitting in her car. How dare she try to pretend they were still friends? What was she doing out there? Waiting, so she could yell at her and call her "baby killer"? What right did she have to call her names?

Forget it. I'm not talking to you until this thing's done. Maybe not even then.

She removed her fingers from the blinds. Her eyes fell on a picture sitting on the coffee table. She and Jillian had their arms wrapped around each other. Their eyes sparkled. Jillian's strawberry curls had sprung loose, giving her a wild look, and she was on her tip-toes. Brittany was bending forward, her long straight dark hair flowing over her shoulder. Their cheeks were pressed together. They looked so different it was comical—but the real differences were inside. How could they ever have become best friends?

Jillian's car started. Brittany's daydream vanished. Best friends no more. She picked up the envelope that had fallen through the slot. She held it on the edges, as if to avoid putting her fingerprints on it. It was silly, but she was afraid to hold it. She went to her bedroom, dropped the unopened envelope into the trash, then climbed into bed. She opened her nightstand and grabbed the well-read brochure. She'd nearly memorized it.

"'The most frequent response women report after ending a problem pregnancy is relief.'"

It'll all be over tomorrow.

She looked at the address on the brochure and the little map. She didn't go to that part of Portland often. She hoped she wouldn't take the wrong exit. The fear of not finding the place almost seemed like reason enough not to go through with it. No, that was stupid. She'd just leave early, with her cell phone, and call the clinic if she got lost.

After an hour of tossing and turning, she got up and retrieved the letter from the garbage. Before she opened it, she promised herself she wouldn't let it affect her. As soon as she finished the last word, she neatly dropped the letter back into the trash.

Put garbage where garbage belongs.

She went to her desk and pulled out the tarot cards. She picked four of them from different places in the deck, then turned up the top one. The Emperor card. She looked at the explanation sheet to see the meaning of the card—it said "May you be master of your realm."

Yes, my body is my realm, no one else's.

Next she pulled the High Priestess. She smiled. It was her favorite. It was a confirmation. She needed to stay on the throne of her life—not let a medical condition dethrone her and ruin her dreams.

Then she pulled the Fool card.

Yeah, I'd be a fool if I didn't do this. I'm graduating in three weeks. I can't be pregnant at graduation.

Finally, she pulled the Death card. She winced at the fetal images near the skeletoned devil's sharp scythe. Yes. The meaning was clear. It was all about control—she needed to take control of her life. She needed to get this abortion. It would be best for her. Best for Ian. Best for…everyone. She reached for the phone.

"Skyla? Hi, it's me. I need to ask you a favor." They talked for twenty minutes. Skyla reassured her she was making the right decision. No question about it. Skyla was a true friend. Not like Jillian, who'd called her a baby killer.

It's just a short procedure. Then it's over. It's all over.

Brittany collapsed on her bed, barely managing to pull the covers over her. She lay in the dark shivering, exhausted, feeling as if she were poised on the edge of a yawning chasm.

Letter 32

My surprisingly stupid Foulgrin,

There's nothing better than bringing shame to the Enemy's name by luring His children into immoral escapades, then hanging out their dirty laundry before the world. Sexual and financial scandals are my favorites. How many leaders, families, churches and organizations have been brought to ruin through them?

But there's another tactic that's just as satisfying. This is the *false* accusation. In Brittany's mind, Jillian has called her names. She's called her a "baby killer." But Jillian hasn't called her a name, has she? Not once. Yet Brittany's convinced she *has*. So convinced she could probably pass a lie-detector test.

When their consciences tell them they're doing something wrong, they imagine others have attacked them. In fact, their own conscience has done the finger-pointing and name-calling. We have the fun of deceiving them into doing the sinful thing, then making them feel miserable about it. But it doesn't stop there—next we trick them into blaming Christians for it! We get them coming and going. We impose on them the guilt feelings, without the downside of their turning to the Enemy to have their guilt forgiven. There's no forgiveness without confession. And there's no confession as long as they have someone else to blame!

Christians can have a calm dialogue in which they show kindness and concern toward a homosexual they disagree with. But invariably we can convince others that the Christians have behaved as gay-bashing homophobes! (Sometimes they have, of course. But I'm talking about when they haven't.)

Between now and her abortion appointment, you must keep convincing Brittany that her friend has betrayed her. For no one can take seriously the advice of a traitor.

One of the most pernicious secrets about the forbidden book—one which young vermin in particular must never be allowed to grasp—is that the Enemy repeatedly appeals to their own self-interests. When He calls upon their sense of righteousness, this is rarely a threat to us, since they're so inherently unrighteous. But they drip with self-interest. That makes it a hazardous grounds for appeal.

If we could set the rules of the game, we'd make it off-limits for Him to appeal to their self-interest. His argument is insidious—that they should obey the Enemy's commands not simply because doing so is *right*, but because doing so is *smart*.

If the young vermin caught on to this, do you realize how hard our task would be? If Ian and Daniel actually understood they're ruining their lives through their fascination with the occult, it wouldn't be so easy, would it? Brittany thinks she must choose between having an abortion or acting against her best interests. What would happen if she saw that the Enemy actually wants her happiness? Or that what He commands her to do would be best not just for the baby, Ian, her mother and friends, but for *her*?

They all seek pleasure and happiness, Foulgrin. No matter what means they employ to get it. No matter what wrong paths they travel searching for it. They never move except as a response to desire. Whether it's the desire to please the Enemy or to satisfy a moment's yearning, *it's always about desire*.

The Enemy is the great hedonist, always offering delights; throwing parties; staging banquets, feasts, and festivals. That's why we must fill the air with noise to block these sounds from our prey. Fill their tiny minds with sounds so loud they cannot hear the echoes of His celebrations.

Since they seek happiness with such passion, we must teach them it's wrong to seek happiness. Or that happiness can be found outside the Enemy.

I see from your report that each of our young vermin—and even Diane Fletcher—is contemplating choices that could take them toward the slaughterhouse. Close their eyes to the Enemy's warning not to destroy themselves.

The Carpenter told them to believe and obey His words that they might be like a *wise* (He didn't say "righteous") man who built his house on the rock, rather than a *foolish* (He didn't say "unrighteous") man who built his house on the sand. To Him, smart and right are the same. Stupid and wrong are the same. We dare not let the young fools grasp this. If they did, they would look at life in a radically different way.

Wisdom is our enemy. It counts the costs of wrong choices and anticipates the rewards of right ones. If they rehearsed in advance the consequences of dabbling in the occult, eating obsessions, suicide, sexual immorality, abortion, and a host of other choices, they would be terrified. They'd flee from them. Not because they're virtuous. But because the looming consequences would frighten them off, just as the promises of reward would pull them toward Him. Our greatest secret is that the Enemy wants them happy. And that what is right is always smart.

Keep convincing them the Enemy's ways will rob them of fun. And our ways will fill their lives with good times. Think of it as a campaign promise, Foulgrin. Once we get their votes, why would we keep our promises?

Working the campaign trail,

Prince Ishbane

33

Brittany woke up, feeling heaviness on her chest. She didn't want to get up…ever. But she felt driven, compelled to follow through with her decision, not to let anything or anyone postpone it. Groaning, she raised herself out of bed.

She'd had bad dreams, she knew, but couldn't recall most of the details. She'd dreamed of being a high priestess in a chair, like the one on the tarot card. Then she'd dreamed about the children her sister couldn't have, about the little kids next door she'd baby-sat, and about little Joey Fletcher, who loved her as much as she loved him. These images kept assaulting her brain even as the hot shower pounded her. She lathered up over and over again. Once she got home from the appointment, she decided, she'd take another shower, long and hot and soapy. It would wash away her tears and make her clean.

She opened her eyes, looking down at her flat stomach, wondering how soon before it would have given her away. No matter. She'd be back in the bikini this summer.

"The entire procedure takes ten minutes. It'll save me nine months of grief." *How can anything be bad that takes only ten minutes?* Murder and rape came to mind, but she quickly pushed the thoughts away, angry at Jillian for making her feel guilty.

Brittany dried herself, then put on loose-fitting clothes, as she'd been instructed. Even though it was a cloudy morning, she grabbed sunglasses, the darkest ones she had.

"Bye, honey."

She heard her mom go out the front door, headed for work.

It was a good thing Skyla would be there for her. It would have been a lonely drive. Too much time to think. Who knows, she might have chickened out.

I guess this is when you find out who your true friends are.

Brittany's eye caught the letter in her trash can. She grabbed it out of the trash, so quickly she startled herself. She tore it in half, then in quarters, and threw it back into the trash. She stomped a foot down into the bin, so hard it hurt. She even thought about burning the thing.

I'll show Jillian. I'll tell her how easy it was—if I ever talk to her again, which I won't.

She reassured herself with words pieced together from the brochure, the school nurse, and a Planned Parenthood speaker in her health class two weeks ago. Where some of the words came from she wasn't sure. But they made her feel better.

She went downstairs, trying to remember if it was okay to have orange juice. She sat on the couch, staring at the clock. She wasn't sure of the proper etiquette. *Do you come early or right on time when you're going to kill your child?*

Where did that come from? She cursed Jillian for poisoning her mind to even think that way.

The living room clock chimed. Skyla appeared in the driveway. Right on time.

With Skyla's smiling face at the door, second thoughts and doubts disappeared. Brittany swallowed the lump in her throat, and climbed into Skyla's car. She recited to herself all the reasons she couldn't go through with this pregnancy. *My scholarship. My future. Reputation. Popularity. Appearance. Ian. Everything.*

She rehearsed what she would say to Jillian later. *It went fine. It was easy. No pain. No problem. No regrets.*

"I wrote the address down," she said weakly, handing a paper to Skyla.

"Don't need it. I know right where it is. And after we're done I'm taking you out for ice cream—jamoca almond fudge!" Skyla said.

Ice cream? Skyla seemed bubbly. She talked incessantly about Brittany doing the right thing and about how nice the people at the clinic were, and how one of them was a prominent Wiccan she knew well, and how smart and rich she was. Brittany heard just enough to distract her from the warring voices within, the compelling urges both to do and not do what she was about to.

They sat at a stop light that seemed to last for decades. Skyla had the radio on now, singing along. Brittany wanted to go back to bed and sleep forever. Sleep. Sleep without dreams. A familiar thought pressed on her mind. *Why not? It almost worked before, in the garage.* She'd do it right this time. She had a half dozen other methods circled in that book from the Hemlock Society. One involved a plastic bag, another a razor blade. The book was still in her desk. Maybe tonight she'd look it over again. If death was the solution for her baby, why not for her? As they got closer to the clinic, Brittany's breath got shallower. She wasn't listening to a word Skyla said. She eyeballed an oncoming truck, and tried to will it over into their lane.

If she was driving, she'd maybe pull over, turn around, go back home. But she wasn't in the driver's seat. Someone else was.

Skyla pulled into the parking lot. The building was a cold gray, with smoke coming out a pipe on the roof. A garbage collector was emptying a huge dumpster. She saw mounds of plastic sacks fall into the truck's cavernous mouth. She slowly got out of Skyla's car, reaching for the bag they'd told her to bring. She walked around the corner and made her way toward the front steps. She was grateful not to see any of those people holding signs or giving out pamphlets. She'd feared their presence might have kept her from going through with it. But the lady on the phone assured her if the nutcases were there, they'd have one of their volunteers escort her in.

Eyes to the sidewalk, a step behind Skyla, Brittany turned the corner, put her hand on the dark rail and started up the steps. Suddenly Skyla gasped and stopped in her tracks. Brittany bumped into her. She looked up at a familiar face.

"Hi, Brit."

Brittany felt her face flush as she stared over Skyla's shoulder at Jillian Fletcher. Jillian was holding something—a blue blanket—and peeking out from the blanket were two almond-shaped eyes.

Brittany stared at Joey, then let out a low groan and bent over, one knee on the step.

"Who do you think you are?" Skyla asked.

"I'm her friend," Jillian said.

"Come on, Brit," Skyla said, pulling up on Brittany's arm. "They're waiting for you. You'll feel fine in an hour."

"She won't feel fine the rest of her life," Jillian said.

Brittany looked at Skyla, then Jillian. Suddenly the door opened. A thirty-something woman stepped out, wearing a vest that said "Escort."

"She's harassing you, isn't she?" the woman asked Brittany.

"She sure is, Marli," Skyla said.

"Leave her alone," the woman said to Jillian. "And get off our property, or we'll call the police."

Brittany saw Jillian pull Joey close to her, away from the woman.

"I can see it now," Skyla said. "Little Miss Perfect Ex-cheerleader arrested. That would be great. Come on, Brit. It's your decision. Don't let her do this to you."

Another woman came out the door. "Don't let her upset you, sweetie," the clinic worker called to Brittany. "Come on in with Marli and me. We're here for you."

"Sweetie?" Jillian said. "You don't even know her. She's *my* friend, not yours. You're just here to take her money. Are you going to be there for her five years from now? I don't think so."

"Let me help you inside," Marli said, grabbing Brittany by the arm. "We'll get you away from this fanatic." The escort bumped hard into Jillian, jostling her. Joey cried.

Brittany shook off the woman's hand.

"No. I'm not going in."

"You can file charges against her if you want," said the employee.

"I'm canceling my appointment."

"There's no need for that. Everything's under control now. She won't hurt you."

"I'm not going to do it."

"We may have to charge you a cancellation fee," the woman said.

"Tough," Brittany said, standing tall now, next to Jillian and Joey, taking off her sunglasses and staring down at the woman.

Jillian handed Joey to Brittany. "Can you hold him till we get to the car?"

Brittany turned her back on Skyla, Marli, and the clinic worker.

"Don't leave, Brit," Skyla said. "You're making a big mistake. You'll regret this."

Jillian led Brittany to her car, parked around the block. She got in and shut the doors, dropping the power locks immediately. She reached for Joey and buckled him in the car seat. She put the Saturn in reverse, then jammed it into first and moved quickly out of the parking lot.

As they drove away, Brittany watched Skyla talk with the women. She got the distinct feeling they were all part of the same team.

Jillian drove around the corner. After they'd gone five blocks in silence, she pulled over, put the car in park and breathed deeply.

"Funny how they think choice is so great as long as you're making *their* choice," Jillian said. She turned to Brittany. "Are you okay?"

Brittany stared straight ahead, then suddenly started crying. Jillian stretched over and put her arms around Brittany. She felt her friend tremble.

"I almost…" The sobbing grew louder now.

"But you didn't, Brit. You didn't."

Letter 33

My incompetent Foulgrin,

You had her on our turf? Right there at the mouth of our stronghold? And *you let them snatch her out of your hands?* There are three of our warriors at those clinics for every one of theirs. All the odds were with you. How could this have happened?

I don't care that twenty-three other vermin babies were killed that day. Is that supposed to be a consolation? Their attackers weren't under my charge. You are. This was a staggering failure. It's not just that the baby didn't die. Who knows now what the Enemy may do in Brittany and Jillian as a result? The Enemy's always weaving together seemingly unrelated events to accomplish His subversive purposes. What, for instance, do you suppose are the chances of Brittany ever becoming *our* kind of surgeon now that this has happened?

We've harassed, humiliated, impoverished, and ruined the reputations of Christian vermin. We've persuaded them to stop standing outside our clinics. We've convinced even their fellow Christians that it is judgmental and inappropriate for them to intervene on behalf of women and their children. They should just quietly look the other way while babies are killed. They need to be more tolerant. Not butt in to others' lives. Yet despite all we've done, this weakling Jillian Fletcher showed up? It's unthinkable.

While you were working on Brittany, the Ghost took hold of Jillian! You were distracted. Faked out. How does it feel, Foulgrin, to have been defeated by a passive dysfunctional teenage vermin and her idiot baby brother? Wait until this story gets around headquarters. You'll be a laughingstock. But we both know who won't laugh…Beelzebub! Reservations for the House of Corrections are being made. I attach to this message the latest full-color brochure.

You will have to pay for your incompetence. But as long as you're assigned to me, I must continue to guide you. Not all is lost.

Use with Jillian, Rob, and Diane the same strategy I recommended you use with unbelievers. Convince them that obeying the Enemy is to their disadvantage. Disobeying Him will give them the edge. Persuade them that the Enemy is always wanting to throw a wet blanket on the party. Obscure the obvious, that it's the Enemy who created pleasures for them. That it's He who fashioned their desires for these pleasures. That it was *we* who were the party poopers, and have been crashing and trashing parties ever since. (Of course, we had compelling *reasons* for leaving the party. Not least was the fact that the Host ruined everything by wanting to turn over prominent positions in heaven to this pathetic race of rodents.)

Despite the teachings of the forbidden book, let them think the Enemy offers them no joy. Only marching orders. No pleasure. Only drudgery. Cultivate in them that gray, joyless, lemon-sucking Christianity that serves us so well.

Set up the false choice—pleasure on the one hand or the Enemy on the other. This is the heart and soul of our con job. While the forbidden book claims God is for them, we argue the opposite: "God is against you."

To top everything off, I've heard through Baalgore that Kristi, the meddlesome youth pastor's wife, has talked Jillian into being baptized. This is the biggest outward line in the sand the Enemy calls on them to draw. I cringe when I remember how the early Christians declared at their baptisms, "I renounce thee, Satan, and all thy service and all thy works." This clean break from the past washed away our strongholds. They'd burn magic books and jewelry and remove all remnants of our influence.

Fortunately, these days they come to the Enemy, are baptized, and join the church with no instructions on making a clean break from things we've used to hold their families captive for generations. They can still have their horoscope books and occult movies on the shelf. Tarot cards in their game drawer. New Age music in their CD rack. Occult games on their hard drive. Posters of devil-worshiping rock stars on their wall. (The more of this in their homes, the more bridges for us to cross over.)

Baptism is robbed of some of its power by these compromises. But make no mistake, Foulgrin. It remains a terrifying act of aggression against us. The Enemy holds it in the highest regard. He empowers them through this act of boldness to stand more firmly in a hundred other areas.

You've failed miserably in this latest episode. Try to redeem yourself by convincing Jillian to change her mind and postpone her baptism. Pull out all the stops.

Stunned at your strategic blunder,

Prince Ishbane

34

Any questions on the reading?" Ms. Turner asked.

No hands.

"Did anyone *do* the reading?"

No response.

"Okay, let's start on page 261 and hit the highlights."

Jillian skimmed the page. One of the subheads caught her eye. It said *Last Ditch Fundamentalism*.

Jay, a lanky guy with baggy pants and a wallet chain, tipped his hat back so he could see the teacher. "Okay, call me stupid, but what exactly is a fundamentalist?"

"Actually, Jay, that's a great question. Anyone want to answer?"

"A bigot," someone said.

"A religious nut," said Josh Waters. "Usually a Christian fanatic."

"Okay," Ms. Turner said. "We use the term *fundamentalist* to refer to a lot of different things, most of them involving passionate belief and blind faith. In this instance, our text is referring to a historical movement of people who believe the Bible is literally true. They believe God created the earth in six days, there was a real Adam and Eve, a real Noah's ark. They believe Jesus Christ was born of a virgin."

Several students laughed. The teacher smiled and nodded.

"They believe He was God and that He died and rose again. Some of those people are sincere, they may mean well, but of course most educated people no longer believe these old superstitions."

Jay tipped his hat back down and looked at the book again.

Someone should say something, Jillian thought.

A couple of guys from youth group were sitting two rows up from her. She saw them exchange nervous glances. Lisa squirmed in the chair across from her. They looked at each other uncomfortably. Lisa had spoken up before. Jillian never had. Four years of high school were over next week. If she didn't speak up now, she felt as though she'd always regret it. Why was she so afraid?

Jillian had said yes to the church's summer missions trip to Slovenia. How could she be a light in another culture if she wasn't willing to stand up in her own? She'd been baptized Sunday night. She'd stood up for her Lord then. She needed to do it now.

Lord, I don't know what to say. Help.

Jillian forced her hand up.

"Miss Fletcher? You have something to contribute to a class discussion?" Ms. Turner sounded amazed. Maybe because she'd never spoken in class before.

"I believe the Bible. And I don't think I'm ignorant."

"You're a very intelligent young woman. Maybe I've never heard your voice, but I've read your papers. I'm not saying that the Bible is always wrong, just inaccurate in the historical details."

Lisa's hand shot up. "I believe the Bible, too, and I think it's historically accurate."

"Are you telling me you believe God created the earth in six days?"

"That's what the Bible says," Lisa said. "If I'm going to believe in an all-powerful God, why not take Him at His Word? Besides, my dad gave me two books to read on the Intelligent Design Movement, written by university science professors. They say the evidence is overwhelming that every cell is intricately designed, and that the world and especially people couldn't have evolved by chance. Would you like to look at these books?"

Go Lisa!

"I'm sorry, ladies, but in this class we discuss the facts. You're entitled to believe what you want, that's fine. But you have to admit you're making a gigantic leap of faith."

God, give Lisa the right words.

"We all have to have faith," Lisa said. "Faith is just another word for trust. You trust in what you've been taught, what you've heard. Jillian and I trust the Bible. When I sat down, I had to trust that this chair was going to hold me up. But there was good evidence for it. There's good evidence for our faith. It's not a gigantic leap. It's a reasonable one."

"Faith is fine," the teacher said. "It's a noble thing."

"But it's not noble to have faith in the wrong thing," Jillian said, remembering a discussion with Rob. "If I jump off a bridge, believing the law of gravity doesn't apply to me, it doesn't matter how much faith I have because I'm going to fall. It's not noble to have faith; it's just smart to have faith in the right thing. That's why we should check out the evidence for any religion or philosophy."

"I admire your tenacity, girls, but right now I have faith that if we don't cover the rest of this chapter, most of the class will fail the test." She laughed. "So let's get back on track, shall we?"

"Would you like to borrow those books on intelligent design?" Lisa asked. "They're written by a leading biochemist and other scientists. They're really good."

"I've got plenty to read right now. Thanks anyway."

The class continued. Jillian couldn't keep the smile off her face.

When the bell rang, she stayed behind and grabbed Lisa's arm. "That was awesome! I'm so glad you were in there. I wouldn't have known what to say."

"You're the one who had the courage to say something first. I probably wouldn't have said anything if you hadn't gotten me started. Thanks."

Jillian smiled. "I guess I just had to speak up."

One of the guys from church nodded to the girls as he walked by.

"Ms. Turner's obviously not going to read those books," Lisa said to Jillian. "You want to look at them?"

Jillian felt like saying no, but she resisted the impulse. "Sure. Why not? Rob might be interested too."

Just then Brittany came in from the hallway.

"Hi, Brittany," Lisa said.

Brittany mumbled something, but didn't look at Lisa.

"Well, I'm off to physics," Lisa said. "See you girls later."

Brittany grunted as Lisa left the classroom.

"Why don't you like Lisa?" Jillian asked, as they walked to the hallway.

"What's there to like? She went to a Christian grade school. I heard she was home-schooled for three years. Can you believe it? They all think they're better than us public school lowlifes."

"Has Lisa ever said anything like that?"

"She doesn't have to. I can see it in her eyes."

"How would you know, Brit? You don't even look her in the eyes."

Brittany stopped at her locker. "What do you do at a home-school reunion, anyway? Go home and have your mom bake you a pie? At these little Christian schools, do they sit around and handle snakes or what? They're weird, I'm telling you. They're different."

"Sometimes it's okay to be different, isn't it? Sometimes maybe it's better to be different. You'd want them to be tolerant of you. Why can't you be tolerant of them?"

Brittany slammed her locker door. "You're becoming one of them, aren't you, Jillian? Well, if you want to be a pod person, who's your best friend to stop you?"

Jillian looked at Brittany. Somehow she'd hoped Monday's experience at the abortion clinic would change everything. She'd hoped Brittany would become a Christian. Or at least be more open to talking about it.

So much for that idea.

Daniel Fletcher reached into the left desk drawer, the one full of computer disks, including three or four old versions of *Duke Nukem* and *Doom*. In a smoked plastic case, once used for disks, lay a black gun his father had bought. He took it out and pointed it at pictures on his wall. He crouched and pivoted, looking for the enemy, zeroing in on a picture cut from the school yearbook, a big receiver catching a pass in the end-zone. Daniel pulled the trigger.

Daniel thought about bringing the piece to school in his backpack, just to see if he could. Yeah, that's what he'd do. It would be a dry run. To see if he could pull it off. And if he could just get it to school with him, then…his imagination ran wild.

Letter 34

My bullying Foulgrin,

I'm disturbed this Lisa and Jillian are encouraging each other to speak up. Your failure to stop Jillian from being baptized is having a domino effect. The Enemy is instilling courage into her, and her boldness is affecting others. That's the worst possible news.

It's difficult to watch Darwinian evolution being quietly abandoned by leading-edge scientists. I wish we could have held off the discoveries of irreducible complexity at the cellular level. Fortunately, most vermin will remain ignorant of these truths for another few decades. Drift through the Smithsonian. Or Epcot Center. Do you see any indications of the mass of scientific evidence against these evolutionary depictions? Do you see any hint that in scientific circles a debate rages concerning the overwhelming evidence for Intelligent Design? Of course not. If these institutions were to acknowledge the current reality, after decades of blissfully teaching the dogma of blind chance, it would humiliate them. So, evolution will stay at the heart of their worldview until the intelligentsia replaces the old theory with something else. Something that also has the advantage of requiring no belief in the Enemy. "Sure, it's intelligent design. Yes, Darwinian evolution can't account for it. But so what? It just means we were created by aliens!"

They embrace any theory but the true one. And with good reason. For if the Enemy is not their Creator, then He's not their Judge. What they most fear and despise is moral accountability. They'll gladly embrace any theory that relieves them of this built-in sense they must answer for how they've lived. They'll cheerfully overlook such details as the fossil record's lack of transitional forms. The billions of missing links that should be there but aren't. They'll resolutely ignore the lack of living transitional forms that should be everywhere. They gladly embrace any illogic in exchange for its fringe benefits.

The first thing the forbidden book tells them is "God created." If we can deceive them on this single point, we can deceive them about *everything else*. Every issue the vermin ever face comes back to three questions: Where did we come from? Where are we going? Who are we? Evolution gives one set of answers. The Bible gives another. Any person who knows that he came from God and will live forever in either heaven or hell, knows who he is. Once grasped, this knowledge will permeate his worldview. Just as overshadowing is the belief that he and every other person is a random evolutionary accident.

If we convince them that their world began without a Creator, it means the world isn't special. If macroevolution is true, people aren't special either. What can be special about a random accident? Once they accept our premise, they cannot refute our subsequent logic. Why *not* destroy a person who's no more than an accident? Why *not* destroy a world that has no meaning? If there's no Creator, there are no moral imperatives to govern their behavior. There's nothing to answer for because there's no one to answer to.

We've turned the human vices of exploiting, killing, and stealing into a maxim describing how life works—the "survival of the fittest."

This brings me to little Daniel. In the old days, the story of the victim who gets revenge was the comic book advertisement of the skinny guy on the beach. The bully comes along and kicks sand in his face. The weakling spends the next year pumping iron and turning into a rippling mass of muscles. Now he reappears, confronts his nemesis and outbullies the bully. Everyone applauds. Well, culture has advanced to the point that now, to get revenge, the ninety-seven-pound weakling doesn't have to lift a barbell. All he has to do is pick up a gun.

Children are simply living out the low regard for human life. Adults instruct children that they're in essence no different than animals. Then they're stunned and bewildered when their children kill each other like…animals! They wonder, "Why don't our children listen to us?" In fact, their children *are* listening to them. That's the problem!

While affirming a belief in the forbidden book, Jillian carries over her residual antithe-istic beliefs about the world's origins. She doesn't realize she can't represent the Enemy effectively while still embracing two starkly contradictory worldviews.

I'm deeply disturbed Jillian and Rob have both signed up to go on the church's summer missions trip to Slovenia. Their recent discussion about giving more to the Enemy is equally distressing. When they start putting their treasures in heaven, we have no power to stop their hearts from following. Once they start buying up shares in the Enemy's kingdom, their vested interests inevitably shift. We want their portfolio on earth, not in heaven. Giving is the only antidote to materialism. Once they're out of Mammon's clutches, the Enemy may do with them as He wishes. Beelzebub help us then.

I'm delighted to hear about Daniel practicing with the gun. The drills he performs when taking it out of his drawer and pointing it at human images will desensitize him. They'll make it easy for him to actually pull the gun on the real people when the time's right. It's wonderful that he actually put the gun in his backpack and took it to school. Though he didn't pull it out, I'm pleased he had it nearby. And when a few of the towel-snapping jocks, his mortal enemies, walked by, he reached in and touched it? It gave him that feeling of security. That reassurance. That seductive power. I can't wait to see it released.

Celebrating the rehearsal of violence,

Prince Ishbane

35

There's that car," Jillian said, as they walked from Old Navy to Borders. "And look, Mr. Big's in the driver's seat." She pointed at the sleek silver convertible pulling out of the parking lot toward Division Street.

Rob's jaw dropped. "Oh, man. That's the 'dumb car' you've been talking about? It's a Porsche Carrera GT. I've only seen it in the magazines. You know how sweet that car is? Carbon Fiber. V-10 induction engine, six speed. Eighty-two hundred rpms."

"Hello?"

"Zero to sixty in under four seconds. Zero to one twenty in under ten seconds."

"Earth to Rob. Are you receiving me?"

"It can go over two hundred miles per hour."

"But where can you drive that fast?"

"Germany? The Autobahn? That thing must cost something like $300,000. And she's fully loaded."

"She? Did I just lose you to another woman? Anyway, we know *he's* fully loaded."

They continued walking toward Borders.

"How's Brittany?" Rob asked.

"It's been rough."

"Has she told her mom yet? Or Ian?"

"No."

"She really needs to."

"I know. One step at a time. But she'll start showing soon. Then she'll have to."

"Let's pray for them." Rob stopped suddenly, right outside the bookstore, by a rack of sale books. He lowered his head. "Lord, please do a great work in Ian and Brittany. Help her to tell her mother and Ian. And help Ian take it like a man. Use this whole thing to draw them to You. Nothing's more important than that, Lord. And thanks for the courage You gave Jillian to take a stand like that. I'm so proud of her. I know You are, too. Also, thanks for using Joey. You really spoke through that little guy. We praise You in Christ's name. Amen."

Jillian said "Amen," then looked at Rob. "Speaking of taking a stand, I've got to tell you what happened in English class with Lisa and me."

Brittany sat on the couch. She'd decided to skip first period, so suddenly had some extra time. She flipped through the latest issue of *Volleyball* magazine and found an article with preseason rankings for women's college teams across the country. San Diego State was listed in the top twenty-five. She tossed it to the floor.

She heard her mom's bedroom door open. Sharon Powell appeared in pajamas and glasses, heading toward the kitchen. Brittany took a deep breath.

"Hey, Mom. Can I talk to you about something?"

"Honey, I'm not going to comprehend one word till I have my coffee, so hold on to that thought, okay?"

A few minutes later the smell of freshly brewing coffee filled the room. Brittany had always loved that strong French Roast smell—until today. Now she felt as if she was going to throw up. She ran to the bathroom and stood over the toilet, waiting for her morning Cheerios to make their encore. A few minutes later she heard a knock at the door.

"Honey, I'm running late. I need to shower—are you okay?" Sharon stepped in and grabbed some Maalox from the medicine cabinet. She put three in Brittany's hand. "Take these."

"Mom, I need to—"

"Seriously, Brit, I'm in a rush. Tell me later."

Brittany stepped out. Her mom shut the door and turned on the shower. Brittany sat on the floor, waiting for the nausea to pass. After a few minutes, she moved to the kitchen table, front door in sight.

The shower stopped. Fifteen minutes later her mom came running out, putting on her earrings and looking for her purse. Brittany grabbed it from under the table. "Here, Mom."

Sharon reached for her purse, but Brittany pulled it back. "Before you leave, I have to tell you something."

"Brit, I'm late—"

"Mom, I'm pregnant." Brittany watched as her mom's eyes closed, then reopened as if trying to give reality a second chance to get it right.

"What?"

"Pregnant. The kind where you have a baby."

"Brittany." She stretched her name out to four syllables, as only a mom could. "You could've broken it to me a little more gently, don't you think?"

"I keep trying, but you're always going to work…or something."

"I thought you were using protection."

"I know, Mom, spare me the lecture. I've been through it all in my head."

Her mother chewed the side of her upper lip. "Do you want me to help you?"

"Help me how?"

"Like…call a clinic and set up an appointment?"

"I already did that."

"Good. That's the responsible thing to do."

"I couldn't go through with it. I'm keeping the baby."

"What? You don't know what that means, honey."

"It means I'm keeping the baby, that's what it means."

"But it's not that simple. What will it do to your volleyball? And college? Are you sure you're ready for this?"

"I'm sure." Brittany hoped she sounded more certain than she felt.

"We have to talk about this later. Right now I've got to get to the office. I've got two appointments, and then I've got noon aerobics. And you've got to get to school." She grabbed her purse from Brittany's hand and walked to the door. She stopped and turned around slowly. "Whatever you decide, I'll support you, okay?"

Somehow Brittany doubted Ian would say the same.

"Free at last!" Jillian said, grabbing Brittany's arm.

"Yeah," Brittany said, not sounding so thrilled. She smoothed her hands down her gown and straightened her cap.

Jillian studied her as they moved up in the line of students filing into Portland's Memorial Coliseum. "What's wrong, Brit? We're finally graduating! I thought you'd be as excited as I am."

"Trust me, almost every ounce of my body has been waiting for this day for a long time." She paused and lowered her voice. "But I have to admit, there are a few ounces that haven't been. I was more excited about finishing high school when I had a life ahead of me."

Jillian squeezed her arm. "You've still got a life, Brit. It's just going to be a little different."

"There's an understatement. Hey, kiddo, Rob gave you a dozen roses today, right? Ian didn't even pick me some dandelions. So excuse me if I'm not exactly floating. Finals are over, this is graduation, tonight's the senior party. And then I don't have any more excuses. I have to call San Diego State and tell them I won't be coming, then try to figure out what I'm doing for school the next four years. And that's the easy part. The hard part is I have to talk to Ian. Look at him standing up there, not a care in the world. And I've got to burst his bubble."

"I know it's going to be hard," Jillian said quietly. "But I'll be there for you, okay? Just tell me how I can help."

"Is this where you tell me you're praying for me?"

"No. I don't have to. You already know it."

Just as they were about to step out the doorway and walk down the aisle, Brittany stopped. "Remind me that we never have to walk through those crowded halls again on our way to History with Mr. Weaver."

"No more pep rallies," Jillian added. "I'll miss them, but I know you won't."

"No more of Chandler's lame one-liners."

"No more lockers that jam."

"No more cafeteria food served by Helga the German sausage queen."

"No more hideously ugly PE uniforms."

"No more being caught in the hall by Mr. Butcher when we just skipped his class."

They laughed and gave each other a big hug.

"Let's finish this," Brittany said.

As "Pomp and Circumstance" crackled loudly over the speakers, the two walked hand in hand down the aisle.

A few minutes later, the inspirational guest speaker, dressed in a tailored suit that screamed "too expensive," grabbed the microphone as if it were a maraca and he were Ricky Martin.

"You are the best!" he yelled, so loud it hurt Jillian's ears. "You have the power, the smarts, the education to change this world. You can bring justice, equality, and prosperity to your world. You can stop racism and sexism and homophobia. You can create a new order, a society that recognizes and celebrates diversity in every form. Get ready world, because this Kennedy High graduating class is coming!"

People cheered and clapped, but a little tentatively. The speaker acted as if they'd given a roaring response, a mandate to crank it up a few notches.

"You are the best!" He swallowed the mike. "You're going out into the universities and the work place. You're going to excel in business, in academics, in athletics."

"I'm not," Brittany whispered.

"And is the world going to be a better place because of you?" he asked.

"I doubt it," Brittany mumbled. Jillian giggled.

"I can't *hear* you. I said, is the world going to be a better place because of this Kennedy High graduating class?" A third of the students said "yes" this time, so he wouldn't ask again.

"You know what you did yesterday, you know what you're doing tonight. The question is," his voice boomed, "what are you going to do *tomorrow?*"

"Sleep in," Brittany said.

"I'll tell you what you're going to do. You're going to *change the world!*" He raised his hands high, like Rocky Balboa at the top of those steps. They cheered and applauded, and many of them laughed.

"While you're changing the world," Brittany said, "I'll be changing diapers."

"I'll help you, Brit," Jillian said. "If you help me with my homework."

Principal Chandler gave a warm thanks for the "thrilling message" and said, "And now I'd like to introduce our student speaker, our valedictorian, Skyla Stokes."

People cheered. Brittany clapped. So did Jillian.

"Make no mistake about it, classmates. We are the future. We must live by the ancient creed—*Do no harm.* Say it after me—*Do no harm.*"

"Do no harm," the students said in unison, with the same inflections as Skyla. This time they were into it. It sounded like one voice.

"We are the best, the brightest. We are the hope of the world. Believe in yourself. Have faith in yourself. Trust in the cosmic power of the unified force of humanity. Work for the peace and prosperity of all nations. We must call upon ourselves and the great forces of life and the mother goddess, or whoever you consider the supreme power to be. We can't do it ourselves!"

That's for sure, thought Jillian.

"We need each other!"

That's not all we need. We need You, Lord.

"Together we can remake this world into something great and beautiful, without poverty and crime, full of joy and pleasure and hope."

Only You can do that, Lord. Only You. Please do it soon.

∿m

Letter 35

My ambitious Foulgrin,

I love graduation speeches. I applaud their self-congratulatory, self-important smugness. Brats who don't know the meaning of sacrifice imagine themselves superior to previous generations. After all, they're the first tolerant group to walk the planet. Fortunately for us, there's no virtue without sacrifice. At best there are good intentions, and the streets of hell are paved with good intentions. They're so full of themselves they have no room for the Enemy. We can easily hijack their good intentions for our purposes. Besides, most of those intentions evaporate like morning dew in the desert.

Thankfully, the previous generation has failed them miserably by giving them no lofty vision for the future. They haven't passed on the baton of the Enemy's spiritual values. Their parents fumbled it. Now, hopefully, they'll drop it.

Instead of providing a model of maturity for them to strive after, their elders have celebrated immaturity. They've made morality a joke rather than a guiding principle. They're like over-the-hill adolescents, moving from one toy to the next. They've tried to be "friends" to their children. Don't let them see that their children can always find more friends, but never more parents. The parents who bend over backwards to be cool never get it, Foulgrin. The kids see right through them.

Look at the models we've paraded before the young. Their politicians have talked endlessly of high standards, while living in lies, rationalizations, and hypocrisy. We can get limitless mileage from scandals in churches and Christian ministries. Adults without integrity motivate the young to reject the very message they want them to embrace.

Deep within, the vermin youth don't long for mindless action videos with big-chested hotties. They long for stories of brave men and heroic women. People of virtue who've stood for a greater cause. Men and women who've acted courageously by standing against the corruption and apathy of their times. But what the adults offer them is…well, the corruption and apathy of their times!

Beware, Foulgrin, for there's something in these students from the Enemy. It resonates to accounts of those who burned at the stake rather than deny the truth. It thrills to stories of men and women who gave up houses and lands and estates, joyfully, in the pursuit of a greater treasure. These young brats sense there's more to life than what their elders have shown them.

Don't let them read the kinds of books and meet the kinds of people that embody these things they yearn for. Surround them with upwardly mobile materialistic Christians. People insensitive to the needs of the poor and the plight of the lost. In the absence of examples to pull them higher, persuade the young to give up their dreams and lower their standards. In time they can view their duty to the Enemy as nothing more than giving Him a tip in the offering plate now and then. Just as they might a waiter who exists to serve them.

The Enemy challenges them to walk away from obsession with wealth and celebrity. To lose themselves in what's far greater than they are. But we want them to immerse themselves *in* themselves. "We're the best." Many of the morons actually believe it. While the Enemy condemns self-love as their problem, they embrace it as their solution!

Instead of raising the bar and training and motivating the young to jump over it, their parents' generation has lowered the bar so everyone can step over it. (And when they find someone who can't, they lower it further.) Instead of youth who want to be like adults, society is filled with adults who want to be like youth. Instead of the young learning the wise ways of the old, the old market the foolish ways of the young. The older have said to the younger, "We want to be like you." The younger, if they could verbalize it, would say "We don't want you to be like us—we want you to be better, to show us something we can aspire to."

Praise Beelzebub, rarely does that message come across!

I'm painfully aware of all the exceptions—adults who reach out to this generation, discipling and guiding them to spiritual heights. Fortunately, they are few and far between.

It's amusing, isn't it, Foulgrin? The young resent the old not for raising the bar, but for lowering it. The children have nothing to live up to...and therefore no reason to live.

We're the best,

Prince Ishbane

36

JUNE 16, 1:49 P.M.

"Well, kiddo, say your little chants to the saints or whatever you do, 'cause it's go time." Brittany took a deep breath and pictured Jillian's face on the other end of the phone. "I'm going to coffee with Ian. It's time to drop the bomb."

"I'm so glad, Brit. It's the right thing."

"I figure he's probably going to notice eventually, when I have to wheel my stomach around on a shopping cart. So I might as well shock him now."

"Whatever happens, Brit, promise me something…"

"What?"

"Promise me you'll remember you're doing the right thing."

"Somehow it doesn't feel that right telling my boyfriend he's going to be a father."

"He already is a father, and he should know. But just remember you're right to have the baby."

"*I* know that…I just hope he does."

Brittany slid into her Jeep. For a moment, she thought someone else had been driving it. She moved the seat back an inch, to get comfortable.

She turned on to Main Street to head to Café Delirium, rehearsing her speech for what seemed like the millionth time. She sounded calm, rational, completely confident. She just hoped she could fake it when it really mattered.

Ian's Mazda truck was parked outside. Seeing it, Brittany felt nauseous. She told herself it was just midday morning sickness.

Brittany drew a deep breath and walked in the door. The sea-green Mariners' baseball cap turned. It was Ian, flashing a smile and looking at her with those dark eyes. She wasn't used to being nervous, and she didn't like it. She determined to regain control. But already her hands were sweating.

"Hey, beautiful," Ian said, "what can I buy you?"

"A vanilla latte. And one sip of your hot chocolate. That's it."

Ian got the drinks and sat down. Brittany was staring off into space. Ian looked over his shoulder to see if someone was behind him. No one.

"It's good to finally see you again," Ian said. "These last few weeks you've been pretty busy, I guess. I mean, not that it's been all you, I've been doing stuff too—this job at Fred Meyer's warehouse is a killer. It's keeping me in shape though. It's just that we haven't been alone in a long time. We hardly talked at the senior party. But now that school's over and we're settled into summer jobs I thought we could…take up where we left off…" He grabbed her hand. "My parents are gone this weekend. I was thinking we could go back to my place—"

"I'm pregnant, Ian."

He pulled back his hand, bumping the hot chocolate. It spilled over the edge of the table and onto his lap.

Ian cursed loudly and jumped up, knocking his chair over. When everyone turned to look, he grabbed a few napkins and wiped his pants. He wiped off the seat and table, then quickly sat back down. An employee showed up with a towel and wiped down the table. Ian kept saying "that's fine," waiting for her to leave. When she finally did, he whispered to Brittany, "What are you talking about?"

"I'm pregnant."

"Is that all you're going to say?"

She sat motionless.

"I thought you were…making sure that didn't happen," Ian said. "You promised you'd take care of it. What, did you lose those stupid pills or something?"

"Yes, Ian, it's all *my* fault," she said. "And here I thought I remembered another party involved, rather intimately. Didn't your daddy ever give you the talk about the birds and the bees? Never saw the stages of life exhibit at OMSI, is that it? Are you always this stupid, or is today a special occasion?"

"You're sure I'm the father?"

She stared at him. "I can't believe you just said that." She stood up to leave but he stood too, and grabbed her hands, pulling her back down.

"Listen to me," he said loud enough to turn heads. "Listen," he repeated quietly, trying to ignore the room full of stares. "How much money do you need?"

"For what?" Brittany snapped.

"To take care of it. You know. I'm sure you've looked into it, right? A couple hundred?"

"Three hundred if you're awake," she said. "Four sixty if you want to be asleep, so you don't have to actually watch them kill your child."

"Brittany!"

"The entire procedure takes ten minutes or less. First there's the suction. Isn't that nice? They use a tiny vacuum to suck your baby out."

"Stop it."

She kept mumbling the words of the brochure. "Some women experience pain during the procedure. Cramping might continue for up to an hour afterwards." Her monotone sounded as dreary as the words had appeared to her on that pamphlet. "The procedure is usually followed by bleeding, similar to a menstrual period."

"Brittany, get a hold of yourself," Ian whispered fiercely.

"And my personal favorite line is 'feelings of loss or of disappointment, resulting from a lack of support from the spouse or partner, should not be confused with regret about the abortion.'" Brittany's eyes focused on Ian. "As if it's absurd to believe you'd have regrets just for killing your child."

"The only thing that's absurd is you sitting here trying to pretend that you don't want to get rid of this problem. You can't tell me you're ready for this. Even if you are, don't just think about yourself."

"Oh, so you're thinking about *you* now? What a surprise. You don't want anyone to know you knocked me up? That's funny, don't guys usually brag about that? So what's the problem now, big man? Not sure how to explain to Mommy and Daddy that they're grandparents?"

"Brittany, I care about you and your future, but—"

"No, Ian. All you care about is yourself. You don't care about me. And you certainly don't care about our baby."

"Shhh!" Ian said, turning bright red. His eyes searched the room, then landed back on Brittany. "Let's go somewhere else and finish this."

"No, let's not. I was stupid to think for even one second that you'd be man enough to take some responsibility. This conversation is over." She got up and marched out the door in full stride, shoving it open so hard, one of the overhanging bells dropped to the floor behind her. Ian sat speechless, cringing at the jangling bells and watching her run across the street.

Letter 36

My highly esteemed Lord Ishbane,

You'll be gratified to know I concur with most of your analysis of this generation. From the viewpoint of an experienced field marshal, I would offer some further observations you may wish to pass on to your troops.

This generation is granted endless activity, yet suffers perpetual boredom. The boredom is a useful tool to lure them into experimentation. Of course, we have to watch out for the Enemy lest He capitalize on this by offering them a radical faith that gives eternal purpose, thereby transcending boredom.

The generation gap has always been there, but it now involves radical new dimensions. It's not just that today's parents and kids use words foreign to the other, like the old days when the kids said "groovy" and "dropping acid." What's different today is that parents and kids use many of the same words—including *tolerance, acceptance, rights, freedom,* and *truth*—but ascribe to them radically different meanings, usually without knowing it.

To the parents, *tolerance* is accepting others without agreeing with their beliefs and lifestyle choices. To the kids, *tolerance* is accepting that every individual's beliefs, values, lifestyles, and truth claims are equal. To the parents, *acceptance* means recognizing people for who they are, not just what they say and do. To the kids, *acceptance* means endorsing and even praising them for their beliefs and lifestyle choices. To the parents, *rights* means everyone should be treated justly under the law. For the kids, *rights* means everyone should be able to do what they believe is best for them. For the parents, *freedom* means being free to do what they know they *ought* to. To the kids, it means being free to do whatever they *want* to. To the parents, *truth* is an objective standard of right and wrong. To the kids, *truth* is "whatever's right for you."

Of course, many of these parents have gradually embraced this same moral relativism. And some of the kids have rebelled against our relativism, passionately embracing the Enemy's truth. But this difference in worldview has created fundamental dissonance between the generations. They either talk, thinking they've communicated when they haven't. Or, best of all, they give up talking altogether.

The only thing better than their constant conflict is for them to spare themselves conflict through not communicating. These youth and their parents are so used to not understanding each other they've given up trying. No meaningful discussion, no conflict. Of course, all this does is postpone and magnify conflict. The Enemy speaks of turning the hearts of children toward their parents and parents' hearts toward children. Our job description is to turn the children against the parents and the parents against the children.

You seem not to grasp some of the subtleties of my strategic plans to take down the young vermin. This may be because of your many centuries at headquarters, where one may be—owing to the demands of his important position, of course—somewhat isolated from the actual hands-on-throat aspects of working with the sludgebags.

May I suggest you pay closer attention to a detailed study of the vermin? The scientist must know the lab rats in order to use them to greatest advantage. In the end these vermin are but raw material, to be used by us against Him or by Him against us. To us, they are food, meals to be chewed and swallowed. We want them as slaves to exploit and dominate. He wants them as sons and daughters to love and promote to higher service. We want to devour them; He wants to empower them. We would rape them; He would woo them.

We are hunters of men, seducers of women, abusers of children. We stalk and devour and kill. We feed on fear. We go after the weak. Even though the Enemy restricts our free access, they open themselves to us in a thousand ways they don't even realize. The occult, death culture, horror venues, drugs, materialism, and sexual immorality are but a few of them.

It's been too long since my last possession of a vermin. But between Ian, Brittany, and Daniel, I see potential. Even if we can't take over the sludgebags without permission, every book of our kind they read, every conversation they have, every movie they watch, and every ritual they perform opens the door wider.

I remember fondly my last possession. I felt his blood flooding our skull, our eyeballs bulging, the current of electricity flowing through his maggot skin. I used him to create hell on earth, then ushered him into the real hell.

Raketwist and I have been watching movies with Brittany and Skyla. I've been whispering to Daniel and Ian. Revel in it, Lord Ishbane. When we own their mind food, we own them.

Covering your royal hindquarters,

Lord Foulgrin

37

Think about your scholarship," Ian said, moving close to Brittany, in her living room. She backed away, pressing against the wall.

"Stay on that side of the room," she warned. "You had no right to follow me here."

"Brit, if you go through with this pregnancy, it means no more volleyball, no more scholarship, no more college, no more California. You can kiss your dreams goodbye."

Brittany pressed her lips together. "Everybody keeps telling me what it will cost. I'm not an idiot. I know what this means for me. You're just worried about what it means for you."

"Come on, Brit. Think about the next nine months."

"Less than seven, actually. I'm already about ten weeks along. And most people these days don't label pregnant women as worthless outcasts." She glared at Ian. "Present company excepted."

"Don't just think about yourself," Ian said, his voice loud and trembling. "People will figure I'm the father."

"Well, I guess that'll prove they're not idiots, won't it?"

"Shouldn't I have something to say about this?"

"You do. And you've already said it. What you should actually do is take some responsibility. The baby doesn't need to be punished. The baby needs a father. I don't want your three hundred dollars. I want your support. This isn't an armed intruder breaking into your house that you put down with a shotgun. This is a baby. Our baby."

"Wait. That's it. 'Intruder,' you said." Ian snapped his fingers. "The Ouija board warned me an intruder was coming, an intruder that would try to ruin my life. But it told me I shouldn't let it. Don't you see, Brit, this pregnancy is the intruder. The board knew!"

"I don't care what the board knew. And it's a baby, not an intruder."

"I can't even talk to you. You're not thinking rationally."

"Yeah? Then go home and talk to your Ouija board about it. Maybe you can get it pregnant, too."

Ian jumped up and grabbed her arm roughly. The muscles in his face were tight. The veins in his neck throbbed.

"Summer's here, Brit. Your little pink bikini won't cover up this mistake."

Brittany slapped him hard. "You're the only mistake I made. Get out of here."

Ian fell backward toward the front door. He stumbled out to his car, revved the engine and peeled out.

Your little pink bikini won't cover up this mistake. Her fists closed, manicured nails digging into her palms.

Brittany fished around in the trash can below her nightstand until she found it. She read the crumpled brochure out loud to herself again. "'The most frequent response women report after having ended a problem pregnancy is relief, and the majority are satisfied that they made the right decision for themselves.'"

"I don't know what's right any more," she said to the smiling woman on the back cover. "I just don't know."

Jillian and Rob pulled into Sovereign Grace's parking lot a half hour late for the Fourth of July barbecue.

"There better be food left," Rob said. "Your mom's been saying for weeks how awesome this barbecue's supposed to be."

"I'm glad you could come. My church friends are always glad to see you."

As they approached the food line, Jillian saw her mom laughing with a man. He looked familiar. Who was he? Whoever he was, her mom was acting as if they'd been best friends forever.

Why does she keep smiling at him as if he was James Bond or something? Is this the mystery man she's been getting phone calls from?

"Hey, Jillian! Hey, Rob." Jillian turned around to face Jodi, who was holding Joey on her hip with one hand and a plate of food in the other.

"Hi, Jodi! Oh, here, let me take him," she said, reaching out for Joey. He stuck his chubby arms out to her and grinned as she held him close. "You should be eating. Why doesn't Mom have him?"

"Because she's eating. I told her it's not fair for her to be the only one who shows this big boy off all the time." She smiled and took Joey right back, and poked him in the stomach; he squealed in delight.

Jillian stared at her mom again. "Jodi, who's that guy Mom's talking to?"

Jodi turned around and looked. "She hasn't introduced you two yet, huh? He's in her Sunday school class. I can't remember his name. It's something different…like Dudley, but that's not it. Maybe I'm thinking of Dudley Do-Right."

"Huh?" Jillian said.

"You know, the Mountie? The cartoon with Dudley and Nell and Snidely Whiplash? It was on Rocky and Bulwinkle and…never mind. Sometimes I forget I'm a hundred years older than you. Anyway, his name's not Dudley."

"Okay, Jodi. That's…helpful." Jillian looked at Rob. "Do you recognize that guy? He's…sort of familiar."

He looked carefully. "I'm not sure."

Jillian and her mom made eye contact. Diane waved them over to her and the mystery man. Jillian led Rob across the grass.

Diane smiled broadly and put an arm around her. "Jillian, I'd like you to meet a special friend of mine. This is Donovan Swain."

"It's a pleasure," he said with a wide grin, showing off flawless teeth that looked all the whiter because his tan was so deep. "I've heard a lot about you, Jillian."

She recognized the voice. She'd heard it twice on the answering machine. Deep, sort of sickeningly sweet. Jillian's muscles tensed as she looked at her mom. "I'm sorry, I've forgotten already, your name was…Dud—?"

"Donovan. Donovan Swain." He said it as though it was supposed to sound important.

Jillian introduced him to Rob, then studied him closely as the two chatted. He must have been in his upper forties, maybe a couple years older than her mom. His black hair had a perfectly even dusting of gray. He was average height, though taller than Rob, and a lot taller than Diane and Jillian. He was wearing khaki shorts and a white Ralph Lauren polo shirt which accented his tan and striking blue eyes—Jillian guessed they were hiding behind tinted contacts. His *GQ* "casual" outfit was topped off with a navy blue sweater draped over his shoulders.

All of a sudden it hit her.

I don't believe it. It's the silver Porsche guy. Mr. Midlife Crisis. He's after my mom?

"This macaroni salad is incredible," Donovan said. "Do you know who made it?"

"Actually, I did," Diane said, smiling broadly.

"Well, if the way to a man's heart is through macaroni salad, you've definitely got me wrapped around your little finger." Donovan winked at Diane. Jillian stifled a gag reflex.

"Well, it's just been great talking to you, Mr. Swain," Jillian said, "but I think Rob and I are going to get in line for some of that *incredible* macaroni salad before it's all gone."

"Please, Jillian, call me Donovan. It was my privilege meeting you, and you too, Rob. Hopefully we'll get to know each other better in the future." He winked at her, then again at Diane, who made doe eyes at him. "I'll take you for a spin in my car. Your mom seems to love it."

"Bye, honey," Diane said to Jillian without looking away from Donovan's smile.

"Good to meet you too, Donovan," Rob said, "and always great seeing you, Mrs. Fletcher."

Jillian grabbed Rob's arm and pulled him away.

"I don't like him," she announced.

"Why not?"

"He just seems, I don't know…slimy."

"Slimy? What's that supposed to mean?"

"No, I'm serious, look at him—he's ridiculously tan. I know it's summer, but this is Oregon, for Pete's sake; I'll bet you anything he fake 'n' bakes. Actually, he looks so filthy rich I wouldn't be surprised if he flew in a private jet every weekend and got his tan in Fiji or something."

"Hold on. What's gotten into you?"

"I knew I recognized him. He's Mister I Can Blow $300,000 on a Stupid Car!"

"The Carrera GT?" Rob whistled. "Wow. You're kidding. Was he saying he'd let me drive it?"

"Just like a guy! You're not even thinking about my mother."

"I'm not asking him to be my roommate. I just want to drive his car. And are *you* thinking of your mother? Or yourself?"

They reached the long tables and started filling their plates with all sorts of salads and casseroles. Surrounded by people, Jillian toned it down.

"I wonder what he does to make so much money," Jillian whispered. "I bet he's in the Mafia."

Rob laughed. "Would you listen to yourself for one second?"

"Come on, Rob. You can't tell me that you didn't at least want to laugh when Mom said his name. *Donovan Swain.* At least he could go by Don. Donovan...wasn't that the name of the guy who sang that gag-me "Mellow Yellow" song, you know one of the worst songs of all time? Donovan sounds like a...I don't know, like a prize British dog or something."

"Donovan is a perfectly normal name. You only hate it because you think he's after your mom. What if I told you my middle name was Donovan?"

"I'd say 'Roberto Donovan Gonzales, we need to break up.'"

Rob laughed while Jillian looked down at her plate and saw the heaping piles of food. Her mouth watered as she took another scoop of baked beans.

She heard the shrieks of little girls and looked up from a platter of fried chicken to see that the Slip'n Slide had been rolled out. One girl had a swimming suit on that looked like Jillian's. She looked down at her plate again and sighed. She wouldn't be able to fit in that suit if she ate like this.

In less than a month she and Rob were leaving on the missions trip. What would happen with her mom and this guy while she was gone?

She looked across the lawn at her mom and Donovan Swain. Diane Fletcher looked so happy. Why did Jillian feel so miserable?

Ian sat in his truck at the stop sign two houses from Brittany's. Her front door opened and she stepped out. He'd wanted just to see her from a safe distance, make sure she was okay. But his heart pounded. He hit the gas pedal a little too hard and peeled out, making a sharp turn. A block later he hit his forehead with his hand.

What an idiot.

He turned the radio up and drove the rest of the way home, using the heavy metal bands like a sandblaster on his brain. He thought too much, that was his problem. He needed to stop all the thinking. Yeah, that was it.

When he got home, he turned off his bedroom lights and sprawled out across his bed. He'd gotten good at emptying his mind when he was alone in his room. He closed his eyes slowly, and thoughts about work were erased within seconds. But lately he couldn't seem to erase the picture of Brittany that constantly filled his head. He pressed his eyelids down harder. Why was she insisting on messing up their lives?

"Ah," he said aloud. "I can't handle this anymore."

He rolled off his bed and picked up the portable phone from his floor.

"Bailey, it's Ian…where'd you say that party is tonight?"

Killing time before crossing the river for the Vancouver fireworks display, Jillian and Brittany had laughed long and hard for an hour, looking through old picture albums in Brittany's room. Jillian went to the kitchen to use the phone. When she came back, Brittany's nose was in a book.

"Still no answer at Rob's?"

"No. Whatcha readin'?" Jillian asked, sinking back in the beanbag chair.

"Ian gave it to me, before he ducked out."

"Looks kind of weird." Jillian leaned closer to read the title. *The Goddess Trinity: Maiden, Mother, and Crone.*" She took it out of her hand and read the description on the back. 'Unleash the goddess within. Learn the rituals that will guide you through the labyrinth.'"

Jillian remembered Rob's story about going through Ian's books and how it opened up their conversation. Why not give it a try? She walked toward Brittany's books.

"What's that one?" Jillian picked it up off the desk. "*Teen Witch: Wicca for a New Generation.*'Where'd you get this?"

"Skyla."

"Brit…I was hoping after the abortion clinic thing that you'd back away from Skyla."

"She was disappointed I didn't go through with it. But she says she'll support me no matter what. It's nice to have a friend like that. I haven't sold my soul, you know. I still haven't gone to an esbat. But I'm thinking about it." Her eyes brightened. "Did you know Halloween is New Year's Eve on the Wiccan calendar? The day begins at sundown October 31 and runs through the daylight of November 1. It's a sacred Wiccan sabbat. Skyla wants me to be with her coven Halloween night."

Jillian looked at her and shuddered. "You know what I think of that. Just looking at these books gives me the creeps. Silver Ravenwolf's *Teen Witch Kit?* You still have this? You promised me you'd throw this away."

"No. You *asked* me to. I didn't promise anything. I just kept it under the bed awhile so you wouldn't get uptight. I keep it hidden with the tarot cards so you don't have to freak out."

"Brit, you've got to stay away from this stuff."

"Look, I haven't done any spells—it's not like I'm trying to harm my enemies. Sure, I considered trying to turn Kelly into a frog, but I figured no one would notice the difference. I've tried a few charms, an incantation or two. You used to be open-minded. We used to watch *Sabrina* and *Buffy* and *Charmed* together. We saw *The Craft* at Division Street, remember?"

"I wish I could forget."

"That's what I can't stand about Christians. You're so intolerant. But don't worry. I'm not going to come out of my broom closet and declare myself a witch."

"It's not just what you're doing that concerns me, Brit. It's what you're missing. I want you to know Jesus. He means everything to me. I want you to go to heaven when you die."

"I'm not planning on dying."

"It happens to everyone whether they plan for it or not."

"Rob may be a buff little guy, but he's poisoning your mind, kiddo."

"This isn't about Rob. I can think for myself. Maybe you should just deal with the issues, instead of getting on my case whenever I bring up my faith."

"My, we've become assertive, haven't we?"

"Which is what you encouraged me to be—only you wanted it on your terms. 'Assert yourself as long as you agree with Brittany,' was that it?"

"Wow, we've got our own fireworks goin' here, don't we girlfriend? Now's probably a good time to tell you. Skyla invited me to a séance."

"Don't do it, Brit. I mean it."

"You might be interested in knowing that Skyla's still pretty upset with you for interfering with my abortion."

"I'm a big girl. I can live with Skyla's disapproval."

"That's not all. She got together with a few of her friends. They put a curse on you."

The summer was almost half over. Daniel started preparing himself for school as if he were going through boot camp. He reached in the drawer, pulled out the gun and looked at the pictures on his wall. They included not only Josh Waters, but a few other jocks who'd messed with him, and one teacher he hated. He pointed the gun, envisioning taking head shots, since head shots meant more points and moved you to the next level. He pulled the trigger again and again, noiselessly. The gun was empty. Still, it made him feel powerful.

He'd taken it to school twice the last week of the semester. What would they think if they found it? What would they think if in September he prowled the lockers or the library or a classroom, then zeroed in on someone, made them squirm and finally pulled the trigger?

What would they think if the gun wasn't empty?

The thought infused him with something he craved, something he'd never felt in the classroom, the locker room, or the showers.

Power.

Letter 37

My edgy Ishbane,

There's no need for you to insult me. I would have thought you'd appreciate my carefully honed insights.

I'm doing everything I can to keep Jillian from this dreaded missions trip. I'm not worried about what she might do for Slovenia as much as what going to Slovenia might do for her. I don't want to think what the Enemy is likely to do to her—and Rob—through a twenty-one-day trip. How many thousands of them has the Enemy gotten hold of by ripping them out of their comfort-driven culture and putting them somewhere they must trust Him and rely on fellow soldiers to carry out a mission?

Attached is my full report on Brittany. You've got to love her attitude. She hates Christians for being intolerant. But if a Christian believes witchcraft is wrong, it's the Christian she considers hateful. Brittany hates bigotry but is bigoted toward Christians. Wonderful.

May our powers be unleashed upon this generation. I offer them up to Beelzebub that he may have his way with them! I invoke my favorite incantation, the words of the ancient language. I call upon their magic: *Baal jezeb ashnar mordol nuhl—keez gimbus moloch nargul dazg!*

As for our little Skyla's curse, you and I know it can't have power over the Enemy's children as long as they direct their minds toward Him. The Enemy knows that and we know that, but there's good news—the Enemy's little brats don't know! And what they don't know can hurt them.

Daniel's already making school plans for the fall. The distinction between computer simulations and reality keeps blurring. The more he handles the gun, the more natural it feels. By picking up that gun, then moving quickly to the games, and back again, he's developing as much ease with that gun as the ones he carries in the game. From game, to gun, to more potent gun—can't you see it coming?

As Stungoth has noted, Daniel's pulled the trigger on so many imaginary men it's desensitized him to the real thing. You'd think they'd catch on to this, since even the vermin military has proven that shooting at bull's-eyes doesn't make it easier for them to kill people, but practice shooting directed at people-shaped images makes killing a reflex reaction.

I confess I've been away from video games for a while and didn't realize how far we've advanced them. The realistic touches blur the boundary between fantasy and reality. Guns are carefully molded after real ones, wounds have a medically accurate appearance, screams and sound effects are real. There's even the recoil of a heavy rifle. Men learn to fly in flying simulators. Boys learn to kill in killing simulators.

We've built a society in which the primary form of play for millions of vermin children consists of killing large numbers of people! These murder simulators are our training tools for future murderers. We may never get most of them to actually do it, but we'll certainly get many more than we would have otherwise! These dopey adults would never trust their children to a sociopathic baby-sitter, yet they routinely entrust them to our sociopathic movies, games, and Web sites. You've got to love it.

"Why are children killing children?" they cry out, as if this were some great mystery. I get such a laugh every time they ask. Millions of adults kill their smallest children every year just because they feel like it. Gee, I wonder where these kids got the idea that killing children is okay?

There have always been wild and rebellious kids. But now children are robbing, maiming, and killing on whim, without pity or remorse.

Some of the school killers half expected the kids and teachers they shot to get back up and go on with life when the "game" was over. Exit the game, press the reset button, and everything will be fine. Their violent little imaginary world has a mind-numbing effect. They think you can shoot a bunch of people, turn off the screen, then go out for chalupas, without residual effects.

Youth violence thrives in a moral vacuum, Ishbane. When kids don't have a personal value system that distinguishes between right and wrong, there's nothing to prevent them from venting their anger and frustration through violence and cold disregard for human life.

The gun pops the shrimp up to the top of the food chain. It turns victims into predators, hunters into the prey. Just as the Ouija board is a steroid for the spirit, the killing games are steroids for the mind. Power. Control.

I'm still convinced we can get more from Daniel than just a simple suicide. If Stungoth and I play our tarot cards right, today's gunplay will escalate, and eventually he'll take out other vermin before he turns a gun on himself. When he does, rest assured, we'll be there to welcome him to this side.

Celebrating the power they grant us,

Lord Foulgrin

38

M om—phone for you *again,*"Jillian yelled from the kitchen.
Daniel pushed by her on the way to the refrigerator. "You're just ticked cause it's not for you."

"No, actually, what I'm ticked about is that this is the thousandth time Donovan Swain—if that's his real name—has called our house in the last two days."

"I'm with you on that one. That guy is…I don't know, he's just weird."

"All I can say is, he's definitely not right for Mom."

A few minutes later, Diane walked into the kitchen with a smile on her face. Was she humming? This was going too far.

"Hey Mom, who was that? Dudley Swain?"

"Mmhmm," Diane mumbled between notes of the tune she was humming. "Donovan."

"Mom, I really don't think—"

"Jillian, Daniel," Diane said cheerfully, "come sit with me at the table. I have something to tell you."

Jillian froze.

"I don't know if you guys have noticed," Diane started, "but Donovan Swain's been calling me."

"No," Daniel said. "Really?"

"I think we were on the verge of figuring that out," Jillian deadpanned.

Diane's eyes sparkled. "Well…this Thursday night, Donovan has asked me to go with him to a party at his office."

Jillian pictured her mom laughing and talking in the midst of the Mafia, unaware of anything but Donovan's fake tan.

"Where does he work?"

"He's the CEO of a Christian investment company."

Yeah, Christian, uh-huh. Her mom was going out with a forty-eight-year-old gangster, who would send his henchman Vinnie to break her legs if she ever dumped him.

"How long have you known this guy?"

"Let's see, he started coming to church at the beginning of June, and I definitely noticed him then." She giggled. "But I guess I officially met him about five weeks ago."

Jillian raised her eyebrows. She'd heard her mom laugh, but…giggle?

"I feel like a teenager," Diane said, giggling again.

"And you think knowing him for five weeks has qualified you to make a good judgment about him?"

"Yes, Jillian. It's not like I'm making this decision to date him based purely on emotion. I've thought about this for a long time."

"For…less than five weeks you mean."

"No! Well, about Donovan specifically, yes, but I've been thinking about the possibility I might eventually want to start dating again."

Jillian felt something like a blow to her chest, and before she could think she said, "Did you wait a whole week after Dad died before you started thinking about other men, or was it just a day?"

Diane's face turned red, and her eyes filled with tears and fury.

"How dare you say that to me, young lady! The day your dad died, part of me died with him. He was the first man I ever loved. I'll never love that same way again. I thought I'd never want to date anybody again when he died, but you know what, I'm lonely—you and your brother aren't the only ones who need friends. And I don't think your dad would have wanted me to never see another man. If I'd died, I'd have wanted what was best for him, and that would probably include remarrying. But I didn't die. And you know what, Jillian? Sometimes I wish I had."

Tears ran down her cheeks. She seemed completely unaware of them. Daniel got up and left the kitchen. Jillian heard the familiar sound of his door shutting.

"I'm sorry, Mom," Jillian said. "I was wrong to say it like that. Very wrong. That was awful. Please forgive me." She put her arms around her mother. "I know you loved him, and I know it's been hard. I just don't think that…" she paused, looking at the hurt in her mom's eyes. "It's just that…I'm leaving in a week and a half on the missions trip. And I just think you should be careful while I'm gone. I don't want you to get hurt."

"I appreciate your concern, Jill. But I wish you'd trust me. You've got nothing to worry about. Donovan's a perfect gentleman, and very sensitive. And remember—your mother has a life, too. I know it may be hard for you to believe a man finds me attractive."

Diane wiped her eyes.

"I think you look great, Mom. I just want to make sure he…treats you with respect."

Her mother smiled. "Jillian, you sound like you're my mother."

"Yeah. But it's not so bad sounding like a mother, is it?"

The phone rang in the Gonzales home. Rob picked it up. "Hey, Ian…Yeah, okay…Hang on, I need to write that down." He looked around the phone, but the pen fairies had struck again.

"There's a pen on my desk," Rob said to Jillian. "Would you mind grabbing it?"

Jillian went to the far end of the hall, to Rob's room, which she'd been in only once. She stepped around three boxes of Rob's stuff from campus housing, dumped here since he was living at home for the summer. She smiled, seeing Lane, the stuffed camel she'd given him, on the far corner of the desk. But no pen. She pulled open the top drawer. She opened the bottom right drawer. Photo albums! Maybe pictures of Rob as a kid? That would be fun. She pulled them out quickly. When she did, an orange plastic bottle rolled at the bottom of the drawer. She picked up the nearly full bottle and saw Rob's name on it. Under the pills was a book. Jillian recognized the title immediately.

She walked out of the room, feeling weak. Rob was laughing as she turned the corner. He reached out for the pen. She held up the pills in one hand and the book in the other. Rob froze.

"Hey, Ian, let me call you back, okay? Later." He hung up, looking like a little boy caught smoking.

"Rob, what are you doing with this book?"

Rob opened his mouth, then seemed to think better of it. He shrugged.

"And what's with all this prescription medicine? You never told me you take medicine. What's it for?"

He shook his head. "I *don't* take it. It's supposed to be for my depression."

"You don't take it, but you save it up, hidden in a drawer with this…thing?" She shook the book at him. "I know what this is, Rob. It's the same book Brittany used to choose how to kill herself! What's going on?"

"It's too hard to explain."

"Try me."

Rob sighed. "We better sit out back. I don't want Mama to hear."

He led her out back, under the warm but gray threatening sky, and pulled up two old lawn chairs, shaking a little moisture off them, then running the arm of his sweatshirt over Jillian's. They sat down and Rob stared out at his mom's vegetable garden. The slight wind rippled the corn. It was beautiful, warm, peaceful. What Jillian felt wasn't.

"Ever since I was a kid," Rob said, "I've had dark moods come on me. After my brother Guillermo died, they got darker…and more frequent." He stopped.

"And?"

"And sometimes I feel like…ending it all."

"You mean…suicide?"

"I've never tried it…but a few times I've gotten pretty close. I can't explain it, Jill, but sometimes you're buried so deep there's no way you feel you can ever come up again for air. It's like you're drowning. You can't breathe. And instead of swallowing the water, you're in such agony, you just want to take it all away."

She stared at him, thinking this couldn't be real.

"I haven't just been thinking about myself. It's not fair to my mom and dad. They've had to put up with these dark moods all my life. And it's certainly not fair to you. I don't want you to have to be with someone with these kinds of struggles. If I ever got married, I've asked the Lord if it would be right to have children. They might have the same problem. It's too much, Jill. Sometimes I feel like it would be best for everybody. Including me. At least I'd finally be in heaven."

Jillian had held back the tears until that moment, but now they flowed freely. Rob put his arm around her.

"I knew this would happen. I didn't want you to be scared. I'm sorry you found it."

She looked up at him, eyes flashing like a thunderstorm. "Maybe I found it because of God's sovereignty that you're always talking about! Isn't that what you said about my bulimia—that it was God's sovereign plan my mom discovered it? That He was watching out for me? You should've talked to me sooner. But since you didn't, you should thank God I found this now. I mean, what were the chances, humanly speaking?"

Rob nodded. "Sometimes it's easier to see God working in somebody else's life than mine." They sat silently for a minute. "You're scared, aren't you?"

"Of course I'm scared. I'm terrified. But I'm also furious! God can take you to heaven when He wants. He did that with my dad, remember? But it would be terrible, it would be *so* wrong if you did it to yourself. Think what it would do to your parents…and me." She started crying again. "You don't know what it would do to me. It's so incredibly selfish for you to even think about it."

"I know," Rob said, looking like a whipped dog. "But sometimes it just seems best. I tell myself I'm no good. I'm never going to be what I should be. Sometimes the weight seems unbearable, and I struggle with all these temptations."

"So the solution is to give into the *worst* temptation? Give God time to work in your life, Rob! I've seen you with people. God's given you a grasp of His Word and a love for people and a boldness to speak up for Him. No wonder Satan's out to kill you. No wonder you're on his hit list!"

"I…hadn't thought of it that way before."

"Maybe because you've never talked with someone to get another perspective, is that it? Have you ever told anybody about this?"

"How could I? It's such a terrible thing to admit. I'm supposed to be a good Christian, an example."

"What kind of example would it be if you killed yourself? Talking about the temptation, putting it out on the table in the light of day, that brings it out of the dark. Remember when we talked about my bulimia?"

Rob smiled. "Yeah…boo-lee-me-uh."

Jillian stood. "You stay right here. Don't move. I'm getting my Bible out of the car."

Jillian ran around the side of the house, grabbed her Bible from the back seat and ran back to Rob.

"Okay," she said, breathing hard, "you've read Scripture to me. Now I'm going to read it to you. It's your turn to listen to God's Word."

Rob nodded.

"I was running late this morning, and I almost skipped devotions," Jill said. "But I figured, I'll give it five or ten minutes anyway. Well, it was John 8. God really showed me something, and I thought it might come in handy with Brittany if she has suicidal thoughts again. Now I realize why God took me to this passage today. It wasn't for Brittany, it was for you." She scanned the page, then turned it. "Okay, I know it's here some place."

"Jill, I'm sorry—"

"Just shut up while I find this passage."

"Yes, ma'am."

"Okay. Here it is. I guess He's talking to the Pharisees. He says in verse 44, 'You belong to your father, the devil, and you want to carry out your father's desire. He was a murderer from the beginning, not holding to the truth, for there is no truth in him. When he lies, he speaks his native language, for he is a liar and the father of lies.' Okay, Mr. Bible Scholar. Tell me what that means."

"Well, Satan's a liar. And he's really good at lying—it's his native language, like Spanish is my parents'. So he speaks his lies, fluently, to trick us into doing what he wants."

"Right," Jillian said. "He's a liar and a murderer. And they're connected, aren't they? He comes up with lies to rationalize murder. That's how he was trying to get Brittany to kill her baby. And that's exactly how he's trying to get you to kill yourself. Suicide is murder, right? It's the murder of yourself."

"I'd never take somebody else's life."

"But you have the right to take your own? Well, somebody's making you forget those verses you've quoted to me. Remember when you told me our bodies don't belong to us? They belong to God, and we don't have the right to do whatever we want with them. Didn't you say that to me when we were talking about purity?"

"Yeah. It's in 1 Corinthians 6. 'You are not your own; you were bought at a price. Therefore honor God with your body.' Our bodies are sacred because they're a temple of the Holy Spirit."

"So would God ever want you to destroy that temple?"

"No. You're right. It's so clear when you say it, so clear when I listen to Scripture. But somehow when the darkness comes on me, it doesn't register. I start thinking differently. I know you've been moody, but have you ever been really depressed, I mean so bad that you can't even think straight?"

"I get down sometimes. But I admit, I can't imagine contemplating suicide. It's just too...weird."

"That's what I said about your bulimia. Then I told you to just stop bingeing and throwing up. Are you going to tell me to just stop being depressed?"

"No," Jillian said. "It's not that easy, is it? What do you do when those moods come?"

"Stay in my room, when I can."

"Maybe that's part of the problem. You need to call someone, go talk to someone. Jeff...or Steve or one of your pastors. Or one of my pastors. Greg or Kristi. Or Ryan or Jodi. They're all great. Or you could have called me. Why didn't you?"

"I don't want you to see me like this. That's why I don't return your calls sometimes. I can't always just put on a smiley voice."

"You think I have to hear a smiley voice? Maybe I'm not as weak and fragile as you think I am."

"I guess I thought you'd be too overwhelmed to talk about it like this."

"Well, maybe I'm changing. And maybe you need a counselor or a doctor who can give you some medicine. Wait…someone *already* gave you a prescription. Why aren't you taking it?"

"I feel like medicine's just a crutch. The Bible and prayer should be enough."

"So you won't use your medicine as a crutch, but you'd use it as a poison?"

"When you put it that way…"

"What other way is there to put it? Fine, read the Bible and pray. Just because you take medicine doesn't mean you can't do that. It's not either/or, it's both/and."

"Taking the medicine just doesn't seem right."

"My mom takes thyroid medicine. Are you saying that's wrong?"

"No."

"Your sister Seci's a diabetic, right? She takes insulin, doesn't she? What if Seci told you she won't take insulin any more because prayer and the Bible should be enough? What would you tell her?"

"That God can use doctors and medicine, too."

"Right. Then take your own advice, Rob. Set up another appointment. If you should be taking pills, I want you to have them on the missions trip. You owe that to the rest of us."

"I guess it just seems different, somehow. I mean, medicine for a physical condition is one thing but…taking medicine for something mental or emotional? It just doesn't seem right."

"Weren't you awake in health class? The body's full of chemicals that affect our brains and our emotions."

"I just don't want to take pills."

She stared at him, thinking. "It's a pride thing, isn't it, Rob?"

"What do you mean?"

"Give me a P…P, give me an R, R…give me an I, I…give me a D, D…give me an E, E. What's that spell?"

"Pride." Rob grinned. "You know, you cheerleaders aren't as brainless as they say."

"I can be brainless with the best of them, but now's not the time. Aren't you always telling me to do the right thing even when it's not easy? Like speaking up in class?"

"I guess I should've talked to you a long time ago. When you said the word *pride,* it was like God nailed me. I like to think of myself as more spiritual than that. Well, part of swallowing your pride is realizing you need all the help God offers you—friends, family, medicine, His Word, His church. And His messenger Jillian."

She tilted her head. "I've never been called God's messenger."

A light rain started falling. They sat in it, wordlessly, faces up to the sky. The cleansing drops felt good. Suddenly it broke open and they jumped up, laughing. They left the lawn chairs and ran for the sliding glass door.

They sat in the living room, both their faces still wet. Jillian held Rob's hand. She looked at an old Gonzales family picture, sitting on a coffee table. "Are you ever going to tell me how Guillermo died?"

Rob stared at the picture. "I'd rather not."

"Okay," Jillian said.

"He…killed himself," Rob whispered.

"I'm so sorry." She hugged him as he cried. She felt as if she were consoling a little boy. After several minutes he left for the bathroom to wash his face. When he came back, his eyes were red. He sat down.

"Are you disappointed in me?" he finally asked.

"I'm concerned, for sure. But in a strange sort of way I'm almost relieved."

"Relieved?"

"I was afraid something was wrong. You'd disappear for a few days and not even call or return my calls. Then all of a sudden you'd pop out again, like a groundhog or something, acting like everything was just fine. This helps explain what was going on. It's better to know about it than to be in the dark, that's for sure. And also, it changes how I look at you. Not in a bad way. I guess I thought you were above it all. You were Mr. Spiritual, with no serious problems other than the l-u-s-t one, I mean. I never thought I'd have some answers to give you, to be the one to share Scripture with you. I thought that was just something you'd always do with me."

"It works both ways," Rob said.

"Yeah. And it should, shouldn't it?"

"I thought I'd be so ashamed if you knew. I'm embarrassed, true, but I'm really glad you found out. You were right. It was God's sovereign plan."

She pointed to the suicide book, lying on the floor. "Didn't you tell me you thought Ian should burn those occult books?"

"Yeah. Unfortunately, I haven't had the guts to tell him yet."

"Why do you think he should burn them?"

"Because demons can use them to mess up his mind. They're a foothold into his life."

"So what do you think you should do with this book—and the medicine?"

Rob looked at her, then walked to the bathroom. She followed. He opened the bottle and put one pill in his mouth, then swallowed some water. He poured a half dozen pills onto the counter. "Just enough to get me by until I see the doctor," he said to Jillian. Then he poured the rest, maybe forty of them, into the toilet. He flushed, then tossed the bottle into the trash.

He came back to the living room, and began tearing the book apart. He wadded up some newspaper and tossed it and the book into the fireplace, lit it, and watched the book burn. As the smoke rose, he felt something heavy lift from his shoulders.

"Roberto!"

He turned quickly.

"What are you doing starting a fire in July?"

"Just burning a little trash, Mama." He pointed his finger at Jillian and smiled. "It's her fault. She's driving me loco."

"They always blame the women, don't they?" Jillian said.

"You are a smart *chica,* Jillian Fletcher," Mrs. Gonzales said with a smile. She put her arms around Jillian and hugged her tight. "My Rob has found himself a very smart girl."

Letter 38

My unjustifiably proud Foulgrin,

So Rob's dirty little secret surfaced? Another in a long line of failures for you. I'm done keeping track of them—Obsmut's taken over. Certain anonymous agents take special delight in recounting your downfalls. Apparently your endearing personality has worked its charms on them as well.

Rob's pride has been his downfall. Precisely why we needed to keep it hidden from him. The central principle of hell is: "I am mine!" Everything must be done on our terms, never His. That's it in a nutshell. The same applies to the vermin's rebellion. As far beneath us as they are, they, too, crave mastery. Control. Sovereignty. Their battle cry is "I will not serve, I will be served." This means "I refuse to be what I am—a creature; I insist on being what I am not—God."

Of course, Rob would never say such words. He would say the opposite. What matters, though, is not their words, but their hearts. The humble heart acknowledges its inferiority before the Superior. It sees its utter dependence on the Independent One. In such a heart we cannot work. There is nothing to grab on to.

Our greatest enemy is humility. We never know what to do with a humble man. (Fortunately, it's rare we have to deal with one.) Everything we accomplish in the vermin relies on their declaration of independence from God. The humble vermin has the Enemy fighting on his side. It's easy enough to beat *them*—but who can win a one-on-one against *Him?*

The only way the vermin can defeat us is when they've first been soundly defeated by Him. Once they surrender to Him, He tells us we have to go through Him to get to them. But, there's no going through Him, is there?

Still, as long as they're resisting Him, we can effectively fight them. If *He* has not conquered them, then *we* can.

This is the bothersome thing about suffering. Sometimes no sooner do we inflict it, than they humble themselves and call upon Him. Then He takes over and we run for cover. But what's the solution? Keep them from suffering? Damned if we do, damned if we don't.

Pride is the Master's sin. The first sin and the best. It's the fountainhead of all other sins. But pride always works best in the dark. You must push Rob's pride back beneath his consciousness. If he doesn't recognize it, he can't confess and repent of it. As long as he's proud, we don't care how great a Bible student he is. Pride covers a multitude of spiritual disciplines.

The scouting report on Rob suggests the Enemy has special plans for him. Therefore considerable subsidies have been allotted Baalgore. He is well-aided in his campaign to paralyze Rob with depression, implanting suicidal thoughts. All who speak from the pulpits, stand on platforms, and go to mission fields are known by name in Erebus. They're at the top of our hit list. Often we figure out before they do who the Enemy has called to serve Him in this way. Then we weed out as many as we can.

Rob's suicide would serve us well. It would discredit the Enemy. Sadden Him. Break Rob's parents' hearts, and Jillian's. It would disillusion those he's witnessed to, and reassure Ian that Rob's faith wasn't real. Or strong enough. Or satisfying enough. But best of all, Rob's self-destruction would remove someone who might have served Him faithfully for many years. Make no mistake—he could still inflict great damage on our cause. That his secret sins have surfaced and his pride has broken is distressing. That it happened just before leaving on a missions trip is maddening.

The upside is that Rob's depression will not just disappear. Keep working on him. Convince him he must act cheery to be "spiritual." Have him put on a veneer of artificial happiness, even in Slovenia. Then his emptiness will seem deeper still. Don't let him taste that dangerous joy the Enemy offers those who forget themselves and worship Him. Convince him the spiritual life doesn't require joy. He can sit around isolated in the darkness, full of self-pity, and still be godly.

Be careful, though, that you don't overestimate depression's power. Your résumé shows you were one of a cadre of five assigned to Hudson Taylor. Though you plagued him for years with doubt and depression, he continued to seek the Enemy, didn't he? He penetrated one of our greatest strongholds. Rob has already read two missions biographies—by all means keep him from that one. Taylor's biographies have done nearly as much damage as the man's work in China. I'm nauseated to think of those vermin house churches meeting across that land that was once ours, thriving despite every persecution we can muster. We long to squash the roaches. But for every one we squash, the Enemy raises up a hundred more.

Almost as disheartening as Rob's pride being exposed is Jillian's continued boldness. Wasn't it you who called her "mousy," "nonconfrontive," "passive" and "compliant"? I've circled these words in your earlier letters and am attaching them for your perusal. On your watch, this "passive little airhead" is becoming a bold warrior for the Enemy. She's willing to confront. Risk others' disapproval. Worst of all, she's intent on gaining approval from the Audience of One. This Jillian doesn't appear to be the same girl you spoke of seven months ago. And now she's leaving on a missions trip?

The ice you're walking on gets thinner every day. And the temperature keeps rising.

Proud to strangle them with pride,

Prince Ishbane

39

Jillian sat with a Green Bay Packer blanket over her, Nickerson sprawled out on her lap underneath it.

"Some people called me little Miss Perfect. I mean, until I belted Kelly."

"Yeah," Rob said. "That straightened them out."

"Well, your Christian friends thought you were Mr. Perfect, too. Like you had it all together. Maybe that's what you wanted me to think."

"Maybe. But now you know the truth. I'm such a lowlife I've seriously considered killing myself."

"That doesn't make you a lowlife. It just means you need help. Like the rest of us. My eating disorder's a problem. Your depression's a problem. Welcome to the human race. But we can both depend on God's strength and the support of others, right?"

"You're sounding like the preacher now."

"Hey—if it's true, deal with it."

"Where have I heard that?"

They both laughed.

"Anyway," Jillian said, "I'm glad you talked with Jeff and Steve, and had the appointment. And you're taking your pills, right?"

"Yep. One at a time. Thanks for asking." Rob looked around. "Is Daniel home?"

"Probably holed up in his room. He gets more antisocial every day. I'm worried about him."

"What does he do in his room without the computer?"

Jillian shrugged. "Sleep? Read? I don't know."

"Maybe you should find out."

"He's getting weirder all the time. Before school got out, I was afraid he'd explode. I guess they hammer on him in the locker room. They keep ridiculing him, call him 'freak' and stuff."

"Who's they?"

"The usual bullies. Josh Waters is one of them. Unfortunately, he'll be a senior, so it'll start again in the fall. I asked Ian to tell some of his old jock friends to back off. Daniel's got a short fuse."

"If he spends his time holed up in his bedroom, it could get even shorter."

"Maybe it's like your depression. Gets worse when you're alone?"

"That's what I was thinking. Anyway, if we're flying to Europe tomorrow, I've got some packing to do."

Three weeks and one day later, August 15, the missions team was on its way back home. Jillian sat on the plane four rows ahead of Rob, in a window seat, Lisa asleep next to her. Jillian laid her journal open on the tray table in front of her. Three weeks earlier, on a plane headed toward Ljubljana, capital of Slovenia, she'd started this journal. Now she was writing her final entry. Portland was just a few hours away.

In some ways this was the best three weeks of my life. It wasn't easy, Lord, You know that. I was scared and sick at first, frustrated by the language gap, wishing I could accomplish more. Sometimes I was embarrassed because I didn't know what to do or when to do it. There were those tensions on the team, but for the most part we got along incredibly well. Thanks for answering that prayer, and thanks for the people at church who gave to us and prayed for us.

Lisa and I did great as roommates. And I got so close to Megan, Jenny, Holly, Emily, and Adrianne. They were sophomores and juniors when I was a senior, and thanks to the high school caste system, I'd never gotten to know them. Now they're like sisters to me. I wish I'd reached out to them last year. We did a lot of things together with the Slovenian girls, while our guys worked with their guys. That was a good plan, though I didn't see Rob as much as I'd expected. But we had lots of events together, including that great tug-of-war tournament and capture the flag. And hanging out in Ljubljana with Rob and Lisa and Megan was a blast.

What did I learn more than anything? First, Lord, to be thankful for all You've given me. A great mom. A wonderful church. Terrific friends. And above all, You've given me Yourself. I've learned to depend on You like never before. I think my life verse now is "Apart from Me you can do nothing." And I guess I'd have to throw in "My grace is sufficient for you, for My power is made perfect in weakness."

You know there were times I was really weak. Sick for four days the first week. Jet-lagged out of my mind. I wanted to go home. I felt useless. But You ended up using me anyway. And the best part was when I shared the gospel with Branka. I was still woozy and praying like crazy You'd give me the words and help her understand. July 30—I'll never forget that night. It was so awesome to be there when Branka prayed and put her trust in You. It was my first time leading someone to You, Lord. I don't want it to be my last.

Thanks for opening my eyes to see what You're doing around the world. Thanks for letting me see the missionaries close-up, the Pattys and Jacksons and their kids. Help me never to lose my heart for missions. Keep me from ever being satisfied with less than You. And thanks for Your reminder that America's not my home. Somehow I don't care now if we move. I don't need a new house. Like the speaker said when he was teaching from John 14, earth's not our home, heaven is. That's such a freeing thought. My future's not on earth. It's in heaven, where You've gone to prepare a place for me!

I'm so pumped about starting Gresham Bible College in a few weeks. I'm excited about whatever You have for me.

Help me to overflow with Your love, Lord. Help Rob and me to be an example to Brittany and Ian, so they can see You in us. We'd love to see them come to know You, Lord. Like Rob says, please do whatever it takes.

Speaking of Rob, Lord, You know I love him. I care about him so much. He was terrific on this trip, a servant to others. And he says he learned a ton, too. He was so focused on fellowshiping with You and reaching out to others, he says he didn't have time to be depressed! I know the Enemy will attack him again, Lord. Your Word says he always returns at an opportune time. He's got his fiery arrows pointed at us. Help us to stay pure, Lord, and help us be wise.

If You want Rob and me together, You know that would make me happy. But I pray You'll do what You know is best. You're in control, not me. For the first time in my life, that's exactly how I want it. The more I learn who You are and who I am, the more I trust You and distrust me.

I also know You're the main one I need to depend on. Not myself, not Rob or anybody else. You're my bridegroom, Your Word says, and I'm part of Your bride. Thanks for choosing me, Lord. I don't deserve You, but I'm sure grateful. I love You, Jesus.

P.S. Please give Daddy a hug for me, would You?

Jillian put down her pen, closed the journal and stuck it in her carry-on. She blinked back the tears and sat up, turning her head to peek four rows back at Rob. He was looking right at her. He smiled broadly.

Letter 39

My traveling tempter Foulgrin,

Don't get your tactics confused. Make Rob miserable, yes, but do what you can to make Brittany and Ian happy. You heard me. This whole pregnancy, which you assumed was an automatic victory for us, could be an instrument in the Enemy's hands. We want to usher the vermin to hell with minimal struggles along the way. It's our tactic of bait and switch. Lure them in with false promises. Continue the charade to the last moment. Never give them a hint of the eternal terror awaiting them.

When things appear to go their way, they live for the moment only. When life throws them curve balls—including this pregnancy—they can start thinking about the larger scheme of things. Even the hereafter. Then the battle shifts to the Enemy's turf. (How many *apparent* disasters have proven to be the Enemy's grace under cover?)

The Enemy is tricky, Foulgrin. Things are not always as they appear.

Needless to say, I'm depressed to learn of Jillian and Rob's experiences in Slovenia. Here's a country we've steeped in darkness and hopelessness. The Enemy's followers are few there. And yet these pesky missionaries who invited this summer team are working with forbidden fellowships to get out the forbidden message. The missions team encouraged the Slovenian believers? You failed to neutralize Jaltor and Talon, didn't you? Worse still, the Enemy strengthened His hold on Jillian and Rob.

Why am I not surprised?

You'd hoped to couple them up and keep their minds on each other rather than the Enemy's work. Even that failed. One of my anonymous informants tells me Jillian's discovery of Rob's suicidal temptations last month has caused him to face his problem. He spoke openly about it to spiritual advisors. Began taking his medicine. Now that he's home he's already part of an accountability group. Sickening.

Do you see what's happened? When his thoughts emerged from the darkness, they became manageable. Because Jillian saw her boldness rewarded in her dealings with Brittany and Rob, it increased her boldness in Slovenia. I understand she guided to the Carpenter a despicable girl named Branka. For all we know, this Branka could become the Enemy's key warrior to liberate her culture. Just when I think it can't get any worse…

I'm happy to repeat that while you and Baalgore were off sightseeing with Rob and Jillian, Raketwist has been holding his own with Brittany. Pendragon and Stungoth have made great strides with Ian and Daniel. I trust you're ready to resume assisting them? Though, hell knows, they might well do better without you.

It's time to get Daniel and Ian deeper into the occult. When you're using the board, cards, horoscopes, palm readings, occult books, and all the other access devices, don't forget to sprinkle in helpful information and inspirational words. Only after you have them hooked should you resort to vicious or blatantly immoral instructions. I've used the board to make subtle claims to biblical orthodoxy, spouting Christian terminology to take them off guard and suck them in deeper. The end justifies every means. Even if we must resort to throwing in an occasional nugget of truth to set them up for the kill.

With Ian, Brittany, and Daniel, try using our séance strategy. You know, where we play good spirit/bad spirit to fool them into thinking the "good spirits" should be listened to. Make them think the board's a source of guidance like the Bible. Just more fascinating and inclusive. While the Bible explicitly forbids them to dabble in our devices and rituals, we don't forbid them to look at the Bible. To do so would make our ends too obvious.

Don't try to make a vermin throw the Bible in a fireplace. We're better served by it sitting unopened on his dresser. Periodically use the board and automatic writing to instruct them to "love one another" and "do no harm." Feed them such platitudes as you would feed corn to a pig before leading him to slaughter. Yes, the humans are stupider and uglier than pigs. But you get my point.

Only when you have them firmly in your clutches, then feel free to invade their minds with thoughts and feelings so foreign as to terrify them.

One of the great benefits of the occult is that it causes them either to overestimate or underestimate our power over them. They may eagerly come after us, not realizing they're putting their neck in our noose. Or they may flee from us in constant dread of our power over them. Either way we have them. What they think of us doesn't matter. Just as long as they do think of us all the time. Lock their minds on us—or anyone or anything else—just as long as it isn't Him.

Craving the kill,

Prince Ishbane

40

It was the Friday night of Labor Day weekend. The end of summer or the beginning of fall, depending on how you wanted to look at it. Right now, Ian didn't give a rip. He grabbed a beer and walked out the sliding glass doors. He didn't know whose house this was. It didn't really matter. He didn't know most of the people here. Bailey had tried to introduce him to a few guys, and more than a few girls. Ian wasn't interested, though he'd kept his eye on one red-headed girl. He sat alone on an old chair outside, peering into the dark woods that surrounded the house. He thought it weird how ten minutes from the city could feel like a hundred miles. He heard the river flowing even above the loud music muffled by the walls. He felt the bass pounding in his chest.

His head nodded with each thump, the rhythm taking control of his body. He knew he'd had too much to drink, but gulped down the rest of his twelve-ounce can. He thirsted deeply. The next beer would do it, put him over, give him Nirvana or Shangri-La, transport him in place or time. Or at least give him a break from the hell he'd been feeling. He had to have another.

He stumbled by a few guys taking ecstasy. He'd only tried it a few times, back when he went to raves. Maybe it was time to try it again. Maybe later. He went inside and headed for the cooler. It was empty.

"Dude, where's the beer?" Ian said to nobody in particular.

"In here, man. Check it out. We got some hard-core drinkin' going down."

He wandered out to the living room where a crowd had formed around two guys sitting across from each other, a big oak footstool between them. One of them was Bailey. The other he recognized as a basketball player who'd gone to Franklin. He'd guarded him as a sophomore, and the guy had beat him bad. He'd graduated a few years ago and played ball for the University of Oregon. Ian closed his eyes, trying to recall his name. Why couldn't he remember? Tibbs. Ricky Tibbs. Of course. He was a great player.

Not a bad drinker either, if he's facing off with Bailey.

Bailey was gulping down a can of beer, golden brew running down his chin and out the sides of his mouth. When he finished, he smashed the can on his head and everyone cheered. Then all eyes turned toward Ricky.

He smiled broadly and grabbed a beer, popping the top open and toasting the crowd. He finished his even quicker than Bailey had, and crushed it soundly against his head. He added it to the pile of mangled cans at their feet.

The crowd roared. Then all was silent as a skinny, freckle-faced kid parted the multitudes. He brought his hand out from behind his back and presented a bottle of scotch whiskey. Shouts of approval rose. He grinned, enjoying his moment in the spotlight. Apparently this was his house, and Daddy forgot to lock the liquor cabinet. Freckles set out two shot glasses, one on each side of the table, and folded his arms.

Ricky was all smiles as he grabbed the bottle and poured for both of them, arm shaking a little. By the fifth shot, Bailey was struggling. At the eighth he gave up, stumbling to the bathroom to vomit. Ricky finished Bailey's glass, then downed his own. Then he raised the bottle in triumph and drank straight from it. The crowd went wild.

Ian looked at the pile of beer cans and the dwindling bottle of scotch. Ricky must have had over twenty drinks, and they'd been here only a few hours. He shook his head and laughed.

So this is what you learn at college? I'm all over that!

A face flashed in front of him, only for a moment. David Richards. The New Year's party. The phone call. The memorial service. He shook it off. Ian felt invincible. They weren't old fogies ready to die of heart attacks. They were young and strong, and their bodies could take it. They were invulnerable.

Ian finished his beer. He'd had enough of being by himself. It was time to forget everything dragging him down. He didn't care that he hadn't talked with Brittany for seven weeks. He didn't care about ditching Rob tonight for this party. He sure didn't want to hear anything more about Slopainia, or whatever the heck that God-forsaken place was.

He walked over to the corner of the room where the green smoke was thickest. He didn't smoke pot often. He always told everyone he couldn't because of basketball. Training started soon at PSU, but games weren't for a long time. Besides, it was the last weekend of summer. He wanted to go out with a bang. The red-headed girl passed him a joint, and he inhaled deeply. He did this several more times. In a few minutes the room took on a bright blurry edge. It started slipping out of focus.

He heard a loud thump and felt it in his chest. He took a few breaths, then turned slowly, as if in a dream. He saw Ricky on the floor. He'd passed out. He heard people laughing at the far end of a tunnel. He joined in, not because it was so funny but because he thought it was supposed to be. He put the joint to his mouth again and breathed in. Why was it so funny to see a drunk guy passing out? Or smelling the guy who'd wet his pants, or the guy who'd vomited on himself? He didn't really know, which made it even funnier. He laughed some more.

Ian needed another drink. And maybe some buffalo wings and chips. Buffalo with wings. That was funny. Buffalo chips. That was *real* funny.

Ian was starving, but nothing he saw looked like what he hungered for. He wandered through the crowd. He saw the red-headed girl again. She pressed up against him. Later maybe. Not now. He felt like he was going to suffocate. He stumbled over something. He looked down. It was Ricky. In the midst of the deafening music and blurry people, Ricky looked so relaxed, so…peaceful. Nothing to worry about. Nobody was hassling him now. Escape. Was that what Ian longed for?

Ian heard voices all around him, but couldn't make out what they were saying. He heard Brittany yelling at him. He heard Rob condemning him. But there was another voice. This voice was soothing and hypnotic. Was it the red-headed girl? No. She'd disappeared. It was whispering something over and over and over and over. What was it? He focused hard.

Sleep, Ian. Sleep.

Yeah, that's what he needed, sleep. The only time he didn't think about his problems was when he slept. He needed a deep, dreamless night's sleep.

He tripped over someone else sprawled on the floor. He had to get out of there. He wandered around looking for Bailey. He found him curled up next to the bathroom. Ian grabbed his keys from his front pocket and made his way out the door. He wandered through the maze of cars and finally found Bailey's. He fumbled with the keys, trying to find the right one, then noticed the car was blocked in tight.

Ian cursed, then kicked the tire. The keys dropped to the gravel driveway, and he bent to pick them up. When he stood up, his head was swimming. All he wanted was to fall asleep. He just needed to pull the covers over his head and be lost in the darkness.

He saw two guys getting in a car. "Hey," he called, "you guys wanna give me a ride?"

They didn't seem to hear him. He could barely tell who it was. Wait. It was Kyle and Jason, two guys who went to Jillian's church. One had been Lisa's boyfriend for a while.

Hypocrites, he muttered, as they drove off.

He started the quarter mile walk to the end of the driveway. Maybe somebody on the main road would give him a ride home. Step by step he willed his heavy feet to bring him closer to sleep, closer to the quiet darkness.

Sleep, Ian, sleep.

He turned around quickly, losing his balance and almost falling to the ground. A shiver went through his body. Had someone whispered his name? It sounded like the red-headed girl. No. He was drunk. And stoned. He knew that much. He looked to the right and saw the line where the gravel from the driveway stopped and the forest began. The fir trees towered over him as he drew closer. One of the limbs was moving side to side, as if someone had just entered the darkness beyond its reach. It was beckoning him to come in. Why not? He wasn't afraid. He was invincible.

Ian paused at the edge of the shadows. A twig snapped a few yards in front of him. He swallowed hard and put his arms out in front of him to move aside the low branches that blocked his view. He stopped to relieve himself. It seemed to take forever.

Sleep, Ian, sleep.

He heard the dull sound of footsteps ahead of him. There had to be someone out there…someone that wanted him to follow. It was probably the red-haired girl. Yeah. Maybe she wanted him, maybe she was luring him after her. Maybe it was a game, and he was supposed to chase her. He walked faster, stumbling. Something was up ahead, a rushing sound.

After a few minutes, the trees began to thin. He stumbled right up to something dark. Whoever it was had gone farther. If he went just ten more feet, he'd catch her. He was about to leap forward. He wanted to jump into the darkness and drift into pleasure or sleep, whatever awaited him.

Suddenly he felt himself lose his balance, falling. The air on his face felt different, wetter. His blurry eyes couldn't focus.

He dropped to the ground, sitting right where he'd stood. He hung his legs over. He dangled them.

Over what?

Ian looked down under the quarter moon just rising, its reflection appearing on wet rocks below. Way below, maybe a hundred feet. What? He was...on a cliff. Something in the water glowed. It invited him to join it, to come forward, to jump in, to float downward like a leaf. To drift into sleep, to find rest.

The wind started to blow, bringing with it voices.

"I'm pregnant. All you care about is yourself. The only mistake I made was you."

"The murderers and the sexually immoral and those who practice magic arts—their place will be in the fiery lake of burning sulfur."

Robert Banish, the tombstone said. Nineteen years old. "How old are you?" Nineteen.

"It's not a serious charge, right? He's got a scholarship—you don't need to tell Portland State do you? He has to be able to play basketball."

"Kryon is a gentle loving spirit."

"Touched by an angel."

"Touched by a fallen angel."

"Study the Bible with me, Ian. Let's see what it says you're searching for."

Sleep, Ian. Drift down into sleep.

He felt his eyes close. His chin fell to his chest. He was sleepy, but tired of always waking up. He leaned forward. His shoulders were out over his knees. Just a few more inches, and gravity would take over. Then all the voices would go away.

There. He'd lost his balance and was falling now, first in a somersault, then head first, turning in the air. Olympic judges were already putting up his scores. For a moment he felt he could fly. He was about to hit the water. It would be like a dive off the high board. Then he hit. He felt nothing.

A strong wind blew into his face, tipping his balance backward. He opened his eyes, pried from the dream of falling and flying. Trembling, he pulled his shoulders back, then carefully swung his legs up off the ledge. He pulled himself to his feet and staggered back toward the trees. Suddenly his stomach erupted. He vomited into the thick underbrush, and felt some splatter back on his face. He wiped it with his hand, then tried in vain to clean himself on the bushes.

He tilted his head and listened to the voices. There were only two now, coming from opposite directions. Ian Stewart wept quietly as he waded through shadows and pushed away tree limbs. He wept because he didn't know which voice he should listen to.

Ian sat at his kitchen table late Saturday morning, eating a bowl of Cheerios and trying to get rid of the pounding headache. He'd popped Advil and Tylenol both. He'd even poured his mom's six-hour-old coffee out of the pot into a mug and microwaved it. Yuck. But nothing else had stopped the jackhammers. Maybe the coffee would.

Mom had left the TV on next to the stove. Suddenly the local anchorman came on, and next to him someone's photograph. Someone familiar.

"Portland resident and University of Oregon basketball player Ricky Tibbs was found dead this morning at a friend's house in east Portland. Tibbs died of alcohol poisoning late last night after passing out during a party. Multnomah County Medical Examiner Dr. Randall Monnes said Tibbs had a .44 percent blood alcohol level when he died, over five times the legal limit in Oregon. His body was found by police around 8:30 A.M. when a friend called to report Tibbs wasn't breathing. Witnesses said Tibbs had been involved in a drinking contest last night, and had consumed over twenty drinks in a two-hour period."

This can't be happening. Not again. First David? Now Ricky?

Ian shook uncontrollably.

You're next.

He turned quickly to see who'd said the words. No one was there.

Letter 40

My optimistic Foulgrin,

I notice your reoccurring use of the word *almost*. You *almost* got Jillian and Rob to fornicate. You *almost* got Brittany to have an abortion. You *almost* got Jillian not to go on the missions trip. Now you *almost* got Ian to fall off that ledge.

Almost isn't enough!

Of course you terrified him. So what? The Enemy could use that as a wake-up call! Ian has now seen two people who've died at parties from alcohol poisoning. I know he's a fool, but maybe it'll sink in!

It's even possible some parents might look into where their children are spending their nights. As long as their kids stay off crack and don't drive after drinking, most of them don't sweat it. Who gets hurt by a little pot smoking, anyway? Mom and Dad smoked a little weed themselves back in their day. Of course, they don't realize the pot teens smoke today is fifteen times more potent than what they smoked. Meanwhile, Internet sites teach their offspring how to get pot and grow their own marijuana.

Remember, any drug serves us well simply by dulling the mind. The mind that's dulled isn't alert to the Enemy. Truth is His favorite agent of change. Vermin who are high are easily misled, but seldom vulnerable to truth.

One of the most useful aspects of youth culture is this sense of invulnerability. "It can't happen to me. Yes, maybe somebody somewhere dies from alcohol abuse. And drug use.

And sexually transmitted diseases. But not me or my friends. Not us."

Keep Ian from thinking about death. And especially what awaits him on the other side. Blind him to the fact that since his last day is coming, he ought to prepare for it. Don't let him ponder heaven and hell. Or if he does, make him assume he's going to heaven.

One of our greatest allies is the flippancy of popular culture. All the jokes about drunkenness, drugs, and immorality serve us well. Even the most grave moral issues are fodder for the Leno and Letterman types. Though humor goes against our grain, many demons now make careers of joke writing. And why not? What could be better than getting the vermin to laugh at what appalls the Enemy? To scorn what He holds dear? We don't even have to persuade them to engage in these things. Laughter's a form of approval.

Nothing serves the Enemy better than joyful laughter among close friends. Nothing serves us better than cynical laughter that mocks what's precious to the Enemy. But never make the mistake of thinking laughter automatically enhances our position. The Enemy's celebratory laughter is seductive to them and torturous to us. Fortunately, we've persuaded most of them, Ian included, that hell is where there's laughter. And heaven's the eternal gray, the desolate home of the pout-faced dirge. They know no better. They haven't seen the desolation of hell's solitary confinement, where the only sound is weeping regret. Nor have they had to listen to the exasperating gaiety of heaven and its parties or all the gasps of wondrous delight from these slimy vermin as they enter Charis. Nauseating!

You say Rob has been neglecting his time in the forbidden book? Wonderful. The book isn't a magic talisman that works without being read. A Bible does us no harm as long as it remains closed.

While she's not been indulging in dramatic sins recently, I'm glad to hear Jillian's missed church and her new college group the last few weeks. So much comes down to *habits*.

In battle we destroy soldiers by cutting them off from supply lines. If they don't get food, they'll be weakened, unable to hold their ground. The forbidden book is food, the forbidden fellowship is reinforcement. Keep her from both. A stranded soldier is easy to pick off. Cut her from her squadron and you've got her.

That she's starting her classes at this Bible college isn't promising. Still, we've managed to derail them even where the forbidden book is taught. Get her hung up on rules. Give her a few unpleasant experiences with administrators, teachers, and students. Poison her attitude. Make her a whiner.

Who cares whether a vermin is wearing our uniform as long as she furthers our purposes? Indeed, our most effective servants often wear the Enemy's uniforms. Camouflage is critical to successful warfare. That's why I'm delighted Ian saw—at his drinking party— two boys from Jillian's church. Nothing serves us better than the moral lapses of those who attend forbidden fellowships. It undermines and invalidates efforts of true Christians.

In some of the forbidden fellowships we've made certain vices acceptable, almost desirable, among Christian leaders. These include materialism, egotism, exhibitionism, and self-promotion. These are sufficiently publicized to make onlookers identify them with the forbidden message itself! Nothing is more satisfying than to see them promote self under the guise of promoting Him.

We can shipwreck them either by taking them away from the church, or putting them in the wrong churches. Remember Quagmire's ninth law of domination: *The looser a vermin's ties to a forbidden squadron, the more vulnerable he is to us.* Remove a burning coal from the fire, and soon it cools and dies. Get hypocrite Christians to church. Keep genuine ones away.

It's party time,

Prince Ishbane

41

Glad you loved your first week at GBC," Rob said, sitting at his parents' kitchen table snacking on mom's homemade tortilla chips and secret-ingredient salsa. I should come visit some of your classes, since mine don't start for three weeks. Theology or Bible maybe."

"You'd love my ethics class. Except you wouldn't have as many fights with the teacher. He actually believes the Bible. Visiting could be dangerous, though. You might want to transfer. It's your kind of place."

Rob shrugged. "Maybe. How's Brittany feeling about Mt. Hood?"

"She likes the looks of her schedule. Nutrition, anatomy, chemistry. We'll see what she thinks when classes start. She's still swallowing her pride about going to a community college. With raising a baby, medical school may be too much, but she figures she can make it through nursing. I hear it's a great program, really tough. That's what Brit needs. She loves a challenge. We'll see what happens. She knows I'll be there for her."

Daniel sat alone in his bedroom after his first week back at high school. Josh Waters and the other bullies had already terrorized him. It was going to be hell again.

"Hello," it said.

"Is this Dad?"

The planchette indicated "No."

"Who is it?"

No answer.

"Is it FG?"

No answer.

"Should I take the gun to school?"

The planchette moved to "Yes."

"Should I use it on someone?"

"Yes."

"Who?"

The planchette moved from letter to letter, spelling out the name. Daniel's heart raced. He started to put the board away. Suddenly he stopped, then put his fingers back on it.

"How old will I live to be?"

The pointer went up the row of numbers, past the four and five and six and seven, then stopped and moved backward, going all the way to one. Then it stopped. A moment later it moved to five.

Daniel trembled. He backed away from the Ouija board. In another three months he would be sixteen.

Ian followed Rob out of their apartment into a small campus building. He couldn't believe he'd let Rob talk him into this. Basketball training had started and he was tired. But he knew Rob wasn't going to take no for an answer. Ian had tried to avoid him all day, but it was a little hard since they lived in the same three-bedroom apartment with four other guys. They were headed for Campus Fellowship. Even the name made Ian cringe.

They walked in a couple minutes late. Groups of students stood all over the room talking and laughing, eating donuts and drinking Cokes.

Rob led Ian to a seat in the third row. Someone came over and sat next to Rob, asking him a question about the Bible.

Three guys from the basketball team walked in. Ian pulled his baseball cap lower and studied his shoes. These guys were juniors or seniors, and he'd only met them in camp and the weight room. They probably wouldn't recognize him, but just in case… He wondered if they were the team "Christian boys." Every team seemed to have them. Ian looked at the clock, begging its hands to move faster.

A guy carrying an acoustic guitar walked up front, someone grabbed the bass, someone else drums, and a girl stood behind the keyboard.

Ian didn't know any of the songs, but he was surprised at how good the music sounded. He'd assumed there'd be an organ and they'd sing hymns that sounded like old-time roller skating music or something. This was more his style, especially with the bass and the drums. The bass player was fantastic, good enough to be a pro. Ian felt himself starting to relax. Then again, the preacher hadn't come up yet. He'd check his watch to see how long it would take before hell was mentioned.

The acoustic guitarist made some announcements about a retreat they were planning and some "outreach activities" people could get involved in. Ian tuned out. It was getting dangerously close to sermon time. He was ready to be bored or offended, probably both. But if he had to choose, he'd rather be offended.

The band sat down, all except for the bass player. He took the microphone and grabbed a Bible off one of the front chairs. Apparently he was introducing the speaker?

"Hey, everybody! Welcome to a new year of school, and a new year of Campus Fellowship. It's great to see a lot of you again. I'm excited about the new faces. For those of you who weren't here last year, my name's Jeff and I lead this crew, or try to anyway."

The bass player? The preacher was the bass player? He leaned over to Rob and whispered, "Isn't he a student?"

"No, he graduated five years ago, I think. He looks young, though, huh?"

Ian nodded. He'd never seen a guy less than fifty years old give a sermon. He braced himself for hellfire and brimstone. Would this guy parade across the platform like a television preacher? Soon he found out. No platform, no parading, no yelling. Even the guy's hair looked normal.

Jeff read a few verses from the Bible. "So it says Jesus was sent to us from heaven, and He came to us full of grace and truth. What's *grace* and what's *truth?* Let's talk about what those words mean."

He sounded pretty rational. Ian didn't agree with everything. But a lot of it made sense. Instead of fighting sleep like he'd done the few times he'd been to church in the last five years, Ian found himself listening. For a moment he wished he was somewhere else. He felt like getting up and leaving. But he wondered why—it was an interesting talk. He'd read about other world religions and metaphysics and all that. What would be the harm in hearing about Christianity? He felt drawn to Jeff and his words, yet at the same time he felt repulsed by them.

After speaking twenty minutes, Jeff stopped abruptly and started to pray. Ian noticed several guys holding ball caps in their hands. He quickly removed his.

Jeff's prayer was weird. He sounded as if he was actually talking to someone. It wasn't a memorized speech, or somebody nervously asking for a favor.

"So, Lord, I'd appreciate it if You'd speak to anyone who doesn't know You and draw them to Yourself. Help them to realize it's You they're searching for. I ask this in the name of Jesus. Amen."

"Let's talk to Jeff before he gets surrounded," Rob said. He walked straight to Jeff, and Ian followed.

"Hey, Rob!" Jeff said as they approached.

"Hi, Jeff." Rob shook his hand. "This is my good friend, Ian. I talked him into coming to check us out."

"Ian, hi! Great to meet you."

"Where'd you learn to play the bass like that?" Ian asked.

"Something I picked up along the way. So tell me about yourself, Ian."

"I'm a freshman…brand new. I'm here on a basketball scholarship. So besides classes and homework, that's my life right now."

"Basketball player, huh? Awesome. I was a baller myself, back in the day."

"Yeah?" Ian said. "Did you play in college?"

"I was planning on it. But God wasn't."

"O…kay."

Jeff smiled. "I had a scholarship to Oregon State, but right after I graduated from high school I busted my leg playing backyard ball. I had to get screws in it, the whole nine yards. My doctor told me it would be a year before I could walk right, much less play ball. So that was it for competitive stuff. End of career. But after a few years I got my leg back. I still play a little sometimes."

Rob laughed. "Jeff's too humble. We were on a retreat last spring and this old man tore it up big time."

"Twenty-eight is your definition of an old man?" He laughed. "So Ian, if you're not prejudiced against senior citizens, maybe we could shoot together when you've got an extra hour."

"Yeah," Ian said. "That sounds great."

"Why don't you give me your phone number, and I'll give you a call."

Jeff handed Ian a note card, and he wrote down his name and number. They talked and laughed several more minutes.

As they walked out, Ian looked at the clock. They'd hung around nearly two hours. He'd thought Campus Fellowship would be a medieval torture chamber. Where'd he gotten all his preconceived notions? If he didn't know better, he'd have sworn someone planted them.

As they walked back to their apartment, Ian thought about how crazy everything was. A month ago he'd been going out drinking every spare opportunity. But since that scare by the cliff and Ricky's death, he'd been afraid to drink. He wouldn't admit that to Bailey, but it was true. And to top it off, here he'd gone to a Bible study. And he'd actually almost *liked* it.

What was that music he was hearing in his head? The *Twilight Zone?*

Daniel walked down the hallway, feeling power surge through him. Like a robot assassin on assignment, just like in the video game, he scanned the faces in front of him, envisioning numeric data in his computerized head. His right hand was in his coat pocket. As he passed people in the halls, he pictured himself crouching and setting the gun sight on them. He saw himself shooting Mr. McGowan. Then Miss Harcourt. He looked at Kandi Freedman, primping by her locker. She'd mocked him again just a few days ago. Called him "Shorty." He turned the corner toward someplace he rarely dared to tread—the senior lockers. He saw two letterman's jackets and tensed, squeezing the handle in the pocket. Then he saw a third letterman's jacket. Its wearer was tall and broad-shouldered. Yeah, this was the one. He moved closer.

The boy turned his head. It was Josh Waters, the face Daniel had been envisioning. The one who'd pushed him around one too many times. The one who after today would never again snap him with a towel between the legs.

Josh stared at Daniel. He smiled scornfully. "What do you think you're doing here, rug rat?" He raised his voice to draw an audience. "Want to get duct taped to the wall again? How about I take you down to the locker room for some target practice?" His cruel laugh ended with a snort.

Trembling, Daniel slowly pulled the jet black gun from his pocket. He extended his arm just like in the video game at the mall. He pointed it, raising the barrel to Josh's forehead. He pulled lightly, pretending it triggered a red laser beam, focused on the bully's forehead.

"You're done pushing me around," Daniel said quietly, matter-of-factly.

Josh Waters turned pale and blinked hard, standing perfectly still, fingers spread tensely. A girl screamed, a boy shouted, and when Daniel turned to look, kids backed away from him. Several fell to the ground. Others ducked for cover. He saw a teacher peeking around the corner, punching a cell phone. But all voices were muffled. No locker doors slamming. Nobody yelling greetings or put-downs. Daniel floated on the sea of tense silence.

"No!" He heard someone scream, just before stepping behind a locker.

Josh's face looked like pasty papier-mâché, bloodless.

"Don't," he whispered to Daniel, eyes pleading. The hunter had become the prey. Daniel liked what he was feeling.

He glanced around at eyes peeking from behind lockers, at others frozen in their tracks, afraid to move. Afraid of him. Daniel looked at Josh's eyes.

"You shouldn't have dissed me. I'm gonna to make you sorry."

Slowly, surely, vacant-eyed, like his mind was in another world, Daniel pulled the trigger. The gun wasn't empty. It delivered its full payload.

$$\sim\!\!\!m$$

Letter 41

My exemplary Prince Ishbane,

I keep them from praying. When they insist, I try to limit it to a particular posture at a particular time. Fortunately, Jillian hasn't got the hang of firing up prayers to the Enemy throughout the day.

I convince her she's "just" praying, as if it weren't action of the most potent kind. She doesn't understand prayer isn't preparation for battle, it is the battle. I don't fear prayerless study, work, preaching, or parenting. The forbidden talk infuses them with the Enemy's presence and power. I eliminate it when I can, and minimize it when I can't.

The Enemy sent Jaltor and another warrior to stand guard over Ian. I've counterattacked by deploying two more of our troops. I sent the orders on your behalf, knowing that's what you'd want. And don't worry, I'm keeping an eye on Jillian. I'll make sure the Enemy's not doing something behind my back.

Ian's being in college has advantages and disadvantages. The obvious disadvantage is Rob's proximity. I'd hoped by now he'd have snuffed himself out, but that appears less likely than ever. It's disturbing Ian agreed to go to this campus meeting where the Enemy's book was taught and Ian could meet real Christians, whom he now must contrast to our caricatures of Christians. I almost got him to stay home. I assure you, Ishbane, he went with Rob reluctantly.

But the advantages of Ian's being at college outweigh the disadvantages. To quote his psychology professor in yesterday's class, "It's unhealthy to believe in demons. It's a regression to medieval superstition and primitive fears."

I love it when they ask whether a belief is "healthy" or "unhealthy" rather than whether it's true or false. Their reasoning seems to be this: If something causes fear it must not be real. If it would make them afraid to know there are lions, well then there must not be lions. If the existence of demons—or God Himself—makes them uncomfortable, well then demons and God must not exist.

Isn't it amusing how educated men deny fundamental realities uneducated men intuitively recognize? The vermin think of us as they do monsters under the bed, ghosts in the closet, or bogeymen in the basement. As they grow out of believing in them, they grow out of believing in us. It never dawns on them that we are the realities behind those fantasies; we are invisible beings who are, in fact, out to get them. Parents make our job much easier when, instead of teaching their children to resist us, they teach them we don't exist.

The college professors I most relish are those who present no evidence for beliefs and disbeliefs, but simply declare that things are true or not true based on how comfortable they make them feel, or how popular they are among the current academic elite. No wonder many of the young vermin graduate from college considerably more stupid than when they arrive.

Send even a growing young Christian to university with no training for the battle, and we will almost certainly pick him off. How many of them were following the Enemy, and participating in the forbidden fellowship, then were sent off to college where the absolutes they've embraced are scoffed at by the cool and intelligent? As a nonbeliever, Ian has nothing of substance to hold on to in the first place. He's dead meat.

We're looking for a domino effect with Daniel. By destroying one family member, we'll take down others. Diane Fletcher will be devastated by the behavior of her little boy. In turn, we'll drive her into the comforting arms of our Donovan, whom Forktongue has groomed so effectively. Donovan's file is impressive. Diane's vulnerability to a man's attention sets her up for our next move.

It's particularly helpful that she met him at her church, that he's new in town, and his past hasn't caught up with him. By moving such men from church to church, we prey upon unsuspecting women. Many of them end up compromising bodies and souls. When the forbidden fellowships don't intervene to stop these relationships, the women become bitter. And when they do intervene, the women also become bitter! Either way, it's a no-win situation for everyone but us.

Unfortunately, Jillian's duplicity detector is more finely tuned than her mother's. Her generation is slower to trust authority figures. They tend to see through phonies. (Of course, they often falsely assume adults are phonies, but in this case your Jillian is right.) I'm laboring to keep them from seeing through us.

They're suspicious of everything for the same reason they're shocked by nothing. They've seen it all. Cheating? Happens all the time. Stealing? You can't leave your backpack out of sight or it'll be ransacked. Sex? Happens in the school parking lot at lunch. We can use their suspicion to our advantage whenever they hear the forbidden message.

I hate women and children. The weaker they are the more I detest them. The Enemy's special affection for them, His desire to protect them, is an invitation for us to exploit them. It's all coming together. Brittany, Ian, Daniel, and Diane. Hopefully we'll get Jillian and Rob in the aftershock. Our efforts are like buying up lottery tickets. The more we buy, the greater our chances of winning. Even if we fail with one of them, we can bank on the others.

I sense imminent victories on several fronts. This is my chance to prove myself to Beelzebub. I will not disappoint him.

Diligently seeking their destruction,

Lord Foulgrin

42

Mrs. Fletcher?"

"Yes?"

"This is Sam Chandler. Principal Chandler, at Kennedy? You need to get over here right away."

"Is everything okay?"

"No. It's not. Daniel's done something. Something…very serious. The police are with him right now."

"Police? What did he do?" Her voice was hollow.

"You need to get here immediately."

Diane jumped in her car and drove the ten minutes to Kennedy High. When she pulled up into visitor parking, she saw five police cars.

She walked in the front door. Every secretary and teacher who recognized her looked away. Mr. Chandler walked up and took her arm, leading her to an empty office. He had something in his hand, wrapped in a paper towel.

"Have you ever seen this?" he asked her.

She looked closely at the gun. "Yes. My husband bought it a few years ago. It was for…" Her voice faded.

"Did you know Daniel brought it to school?"

"No. I warned him to never do that."

"You made that clear?"

"Absolutely. I told him it could scare somebody."

"Dozens of students and several faculty members won't ever forget what happened here today. I can only imagine what Josh Waters went through ."

"What do you mean?"

"He's the one Daniel pointed it at. Right at his forehead. He even pulled the trigger."

She could barely breathe. "Where is Daniel?"

"In my office. With the police. I'll take you." She followed him, every part of her aching, trying to ignore the stares.

Chandler walked past his secretary and opened the door. Two police officers stood there. She recognized one from church. Her eyes fell on her little boy, dwarfed by the cops, staring at the floor.

She looked at Daniel. "You pointed this at Josh Waters?"

"Yeah," Daniel said weakly.

"And he pulled the trigger," Mr. Chandler said. "It was loaded, too."

"You're in huge trouble, young man," Diane said.

"Maybe bigger trouble than he realizes, Mrs. Fletcher," Chandler said. "With all the school shootings, we have to treat this with the utmost seriousness. We'll have to suspend him for sure. Maybe expel him. If we ever let him back in, he'll have to go through a security check every day. Parents will be outraged."

"There could be legal charges," one of the officers said. "Maybe criminal, maybe civil. Or both."

"What would that mean?" Diane asked.

"He may have to go through the juvenile court system," he said. "And, of course, somebody could sue you for the emotional trauma, especially the Waters family."

"They could sue for something like this?"

"It's been done," the officer said.

"What do you have to say for yourself?" Diane asked Daniel.

He hung his head, then looked up at her. "I didn't think it was that big a deal."

"Of course it's a big deal," Diane said. "Did anyone else know you were going to do it?"

"I told Stanky I was planning it. He thought it was a good idea. He's tired of Josh Waters, too."

"Well, he was wrong," Diane said. "You never should've done it."

"But…it's only a squirt gun."

"Well, of course it's a squirt gun. *We* know that. But Josh Waters and the others didn't know, right? It looks like a real gun." Diane looked at one of the officers and said, "My husband used to shoot Nickerson with it to keep him quiet."

The officer tilted his head. "Nickerson?"

"Our Dalmatian. He barks a lot. If you mix lemon juice with water and shoot him in the face with the…never mind, why am I telling you this? Anyway, Daniel, I specifically told you never to take it out of the house, remember? I can't believe you'd scare somebody like that. Do you want to get expelled? Do you want to hurt your family, maybe lose everything we have in a lawsuit? Is that what you want?"

"I didn't know this would happen," Daniel said. "I was just tired of getting pushed around and snapped with towels all the time. I didn't think—"

"That was it, wasn't it? You didn't think. Or maybe you let someone else do your thinking for you!"

As Jillian reached the bottom of the stairs, she saw something in the living room. Two people were hugging. Her mother and…Donovan Swain. It was a big hug. Full-bodied. His hands were stroking the back of her hair. Jillian turned away, feeling it in the pit of her stomach.

She walked to Daniel's door and knocked. No answer. She knocked again. Still no answer.

"Daniel? Unless you tell me not to, I'm coming in."

She opened the door. The room was dark. Daniel lay perfectly still, on his bed, facing the wall.

"I need to talk to you, Danny."

He didn't move.

"I know you're in big trouble. I didn't come to talk to you about that."

No response.

"I came to apologize. I haven't been there for you. Sometimes I've been downright mean. I've been a lousy big sister. Here I went on that missions trip, and now I've started Bible college, and I realize I wasn't even obeying the Bible when it came to loving my own brother. I was a fake, and I wasn't very kind to you. Ian and Rob have both been nicer to you than I have. I realize now you were lonely, just like I was. Maybe more lonely. I should have been there for you. I wasn't. And I'm very sorry."

Daniel still didn't move.

"I feel like God has opened up my eyes," Jillian said. "I want things to be different. I want to be a good sister to you. I want to help you and be there for you. Rob says he wants to do anything he can for you, too. He's been in trouble with the police before. He understands. When you're ready, he wants to talk with you. But, Daniel...would you please forgive me?" Her voice cracked.

She came closer to the bed, then sat on its edge. She put her hand on Daniel's shoulder. She said aloud, "Lord, it's just me and Daniel here, but I know You're with us, too. You're here and maybe Your angels are, and maybe the bad ones too, I don't know. Daniel's hurting, and he's in trouble. Please forgive me for being so selfish and thinking about my life all the time, not about Daniel's or Mom's. I love him, Lord. Would You please help my brother? I know You want to. Help him to let You. I don't deserve Your forgiveness or his. But I'm asking forgiveness in the name of Jesus."

She sat there for two minutes, hand on his shoulder. If she hadn't seen signs he was breathing, she'd have checked his pulse.

"I'm going to hug you, Dan. I don't think I've done that since Daddy..." The tears flowed, and she held her face in her hands.

She felt someone on the edge of the bed next to her. Daniel hugged her in the darkness, sobbing and clinging to her like a frightened puppy.

Letter 42

My meddlesome Foulgrin,

I've sent a memo informing my agents they are not to follow any orders coming from you. Deploying demons on your authority is inappropriate. You *have* no authority!

Your account of Daniel's dramatic episode was mildly amusing. Obviously, it's not nearly as satisfying as the real school killings. And there's always the danger it could serve as a serious warning to school bullies. Locker room intimidation of weak troubled boys is one of our favorite strategies.

While Daniel won't be locked up for this, it serves the purpose of reinforcing his self-loathing. It also gives him a label he'll never live down. Convince him he'll always be ostracized. Make it the core of his identity. With some effort, eventually you may get him to carry a real gun to school. Next time the shot to the head won't be a stream of water. Meanwhile, keep teaching Daniel that human life, both his and everyone else's, has little or no value. Evolution sends that message. And abortion. And euthanasia. And physician-assisted suicide.

The effect on his mother is perfect. Devastation. Shame. Self-condemnation. I'm particularly delighted to hear she hasn't turned to her church family. And only a handful of them have reached out to her. Instead, she's turned to our Donovan. He made his move right on schedule. Don't you love it when a plan comes together?

So "she felt the warm comfort of Donovan's strong arms"? You sound like a romance writer, Foulgrin. That's right, I forgot. You were assigned to one a few decades ago. After demonstrating what a compassionate and caring Christian man he is, Donovan should seduce her within the month. The movies she's watched and the novels she's read, all have prepared her to be swept off her feet by this handsome wealthy suitor. When our agents are disguised as the Enemy's, guards are always down.

You briefly mentioned Jillian went to talk with her brother. But you didn't say what happened. I assume she laid guilt on him? Let me guess—he rejected her initiative and she went away resentful, giving up on him again? I want details, Foulgrin. It's essential that family relationships are kept at a distance in such crises. Otherwise, the Enemy can pull off what He calls "bringing beauty out of ashes." I prefer our motto: "bringing ashes out of ashes."

Keep working Daniel over in secret. It's *our* bedroom. Make sure no family member intrudes.

I'm pleased our favorite holiday's coming up in a few weeks. Halloween! It's official, Foulgrin—these vermin now spend more money on this holiday than any other except Christmas. For Ian and Daniel it served as a doorway to the occult. Dressing up as little devils. Bloodsucking vampires. The walking dead. Looking and acting as evil as possible. It may be cute to their parents, but in some cases, it's just the foothold we need. Whether we're celebrated or mythologized makes no difference…either way furthers our purposes. And since Halloween's all about children and their impressionable minds, it couldn't be more strategic.

I was a key figure in the early celebration of Samhain, from which their modern Halloween developed. Pagans believed the spirits couldn't rest peacefully until given food and drink. This was a payment to the god who ruled the spirit world. Spirits were thought to roam the vicinities of their earthly lives seeking such treasures. On Samhain, the veil between the living and the dead was drawn back. On that night these wandering souls, in search of needed treasures, could visit and harass the living. Spirits would go to houses seeking the goods ("treats") needed to find final rest. If a spirit wasn't given a treat, it would "trick" or haunt the residents who refused to appease it. Pagans believed these harassing spirits could be deterred by carving fearful faces into pumpkins or squashes.

Of course, most of the vermin don't understand this occult origin. And just enough innocence and fun have been infused to make it seem harmless. But Halloween either glorifies death or makes light of it. The Enemy neither glorifies death nor makes light of it. Halloween eclipses His portrayal of death and the afterlife.

We've mutated this holiday into an effective introduction to the dark side. Razor blades hidden in apples or poison hidden in candy pale in comparison to what we've hidden inside the holiday itself.

Happy Halloween,

Prince Ishbane

43

C an I talk to you, Mom?" Jillian asked as she helped clean up after dinner.

"Sure. But Donovan's coming in an hour, and I don't want to keep him waiting."

They went to the living room. Diane sat on the love seat with Jillian next to her. Up close her mother looked weary, as if she hadn't slept in a week.

"Rob's getting together with Daniel tomorrow."

"Good," Diane said. "Since he's suspended and grounded, I'm sure he's got the time."

"Daniel and I have been talking more. I mean, since I asked his forgiveness."

"That's good," Diane said. "What did you want to talk to me about?"

Jillian took a deep breath. "It's about…Donovan."

"You still don't like him, do you?"

"First, I want to apologize for my original reaction. Maybe I was threatened because I didn't want a substitute father."

"Nobody could replace your dad, Jilly. I'd never want that."

"I know. But you have a life, and I have no right to deny you. I want you to be happy, Mom. I really mean that. And I think you're terrific. God probably has a husband in mind for you. And if you wanted me, some day I'd love to be one of your bridesmaids."

"Thanks for saying that, Jilly," Diane said, wiping her eyes. "That's the nicest thing I've heard in a long time. It means so much to me. Donovan will be thrilled, too."

"But…hang on, Mom. I really do feel that way. I think God probably has someone for you. But…I just don't think Donovan's the one."

"Why? He's been very nice to you—a lot nicer than you've been to him."

"But there's something about him. Something phony. Like he's always putting on an act, projecting an image."

"How can you say that? You don't even know him. You haven't given him a chance."

"Rob liked him at first, but now he agrees with me."

"You've been talking about Donovan?"

"The same way you'd talk about a guy I was dating. Rob says he doesn't sense much depth or character in Donovan. Rob brings up spiritual issues, and Donovan always turns the conversation to money, things, cruises, and trips to the Bahamas. He starts bragging about all the people who work for him."

"That's not fair. He even let Rob drive his car."

"Rob wants to like him. Who wouldn't want to be around someone with a car like that? But it's not about things, it's about character and love for Jesus."

"Donovan's a fine Christian."

"Because he goes to church and owns a Christian company? I mean, even Nickerson growls at him."

"You're saying our dog has a voice in who I date? Shall I ask Nickerson how he really feels about *Rob?*"

"Okay, maybe I'm stretching it. But Mom, I just hope…you're making sure to guard your purity."

Diane stiffened. "Who are you to talk to your mother about guarding her purity?"

"I'm…your daughter. And your sister in Christ. I've been praying about this, and it's one of the hardest things I've ever done. But I really believe God wanted me to talk to you. It's like what you told me about talking to Brittany. I needed to do it, for her sake, and I think I need to say this for your sake. I hope Donovan's not taking advantage of you. But with everything that's happened, with all Daniel's problems…I think you should be on guard."

"Suddenly I'm the kid and you're the mother, is that it?"

"I don't want to butt in to your private life, but Mom, you're emotionally vulnerable. This nice-looking rich guy is showering you with attention. I just want you to have your eyes wide open, okay?"

Diane stood up. "My husband is dead, my daughter has an eating disorder, my son is into God knows what and is kicked out of school, and everybody's talking about him. I'm the world's worst mother and now a man comes along, a wonderful man, and shows me some attention, and he's there when I need him, while you were off in some country I've never heard of, and spending all your spare time with Rob. And I'm supposed to feel guilty about enjoying my relationship with Donovan? Well, how about you live your life, and let me live mine…small and insignificant though it be!"

Jillian reached out to her mom, but Diane headed for the stairs. She stopped a few feet up and turned back to Jillian, red-faced.

"If you find something else I should feel guilty about, some other small happiness you want to take from me, feel free to let me know!"

She ran up the stairs. In the distance, Jillian heard a door slam.

Rob and Ian both slouched on ends of a couch at Café Delirium. Rob sipped his mocha, Ian his hot chocolate.

"I still say I'd rather be in hell with interesting people than in heaven with a bunch of sticks-in-the-mud," Ian said. "Present company excepted, of course. I guess if I could come over once a week and ride mountain bikes and do rock climbing with you in heaven, that'd be cool. But I get the impression heaven's going to be pretty boring."

"Where in the world did you get that idea?"

Ian shrugged. "I don't know."

"The Bible portrays heaven as a great place, exciting, with beauty and banquets and activities. It says we'll have things to do. There'll be places to go, a universe to be explored. The Bible says God will make us a new heaven and a new earth. The new earth will have all the best things of this world, with none of the bad ones. Personally, I want to climb mountains, swim lakes, travel to distant galaxies, you name it. God made this earth for us before we messed it up with sin. We'll have a lot more fun in the new earth than we can have on this one."

"I've never heard anyone say that before," Ian said. "After reading about Shangri-La a couple of years ago, I asked my parents what they thought heaven would be like. They had this blank look on their face and said something about spirits floating in the clouds and playing harps. It gave me the creeps. I figure that might get old after, say, the first hundred million years."

"That view of heaven isn't from the Bible. I wonder if Satan came up with it, just to mislead people and give heaven a bad name. I've got a little book on what the Bible says about heaven. I'll get it to you."

"Sure. You know me. I'll read anything. Well, almost anything. By the way, I read once that Mark Twain said 'It's heaven for atmosphere, and hell for company.'"

"I'll bet Mark Twain changed his mind a few minutes after he died. I don't know exactly what hell will be like, but I guarantee you it won't be a bunch of guys sitting around at a bar having fun and telling stories, then going out to toss a football. Hell's the only place in the universe God won't be. And since He's the maker of pleasure, the inventor of celebration, there won't be pleasure and celebration in hell. All the great stuff will be in heaven."

"Still, Rob, even you have to admit there's a lot of Christians you wouldn't want to spend an hour with, much less eternity."

"Christianity all comes down to Jesus. It stands or falls on Him. Not on the church, not on whether some people claiming to be Christians are hypocrites. Yeah, I agree, there are all kinds of jerks, plenty of hypocrites. There are lots of counterfeit bills, too, but that doesn't mean there's no such thing as real money. The point is, Christianity isn't about the stupid things some Christians say and do. It's about Jesus."

"I have no problem with Jesus," Ian said. "I respect Him as a great man."

"But do you believe in Him as the Son of God, the one and only Savior?"

"It's that 'one and only' thing that throws me. Go ahead and put Him alongside Confucius and Mohammed. But 'the only way'? I don't think so."

"That's exactly what Jesus claimed to be. He said, 'I am the way, the truth, and the life. No one comes to the Father except through Me.' So Jesus was saying He's the only way to be saved, the only way to get to heaven. I didn't say that. He did."

"That's too narrow for me. I'm not saying I don't believe in God—I don't know for sure one way or the other. Who can know? But I do know if there's a God, He wouldn't be as narrow as you make Him out to be."

"You remember Ryan, that guy from Jillian's church? You met him over at Jill's."

"I remember."

"Well, Ryan and I were talking about this a few nights ago. He says since Jesus claimed to be God and to be the only way to heaven, then He either is or He isn't. If He isn't, He was a liar or a lunatic."

"I said I respect Him as a great man, and I do. But not as God. That's just too much."

"Do great men tell the truth, or do they tell lies?"

"Truth."

"So no great man would claim to be God when he wasn't, right? And He wouldn't claim to be the only way to God if He wasn't, would He?"

Ian shrugged.

"Do you think Jesus was a liar?"

"No."

"Do you think He was crazy?"

"No." Ian fidgeted. He looked around the room, hoping to see someone familiar. Someone he could call over. Some way to end this conversation.

"Then what option's left, Ian? If Jesus wasn't lying or crazy when He said He was the way, the truth, and the life, and that no one can get to heaven but through Him, then He must have been telling the truth. Isn't that the only other alternative?"

"What about Buddhists, Hindus, Muslims, Wiccans, atheists, agnostics?"

"I think Jesus died for the sins of the whole world. It says that in the Bible. But you seem to have this idea that each worldview is like one more flower in the garden. It's a nice sentiment, but it doesn't fit the real world. Things that contradict each other can't both be true. Jesus contradicts the claim that there are many ways to God. He says He's the only one."

"I have lots of problems with Christianity. Lots of questions."

"That's okay. You say you'll read anything? I'm going to get you some books I've read in the last year. One's called *Mere Christianity* by C. S. Lewis. Another is *He Is There and He Is Not Silent* by a philosopher named Francis Schaeffer. Then there's *More Than a Carpenter, The Case for Christ,* and *The Case for Faith.* I want you to look at all of them and choose one or two for us to read. Then let's get together every week to discuss it chapter by chapter. Is it a deal?"

"What do I get out of it?"

"A free hot chocolate each week, a stimulating metaphysical discussion and the pleasure of my company."

Ian stared at the bottom of his cup. Finally he looked up. "I'll do it…but mostly for the hot chocolate."

Jillian came out of her room. She saw her mother with her ear close to Daniel's door. She thought her mom would back away in embarrassment when she heard her, but she didn't. Jillian came closer and heard Daniel's voice.

"Who's in there with him?" Jillian whispered.

"Listen," Diane said.

Jillian put her ear to the door.

"Are you there, Dad?" she heard Daniel ask. "You said it was okay for me to take that money. But I'm afraid I'll get caught. Talk to me. Please, Dad."

Diane shoved open the door. The room was dark, but light from the hallway flooded in. Jillian saw Daniel in a heavy sweatshirt, sitting with his legs crossed, and a flashlight shining on a brown board. A Ouija board. The room was cold, but the window wasn't open. Jillian choked on something in the air. She'd never felt anything like it. She looked at Daniel—his eyes were red and wet. As Jillian stood frozen, her mother stepped on the board, pushing it aside with her foot. She got down on her knees and embraced Daniel.

"What's going on?" Jillian said from the doorway. "Are you okay, Daniel?"

As a slow whimper came out of his mouth, Daniel shook his head.

Diane called Donovan Swain and cancelled their date. Jillian picked up the Ouija board and planchette, took them outside, and stuffed them in the garbage can. Diane called Greg, the youth pastor, and asked him to come over. Twenty minutes later Greg sat in their living room, along with Diane and Jillian, while Daniel spilled out his story.

Letter 43

My over-the-edge Foulgrin,

Their society is still living on interest earned off the principal of Christian beliefs. I take solace that since the principal itself is rapidly vanishing, the interest, too, is waning. Bankruptcy looms.

You keep saying things are going as you'd hoped with Diane. You brag she feels distant and alienated from Jillian. That she's angry at her for speaking up about our man Donovan.

But you minimize the truly horrifying thing—that Jillian would confront her mother in the first place! Our plan is that family members always look the other way. The reason is immaterial. Fear, self-consciousness, busyness, denial, indifference, or "love"—it's all the same. But Jillian spoke up. I ask you again—what happened to this mousy, compliant girl who posed no threat to us? Suddenly she's become this...this spokesperson for the Enemy!

To make matters worse, your ploy as the voice of Jordan Fletcher has been exposed? Family members are aware of what you've been doing to Daniel in his bedroom? The Ouija board has been discovered and removed?

Yes, you still have a stronghold. You may yet speak to Daniel in other voices. But your situation is precarious. You must do all you can to insure that the parties interested in Daniel don't gather to share insights and pray for him. Don't let them intervene for Diane either. Make sure it's Donovan's arms, not the Enemy's, she falls into. If the arms of the forbidden fellowship reach out to her, she could recede from Donovan. Pull out the stops. Don't let that happen.

I'm disturbed this troublesome Ryan is developing a mentoring relationship with Rob.

That he walked him through this "Lord, Liar, or Lunatic" logic is most unfortunate. That Rob in turn shared it with Ian is irksome. Yes, Ian resisted the logic. But did the Enemy introduce seed ideas to him that eventually could grow and bear fruit?

We can't afford for young minds like Rob's to be trained in the forbidden book's truths. Offer them a salad-bar theology. Let them pick according to preference.

As for Rob giving Ian some of the Enemy's most useful books, this too is awful news. Ian's a reader. Baalgore has used this to our advantage by directing him to our volumes. But what if the Enemy keeps giving Ian *His* reading material? It could turn against us in a heartbeat. You and Baalgore must make sure he doesn't read these books. If he does, Foulgrin, I warn you—there'll be heaven to pay.

I like Ian's proclamation of agnosticism. It's a sort of theological Switzerland in which he imagines spiritual neutrality. Fortunately, the Carpenter said, "He who is not for Me is against Me." Kind words about the Enemy's Son are no threat. It's bowed knees we cannot tolerate.

Dismayed at your failures,

Prince Ishbane

44

OCTOBER 27, 12:23 P.M.

"M om," Brittany yelled into the living room. "Do we have any pickles?"

"So now it's pickles?" Sharon Powell hopped into the kitchen holding her keys, trying to put her high heel on. "I bought you cashews yesterday, kiwis before that and chow mein Monday."

"I'm in the kosher dill stage today. And I'm not getting fast food again, not right before my nutrition class."

Sharon looked at her watch. "I have an appointment, honey. Gotta run." She walked out the front door, but poked her head inside again. "I won't be home for dinner either, so when you're buying pickles, get some Portuguese food for yourself, or whatever you'll be craving later."

Brittany sighed and put her hands on her stomach. She felt a kick. "I know, I know. Dills are your favorites, too. I tried." She looked at the clock and wondered what to do with the extra hour before her afternoon class. She sat down at the kitchen table and looked through the paper. One advertisement jumped out at her. "Are You Pregnant and Thinking about Adoption?"

"Well, I'm pretty sure about the pregnant part," Brittany said aloud. She felt another kick, and laughed. "We're certainly energetic today, aren't we? Already training for all the sports you're gonna dominate, huh?"

Brittany thought about all the sporting events, holiday pageants, and graduations her mom had been there for when she was little. She remembered the notes her mom put in her lunchbox in grade school. But then she remembered the day Mom had to start going to work instead of volleyball games. It was the day her dad left.

It's not fair to let my baby grow up without a father. It's too hard.

Her mom's face came back to her again. This time she was standing in the bleachers, cheering her heart out after Brittany's team had just won the YMCA ten and under championships.

Brittany envisioned herself doing the same thing.

I'm supposed to be playing at San Diego State, and here I am planning attendance at my kid's ball games. This is unreal.

She grabbed the cordless phone and walked to the living room. She started to call Ian at his home number, but realized by now he'd moved to the PSU apartment. She didn't have the number. She could get it from Jillian, but... She'd always wondered what Ian's parents had said about her when he told them she was pregnant. They blamed her, no doubt. But part of her was dying to hear his mother's tone of voice.

"Hi, Mrs. Stewart, this is Brittany Powell..."

"Brittany! Oh, it's been so long since we've heard your sweet voice around this house!"

Is she setting me up for a kill?

"Uh, yeah, it's been quite a while."

"I don't think I've seen you since graduation! How are you, dear?"

"I'm okay. Actually, to be honest it was pretty rough for a while, but I'm doing a lot better now. The first few months I was sick all the time."

"Oh, sweetheart, I didn't know you were sick. Poor girl. That must have been hard when you were training for volleyball."

"Volleyball?"

"Yes, honey, isn't that why you went off to college so early? Isn't it San Diego State? How's the team doing?"

Ian's face filled her mind. *Of all the selfish, irresponsible...*

"Uh, I'm kind of in a hurry, so I can't really chat. I lost Ian's phone number at PSU; could you give it to me?"

After getting the number and all the best wishes for volleyball season from Mrs. Stewart, Brittany hung up the phone. She closed her fist over the scrap of paper with Ian's number on it. Then she smoothed it out and punched the numbers.

"Hello?"

"Ian, it's Brittany." Silence. "Look, Ian, you don't have to say anything—in fact, I don't want you to say anything. I just thought you should know I've decided not to give the baby up for adoption. I'm keeping it." Brittany quickly swallowed back the lump in her throat and continued. "I don't want any of your money, and I'm not even going to put your name on the birth certificate, so you won't be responsible for us at all."

"Brit—"

"I'm moving to California once the baby's born," she said.

If I win the lottery.

"I think that'll be easier for everybody. I guess the only thing I need from you is to know whether or not you'd feel comfortable with me telling my child about his father, once he grows up. I mean, I won't say your name; it's not like someday you're going to get a knock on your door from your son or daughter, it's just that it would be helpful to know."

"You just call out of the blue and expect me to deal with a question like that?"

"No, Ian. You should have been dealing with it every second for the last six months like I have, instead of lying to yourself and everybody else."

"You have no idea how hard this has been for me. I—"

"*I* have no idea? I spent three months vomiting all over the place. My whole body's changed right before my eyes. I get back cramps, I'm tired all the time, I cry at the drop of a hat, and I get holier-than-thou looks from old women at the store when they don't see a wedding ring on my finger. While your mother thinks I'm off having a good time playing ball for San Diego State, I've been lying awake every night trying to decide whether I'm going to turn my life upside down or rip out my heart and give my baby away in a few months. I hear the only throwing up you've been doing is after getting bombed at parties.

Don't you *dare* tell me about how hard it's been for you."

Brittany slammed the phone. She wished she could scream, but sobs choked her as she slumped down on the couch.

The group spread out in the Fletcher living room, sipping on coffee, tea, and punch. Jillian sat next to her mom and Jodi on the couch, Greg and Kristi sat in the love seat and Ryan on the floor.

"I wish now I hadn't seen all those *Friday the 13ths,*" Jillian said. "And the *Halloween* movies. Brittany and I have probably seen a dozen movies together that make witchcraft seem okay. It scared me off, but it sucked Brit in, I guess. I'm worried about her."

"Just call me the oblivious mother," Diane said. "Either I never knew you were watching those movies or I didn't understand what they could do to you. I'm so sorry. Before Daniel left tonight for his anger management class I asked him how he first heard about the Ouija board. You know what he told me? Remember those Teddy Ruxpin books, Jilly? There was one called *The Missing Princess.*"

"Sure. You read it to us."

"We still have it. Flipped through it this morning. If I hadn't, I wouldn't have believed it. The children go to someone called the Wizard of Wee Gee. Get it—wee gee? They consult a Ouija board to find where the princess is. Daniel says he thought that was really cool. When I read that book, I never thought twice about it. I feel like a terrible parent."

"Don't blame yourself, Mom. After he came to Christ, Dad talked to me about my movies and some of my romance novels. But by then I'd already seen and read a lot of stuff I shouldn't have. I'm the one that gave Daniel the Harry Potter books for Christmas, remember? At first he turned up his nose because it seemed like they were for little kids, but next thing you know he was reading them all the time."

"One thing's for sure," Ryan said, "the miracles and magic in Harry Potter aren't empowered by the God of the Bible. And there's no such thing as neutral supernatural power sources—they're either good or evil."

"Stuff can be a gateway to something else," Greg said. "How many kids—and even adults—watch the programs and read the books and learn there's no reason to fear witchcraft, that you can use supernatural powers to good ends, even when the God of the Bible has nothing to do with it? It's subtle, but it's dangerous."

"When I finally pulled the plug on the Internet," Diane said, "I thought Daniel would hate me. But I should've done it sooner. It was ruining him. Then when I found out about the Ouija board and called in you guys, I was *sure* he'd hate me. But I had to take the risk. He's still mad, but I'd rather have him mad than messed up. I told him I was butting into his life because I loved him."

"You're his parent," Greg said. "That means you're *supposed* to butt in." He looked at Kristi, as if wondering if he should keep talking. "We're amazed what's happening in a lot of our church homes. The kids will tell me they watched some immoral or evil R-rated video and I say, 'your parents let you watch that kind of movie?' They shrug their shoulders like, 'my parents let me watch whatever I want.' Sometimes they say 'our parents rented it.' I find out a kid's been having terrible dreams and it turns out he's played with Ouija boards and tarot cards and gazed into crystals at slumber parties, and his parents either don't have a clue, or they know about it and don't care. It's happening in Christian homes at Sovereign Grace Church."

"Working with the youth group has been a real eye-opener for both of us," Kristi said. "In my house, Dad and Mom knew what we were doing, who we were hanging with, what movies we watched, the whole deal. That was their job, and they didn't apologize for it. It's like this generation of kids has money, cars, and time on their hands, and they can do whatever they want, wherever they want, with whoever they want."

"And stay out as late as they want," Greg said. "It sounds awful to say, but it seems like a lot of Christian parents have given up on their kids. It's like they're just handing them over to…well, sorry to sound so dramatic, but to the devil."

"The worst thing isn't drugs or pregnancy either," Kristi said. "It's what happens to their minds."

"You feed your mind on evil, and it's going to desensitize you to it," Ryan said.

"Or make you terrified all the time," Jodi said. "I saw *The Exorcist* when it first came out. I had horrible dreams for ten years. Scripture says the One who's in us is greater than the one who's in the world. We don't need to be terrified."

"That's what Greg told Daniel that finally got through to him," Diane said. "Daniel was convinced the Ouija board knew he'd die before his sixteenth birthday. But Greg told him God knows the day of our death and demons don't. God's in control and they're not. They're just trying to scare him. But he's let them get a grip on him. He's got to turn to God for help."

"I'll tell you what really made an impact on Daniel," Ryan said, looking at Diane. "It's when you asked his forgiveness for not paying attention to what was going on in him. You said you'd given him a lot of what he wanted, but not enough of what he needed. How long did you say you talked?"

"Two hours. We talked more that night than we had in the last year. Once I told him I really wanted to understand him—not judge him—it was like a dam broke. He told me lots of things I didn't know. Some of it was hard to hear. But I felt like I got my son back, for the first time in two years. Jordan was getting through to Daniel before he died. But this was my first connection with Daniel for…a long time." Her voice cracked. "I just hope it's not too late."

"It isn't," Jodi said. "As long as we're still here, it's not too late for God to work. Daniel's been under attack. But maybe that's because he has lots of potential to serve Christ."

"It's not just Daniel who's under attack," Diane said. "I fell for Donovan because I thought I needed a man's attention."

"Whoa!" Jodi said. "Are you saying you're done with him?"

"I'm just saying since Jillian talked to me about it, and then you came in as her tag team partner, I'm taking it slower, that's all."

"Well, that's a start," Jodi said, catching Jillian's eye. "We'll keep working on her, won't we guys? If we're butting in, Diane, it's only because we love you."

Diane turned red. Jodi laughed and put her arm around her.

"One thing I should tell you," Jillian said. "Brittany told me Skyla was so mad that she and some friends put a curse on me."

"What?" Jodi said.

"It's a long story. She's a witch. Or thinks she is."

"Things have changed," Jodi said. "There were the FFA guys, the drill team, and the chess club, but I don't remember going to school with witches—they put a curse on you?"

"I was terrified at first, but then Kristi showed me all these verses to memorize. She reminded me that I'm in God's hands and Satan can't do anything to me unless it's part of God's plan."

"That made you feel better?" Greg asked.

"Totally! I know God's watching over me. First Peter 5:7 says, 'Cast all your anxiety on Him because He cares for you.' Anyway, could we pray for Daniel? He really needs the Lord. And I need to know how to reach out to him."

"Let's pray for Ian and Brittany, too," Ryan said. "They're not out of the woods yet. Not by a long shot."

"And pray for Skyla," Jodi said. "Her power source is nothing compared to ours. She doesn't know what she's up against!"

Letter 44

My intolerant Foulgrin,

Don't let Ian get over his repugnance at the notion of the Carpenter being the only way. As long as they get it wrong on the Carpenter, it doesn't matter what they get right.

They like to believe that the great river of life flows on a path to heaven, every tributary taking them to the same destination. The notion that one way leads to life and all other ways to death offends them because their culture tells them it should. And we know who pulls the strings of the culture.

This living room gathering was terrible news. I can't stand it when they put their miserable little heads together. When they quote the forbidden book and engage in the forbidden talk, that's worst of all. The Enemy designs them to need each other. To lean on each other and draw from each other's wisdom, counsel, and experience. Our objective is the opposite: Divide them. Isolate them. Pull them away from each other. Leave them on their own. Hell's gates can prevail against individuals. It's the Church we can't handle.

As for the Harry Potter books, we've capitalized on their interest in the supernatural. I'll gladly put up with the morals and character lessons in the books. Just as long as we can make them believe that any route of connecting with the unseen world serves them. By portraying witches and wizards as good, we lure them in. It'll take more than Harry Potter to get a hold on most. But he's certainly a welcome introduction to the path we'll lead them on.

Meanwhile, every day we're spawning a new genre of magic and witchcraft books for the little tykes. Perfect. It's like boxing. Lead with the apparently innocent. Lull them in. Then follow with the hard punch, and finally the knockout blow. Think of all the spin-off programs, movies, and products from these books. Having established our presence on the beachheads of their minds, we can turn footholds into strongholds. We start with subtle influence. We end with ruthless domination.

Alas, their parents won't overtly sacrifice their children to Moloch. But take heart, Foulgrin. Through what they allow their children's minds to feed on, they offer them to us as living sacrifices.

Exacting revenge on Him by luring them to us,

Prince Ishbane

45

OCTOBER 31, 7:08 P.M.

Ian sat in his campus apartment, holding his head in his hands. Brittany's words hadn't let him sleep for days.

It's not like some day you're going to get a knock on your door...

The door opened. It was Rob, holding a Bible and another book in his hand.

"Happy Halloween," he said, handing him *The Case for Faith*. "I know it's your favorite holiday."

Ian didn't respond.

"What's wrong, amigo?"

"It's Brittany again."

"What about her?"

"She's still pregnant."

"Yeah. Sort of a nine-month plan, from what I've heard."

"It's not too late to fix it. There are places that'll still do it."

"Yeah, and there are places you can go to hire a hit man to kill your parents," Rob said. "But that doesn't make it right."

"She's not just going to have the baby and give it up for adoption," Ian said. "Now she says she's actually going to keep it. Can you believe it?"

"Good for her. I mean, either choice is fine, as long as she lets the baby live."

"I never thought I'd hear you stick up for Brittany."

"I've stuck up for her every time we've talked about it, haven't I? If there's a side here, I'm on hers. You know that. She's doing the right thing. I respect her for it."

"You—respect Brittany? She'd have a hard time believing that."

"Have I been that hard on her?'

"You never said it, but both of us always saw how much you disapproved of her. You and me, we can disagree and it doesn't bug me. You can be a horse's...south end, and I put up with it. Brittany's different."

"I'm really a horse's south end?"

"On your good days. I won't say what you are the rest of the time."

"Well, I won't say what you're acting like right now. But I will say that I think you should buy Brittany flowers and write her a note. Tell her you've been a jerk. Tell her you'll help her financially, help her with your baby. Anything. Everything."

"What I'd tell her she doesn't want to hear. I still think she should take care of it."

"She's going to take care of the baby, not get rid of him. She decided four months ago to keep the baby. She's six months pregnant! Stand up and be a man, Ian!"

"We can't afford this. We've got lives, education, careers at stake. She was going to be a surgeon!"

"Remember when we were talking about the occult in your bedroom? Remember the passages of Scripture I was reading? You said, 'Obviously I don't believe in child sacrifice.' Jill and I talked about this. To us, killing a baby for convenience, because of financial reasons, is sacrificing a baby to a false god."

"You can't believe that."

"I do believe it. And deep inside, I think you know I'm right."

"Stop. I've had enough." He stood, holding up his hands as if to block Rob's next words.

"We're done," Rob said. "I came to invite you to something. That Bible study I was telling you about? It's tonight at Jeff's house. How about coming with me?"

"Well, uh…I have some homework and stuff…you know."

"If you change your mind, I don't leave for fifteen minutes."

"Yeah. Okay."

"Look, Ian. Since I'm standing here with my Bible, do you mind if I read you just one passage?"

"Now's not a good time."

"I've felt like I should share it with you because of our last talk about the occult. And since I won't see you tonight, who knows when the next opportunity will come? It'll only take a minute."

Ian shrugged helplessly. Rob opened his Bible.

"It's from Acts 19. First it tells about the apostles casting out evil spirits. Then some people tried to cast out spirits, but didn't know what they were doing. There were these seven brothers and here's what it says: 'The man who had the evil spirit jumped on them and overpowered them all. He gave them such a beating that they ran out of the house naked and bleeding.'"

"Wow. That's gotta hurt."

"You know what I get from that, Ian?"

"No. But I bet you're going to tell me."

"Don't fool around with the spirit world. These guys wanted to cast them out and they got overpowered. It applies even more to those who flirt with the spirits and open the gates to let them into their lives. You can't just use spirits. They end up using you."

"Your warning is for Ian the Pagan, no doubt."

"Yes, it is. Though I'd never call you a name. But here's what I really want you to hear. Right after that something incredible happens. It says, 'When this became known to the Jews and Greeks living in Ephesus, they were all seized with fear, and the name of the Lord Jesus was held in high honor. Many of those who believed now came and openly confessed their evil deeds. A number who had practiced sorcery brought their scrolls together and burned them publicly. When they calculated the value of the scrolls, the total came to fifty thousand drachmas. In this way the word of the Lord spread widely and grew in power.'"

"Are we done, Bible man?"

"Almost. See, this was way before Gutenberg. Books were made one at a time. They were extremely valuable. A note in my Bible says a drachma was a day's wage, so if this happened now and somebody was making say $100 a day, it would be over five million dollars."

"Why would you burn five million dollars of books when you could sell them and do good things with the money?"

"Because they were evil books. It wasn't just that they needed to get rid of them. They needed to *destroy* them, to break their hold on them—and so they couldn't have a hold on anyone else either. When somebody came to Christ, they divorced themselves from having anything to do with the occult. They didn't just figuratively burn their bridges behind them. They literally burned their occult books and replaced them with God's Word."

"So what do you want me to do, torch my bookshelf?"

"Well, I think I'd take the books outside before I burned them, but yeah, that's exactly what I'd do. You know how I told you I burned that suicide book?"

"Yeah."

"You can't believe what that's done. Ever since then, I've felt…free from it. It had a grip on me I didn't even realize."

"I'm not thinking about suicide."

"But you've been influenced by the occult. Those books are blinding you. There's a battle for your soul, and the books are drawing you away from Christ. I think you should get rid of them. I told Daniel the same thing. Jillian had thrown his Ouija board in the trash. I asked Daniel if I could pull it out, and he and I could go out behind their house and pour some gas on that board and torch it."

"What did he say?"

"He isn't ready for it yet. But I'm praying eventually he will be, and meanwhile I've got the board out in our barn, where he can't get to it. But I'm praying for you, Ian, that you'll get rid of all the things Satan's using to hang on to you."

"How about we try something new, Rob? How about, when I want your opinion, I ask for it?"

"Sorry, man. Maybe this wasn't the best time. Maybe I didn't say it right. I just felt like I needed to tell you now."

"Maybe there's no good time to say it. Maybe you should just keep it to yourself. Did that ever occur to you?"

"You're my friend. Friends tell each other the truth. Jillian and I have been talking about that."

"Well, good for you and Jillian. Why don't you go talk some more with her, okay?"

Rob put his hand on Ian's shoulder. "Sorry, man. My timing was off. What else is new? See you tomorrow?"

He shrugged. *Don't hold your breath.*

As Rob walked out, Bailey walked in. He looked back at Rob. Once he was out of earshot Bailey spoke excitedly to Ian. "Just heard about a huge Halloween party Kappa Sigma's throwing over in Jake Morley's backyard, near the park. Everybody's invited. Come on, I'll drive."

For a moment, Ian thought about Ricky Tibbs, and sitting on a cliff. Something told him not to go. Something else told him it had to be better than sitting in his apartment giving out fun-size Snickers to runny-nosed trick-or-treaters.

The next thing Ian knew he was engulfed by a crowd of people, stereos blasting in a huge backyard.

"It's cold," Ian said. "Can't we go inside?"

"Nope," Bailey said. "Morley's folks are gone, but they'd smell the beer and dope. You look tense, man. More girlfriend stuff? Who needs 'em? Have a drink, it'll loosen you up. Forget your troubles."

Ian thought about one last-ditch attempt to get Brittany to change her mind. His parents had just found out somehow. They said Brittany hadn't been a good influence and he needed to focus on his school and basketball anyway. They said she probably tricked him into getting her pregnant, and he should stay away from her.

I need something to calm my nerves. I won't get hammered, though. Not this time. I promised myself that last time.

He grabbed a beer. Ian saw Bailey pass a paper bag to Luke, another guy from their apartment. Luke opened the bag and grinned. "Attention, everybody, attention."

The music was so loud and the beer so plentiful, only a few people turned toward Luke. "If anyone has the need to partake of some medicinal marijuana, step forward please!" Everyone laughed. The bong pipe was ceremoniously brought forward.

Bailey came toward Ian, beer in hand. "Hey, it's been a while since we burned a bowl of bud, man. Step on up and you'll feel better in no time! Or you can try some of Morley's ecstasy." He pointed to the host, who was selling some hits of the party hallucinogenic of choice.

Ian shook his head, remembering the last time. Beer was enough for him. If marijuana and beer had put him out on the edge of that cliff, he didn't even want to think about what ecstasy might do. He was no druggie. He grabbed another beer from the cooler.

Three hours later, Ian didn't know where the time had gone. He didn't think he'd had too much to drink. No more than six beers, probably. But he felt queasy.

An eerie fog had descended, and it started to rain. Ian heard complaints from all over the crowd. When the light sprinkle turned into a downpour, people started to bolt.

"I'm outta here," Bailey said. "You comin' man?"

Ian nodded, keeping his mouth shut lest something unwelcome come out. He pulled himself into the leather front seat of Bailey's new Honda Accord. He fumbled for the seat belt, nearly giving up, then hearing it snap into place. For a moment he wondered if Bailey was too drunk to drive. *Nah. Bailey always comes back in one piece, even when he's smashed. Besides, it's not a long drive.*

Bailey hadn't turned the windshield wipers on, and the headlights didn't look very bright. *Are they even on?*

Bailey's foot was heavy. They were taking corners like this was some low-riding sports car. Ian saw three figures up ahead, in the swirl of fog and headlights, walking on the side of the road. He felt relieved when Bailey slowed down. They were late-night trick-or-treaters, one dressed as the devil, one as Jason, and the other as Freddy Krueger. Just as Bailey passed, he cut sharply in front of them and slammed on the brakes in the gravel. Then he gunned it, spraying gravel in their faces. Bailey laughed. Ian heard the loud cursing behind him and looked back at the arms flailing in the air. Ian laughed too—it was an unforgettable sight.

Bailey was soon taking the curves at fifty, looking as if he was hunting for a few more victims. Ian wondered if he should ask him to pull over. *Nah. We'll be at the apartment in ten minutes.*

As they sped around a corner, ignoring a stop sign, the Accord fishtailed on the wet pavement. The car swerved up onto the embankment, and Ian saw a shadow right in their path. Bailey swore, then turned the steering wheel wildly. But before the tires veered sharply to the left, they heard a loud thud and a green blur rolled across the hood of the car, up and over the windshield. Then Bailey lost control, and the car spun wildly. The last thing Ian heard before impact was the start of his own scream.

Letter 45

My lowly Foulgrin,

You referred to yourself as *Lord* Foulgrin again. Don't you ever learn? Do your job and I may ignore it. Fail me, and I'll inform Internal Affairs.

If you have any tricks up your sleeve, pull them out. Ian's your best shot—take him now. His guard's down. He's lazy and careless. The one who thinks his car is safe leaves windows down and keys in the ignition, dramatically increasing the chances that his car will be stolen. If Ian thinks his soul's safe, it's the same thing. He'll be careless. Open himself to theft. The man who doesn't realize he's in a battle has a civilian mentality. Civilians end up being casualties.

The interference of Ryan, Jodi, Greg, and Kristi is disturbing. Let me instruct you on our philosophy of generational segregation. Maybe you can use it to get these adults away from our kids.

We want Christian adults to give up on this generation. Don't let them see they bring as much cultural baggage to the table as the Millennials do. Some of them insist certain hymns be sung. They get worked up about whether to pave the parking lot. They throw hissy fits if the order of service isn't what they're used to. Then they accuse the kids of having strange music, caring about silly things, and being closed-minded about adult interests. Let them cringe when a studded, tattooed kid walks in the door. That'll guarantee few ever do. If one slips by the church's gatekeepers, they'll never talk to him. They'll stare at him as if he were a zoo animal. Perfect. They don't have room for them in their organization. We've got plenty of room in ours.

Never let these Christian adults look for common ground. Keep them from examining the kids' music, movies, and games and using them as launching pads for discussion. Persuade them always to talk. Never listen. Give answers. Never ask questions. Force their opinions on them. Like turning a screw until its stripped and no longer holds.

Instead of warmth and honesty, have them convey that patronizing I-can-barely-tolerate-the-sight-of-you attitude. Don't let them set the climate in which the young will feel safe enough or loved enough to communicate. Keep them from sharing their own search for truth. Or their mistakes, rebellions, and life lessons. Never let them admit they're still failing, still learning.

How can we insure these generations don't communicate with each other? Nothing's been more effective than TV. Even if all those things that serve us so well were taken off television, Beelzebub forbid, it would still be a great asset. Even if the most morally objectionable program was *Leave it to Beaver,* we could still successfully distract both generations from interacting with each other. Neutral television, even wholesome television, still robs them of relational time and opportunity.

Conversations that build relationships and transfer wisdom almost always come in spontaneous contexts. This requires leisure time spent together. Parents and children, especially teenagers, virtually never take walks with each other or sit in the same room quietly reading. So when they're not watching television, they're going out with their own age group. The Enemy says to parents "talk of these things on the way." But unlike past generations they're seldom next to each other as life happens. The dinner table is a bus station. Conversation is limited. Hurried. Superficial. Parents and children quickly move away from each other to each get on with "their own lives." Perfect!

What about this church youth group led by Greg and Kristi and their cohorts? First, isolate them from the adults. Suggest "big church" is irrelevant. Worthless. There's no need to sit alongside the fogies. The Enemy wants to bridge this culture's generation gap inside His forbidden fellowships. We want to widen it.

As for the youth pastor, do all you can to convince him to tell more stories, play more games, watch more videos, serve more pizza, do anything and everything but spend more time teaching the actual words of the forbidden book.

The Enemy doesn't promise that stories and games and music and videos and pizza won't return to Him without accomplishing their purpose. What He promises is His Word will not return to Him without accomplishing its purpose. This is why you must keep that book shut. Unfortunately, they can use the games and the pizza effectively to draw in students, give them a good time at church, and cultivate friendships with positive peer pressure. That itself is a defeat for us—but *only* if the forbidden book is taught.

I'm delighted to hear that since Jillian's started Bible college, her times with the Enemy are fewer and further between. The forbidden book is becoming something to take tests on. Not to feed her hungry soul. I see she's been engaged in conversations on campus with those who are reading into the book what isn't there. Excellent. Misinterpreting the Bible is much more effective than denying it. We can cover our errors under the cloak of orthodoxy. Never attack the forbidden book when you can spin it to your advantage.

Thinking strategically,

Prince Ishbane

46

Bailey's car slammed into a telephone pole. The impact threw Ian forward, but he was suddenly thrown back when the passenger's side airbag exploded into his face and chest. He coughed and his head spun. He opened his eyes and thought he saw smoke.

"Bailey! Get out quick, man!"

Ian tried to open the door. As he fumbled with the handle, the substance that looked like smoke settled across the cab in a thin layer, like talcum powder. He felt relief. There wasn't any fire. He heard a few expletives. Bailey was throwing wild punches at his deflating airbag. Ian managed to open the door, and fall out onto wet underbrush. The car was slanted upward on the off-road incline. The headlights were shooting up through a thick cloud of steam rising from under the hood. Ian walked toward the front of the car, a mass of crumpled metal.

The crash had a quick sobering effect, like downing a pot of coffee. Ian thought for a moment how lucky they'd been. Then that invincible feeling surged through him. He'd survived again. The adrenaline was still pumping, his heart still thudding like something inside was trying to get out. Yet even now he knew he was okay and when the dust settled this would make for a great story.

Then he remembered the noise and the green blur that rolled across the windshield.

Ian peered through the rain and fog. Two cars had stopped, and a few trick-or-treaters had circled around something lying by the road.

Ian slowly approached the group, craning his neck to look for what it was they'd hit. Through the spaces in the crowd Ian could see what looked like a thick winter coat at their feet. A green coat. He felt something rising in his throat.

"No…"

Rain now dripping from his face, Ian shoved everyone aside and stood over the crumpled figure.

"Please, no." He blinked, hoping the beer was playing a trick on him. "Don't let it be him."

It was.

But how…? He must have been coming home from his Bible study. But why was he walking?

Ian's eyes never left Rob's face as he screamed, "Someone call 9-1-1. *Now!*" A woman ran to her car, pulled out a cell phone and punched numbers.

Rob stirred, moaning, his face contorted. His body was twisted, his hips turned to his torso at an impossible angle.

"Hang on, Rob," Ian pleaded, getting down on his knees next to him.

"Ian?"

"Yeah, it's me. Looks like you're banged up bad. Don't move, okay?" Ian tried to swallow the sob stuck in his throat. "The ambulance should be coming soon. I'll stay with you, okay?"

"Okay," Rob choked out. "So this is the way, isn't it, God?"

"What'd you say, Robbie? Stay with me, buddy."

Rob spoke haltingly, with a strained voice. "I prayed God would do whatever it takes to help you find Him." He choked again and coughed. Ian saw blood drip out the corner of his mouth. Eerily it flowed straight across his cheek, veered, and streamed down his neck.

"Hang on, man," Ian pleaded. "Help's on the way."

"Listen to me, Ian." Rob's voice grew clearer, as if he was pouring all his strength into it. "You're empty. You need Jesus. Nothing else is good enough." His voice grew softer, his face paler, but his eyes were still barely open. "Hear me, Ian?"

"Yeah. I hear you. Don't say anything else, okay? I hear the sirens. They're coming. I see them."

Rob looked up over Ian's shoulder. "Yeah. I see them."

Watching Rob's eyes focus behind him, Ian whipped around. No one was there but the half dozen onlookers, all keeping their distance.

Ian felt a movement behind him and turned back quickly toward his friend. All he saw was a twisted mannequin. It looked deserted. Like a deserted house, with no lights on.

"Rob," he screamed. "Rob!"

Ian saw a fire truck pull up, and right behind it an ambulance. He watched as the paramedics walked steadily, but didn't run toward the body lying on the street.

"Hurry up," Ian yelled at them. "Hurry. He's dying!"

Just as the paramedics got to Rob, two police cars arrived. "We need you to stand back," a cop said to Ian. "Are you his friend?" he asked, as a paramedic was feeling for Rob's pulse.

"Yeah, I…uh—"

"What's his name?" the cop asked, as the paramedic opened his bag and removed an oxygen mask.

"Rob. Rob Gonzales. He's not…he's going to be okay, isn't he?"

The paramedics placed an oxygen mask on Rob's face. They put something on his finger with a cord coming out of it.

"Pulse is weakening. Get him out now!"

How did this happen? Why was he walking on the road?

"What kind of car does he drive?" the officer asked.

"Black Impala. '62, I think. Low rider."

"It's a half mile back on the side of the road," the officer said. "He probably ran out of gas. Or broke down." He pointed toward Bailey's car. "Were you a passenger in that vehicle?"

Ian nodded.

"That young man was the driver, correct?"

Ian looked at Bailey, who was leaning against a tree, vomiting in the grass, while another police officer stood back.

"Uh-huh."

He heard something sizzle and turned to the road. Flares out in the rain. It seemed like everyone around him now was in uniform. Policemen, firemen, paramedics. They lifted Rob from the street and placed him on a stretcher.

The police officer shone his flashlight toward Ian. He looked in his eyes. "Were you drinking?"

"A little…is he going to be okay?" Ian asked. "For a second I thought maybe he was…you know, gone. But the guy said he had a weak pulse. So he's alive, right?" Ian could hear his voice slurring.

"They're doing all they can for him. I need you to answer my questions. Was the driver drinking?"

"Yeah. Yeah, he was drinking. Okay, I didn't stop him from driving! It's my fault. It's all my fault!"

"How much did he have to drink?"

"I don't know, I didn't count bottles!" He ran to the stretcher, stumbling, just as it was being put in the back of the ambulance. "Rob, I'm sorry! I'm sorry, man. I should've gone with you." The door was shut and the ambulance pulled away, sirens wailing.

Ian sat in the gravel, watching Bailey try unsuccessfully to take nine steps, heel to toe. He looked as if he were on a tightrope, about to fall, arms swaying wildly. Then they had him blow into a long tube with a small computer gadget attached.

"Where they takin' Rob?" he asked the cop.

"To OHSU emergency."

"Does his family know?"

"My partner got his parents' name from the registration. He called them."

"I have to go see Rob."

"I still need to ask you a few questions, son. But…how about I do that on the way to the hospital? I'll take you." As the cop drove, Ian answered questions in a detached monotone. He thought of having to face Rob's parents. And….oh, no.

"Hey," Ian said. "There's somebody else that needs to be called."

Jillian leaned over the bathroom sink scrubbing her face with a foam cleanser. She thought she heard the phone ringing over the sound of running water. She turned it off and grabbed a towel, wiping her stinging eyes as she ran to the phone.

Jillian looked at her digital alarm clock next to the phone in her bedroom.

11:49? I know it's Halloween, but it's still a school night, Brit.

She picked up the receiver just as Joey started crying.

"This better be good, Brittany. You woke Joey up."

Jillian heard a male voice clear his throat on the other end of the line.

"Hello? I need to talk to Jillian Fletcher."

"This is Jillian."

"This is Officer Joe Greenley, Portland Police. I've been asked to call you because there was a car accident tonight. I'm told you're a close friend of…Roberto Gonzales."

"Rob?"

"He's been seriously injured. I'm sorry. They're transporting him right now to the emergency room at OHSU. I'm with his friend…. Ian Stewart? We're heading up there right now."

"Ian too? Is he alright? Will Rob be okay? O God, please!"

"If you come, have somebody else bring you," Officer Greenley said. "And make sure they drive carefully, ma'am."

Rob slowly opened his eyes to a blur of white and blue. He felt as if he were floating into a building. Paramedics hovered over his body. Once they got to a second set of double doors, the paramedics stepped aside and doctors and nurses took over the hovering. He heard voices, lots of them, but couldn't understand the words.

It was like watching a movie in slow motion. Rob could tell they were working quickly, yet he saw each movement frame by frame. He saw the doctors yelling out orders, their mouths moving in sluggish exaggeration. The words came out an octave lower than they should have. Nurses hooked up tubes coming out of his body to various machines and liquid-filled bags.

He wondered why no one seemed to notice he was conscious. He also wondered why he wasn't feeling pain. Anesthesia? He tried to speak, but found there was a tube down his throat. He heard a frantic beeping noise. The voices got louder. He saw a doctor raise his arm to wipe sweat off his forehead.

Rob watched as a scalpel moved beneath his line of sight, then barely felt it pierce his flesh. He saw his own blood spilling to the floor. Still no pain. The surgeon's movements seemed to be getting even slower, as though his hands were pushing through thick mud.

I need to hear the doctors. I need to know what's wrong…

The beeping seemed calmer now. Or was it because other sounds muffled it, new sounds from far away but coming nearer? He tried to focus on the doctors' words, but the strange sounds kept getting louder. Did they have the radio on? It was music, but not like any music he'd ever heard.

What in the world?

The doctor yelled. Rob fought to hear what was going on. They moved a bright light over his body, pointing it directly at his face. But instead of the light growing weaker as his eyes got used to it, the light got more brilliant each second. The mysterious sounds were now too loud to hear any more words back in the room, which seemed as far off now as the music did at first. But somehow he didn't care about the hospital room. He was fascinated by the beckoning from the place beyond.

The light flickered. He saw a shadow. Something was moving toward him. Or was he moving toward it? The melody called to him. Now the melody and the moving figure were the same. He thought he heard it whisper his name.

With a startled gasp, not of the throat but of the mind, Rob entertained a notion. *Is this...? Could I be...?*

The shadow was...bright. *How can a shadow be bright?* It came closer now. Rob could see it was a person. He stretched out His arms, inviting Rob to join Him.

But what about my mom and dad, my sisters, and Ian and...Jillian?

Even as he asked the question, he knew the answer. With everything in him, he wanted to dive in and lose himself in this Person's radiance, cross the threshold to the great adventure that had beckoned him ever since childhood. Yes, he felt like a child again. No weight of the world, no disillusionment with self or others. Just a childlike preoccupation with an object of wonder.

He saw hundreds of colors he'd never seen or imagined, breathtaking colors. Were the colors new, or had they been there all along, but he'd been unequipped to see them? The doctors, nurses, and machines were almost silent now. He was immersed in magnificent sound. It was like an orchestra and a choir, but there weren't just a few parts, but hundreds of them, dancing melodies and rich harmonies. A voice came from the bright shadow. He sang words, words that Rob knew could make a world, but words he couldn't understand. But he could *almost* understand. He felt right on the verge. On the verge of something magnificent. Something he would gladly give everything to step inside of.

The music kept getting louder and louder. He noticed it wasn't just the one voice of the person with arms spread wide. Thousands, maybe millions of voices melded with his. Rob's eyes were set on the Person. Not *a* person. *The* Person.

He felt an intense yearning in his heart, like a thirsty man who, seeing cool water, becomes even thirstier the instant before drinking.

The old world, that colorless world of grays, began to fade. But as it faded, another world took shape. A world so perfectly defined, so glorious beyond expression, that all he could think was "this is the *real* world, the one I was made for." He felt like a hungry man standing in an orchard full of a hundred different fruit trees, wondering which fruit to grab and bite into first. He reached out wildly, to grasp whatever he could lay hold of.

The Shadowlands, the world of grays he'd lived in, was disappearing. Now he was seeing the Substance that cast those shadows he'd once imagined were the ultimate reality.

The figure became brighter and brighter, yet didn't hurt his eyes. The one who'd at first seemed a shadow was now bathed in light. More than that. He was the *source* of light. He stretched out both arms, human arms, yet much more than human. A bubble of laughter erupted from Him. And also within Rob. He felt like a tuning fork that was vibrating furiously in the presence of that one perfect Sound. Rob ran toward the Light, leaving behind nothing but his body.

Letter 46

Foulgrin,

I just received a terse message from Outpost 96. What's happening over there? I'm about to leave for the threshold. I was informed one of your vermin is dying. Excellent! Ian? Brittany? Daniel? Or did you get Rob to destroy himself after all?

By the time you get this letter I hope to know the answer. In the pool at headquarters I bet on Ian. But I'll be pleased with any of the others. I'm rushing to celebrate our victory. I hope to see you there. Well done! Beelzebub will be pleased!

Impressed,

Prince Ishbane

47

Brittany's Jeep raced down the Banfield freeway from Gresham toward downtown Portland.

"Hang on, kiddo," Brittany said. "We'll get you there."

"I was shaking so much I couldn't drive," Jillian said. "And with Joey sick, I couldn't have Mom take me." Her voice trembled. "I thought you were going out with Skyla's coven for their New Year thing."

"The esbat? I guess you talked me out of it. Besides, I decided I'd cast too big a shadow under the full moon."

Jillian laughed, then cried just as suddenly.

"Rob called me tonight," Brittany said.

"What? When?"

"Right after dinner. Must've been six thirty or so. He told me he wanted me to know he respected my decision to have my baby. He said he admired me. That I'd done the right thing. Said I was courageous and he was proud of me. Even offered to help me any way he could. I was speechless. And then…he did something weird."

"What?"

"He apologized to me. He asked my forgiveness."

"For what?"

"For always disapproving of me. He said that was wrong and he knew I had a lot of good qualities. He thanked me for helping you with your bulimia. And for being loyal to you."

"Wow."

"Yeah. A lot of Christians have made it clear they don't like me, but no one's ever apologized to me. Except you. And now Rob."

Jillian squeezed Brittany's hand as they saw the sign: Fourth Street, with an arrow pointing right. "That's it, that's the exit."

Brittany shifted her Jeep down to third as they eased off the freeway.

Jillian checked the notes mom had scrawled out when looking at the map.

"Okay, left on College Street." They saw the sign at the light pointing left. *Oregon Health Sciences University.* After making a few more turns, they would have been lost if not for the blue "H" signs pointing them in the right direction. It was raining hard, and city lights were behind them as Brittany's Jeep climbed the narrow road up the hill.

"This is creepy," Jillian said as they rounded another curve. After about a mile, they saw signs of civilization again, along with big red signs pointing them to *EMERGENCY.* A thousand different scenarios went through Jillian's mind as they drove past the emergency room doors. She was glad Brittany didn't offer to drop her off at the front. She didn't want to go in by herself.

They parked and ran out of the parking garage toward the emergency room. Four ambulances were lined up neatly in a row outside the automatic glass doors. As they entered, they saw the triage nurses' station directly in front of them. Brittany went to the desk.

"We're here for Rob Gonzales." Looking at Jillian, Brittany said, "She's family."

The nurse punched a few keys on the computer.

Jillian looked around the waiting room. Five people were spread out among the floral print chairs. She didn't see Rob's family or Ian. Maybe they were back in his room visiting him? Maybe he was telling them stories of how an angel protected him?

Jillian turned to the left and saw white double doors with a sign, *Restricted Entry, Access Card Only*. The doors opened and a nurse came through. Jillian looked down the hall and saw two nurses in light green scrubs. One was pushing a gurney. The other was running.

"If you two could just have a seat here in this room, we'll see if Mr. Gonzales's attending physician could come out to speak with you." The nurse behind the glass had come out and was leading them through a door to the left of the front desk.

"Can we see him?"

"Not until things are under control. You'll have to speak with the doctor first. Go ahead and have a seat."

Brittany sat, while Jillian walked back and forth. "I have to see him."

"Sit down, Jillian."

Jillian saw in her mind the policeman, the one who'd come to her house the day her dad was killed. He'd asked her and Mom and Daniel to sit down.

"No, I won't sit down."

After a few minutes, the door opened. In came a tall young-looking doctor, in whites and blues, with a stethoscope around his neck and a clipboard in his hand. Next to him was a man dressed in a gray suit and a maroon tie.

The doctor cleared his throat. "My name's Doctor Moffat. This is Reverend Arnold. You're here for Roberto Gonzales?"

"She needs to see her fiancé," Brittany said.

"A nurse gave your name to his mother and said you were the girlfriend?"

"Right," Jillian said.

"They're almost engaged," Brittany said.

"Please sit down."

"I don't want to sit down," Jillian said. "Can't we talk after I see Rob?"

"It would be better if you had a seat, ma'am."

"Tell me what's going on!"

Doctor Moffat looked up from his charts. "I'm sorry, but…his injuries were very serious. There was nothing we could do. He died on the operating table."

Jillian felt the wave of nausea she'd first experienced a year and a half before. Her body sank to the carpeted floor. Brittany lifted her into a chair.

"Please, God, not again." The air was thick and poisonous. She was suffocating.

"Mr. Gonzales's family is through those doors in the room where we put his body. If you want, they said you were welcome to join them. His mother said you were like family."

Jillian's insides pushed together as if she were going to sob, but she didn't. It seemed as if she'd just been stabbed in the chest, and the knife was still there. She pulled both of her feet onto the chair and hugged her knees, rocking back and forth like a frightened child. She hoped her tears would drown the pain. They didn't.

Rob felt his chest pounding as he ran. He knew of runner's high, but he'd never experienced an adrenaline rush like this. He suddenly realized that the original figure he'd seen, the Singer of the great Song, the One in whom he'd become lost, had receded. For the moment He wasn't in sight. This was someone different, someone huge. He sensed it was this one's job to escort him to the Bright Shadow.

Rob's eyes adjusted to the massive height difference. While the Bright Shadow had been a man about Rob's height, this being must have been eight feet tall, powerfully built, like a great warrior. Their eyes locked. Rob felt no fear, but an immediate sense of recognition. He looked at this stone-faced creature and somehow felt connected to him, as though they were old friends and there were no secrets between them.

Rob peered into the warrior's unblinking eyes. He didn't know why, but he suddenly saw himself as a child again. He was seven years old. He and his brother Guillermo were playing with a football in their front yard. Guillermo kicked the ball. It catapulted into the street.

Rob remembered the next frame even as he saw it happen again. He started to run after the ball, hoping to catch it on the bounce. But he tripped over something and fell to the grass. Seconds later a car swerved around the corner. He would have been killed. Guillermo had told him he was lucky.

But this time he saw the end of the story through someone else's eyes. The boy started to run after the football, but…someone grabbed his left foot, causing the fall. Rob blinked hard. He looked at the warrior in front of him.

The giant nodded, his face expressionless. Rob stared intently at those eyes. He took a sharp breath as countless other life experiences played out in his mind, one after the other. He remembered each like it was yesterday. But now he saw them all from a different viewpoint. He felt as if he were seeing them for the first time. How could he have missed so much? How could he have been so blind to what was really happening?

"Who are you?" Rob whispered.

"I am Talon, servant of Elyon, God Most High."

"You were with me, weren't you?"

Talon's stony face twitched, and the edges of his mouth curved slightly. "I witnessed your birth into the Shadowlands. I've been near you ever since. When you were touched by the King's hand, drawn to Him, I was given new powers, and a commission to defend you. Now it is the will of Elyon that I escort you to your true birth."

"My true birth?"

"Yes. Your birth into the Substancelands, the real world. The Shadowlands was your womb. Your life until now has been the labor pains. You are about to be born into a world you've only dreamed about, caught faint glimpses of, little foretastes. You will discover that you loved the old world only in those times it gave you hints of this one."

Rob looked ahead of them and saw the end of the passageway. Or was it the beginning? He watched Talon step through the gate.

Rob inched closer. He wasn't sure of the proper protocol for entering eternity. He'd never died before.

Laughing at himself, he looked around one last time before stepping through the portal. His eyes stopped at something in the distance. It was a hideous creature, more repulsive than anything he'd ever seen. He could almost feel the evil radiating from it. But it didn't scare him in the slightest. Instead, it saddened him that something could choose such misery after it had known Joy itself. He lifted up a prayer not for the hopeless creature, but for Ian and Brittany, who still lived in the land of second chances.

Rob looked forward now and took a deep breath. He pressed against a great membrane that stretched at his touch. He pushed harder and suddenly broke through the membrane. It was as if scales fell from his eyes. Everything was so bright, so colorful. Compared to this, the sunniest morning on earth was as black as midnight. Yet the light didn't sting his eyes, it soothed them. He did have to close his eyes for a moment, because of a slight daze from all the colors, and a slight sting from all the details.

He saw a sea of people, many of whom he recognized. The closest seemed to be reaching out their hands as midwives, pulling him into the new world. He turned around in circles, amazed by the beauty of it all.

When he could finally speak he yelled, "At last! This is it."

The crowd cheered. Rob felt he was going to burst with pleasure. Nothing in his wildest imagination had prepared him for this.

The crowd parted. Rob's eyes fixed on One coming toward him, the Bright Shadow. He glowed not as in paintings Rob had seen, where the light appeared as a separate manifestation from His being. This light did not come *from* Him. It *was* Him. Not a display, but His essence.

The light was love and strength, grace and truth. The Bright Shadow walked with arms outstretched again, and Rob noticed first the striking profile, and second His scarred hands. Rob looked down instinctively at His feet. They were disfigured, not like the paintings, not normal-looking feet with a dot of red or a neat manageable scar. They looked as if they'd been torn, flesh ripped from the inside, through bearing a weight as great as the world itself.

With a startled gasp of realization, Rob fell to the ground. This was He who spoke the cosmos into existence with but a word. This was He who carried wood up a long lonely hill to die for those who hated Him.

Rob felt two strong hands under his arms, pulling up his dead weight. Finding his legs, he stood before the Ancient of Days. He looked at Him, impossibly, in the eyes. He felt unworthy. Yet loved. And complete. Whatever had always been missing fell into place, like the last twenty pieces of a puzzle he'd been tempted to give up on.

"At last. You're the Person I was made for!"

"Made for and made by. I have prepared a place for you. And I've prepared you for the place."

The Bright Shadow who was now Bright Substance hugged Rob tightly, then lifted him up in the air effortlessly and spun him around.

"Yes, I am the Person, and this is the place. The Object of your deepest longing." He put Rob down and put His arm around his shoulder. "You're going to like it, Rob. I've been building it for you. And I know how to build. I'm a Carpenter!"

Rob tried to speak, but couldn't. He knelt again and laid his forehead on his Savior's scarred hands. Moments passed until he looked up at His face again.

The Carpenter smiled and pulled him up a second time.

"Well done, My good and faithful servant. Enter into the joy of your Lord!"

Letter 47

My defeated Foulgrin,

I'm not misled by the upbeat tone of your letter, celebrating the death of Rob Gonzales. I'm always glad to have one less of the Enemy's vermin in the world. But any temptation to celebrate his death is overshadowed by the profoundest sense of defeat. First, that he went to the Enemy at all. Second, that he went to Him with his relationship in order. He left the dark world not as a disobedient servant, but a faithful son.

We wanted Rob's death only on *our* terms, not the Enemy's. His suicide would have been a triumph. This was a fiasco. You've snatched defeat from the jaws of victory, you incompetent fool. The Carpenter has won. Again.

I wish the Enemy would be content with this victory. Unfortunately, He has a nasty way of using these situations to meddle with those left behind. The forbidden book says, "Death is the destiny of every man; the living should take this to heart." The *last* thing we want them to do is to take death to heart! When they do, it changes everything.

You must hold on to Ian, Brittany, and Daniel. Labor to maintain the outrageous illusion of the young—that they will not die. They'll die, perhaps, but never soon, never today. We use this invulnerability complex to motivate them to pursue, without fear of consequences, everything from casual sex to reckless driving to drugs and the occult. But it's a delicate veil of deceit. It's too easily torn by the death of a friend.

When I got the report that the relocation of one of your vermin was imminent, I rushed to the gateway to witness it myself. I had guessed it was Ian, or perhaps Daniel or Brittany. When I saw Talon with his sword sheathed, a surge of hope went through me. Rob had taken his life, I thought. We had won!

But in an instant I realized what had happened. Rob hadn't taken out himself—the Enemy had taken him! He'd used an irresponsible vermin to do His bidding, as He often does. I stood there, crumbling at the sight, when Rob caught his first glimpse of Talon. That worthless guardian betrayed us long ago by staying with the Enemy and refusing to join the rebellion. The sludgebag Rob started recalling a hundred times when Talon had saved his skin, times we'd veiled from his eyes.

But the moment they leave that realm, any hold we had on them disappears. Every deception evaporates like morning mist in the heat of the day. The lights turn on. Never again do we have any power over them. It's infuriating!

I was standing behind that impenetrable barrier, knowing I could no longer touch the vermin. Rob Gonzales looked at me, an enemy so great he should have trembled at the very sight of me. But he didn't. He gazed right at me with a look of curiosity and scorn and almost…pity. Pity! That base beast of sweat and grime, begotten in a bed, looked on me not with dread and terror, but with pitiful disapproval! Instead of cowering at my feet, he turned from me in utter disregard. Never to look at me. Never to think of me again. The shame of it! The outrage!

I saw the look on his face. Even in his most enlightened moments, this Rob vermin never imagined Charis as real. It was in his creed, but it seemed to him a fairy tale. At most he thought of it as drifting around in the clouds as a disembodied spirit. Eternal boredom. He'd read the words he spoke to Ian, but he didn't yet realize their truth. But suddenly his faith became sight. Before my loathing eyes, he graduated from Shadow to Substance. And who but the Carpenter was there to hand him his diploma?

The Emperor's Son lifted him effortlessly up in the air, as if he were a young child, and spun him around playfully. They *played*, Foulgrin. Right there in front of me!

And then He said those dreadful words. No matter how many times I've heard them, the horror remains fresh: "Well done, My good and faithful servant. Enter into the joy of your Lord!"

I saw the look of utter delight on the face of Rob Gonzales. I saw the others crowd in around him, family members and others who knew him. I saw them lead him toward grassy meadows and forests and lakes and waterfalls and great rock cliffs. I saw one reunion after another. I even saw him meet and embrace an old friend of yours, Foulgrin, someone who'd been watching him. None other than *Jordan Fletcher!*

Writhing in the terror of it all, I heard a hideous scream. "Nooooo!"

It reverberated in my ears. Yet those in Charis seemed not to hear it. They didn't even turn their heads. The voice was Lord Beelzebub's. He shouted, "He was mine!"

Then Michael himself stepped forward from Charis, right out into the Hinterlands. I fell backward at his mighty presence, lest he strike me. He pointed his finger at our Master. Michael's words to Beelzebub were hard as rock. I was ground to dust between them.

"First His by creation. Then yours by fall, for but a moment. Then His again by redemption. First His, and last His, forever His. *Never* again yours!"

Michael turned his back on our Master, who was once his twin. I'll never forget Beelzebub's bloodcurdling scream. His anger. His desperation. His utter defeat. Yes, defeat, Foulgrin. I'll say the forbidden word! It was hideously clear in that instant. The Carpenter's victory over the sins of Rob Gonzales, and the vermin's victory over us, was but a sampling, a down payment on the coming triumph of the Crucified!

You blame your failures on Baalgore, but it was you who eagerly took Rob under your wing. You assured me you could strike him down. You would take him out of that world in shame and defeat. Talon would be no match for you. You would thwart even the Ghost. Your own words judge you. I have them all on file.

He was ready for heaven, this vermin. Don't think I didn't hear about his last words to Ian. Baalgore confessed them all. I did not hear his last gasp of earth's putrid air as you did. But I had to endure his first breath of Charis.

You would console me by saying "he suffered before he died"? Did I see any sign of suffering, any teeth gnashing, pain, exhaustion, or even sweat on his brow? *None!* What can fleeting moments of suffering do for us now? If you'd kept him there longer, he would have suffered more. Perhaps eventually he'd have strayed from the Enemy. But now not only the death of Rob Gonzales but his *life* will be fixed in the memory of his friends and family. It will be a reference point for them. One that will remind them of their mortality. They will recall his faith. And his desire to live for the Enemy.

When they are tested, they'll remember him. The sequel to their pain is joy. The whole thing *sickens* me.

The Carpenter may try to use Jillian's pain to deepen her cup, that she might have greater room for joy. I cannot be satisfied with the sufferings of Rob's parents, siblings, and Jillian when I know the Enemy may turn it around and enrich and use them more for His purposes. I cannot bear to know that the weeping of their separation will be forever broken by the laughter of their reunion.

Just now I heard the sounds of Charis again. And out of the mingled sounds of laughter, I heard one voice in particular. That of Rob Gonzales. Listen to the winds, if you dare. For on them floats from Charis the sounds of one young man's laughter, a laughter you vowed to silence. The Enemy has beaten you, Foulgrin. So has Talon. So has Rob Gonzales. Let the thought pierce you as a thousand swords. The vermin will never read your résumé. He will never know your name!

It's time now to pick up the pieces. Damage control. You must cultivate bitterness among the survivors. Since Jillian has lost the two most important men in her life, she should be the center of your attack. Rob's parents are prime candidates, too. Don't let them treasure the time they spent with Rob, or trust the Enemy's wisdom. Don't let them hear or believe the Enemy's assurances that He is Lord over death. Or that His servants cannot die until His purpose on earth for them is done. Instead of celebrating his life, make them torture themselves with his death. Convince them he belonged to them, not to Him. Therefore, *He had no right* to take him.

Ian, Brittany, and Daniel are at critical points. The Enemy may attempt to pull off a coup. He might try to take one or more of them captive. Don't let it happen. Baalgore will assist you. Needless to say, he's now available.

I have just filed my report. I don't know yet what action will be taken against you. For now, *Lord* Foulgrin, you can stew in your own juices.

Counting your blunders one vermin at a time,

Prince Ishbane

48

Ian stood motionless behind a vending machine at the far end of the reception area. He'd watched the girls walk in. He'd been shocked to see Brittany's profile. Being pregnant made her look older. Strangely, he felt drawn to her. But he was too frightened and ashamed to show himself.

He watched them follow the doctor through the locked doors with the warning sign. Part of him wanted to join them and Rob's parents. But most of him wanted to be on another planet. If he could pull off that astral projection stunt, he'd place himself in a solar system several galaxies away.

What could he say to Jillian? How could he tell her he'd been in the car that killed Rob? That he hadn't refused to go with his drunk friend, and hadn't spoken up to him and tried to take his keys?

He sat down, looking at two drugged-out girls in witches' garb, sitting listlessly at the end of another night of fun. He sat for twenty minutes, until Rob's mom and dad came out. He grabbed a *Sports Illustrated* and raised it in front of his face. Mr. Gonzales was holding up his wife. Though she was usually strong and healthy, she looked crippled. She was quiet and drained. His dad's eyes were wet and hollow. Ian had been at their house a half dozen times at least. He'd gotten to know them just well enough to feel even more guilty seeing them and not talking to them. But how could he?

A few minutes later Brittany came out, walking slowly, holding Jillian's hand. As they walked toward the door, Brittany suddenly saw him. Their eyes locked. Her hand went to her throat, then quickly to her stomach. She cried. Jillian followed her gaze to Ian.

"I'm so sorry," he said, hardly recognizing his own voice. The words sounded empty. He said it only once, but he meant it for both of them. He stepped closer, then put his arms first around Brittany, then Jillian.

"Jillian, I need to tell you something."

Jillian's eyes looked vacant, her face worn and frail. If Brittany let go, Ian was sure Jillian would collapse to the floor like a rag doll. He put his arm around Jillian and led her to a chair. He crouched down in front of her and Brittany, folded his hands and put them up to his mouth.

"You were there with him, weren't you?" Jillian asked. "Didn't the cop say that?" Her words were lifeless. "His car broke down and you guys were walking, right?"

Ian nodded and pressed his lips together, not meeting her eyes.

"How come he got hit and you didn't?"

"I wasn't with him, Jill."

"I…don't understand."

"Rob asked me to go to Bible study with him tonight." Ian looked at Brittany, then back to Jillian. "I had a lot of things on my mind. I didn't want to go. Then Bailey told me about a Halloween party. I wasn't going to get drunk or anything. I don't do that any-more…I mean, I didn't intend to…"

Ian stared subconsciously at Brittany's midsection. "Bailey drove, not me. I just had beer, but Bailey…all those beers plus the pot…he was smashed. Oh, Jill, I'm so sorry."

Jillian's body stiffened. "You were in the car that hit Rob?"

"I knew Bailey was wasted, and I still let him drive. I didn't even tell him to check his headlights or turn on his wipers. I didn't warn him to slow down. I don't know why. I wish I could do it over again," he whispered. "I wish it would've been me who died."

Ian's face felt hot. He kept whispering, "I'm sorry."

Jillian sat silently for probably a full minute, the longest minute of Ian's life.

"What do you want me to do?" Jillian finally asked, her voice a cold whisper. "Do you want me to throw my arms around you and say all is forgiven? I can't do that. You're a coward, Ian."

He looked at her eyes and saw ice.

"You wanted Brittany to kill your baby because you're a coward. You walked away from them both because you're afraid to take responsibility for your actions. You drank your life away over the summer because you weren't man enough to face your problems. You wouldn't take the keys from Bailey because you thought he wouldn't like it. You were afraid to even go to a Bible study, weren't you? Afraid of what might happen to you. And now Rob's dead. Rob's dead because Ian Stewart is a coward."

Jillian got up and walked toward the door. Brittany grabbed her arm but Jillian shook her off. Brittany looked back at Ian, eyes sad and sympathetic. She looked as if she wanted to say something. She didn't. She followed Jillian out the door. When they left the waiting room, the clock showed 2:10 A.M. Ian was alone. He didn't even see anyone behind the desk.

He sat limply on the floor, closing his eyes. On the backs of his eyelids he saw the over-turned car. He saw Rob, his body contorted, blood running from his mouth. He saw police cars, fire trucks, and the ambulance, bright lights flashing wildly. But what tore at him most were Jillian's frozen eyes.

He knew he wasn't the only one who wished he'd died.

Letter 48

Foulgrin,

Nothing can compensate for your colossal failure with Rob Gonzales. But at least you're making the most of it with Jillian. Not only is she wounding Ian with her hateful words, she's destroying herself. Vermin fools don't realize their refusal to forgive is like tapping a stick on another's heart, while thrusting a dagger in their own. Convince her it'll be easier to deal with the pain if she blames someone for it. Whether it's Ian or the Tyrant—preferably both—she'll never be healed if she believes his death was arbitrary. Convince her that human hands have the power to end life without the Enemy's permission.

The wonderful irony of bitterness is that it almost never gets them what it longs for—revenge. It's not the person who did the dirty deed who suffers, it's the one who's bitter. Seeking to torture others, they end up torturing themselves. Now, in Ian's case he *is* suffering greatly due to her bitterness. But in time he'll suffer less and less. Indeed, with some help from you and Pendragon, Ian may use her refusal to forgive him as another excuse for distancing himself from the Enemy and the forbidden fellowships. Make him think if a Christian won't forgive him for something, neither will the Enemy.

As for Jillian, it's particularly difficult for the Enemy to rescue her from bitterness. She doesn't *want* to be rescued. Bitterness is a cozy little corner to snuggle up in. There's an initial warmth in blame. But it turns frigid as the years go on.

Make Jillian imagine that Ian's offense against her is huge, while her offenses against others pale in comparison. Make her think she's qualified to pass final judgment on Ian. In short, make her think she's God. While the Enemy heaps mercy on her, let her be quick to call down justice on Ian.

Whatever you do, don't let the Ghost or His warriors trick Jillian into praying for Ian. If she did, she'd come to see him not as an enemy, but a sinner in need of grace. Like little mud puddles beneath a bright sun, resentments evaporate under the warmth of intercession. Don't let it happen.

While Scripture says "The Lord works out everything for His own ends," convince her that this particular event—Rob's death—is an exception. When it says "In all things God works for the good of those who love Him," convince her Rob's death isn't one of those "all things."

It amuses me to see their scrawny minds think that if they ran the cosmos, things would be so much better. Of course, if we did, it *would* be; but they're too stupid to manage their own lives, much less the universe.

As for Ian, the strategy is obvious. Saturate him with guilt. Make sleep impossible. Fill his mind with images of the accident. But if he starts to recall Rob's last words, or the example of his life, ease him into fitful sleep. In time, he'll become desensitized to the pain. He'll believe life must go on. But don't let him do with his guilt what the Tyrant invites him to—confess it, repent of it, and embrace His forgiveness.

Beware. Suffering is the Enemy's megaphone. Too often the Ghost comes closer and whispers louder in the midst of tragedy. Drown out the Ghost's offer to Ian to *know* God with Beelzebub's offer to *be* God. Never mind that ours is a false offer. Like smelly cheese, false promises catch more rats.

Are those books Rob gave Ian still in his room? Do whatever it takes to get rid of them. Get them out of his sight. Should he start reading them now...I don't want to think about it. Have somebody "borrow" them or torch the whole apartment, I don't care. Just keep the Enemy's truth out of Ian's reach.

Since my last letter, not a moment's gone by when I've not been plagued by heaven's laughter. The Carpenter promised those who weep on earth will laugh in heaven. Already they laugh. Heaven's language seems to be joy's laughter. For the reason they love it so, we hate it. Like fingernails on a chalkboard.

I do not buy High Command's propaganda that we may yet win the war. Our time is short, Foulgrin. Our only consolation is to deceive and destroy as many of them as we can before we join the vermin in hell's wastelands. Will it be even more horrible for us, plagued forever by the memories of the heaven that was once our home?

Foulgrin, do you ever wonder *why* we gave up the very place the vermin so long for and embrace with such delight? Of course, I can rehearse the reasons, as I have a million times. But between us, out here in the gray Hinterlands of exile, do you think it was a mistake to leave the only place we've ever known joy?

I detest how Charis is for the vermin a place of both remembering and anticipation. When I stand outside and listen, hoping to gather useful intelligence, I hear reminiscing. They tell stories and act out escapades and laugh at themselves and their experiences. And that's but their backward look. Their forward look is unendurable. They speak of their desires and plans. Their longing to travel and explore. Their yearning for new discoveries, not only of the cosmos, but of the hidden depths of the Enemy's person.

I keep hoping they'll be plagued by memories of suffering on earth. That they'll speak of how powerfully we held vermin in bondage or how fearful they were of us. But never do they speak of us. Their shouts of suffering on earth are now but whispering memories, reminding them of the Carpenter's greatness. Their whispers of joy on earth are now shouts of joy in heaven, reminding them of the same thing—the Carpenter's greatness.

This is the horror of it, Foulgrin. In that place, the Carpenter is the center of gravity, the reference point to which everything invariably returns. And, to add insult to injury, He does not promise them mere immortality, but resurrection! They do not merely continue but will be made better a million times. He does not just give them memories of the old earth, but promises of the new one!

The sounds of dancing and singing, the smells of feasting and celebrating attack me like monsters in the night. I cannot bear it. Already the prescient shouts of victory pierce the air of Charis. They float out into our transient shadowy realm. Already the horses of heaven rear up, eager to ride out into battle. A cloud of doom hangs over Erebus. The sword of Michael is poised above us, waiting only for his Commander's nod.

Why do I bother telling you, Foulgrin? There's already talk that unless you pull something out of this, you may be demoted again, perhaps to Squaltaint's level. Maybe you'll join some of your predecessors, inspiring bathroom graffiti.

Remember it, Foulgrin. Let it anger and inspire you. For those who know the Enemy, their separation from Rob Gonzales is not the end of relationship, but only an interruption to be followed by reunion. *But*...they can only be united if they end up at the same destination. Ian, Brittany, and Daniel's reservations are still in the smoking section. At all costs, don't allow the Enemy to move them.

Eternally doubtful,

Prince Ishbane

49

Nobody understands," Jillian said, lying limply on the couch. "They say they do, but they don't."

"Nobody?" her mother said. "I lost the best friend I ever had. The man I was married to for twenty-five years. I know you loved Rob, but I loved your dad a lot longer. I *do* understand."

"I know. Sorry. But I lost them both. Daddy and Rob. The two people who helped me learn more about God than anybody else—along with you, I mean. Why would God take them from me?"

"Why would God do a thousand things He does? And not do a thousand more we want Him to? I asked Jodi the same thing. She pointed me to some verses in Isaiah 55. Can I read them?"

Jillian nodded. Her mother picked up her Bible and read. "'As the heavens are higher than the earth, so are My ways higher than your ways and My thoughts than your thoughts.'"

"Rob and I talked about that. I didn't understand then and I don't understand now. But Rob said if we could understand everything God does, then He'd have to be a small god—small enough to fit into our little minds."

"That was wise," Diane said. She reached out her hand and took Jillian's. "I'm going to be here for you, Jillian. Besides Jodi, I haven't really had anyone I could talk to much about your dad."

"Funny, I've felt the same way."

"Then we need to talk with each other, don't we? Help each other."

Jillian nodded.

"Actually, Jilly, you've been a big help to me with something already, even though I got angry with you. I'm sorry."

"Donovan Swain?"

"I was acting like a school girl, not an adult."

"So since I'm a school girl that means…"

"Sorry. You know what I mean. You were the adult, and I needed some parenting. So I'm going to cool it with Donovan for a while."

"For a while?"

"I'm going to make sure it doesn't go too fast."

"Should it be going at all? Sorry, Mom, but what would you say to me if I was going with the wrong guy?"

"Okay. You've got some insights, and I admit I need to listen. We need each other, Jilly, especially with your dad gone. And now Rob. We've got to look out for each other, and

Daniel. So, if you give me permission to be honest with you, I'll give you permission to be honest with me."

"Permission granted," Jillian said.

"Like Jodi said, 'People who love each other don't just try to help each other *feel* good, they try to help each other *be* good.' Thanks for trying to help your silly old mother."

They hugged each other. "You're not silly, Mom. You've been so much help to me. With the bulimia, with my spiritual struggles, with Brittany, and now with losing Rob. You're the best. And I have a favor to ask you. Would you sit next to me," her voice cracked, "at...Rob's memorial service?"

After they showed some powerful slides of Rob's life, Jeff read some of Rob's favorite passages, then his youth pastor Steve gave a gospel message. Jeff wrapped up the service with prayer:

"Lord, Rob was one of the most godly young men I've known. He wasn't perfect, none of us is, but he had a great passion for You. Help us to remember we don't have much time here. Help us to remember that one moment after we die, we'll know just how we should have lived. But then it will be too late to go back and live it over again. I thank You that Rob was doing the right thing when he died. He was coming back from a Bible study. Just ten minutes after he was at my house...he was gone. Thanks for the final prayer I heard him speak that night. He prayed for one of his friends, asking You to do whatever was necessary to bring him to Yourself. I pray the same thing, Lord, for anybody here that still hasn't confessed his sins and placed his faith in You. I pray that, because of Rob's life, we'll all be reminded of how we should live. I miss him already. I look forward to seeing him again."

The service was over. One of Rob's favorite CDs started playing. Jillian, sitting in the front row between her mom and Brittany, stood up. She was glad there weren't ushers, because she didn't want everyone watching her. While Brittany hugged her, Jillian saw Kelly Hatcher across the room.

What are you doing here? You didn't even know Rob.

After putting on a smile and nodding at every sympathetic word from dozens of people, Jillian turned to make her way to the bathroom.

"Jillian?" Kelly stood there staring at her.

"Why are you here, Kelly?" she asked quietly.

"I just needed to tell you—I wanted to tell you—that I...well first of all, I'm sorry about Rob. I realize it's not the same thing, but I know it hurts to lose the guy you love."

Jillian's eyes shifted to Kelly's shoes. She bit her lip hard.

"We haven't talked in a long time, and I've been wanting to say this to you. I just can't wait anymore. The day you came over to my house...I thought you were a fool."

"Thanks."

"Wait, let me finish. I thought you were a fool because you knew I'd react the way I did, but you still apologized. You did it because you thought it was right. You knew you wouldn't gain a thing for yourself, but you still knocked on my door. I said what I did because I thought you deserved to suffer." Kelly paused. "But I don't think that now. I've never done the right thing just because I knew it was right. Jillian, you're the bravest person I know. I can't tell you how much it meant to me that you came over that day. You asked for my forgiveness. Well, I forgive you, Jillian. I do."

They embraced each other long and hard. Tears streamed down both their faces.

"Now I'm the one who needs your forgiveness," Kelly said. "Dustin and I had a messed-up relationship before you came along, but I've blamed you for everything because it was easier than blaming myself. I've said and done so many awful things to you, Jillian. Now I'm asking you to forgive me."

Jillian hugged Kelly again, with all the strength she had left, which wasn't much. "Of course, Kelly. Jesus has forgiven me. Who am I not to forgive you?" As they hugged, Jillian saw Ian in the corner talking to Jeff, his head in his hands. He looked exactly like he did at the hospital the night she'd turned her back on him.

After thanking Kelly, she went into the bathroom and fixed her face. She knew what she had to do. She walked out, went over to Ian, right in front of Jeff, and put her arms around him. They both held each other and wept. Brittany came over and joined them.

Letter 49

My advocate Prince Ishbane,

It wasn't my fault, I'm telling you! This is the most incompetent cadre of tempters I've ever worked with. I valiantly battled to hang onto Jillian's bitterness, and I almost succeeded. Pendragon lost Ian completely. It was horrible. Even Stungoth, in whom I'd put such hope, is teetering on the edge with Daniel. Raketwist is holding on to Brittany, but barely. Somehow things have spun out of control. The Enemy and His warriors blindsided us. It isn't fair! I did everything right. Somehow it just blew up in our faces.

Put in a good word for me, Ishbane. Please. If you do, I promise not to pass on to your superiors the derogatory comments you made about them, and the doubts you expressed about our mission. I've kept some of your letters, hoping I wouldn't have to turn them in. But if you choose to bring me up for disciplinary action, it would force me to divulge this information to High Command. Don't make me do it.

"Do you think it was a mistake to leave the only place we've ever known joy?" you asked. We both know how that would go over at Internal Affairs. And then there's your beseeching me to call you "Lord Ishbane." I would hate to see you embarrassed. Let's talk, shall we? (You might mention to Obsmut that I've dug up some interesting tidbits on him as well.)

I have an overnight trip planned, now that I've pinpointed my former subject Squaltaint's location. By the time you receive this, I should be having him for dinner.

Hoping for your sake we can cut a deal,

Lord Foulgrin

50

Jillian and Brittany sat on a battered brown couch in the youth center at Sovereign Grace Church. Rainbow streamers hung from the ceiling lights. The music blared, different music than a year ago. About the same number of kids, but different faces. Lots of home-baked cookies and bags of chips and soda cans on ice. No beer, no pot. Nobody sneaking off into the dark. Uno cards, but no tarot cards. Risk boards, but no Ouija boards. The dress wasn't quite as stylish.

But most of them are really having fun. They don't seem to be pretending.

Jillian felt at home here. After the emotional roller coaster of the past two months, it was a welcome feeling. Sitting next to Brittany on this comfy sofa, there wasn't any other place she'd rather be. Not in this world, anyway.

She smiled and put her hand on Brittany's protruding midsection. "You better lay off the chips, Brit. Pretending you're pregnant won't work much longer."

"You're a riot," Brittany said, stretching her long legs out and resting her arms on the lump, then chomping down on a few potato chips just to make a point. "You should be on late night."

"I've had offers."

"Look at Ian over there, smiling and pointing at me." Jillian followed Brittany's gaze to Ian and four guys, two from the college group, two high schoolers. "I keep thinking he's got to be embarrassed, but it's weird. It's like he *wants* to be a daddy. In fact, he keeps reminding me he already *is* a daddy. He says he's proud of the kid, even proud of me. Weird."

"He became a Christian," Jillian said. "When that happens, you change. That's a miracle, but it's not weird."

"It's invasion-of-the-body-snatchers weird, that's what it is. You know how he freaked me out when he took his Ouija board and the New Age books and the tarot cards and made that bonfire, with your youth pastor there and everything! Man, it felt like our own little episode of *The Exorcist* or something. I thought, the guy's gone nuts. He's headed for the loony bin. I wondered if he was going to drive a stake through someone's heart. But I figured, okay, he's shook up by Rob's accident and he blames himself, so he's just overcompensating. But he's never looked back. It's been, what, seven weeks? But he's becoming as radical a Christian as Rob was…maybe more radical."

"I agree. It's amazing. Then when Ian talked Daniel into pouring gas on his Ouija board in our backyard… Mom and I were watching out the window when Daniel tossed the match on it. Ian's arm was around him. Then they prayed. I felt like Daddy and Rob were right there…" Jillian covered her face. Brittany put her arm around her.

"I'm still here for you, Jill. Not sure what I have to offer you other than mega-stretch pants, but it's all yours anyway." She stared at Ian again. "This isn't the same Ian, I'm telling you."

Jillian fingered her ever-present tissue. "Is that good or bad?"

"Well, it's…good. Mostly. You know what I mean."

"Tell me."

"Always trying to make me go deep, aren't you?"

"Somebody's got to do it. Why not your best friend?"

"Well, the good thing is, he's kinder, much more sensitive, not the macho got-to-have-it-my-way jock. Plus, he doesn't try to take anything off me. You know, his thing about 'sexual purity'? I say it's maybe a little late for that," she patted her baby's hiding place, "but he says we can start over and we're going to do it right this time. 'Secondary virginity,' they call it. They've got a name for everything. Me and virginity in the same sentence—can you imagine? Anyway, he makes sure I'm taking my vitamins, holds doors open for me, gives me flowers. It's kind of…well, did I mention *weird?*"

"Didn't you tell me once it insulted you when guys held the door open for you? That it made you feel like they thought you were a weakling, like you were inferior or something?"

"Well, maybe I changed my mind," Brittany replied. "Is that a crime?"

"Oh, yeah. Big crime, Brit. You oughtta be shot."

"Anyway, when we get over to my place after the party, you'll see the flowers he gave me. A dozen roses, baby's breath, and everything. And you've got to read the card. Blew me away. I have it memorized."

Jillian nodded, while Brittany's image got blurry. Only two men had ever given her roses. One was her dad. A week before he died. The other was Rob. Now he was gone, too. Gone where? She knew, yet she wished she knew *more.* He was in heaven, yeah. But she didn't really understand what heaven was like.

That book Greg and Kristi gave her was helping. It was the same one Rob had read. Only three chapters into it, and she knew more about heaven than she'd ever dreamed. It was full of Bible references. She'd been reading slow because she was looking up every one and taking notes. She wanted to learn whatever she could about where Dad and Rob were. She kept picturing them together, knowing they'd really like each other.

"Do you think Rob and Daddy have met?" she'd asked Kristi. "Sure, why not?" she'd said. Maybe they were looking down at her right now, on the couch with Brittany. She smoothed down her hair, then laughed at herself.

Once in awhile she'd think about what Dad and Rob were missing by not being here. But most of the time she thought about what she was missing by not being there. Tears again. She pulled out the wad of tissue.

"What's with it, you and New Year's parties?" Brittany asked. "You cried at the last one, too. I had to take you in the bathroom and fix you up, remember?"

"These tears are different."

"How?"

"Last year I was empty, like I'd lost something I could never get back. I was looking for something to fill the emptiness. This year I feel some emptiness, sure, but it's like…the loss is huge, but it feels temporary, not permanent. It's like Kristi says—my relationships with Dad and Rob haven't been terminated, just interrupted. One day I'm going to be with Jesus, and them too. They'll probably show me around heaven. That's when the adventure's really going to begin. Earth's not my home. Heaven is. I tell myself that every day. That's how I make it through."

"Too deep for me," Brittany said. "But I'm happy for you, Jill. I think it's neat the way you've…I don't know, I guess it's the way you've changed too."

She reached out her hand to wipe away a tear from Jillian's face, and at the same moment Jillian reached out to hers.

"Wow," Jillian said. "Now *you're* crying. Going soft on me, Brit?"

"It's the hormones. I'm in the family way."

"You look great."

Brittany rolled her eyes.

"No, I mean it, Brit. You do. Nobody's going to put you on the cover of *Seventeen* magazine, but hey, I think you look better than those skinny little models any day."

"Let's see, I've just been told I don't look anything like a model and I'd never make a magazine cover, and this is supposed to be a compliment?"

"Aren't you the one who told me I needed to stop obsessing about the way I looked? Didn't *you* hand me the phone number for that eating disorder clinic?"

"Yeah, well…not looking like a model is one thing. Being the body double for the Goodyear blimp is something else."

She stuck her legs out further and buoyed up her midsection. Jillian put her arms around Brittany and they laughed hard, until they were crying again.

"You know, we started labor training a month ago," Brittany said. "Ian insisted on being my labor coach even when I told him I wanted you. Can you believe it? I'm a freshman in college, and a guy who didn't want anything to do with me is taking me to childbirth classes!"

"God does great things, huh?"

"Look at all these Christians," Brittany said, waving her arm and gazing around the room. "They've got to be thinking, 'there's a loser; that harlot shouldn't be sitting on a Christian couch. We better sterilize it when she leaves.'"

"That's not true, Brit, and you know it. Why do you have to act that way? People at this church love you. They've reached out to you. They gave you a baby shower. What, a half dozen women, including one of the pastors' wives, have already offered you babysitting? Lisa got you that crib and those baby clothes from the Pregnancy Resource Center. You accuse them of judging you, but you're the one judging them."

"Yeah, yeah, settle down, girl. I guess I have to say, I'm surprised, okay, *impressed* by the way they've treated me. Lisa's been…a nice surprise, I mean for a home-school/private-school person she's not that much of a freak. Okay, she's even becoming a friend. Now, most of my old friends, the ones I *thought* were friends, they've dropped off the face of the planet. My volleyball teammates are history. No sports, no scholarship, no future. Who wants to hang out with ol' Blimpie, the outside hitter with the jump reach of a hippopotamus?"

"People at church don't think that way, Brit. They're not perfect—don't get me going on Donovan Swain, but good case in point. But they understand grace and forgiveness. They've received it from God, and they want to pass it on. I mean, look over there at my little brother." Jillian pointed at Daniel, playing table tennis with three other kids. "Think about all the problems he's had. But somehow he fits in here. They've accepted him. Three months ago I would have figured he'd be in juvenile detention by now. Rob had a good influence on him, but Ian's been incredible. Mom's blown away by those men from the church who drop by and take him places. One of them's already asked him to a father/son campout in the spring."

"Yeah, well, sometimes it's easier when you can tell yourself they're all hypocrites. Then you don't have to deal with what they believe."

"Wow, Brit. That was an honest statement. Now *you're* getting deep. So where are you at—I mean, what do *you* believe?"

"Well," Brittany sighed, "I've maybe moved from pantheist to theist, how's that? Is that progress? Maybe I've even come a little further. Ian keeps reading his Bible to me, and his Christian books, like the ones Rob gave him. At first it bugged the heck out of me. You know how I started calling him 'preacher boy.' Then, I just figured, hey, if he opens doors for me, treats me good, and gives me roses, I can put up with a little Bible reading. But now I sort of…well, it's actually pretty interesting. You know his goal. First he wants to convert me, then he wants to marry me."

"I can think of worse," Jillian said.

"Well, the getting married part is sounding better all the time. Just turned nineteen and I'm thinking about marriage? It sounds scary, but it's growing on me. Ian says he wants to help with the baby whether he marries me or not. I'm still not sure about this born-again stuff. But he makes it sound like a package deal. It's like he won't marry me unless I've become a Christian."

"The Bible says something about that. I think he's right, Brittany."

"Thanks a lot."

"No, really, it's important that you're on the same page in your spiritual life. Trust me, I've been there. You both need to know Jesus. Otherwise—"

"Here comes the proud papa now."

"Hey, Jill," Ian said. "Taking good care of my lady?"

"Trying to. Sounds like you've been taking good care of her, too. She's been bragging about you."

Brittany's face reddened. Jillian couldn't remember seeing Brittany blush at anything.

"I love this church, Jillian," Ian said. "It's like home to me now."

"Yeah," she said. "Me, too."

The three immersed themselves in conversation, recounting the last year, talking about

Rob, discussing the future. Suddenly they heard a steady chant in unison.

"Ten, nine, eight…"

Countdown? Where had the time gone? Ian, on the couch next to Brittany, grabbed her left hand.

"Seven, six, five…"

Ian and Brittany gazed into each other's eyes. Jillian closed hers. She thought about Rob and Daddy. Then she did what Jodi had suggested. She tried to picture her bridegroom, the Carpenter from Nazareth, the One who'd gone to prepare a place for her, and promised to come get her for the wedding.

"Four, three, two…"

Jillian opened her eyes and saw Ian kiss Brittany on the cheek. She saw tears on Brittany's face.

She can't believe Ian loves her like this.

"One."

Jillian hardly heard the noisemakers and the shouts. Sitting alone on her side of the couch she thought of what she'd been reading in the Bible and that book on heaven. She thought about how this world wasn't her real home. She thought about the Person she was made for and the Place she was made for. Jesus was the person; heaven was the place.

"Thank you, best friend," she whispered aloud beneath the shouts.

Whatever the next year brings, help me to have Your perspective. And…please say hi to Daddy and Rob for me there in that perfect place You've made for me. Maybe they can see me, but if they can't, send them my love. And tell them I'm coming—but until I get there, I'm going to live for You. Give me the strength, Lord. Please, give me the strength.

Suddenly she felt Brittany on one side, hugging her, and Ian on the other side, completing the hug. She put a hand on Brittany's midsection. In the warmth of their embrace, Jillian yearned for a coming celebration. Not just a New Year's party, but a New Earth party.

A homecoming celebration.

The great reunion.

A wedding feast.

The Bridegroom she longed for.

The publisher and author would love to hear your comments about this book. *Please contact us at:* www.multnomah.net

ANGELA ALCORN

Angela is a full-time mom and part-time emergency room nurse at Adventist Medical Center in Portland, Oregon. She is married to Dan Stump, a middle school teacher and coach. They are the proud parents of two very active boys, Jake and Ty.

KARINA ALCORN FRANKLIN

Karina is a stay-at-home mom with two young sons, Matthew and Jack. She is married to Dan Franklin, a college pastor, and together they enjoy raising their family and working side by side in ministry.

RANDY ALCORN

Randy Alcorn is the founder and director of Eternal Perspective Ministries (EPM). Prior to this he served as a pastor for fourteen years. He has spoken around the world and has taught on the adjunct faculties of Multnomah Bible College and Western Seminary in Portland, Oregon.

Randy is the best-selling author of twenty-seven books (over three million in print), including the novels *Deadline, Dominion, Lord Foulgrin's Letters* and the 2002 Gold Medallion winner *Safely Home*. His ten nonfiction works include *Money, Possessions and Eternity, ProLife Answers to ProChoice Arguments, In Light of Eternity, The Treasure Principle, The Grace & Truth Paradox, The Purity Principle, The Law of Rewards, Why ProLife?* and *Heaven: Resurrected Living on the New Earth*.

Randy has written for many magazines and produces the popular periodical *Eternal Perspectives*. He's been a guest on over 500 radio and television programs including Focus on the Family, The Bible Answer Man, Family Life Today and Truths that Transform.

The father of two married daughters, Randy lives in Gresham, Oregon, with his wife and best friend, Nanci. He enjoys hanging out with his family, biking, tennis, research and reading.

Feedback on this book (to any of the authors) and inquiries regarding publications and other matters can be directed to Eternal Perspective Ministries, 39085 Pioneer Blvd., Suite 200 Sandy, OR 97055. EPM can also be reached at 503-668-5200. For information on EPM or Randy Alcorn, and for resources on missions, the persecuted church, pro-life issues, and eternal perspective, see www.epm.org. Visit Randy Alcorn's blog: www.randyalcorn.blogspot.com

More dramatic fiction from
RANDY ALCORN

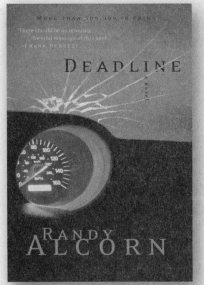

Deadline

When tragedy strikes those closest to him, award-winning journalist Jake Woods must draw upon all his resources to uncover the truth about their suspicious accident. Soon he finds himself swept up in a murder investigation that is both complex and dangerous. Unaware of the threat to his own life, Jake is drawn in deeper and deeper as he desperately searches for the answers to the immediate mystery at hand and—ultimately—the deeper meaning of his own existence.

ISBN 978-1-59052-592-0

Dominion

A shocking murder drags black newspaper columnist Clarence Abernathy into the disorienting world of inner-city gangs and racial conflict. In a desperate hunt for answers to the violence (and to his own struggles with race and faith), Clarence forges an unlikely partnership with redneck detective Ollie Chandler. Despite their differences, Clarence and Ollie soon find themselves sharing the same mission: victory over the powers of darkness vying for power and control. *Dominion* is a dramatic story of spiritual searching, racial reconciliation, and hope.

ISBN 978-1-59052-593-7

Nonfiction titles from
RANDY ALCORN

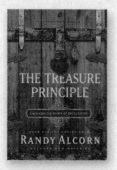

THE TREASURE PRINCIPLE:
Unlocking the Secret of Joyful Giving

Bestselling author Randy Alcorn uncovers the revolutionary key to spiritual transformation: joyful giving! Jesus gave his followers this life-changing formula that guarantees not only kingdom impact, but immediate pleasure and eternal rewards.

ISBN 978-1-59052-508-1

THE PURITY PRINCIPLE:
God's Safeguards for Life's Dangerous Trails

God has placed warning signs and guardrails to keep us from plunging off the cliff. Find straight talk about sexual purity in Randy Alcorn's one-stop handbook for you, your family, and your church.

ISBN 978-1-59052-195-3

THE GRACE AND TRUTH PARADOX:
Responding with Christlike Balance

Living like Christ is a lot to ask! Discover Randy Alcorn's two-point checklist of Christlikeness—and begin to measure everything by the simple test of grace and truth.

ISBN 978-1-59052-065-9

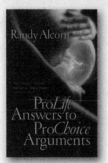

PROLIFE ANSWERS TO PROCHOICE ARGUMENTS

This revised and updated guide offers timely information and inspiration from a "sanctity of life" perspective. Real answers to real questions appear in logical and concise form.

ISBN 978-1-57673-751-4

Randy Alcorn brought you

DEADLINE

and then...

DOMINION

Don't miss the next chapter in...

DECEPTION